W9-COR-440

DONOVAN'S WIFE

BY THE SAME AUTHOR

FICTION

Get Out of Town
So Fair, So Evil
Tears Are for Angels
(*under the pseudonym Paul Connolly*)

The Kingpin
The Devil Must
The Judgment
Facing the Lions
Unto This Hour

NONFICTION

Kennedy Without Tears
JFK & LBJ: *The Influence of Personality Upon Politics*
A Time to Die
On Press
One of Us: *Richard Nixon and the American Dream*

DONOVAN'S Wife

TOM WICKER

WILLIAM MORROW AND COMPANY, INC. ★ NEW YORK

It is the policy of William Morrow and Company, Inc., and its imprints and affiliates, recognizing the importance of preserving what has been written, to print the books we publish on acid-free paper, and we exert our best efforts to that end.

Library of Congress Cataloging-in-Publication Data

Wicker, Tom.
Donovan's wife / by Tom Wicker.
p. cm.
ISBN 0-688-10627-7
I. Title.
PS3573.I25D6 1992
813′.54—dc20 92-7729
CIP

Printed in the United States of America

First Edition

1 2 3 4 5 6 7 8 9 10

BOOK DESIGN BY LINEY LI

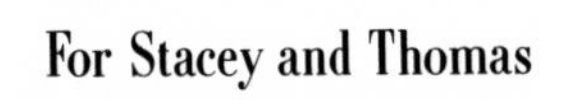
For Stacey and Thomas

The author is grateful for the cheerful cooperation of Julian P. Kantor, curator of the extensive archive of political commercials maintained at the University of Oklahoma, in Norman, Oklahoma.

Another such victory and we are undone.

—King Pyrrhus,
after defeating the
Romans at Asculum

1.

The subcommittee hearing was already under way when Milo Speed walked along the echoing corridor of the Sam Rayburn Building, past a waiting line of spectators. A portly Capitol Hill policeman saw him coming and swung open one of the big oak doors. Speed went past with a nod of thanks, trying not to notice the murmurous stir—whether of recognition or resentment he did not wish to know—among those he had bypassed. The policeman pointed to a vacant seat in the fourth row.

"Mister Chairman," an authoritative voice was proclaiming through what otherwise would have been the cathedral silence of the hearing room, "in this case, I can assure you that what's good for Cramer, Wentz, and Marbury—"

Spectators jammed the seats. In upper and lower rows upon the semicircular rostrum at the front of the chamber sat a full complement of the House Energy and Commerce Committee's Subcommittee on Business Operations, Plans, and Productivity. The attendance was impressive, a tribute to the drawing power of the witness; but Speed, glancing over his shoulder as he edged into the row, had no difficulty locating Representative Victor T. Donovan. He was seated in the bottom row, near the center of the rostrum, as befitted his seniority.

"—really is good for the country!"

Speed struggled toward the open seat, past the hunched-up legs of bemused spectators and the ample form of Frank V. Stratemeyer, the Washington representative for Bigger Bang, an association of military industries.

"And vice versa, of course," the witness declared.

The congressmen on the rostrum, Speed saw without surprise, appeared absorbed in the testimony. Television lights, after all, were burning whitely; the bloody eyes of the cameras glowered above their bony, stilted legs, and a rank of still photographers crouched beneath the paneled rostrum, ready at the least hint of blood on the floor to spring out like wolves from their lair.

"Because at Cramer, Wentz, and Marbury, Mister Chairman, it's our firm conviction—"

Between the stills and the spectator seats, at two long tables—where, if Milo Speed had chosen, he could have claimed a prominent place—the men and women of the working press sat elbow to elbow, scribbling their notes and doing their best to look as bored as the ethic of their trade decreed.

"—that you can't separate the interests of this country from the interests of business!"

Bullshit, Speed thought, but in that setting, he knew, it was effective bullshit—particularly from the formidable occupant of the witness chair: J. Conrad Cramer, the renowned financier "profiled" by *New York* magazine as the "Takeover Tycoon."

"Aren't you ever on time?" Frank V. Stratemeyer's whisper seemed to strew gravel on the floor.

"Sorry . . . sorry," Speed mumbled hypocritically, wishing he had stepped on the lobbyist's foot. He eased into the vacant seat as the Takeover Tycoon's reverberant words filled the room.

"And if every American was as sensitive as this subcommittee to the importance of a healthy business climate—"

J. Conrad Cramer was a diminutive man whose feet barely

touched the floor beneath the witness chair. He nevertheless wielded a voice that could quell a stockholders' revolt and a presence that meant he'd rarely face one.

"—every American would be better off!"

One of the nation's wealthiest men (though mostly on paper, Speed suspected), J. Conrad Cramer was the most fawned-upon "risk taker" in a society that revered the breed, a hero to *Time* magazine ("Neither Adam Smith nor Horatio Alger could have imagined hard-plunging, high-rolling Connie Cramer"), a wheeler-dealer (in Speed's jaundiced opinion) who juggled bank loans, junk bonds, and stock holdings while buying and selling companies—as well as politicians—like so many collectibles at a flea market.

"In Allied Ventures we saw opportunity," J. Conrad Cramer now informed the subcommittee, adding in tones that echoed to the corners of the room: "We saw what no real American businessman can ignore, Mister Chairman—"

Speed stopped listening—partly because he'd heard more than enough self-serving platitudes in a long lifetime, mostly because he really didn't need to hear J. Conrad Cramer's prepared pieties. Zealous press agents were sure to produce printed texts for the press galleries, underlining the parts they hoped to have quoted on the evening news and in the next day's papers.

"—we saw opportunity going begging!"

Looking about the chamber, Speed noticed that Victor T. Donovan did not appear to be listening either. Seeing him glance to the other side of the hearing room, Speed looked that way and saw with a painful catch of his breath that Josie, the congressman's wife, was there in a front-row seat. Abruptly, unexpectedly, the *first* time he had seen her came back to him with brutal clarity.

Sometime between late Nixon and early Carter, Speed had gone reluctantly to one of those Washington cocktail parties at which Nancy, then his wife, said that everyone looked "at the bird on your shoulder," hoping to see someone more important just beyond. He had turned away from the bar, holding a drink in each hand, to find Josie standing so close behind him that he almost spilled vodka on her. She radiated an earthy vitality, he thought at once, as if she might glow in the dark.

Josie held her place and took one of the drinks out of his hand. "You weren't going to drink both, I hope."

It had not been exactly love at first sight. Speed only thought, immediately: *I'm going to fuck her eyes out.*

"One was for my wife," he managed to say, thinking: *Soon. Tonight. Tomorrow.*

"You *would* be married," Josie said. "Wouldn't you?"

He lost himself, as if diving into the surf, in the depths of her sea blue eyes.

"But I'm not dead."

"I can see that. I could tell."

Not looking at the bird on her shoulder but at the touch of her tongue on her dark, full lips, Speed was nevertheless aware that Nancy was making her way toward them through the chatter, mostly of men in dark suits to listening women.

"I'll call you," Speed said in the last possible moment, just before he reached to draw Nancy to his side. "This is my wife, Miss . . . uh . . ."

Josie had put out her hand without a hint of hesitation. "I'm Josie Donovan. My husband works for Congressman Meldrim Hooks."

Married, too.

But Speed did not fail to pick up the clue she had dropped, the clue he would need to find her the next morning, when dutiful congressional aides would be at work on Capitol Hill. When he did call, from a phone booth at 9:00 A.M., Josie answered on the first ring.

"You're not dead either," Speed said. "I could tell."

In a motel room in Arlington, after a lingering lunch, Josie told him what had caught her attention at the cocktail party: "Someone said you were the best young reporter in Washington."

"*That's* not saying much." Even then he was more flattered to be thought young than a good reporter.

"And a great swordsman to boot."

At the time Speed had been taken aback, because he had been complicitous, rather shamefacedly at that, in only one or two love affairs, short and unsatisfactory. He had, in fact, before meeting Josie, almost definitely decided to be faithful to Nancy.

"Who told you that?"

"Somebody who said she heard it from somebody."

Speed was discomfited that anyone knew of his private doings. But he was too entranced with Josie to dwell on the matter.

"Umm," he murmured into her cleavage. "Is it true?"

"Show me again, so I can make sure."

Speed had not hesitated. In his first tryst with Josie he was learning with shocks of pleasure that her shining vitality, which had struck him so forcefully at the cocktail party, fed on an exuberant carnality he had never known or suspected in a woman. He had not thought it possible that his own desire for intimacy, freedom from himself, could be matched or exceeded in the other sex.

"It's true," Josie murmured in his ear. "Oh, my God, Speed . . . is it ever true!"

Josie was not a ravishing beauty; she just gave that impression. Her mouth was a little too full, her chin perhaps too challenging; her brows were a mite low over eyes startlingly blue, her forehead a bit too high beneath lustrous but carelessly combed dark hair. Then, too, Josie was shaped unfashionably for the age, though agreeably to Speed—more along the lines of Venus de Milo than of the *Town and Country* models Nancy starved herself to resemble.

Across the hearing room Speed could see that even after the passage of years, when she had to be pushing forty, Josie still had what he knew to be rarer than dollface beauty or clotheshorse bones. Josie still had an electric field of presence, an aura almost visible in the air about her, like the halo—Speed had whispered in a long-ago spasm of passion—over an angel in a stained glass window.

"You may be a great lover," Josie had replied, "but you'll *never* make a poet."

There had been nothing else remotely angelic about Josie. What shone about her, what had been new and miraculous to Speed, was her delight in the wonder of herself and of him, in the giving and taking of love, the myriad ways in which, in their long, hungry motel-room afternoons, they had clutched and caressed each other against the world that sped past uncaring, beyond the drawn blinds, the disconnected phone, on the roaring highway of modern America.

"—seized it by the horns, Mister Chairman. We seized that opportunity when we saw it, and isn't that the American Way? Isn't that—"

He had tried often enough, Speed thought, with the sense of shame never far from his consciousness, to find again what they'd had—whatever it was. His life, for a while after Josie and Nancy, had been a procession of women, a long, tumescent search for what he once, so briefly as to seem almost a fantasy, had found with Josie—at least remembered having found.

But even if that had been real, he had come to wonder whether it *could* be found again, whether only self-delusion and his pervasive sense of loss had led him so persistently and fruitlessly through so many tumbled beds and female bodies—some yielding, some grasping, some hard as truth, none finally easing for long his loneliness, all leaving in him the sour tastes of waste and betrayal, not least of himself.

A woman in the seat behind Speed's whispered in his ear, loudly enough for heads to turn in the rows around them:

"Slumming, huh?"

Speed was used to being recognized, but he dreaded having attention called to his presence—less from false modesty than because he was never sure he would meet expectations. His instinct was to ignore the whisper. But he had turned his head just far enough to recognize from the corner of his eye the blond hair and brown eyes of Gabriella Lukes, who was rated the most beautiful lobbyist in Washington, against little competition.

In his searching years Speed had made what he now regarded as a mistake of taste, taking Gabby Lukes to New York for a weekend that turned out—so it seemed—to be an age. In common decency, therefore, he was compelled to reply.

Hoping to sound dismissing, he whispered over his shoulder: "Just kibitzing."

Actually, in one of his twice-weekly columns (distributed to more than three hundred leading newspapers, said the publicity blurb that accompanied Speed's ten-year-old mug shot), he had called J. Conrad Cramer "a financial bloodsucker, a parasite on the national economy"—proving it, so Speed thought, with ample, if elsewhere ignored, evidence. From the subcommittee's inquiry into the multibillion-dollar takeover of Allied Ventures Ltd. by Cramer, Wentz, and Marbury, Speed thought he might be able to mine more nuggets in that vein.

None too hopefully, he tuned back in to J. Conrad Cramer's spiel.

"—uppermost in our minds, Mister Chairman—almost our only concern, I may say—was the best interests of Allied stockholders we considered long-suffering."

Speed promptly tuned out again. In his opinion, the only stockholders—if any—for whom J. Conrad Cramer ever had given a damn were those who might muster the nerve and power to vote him out as chairman and CEO of Cramer, Wentz, and Marbury.

To Speed's right, Frank V. Stratemeyer shifted massively in his chair, as if fantasizing a new weapons system. Speed shied away to his left; such unwanted proximity caused him for a moment to regret passing up the press table seat to which his years and eminence entitled him.

On the other hand, sitting up there with the working press would have put Milo Speed down on their level when he had spent too many years and too much effort getting out front, professionally and otherwise. But he had not been hungry enough for celebrity to appear often on television, so he also feared that some of the bright young upstarts at the press tables might not even know who he was. Speed did not *like*, but nevertheless *wanted*, to be recognized.

He especially feared that some at the press tables might even momentarily question his right to sit among them. He knew he had only to speak his name to prove his right, but Speed firmly believed Woodrow Wilson's dictum: There was such a thing as being too proud to fight.

And sometimes, he thought wearily, *I feel as if I had been around to hear him say it.*

★

"It was as if, Mister Chairman," J. Conrad Cramer roundly declaimed, "my associates and I had glimpsed a handsome house in disrepair, just waiting for good carpenters to rebuild it."

The Honorable Victor T. Donovan, apparently still not listening, was bent over something he was writing, a display of effort that faintly surprised Speed. Just the day before, he had reluctantly stroked the congressman through an expense account luncheon, setting him up as a possible leak but also confirming Speed's view of him as too dull to cut butter.

Victor T. Donovan had arrived in Washington as a young graduate of Stanford Law School, the competent and devoted administrative assistant to an elderly member of the House who had concerned himself term after term only with the promotion of beef and sugar beets and the protection of air bases, his far-off district's prime assets. Upon the Honorable Meldrim Hooks's demise at eighty-eight—the old gentleman, fittingly, had choked on a slice of well-done roast beef lodged in his windpipe—Victor T. Donovan had been handed the House seat, his loyalty, patience, and unavailing Heimlich maneuver rewarded without deleterious effect on beef, sugar beets, or the Air Force.

"—in our determination to reorganize and revitalize Allied Ventures—"

Not least because Victor T. Donovan's age, intelligence, and looks were a notable improvement on those of the late incumbent, the governor who had appointed him, as well as Washington optimists, had expected great things of him—perhaps a seat in the Senate, at least party leadership, maybe even national office. But like many another young phenom predicted to light up the political sky, Victor T. Donovan had learned quickly that the brighter he shone, the better target he presented, and he had settled into a congressional career as undistinguished and unexceptional as that of his predecessor, exemplifying the ancient wisdom of the House: "If you want to get along, go along."

A handsome man, grown only slightly jowly, the Honorable Victor T. Donovan had gained with the lines in his face an air of dignity where once there had been only blandness. Speed had to admit that he at least *looked* like a congressman; in fact, he looked like a senator, maybe like a President—possibly even a Supreme Court justice. And since he held a safe seat in a one-party district in a sparsely populated state, he would be a committee chairman someday.

But as far as Speed could see, or cared to see, the passage of years had left Victor T. Donovan little more than the bland and obtuse careercrat Speed and Josie once had so easily circumvented. In those years Speed had developed something like contempt for Josie's husband, and Victor T. Donovan's later ascent—if that was what it was—to a seat in the House had not diminished it.

"He's cautious," Josie had conceded one night as they drank vodka in Speed's bed when Nancy was away on a visit to her mother. "Even dull sometimes. But his father used to be the state attorney general, you know. Vic was third in his law class at Stanford. He might surprise everybody one of these days."

"But not you." Speed touched her where and as he knew she loved to be touched. "Not this way."

"No . . . oh, Jesus, no . . ." Josie moved with his hand. "*Never* that way."

Seeing her again, remembering so vividly, caused him to ask himself again—as he had long ago thought he had stopped himself from asking: Why was Josie still Victor T. Donovan's wife? The wife of a congressman, and a second-rate congressman at that? In a city where both were a dime a dozen?

Speed could think of no answer except the perversity of things, for which he had a hard-earned respect. Nothing else, he told himself, could have kept a woman so vibrant with life linked to a dull man with a stagnant career. Even in the harsh glare of the TV lights, even seated fifteen ranks of seats distant, he found himself shivering at the sight of Josie, as for years he had not let himself do.

"—the duty of American business, to *build*," J. Conrad Cramer declared.

In the white light of the hearing room, with the witness's

paeans to the American Way echoing off the walls, Speed tried manfully to stop remembering. He knew that was the worst thing he could do; inevitably he would end up as before, dreaming of Josie in the night, of that voluptuous presence, that devouring pleasure in which he could lose his hurts and disappointments, his demeaning and irrational fears—only to wake in darkness, silence, the oppressive emptiness of his room and his life.

"At Allied Ventures, Mister Chairman," proclaimed J. Conrad Cramer in his drill sergeant's voice, "we'll make the American Dream come true!"

Speed listened reluctantly as the Takeover Tycoon came down the homestretch in resounding fashion, with still another recital of an oft-told tale: how he had risen to fame and fortune from a boyhood job selling his aunt's homemade doughnuts door to door, out of a towel-lined laundry basket at twenty-five cents a dozen, from which he was allowed to keep a nickel commission.

"And that, Mister Chairman, is what we mean when we say, 'Only in America!' May it remain that way, for your grandchildren and mine!"

The audience burst into furious applause, and the stills sprang into flashing action. The witness gathered up his papers, receiving whispered accolades from a blue suit seated on one side of him and a gray suit on the other. Above the rudely popping and clicking stills, Speed could see Chairman Hartley G. Flander square his shoulders, adjust his tie, and hold his head back for a young woman who swiftly materialized to powder his gleaming forehead.

Gabby Lukes, too persistent to have been brushed off as Speed had intended, whispered in his ear: "Two to one it was an insider deal all the way."

Speed usually tried to avoid Gabby, wondering how he could have allowed himself even briefly to be attracted, but he was amused that J. Conrad Cramer's Horatio Algerish tale had not deceived so cynical an observer. He whispered back: "Does Cramer do any other kind?"

This exchange apparently had been loud enough to be overheard by Frank V. Stratemeyer.

"You press guys," he muttered to Speed, while continuing to clap. "Don't you realize you're out of touch with America?"

Frank V. Stratemeyer's organization, Bigger Bang, had tried often to plant in Speed's column its patriotic defense of the Rough Rider Armored Personnel Mover (RRAPM), a high-priced turkey so unmaneuverable that after the first half dozen underwent combat testing, the Israelis sent them back.

Speed said: "You may be right, Frank. I'm so out of touch I'm dead against that Rap'Em you keep trying to unload on the taxpayers."

Frank V. Stratemeyer drew himself up, no small matter. But before he could answer, Chairman Flander rapped the gavel deferentially, and the last of the applause died. The stills slunk back to their menacing crouch under the rostrum.

"Mistuh Cramuh," the chairman drawled, "I speak fuh this en-tiah subcommittee when I say that seldom have I hud the princepuls of the Amecan Way so ably set foth."

Speed quickly lost interest again, as Hartley G. Flander droned through his allotted five minutes of "questions" that were mostly tributes to Cramer, Wentz, and Marbury. Rather like a homing pigeon, Speed's attention returned again to Josie Donovan—not, he realized with an unwelcome start of surprising pain, that it ever had been as far from her as he'd tried to pretend.

On the many unavoidable occasions when they'd met at cocktail parties or dinners or political events, neither had said or implied anything personal, ever; now he saw that Josie didn't even know he—or anyone else for that matter—was in the hearing room. She seemed oblivious of the audience but vitally engaged with the proceedings.

Josie always had had a way of tightly focusing her attention, narrowing it to the dimensions of whatever or whomever she was attending to. Even now, though it had been years since Speed had felt the feverish current of that intensity, he could sense it across the room and through the crowd, recall how once it had caused him to do and say foolish things.

"You're the only woman," he had even declared, as in ecstatic satiety he had struggled out of bed in some motel room strewn with their fallen clothes, "who ever made me wonder if I ought to divorce Nancy."

Even as he said it, he had thought with pained regret of his wife's hard little breasts, her delicate sexual tastes. But Josie had only laughed out loud, covering a selected portion of herself with a triangle of sheet.

"You? Divorce the Girl Next Door?" In private, she always referred to Nancy as the Girl Next Door, though they got along decently when their paths crossed socially.

"What's so funny?" Speed had been affronted that what he thought a heartfelt remark had provoked her laughter.

"You're too proud. You'd never admit you'd failed at marriage. Or that *anything* was beyond you. She'll be the one that'll get the divorce."

He could think of only one reason Nancy might. "Because I'm playing around with you?"

Immediately he wanted to call back the words, the unthinking euphemism. He did not wish to suggest that he was merely "playing around" with Josie. He was not sure what he *was* doing, but he knew it was not "playing around."

Josie took no notice. She drew up one bent, beautiful leg—clearly for his eager eyes—as if to examine her thigh for bruises or teeth marks he might well have left. Her own eyes were startlingly sky blue—though often they were sea blue and sometimes what he thought of as vein blue—against the spread of her dark hair on the disheveled bed. Josie's eyes could change with the light.

"Because she can't stand the pace," she finally said.

Hartley G. Flander's voice broke vaguely into Speed's consciousness. The chairman was rambling on about the American Way, pausing only occasionally for ritual answers from the witness. Speed quickly took another mental walk, pondering the inexplicable.

Who could ever know what went on between a man and a woman? Who knew, really, what happened between lovers, friends, husbands and wives, sons and mothers? It made little difference as long as they were male and female. What happened between the sexes was mysterious, fascinating, compelling as death, making life interesting, perverse, as nothing else could.

". . . now call upon my able and distinguished friend, the rankin minotty membuh . . ."

Hartley G. Flander's able and distinguished friend had no more pungent questions for J. Conrad Cramer than the chairman had had; Speed stayed with his own thoughts.

How, for instance, had he and Nancy kept going as long and as well as they had, with no children to provide the usual family cement and years after Nancy's restraint had killed what physical interest he had had in her, hence in their marriage? In the end, as Josie had predicted but nevertheless to Speed's consternation, Nancy had left him—not for any of the infidelities and deficiencies with which she might have charged him, but for her own puzzling (to him) purposes.

"Just occurred to me one day," she'd said in her distant manner—with no special emphasis or advance warning—over dinner at Rive Gauche. "Like in the funny papers, this little light coming on over my head? What about me?"

Speed had not at first understood. He had often not at first understood Nancy, especially in the years since they had moved on from the small-town milieu in which they had been reared together and in which she had been comfortable.

"Well . . . *what* about you?"

"My life, I mean."

Speed then thought, mistakenly, that he had been around that track a time or two. "You should get a job, Nan. I've been telling you for years."

"That's not it." Nancy suddenly seemed a slight, lost figure, hunched at the table as if unwilling to be noticed. She sounded as if she were reading from the menu. "I can get a job. But I've got to have a *life*."

Then Speed understood. He ate duck à l'orange and sipped Côtes du Rhône, shocked, delaying, pondering how to proceed. But he could think of no reply.

After a while, her small voice unexpectedly strong, Nancy said: "Not your life, Milo. My own. Pour me some more wine?"

Speed filled her glass, refilled his own. "Don't do that to

me, Nan." He was frightened, incredulous, resentful. First Josie, now this. He felt his roots being pulled up. "I don't deserve it." Though he feared he did.

"*I* deserve it." Nancy drank wine. "That's the point."

Hartley G. Flander's gavel and mellifluous voice recognized still another able and distinguished gentleman and called Speed back to the hearing room. This time it was not hard to do; he abhorred the memory of that scene with Nancy—he had never set foot again in Rive Gauche—not for what she had done but for why she had done it. He hated the idea that what he had offered her had not been enough, and he missed—if not Nancy herself—the settled life she had embodied.

"Mister Chairman," the Honorable Victor T. Donovan said, "I wonder if the chair would do me the honor to yield about three minutes extra time? I estimate I may need that long for a few little questions I have here."

"Thout objection, so awdud."

The chairman settled comfortably in his chair and Victor T. Donovan turned to the witness. "I want to ask Mister . . . ah . . . Cramer first. . . ."

He paused, looking down at papers in front of him. Just as it dawned on Milo Speed that the congressman had offered J. Conrad Cramer none of the usual deferential greetings or the customary congressional hypocrisies, the Honorable Victor T. Donovan added mildly:

"After your boyhood success selling doughnuts, didn't you make your first real money operating a porno theater?"

★

"What the shit?" said Darwin John, as on his megascreen TV the stills leaped from under the rostrum like football linemen coming off the snap. "Did I hear right?"

Bedlam was erupting in the hearing room in the nearby Rayburn Building. Graphically depicted on the enormous television suspended from Darwin John's office ceiling, half the stills had clustered in front of J. Conrad Cramer and the other half, flashing, clicking, and scrambling, had turned on Victor

T. Donovan. An alert director, quick-cutting adroitly, caught in close-up a wide-eyed Hartley G. Flander bucking upright in his high-backed chair.

"Oh, you heard right, Chief."

Floyd Finch, like everyone who knew Darwin John, called him Chief because that's what he was—the feared and revered national chairperson of Victor T. Donovan's political party, an unchallenged Colossus astride more than half the nation's politics.

Finch, a veteran of the party staff, spoke without taking his eyes from the televised confusion, against which Hartley G. Flander was vainly wielding his gavel: "Rafe Ames *said* if we watched, we were in for a shock."

On the screen, as the blue and gray suits on either side of J. Conrad Cramer appeared to be restraining him, the entrepreneur was shouting something—uncaught by the mikes or perhaps censored by the engineers—at Victor T. Donovan, who sat quietly above the milling stills and the audience commotion. Even the working press at their privileged tables were turning to one another or to watch J. Conrad Cramer, as if they had been shaken from professional ennui.

"I wouldn't say shock," said Darwin John, who already regretted his outburst at Victor T. Donovan's unexpected question. It was part of the chairperson's cultivated mystique never to appear surprised. "I always said Connie Cramer was a fishy little prick."

Darwin John was stretched at full length on a leather sofa that had cost the party enough to pay for a small-city mayor's election. His hands, as he watched J. Conrad Cramer subside into the advisory embrace of the blue and gray suits, were clasped behind his head, around which gamely semicircled a wispy gray tonsure, and from which—his only defect as party chief—TV highlights would bounce like Halloween sparklers.

"You sure had that right, Chief," Floyd Finch said fervently, though he had never heard Darwin John mention J. Conrad Cramer except as a substantial party contributor.

On the huge suspended screen, framed between the blunt toes of Darwin John's shoes—procured in London, of sturdy material endangering no species that might have political clout, and propped like giant brown rabbit ears on the sofa arm—the stills started to drift sullenly back to their crouch beneath the rostrum.

"Aw-duh!" Chairman Flander bellowed. "Aw-duh! Aw we'll cleah this chambuh!"

The camera shifted to the carefully expressionless face of Victor T. Donovan, waiting on the rostrum.

"Handsome sucker," said Darwin John. "Unless that's a rug he's wearing?"

"Don't look like it to me." Finch nevertheless took out a small notebook. "I'll check it with Rafe."

Floyd Finch was a thoroughgoing detail man. Unfortunately, in Darwin John's experience, detail men sometimes couldn't see the woods for the trees, and Finch was no exception. Like now, with this Ames bozo playing him like a bagpipe.

"Great TV." Floyd Finch leaned forward, pointed elbows on skeletal knees, translucent hands dangling lengthily in front of unpressed trousers. "Confrontation. White hat and black. I don't have to tell you, Chief, that's the name of the game nowadays."

"What you don't have to tell me," said Darwin John, "is what you're trying to *sell* me. You and this Ames dingleberry."

From the TV speakers came at last the carefully restrained voice of J. Conrad Cramer: "Mister Chairman, I must say I find completely incomprehensible a question coming out of left field like that. We at Cramer, Wentz, and Marbury are in the business of creating jobs and opportunity, and we came here to discuss our contribution to good old American know-how—"

"Sweet Jesus," said Darwin John to the screen. "Give me a *break*!"

The pieties of the nation's entrepreneurs, with many of whom he dealt every day, in every way—sometimes even publicly—had ceased to impress the Chief sometime before the Chrysler bailout.

Victor T. Donovan, also displaying impatience, interrupted

the witness: "I didn't ask you about know-how. I asked you about a porno theater pouring smut into the eyes and ears and minds of good Americans."

Floyd Finch smacked a bony fist into a thin palm, with a sound like popping gum. "Look at that eye contact, Chief!"

"What I see," said Darwin John, "is an uppity congressman that's about to get his ass handed to 'im."

"Like he's about to bust right through the screen," Finch went on, in a rare display of independent opinion. "Right into the room with you, including the can, you got a set in there."

Floyd Finch had never been allowed in Darwin John's private bathroom; no one except the cleaning woman ever was.

Meanwhile, J. Conrad Cramer's patient tone had vanished: "I simply have no idea what you're talking about, Mister Congressman."

Too smart, thought Darwin John, *to use the asshole's name. Give him the kind of publicity he's after*.

"Then I'll repeat the question. Didn't you make your first money—"

"I heard you," J. Conrad Cramer said. "I just thought maybe you were reading from the wrong set of notes. But—"

"Oh, these are the right notes."

Victor T. Donovan had interrupted again, an imposition to which, even at television range, the further stiffening of J. Conrad Cramer's slight body signaled how little he was accustomed.

"And they contain some facts, Mister Cramer. My staff has ascertained, for instance, that you began your pursuit of the American Dream"—the congressman's voice was heavy with sarcasm—"in San Francisco, when you took over the T and A Theater in North Beach. With live sex acts on stage."

Once again the hearing room burst into noisy chatter. A few of the working press, no doubt wire service men heading for phones, ran out of the room. The blue and gray poured a lava flow of advice in nearly visible streams into the ears of J. Conrad Cramer.

"I'd say Donovan's got guts, Chief. Wouldn't you?"

Not, thought Darwin John, that that was such a great asset.

Like for damn sure there went a few K that Cramer's PAC might have slipped a cooperative congressman for a little discretion.

"Guts win prizes, Floyd. But damn few votes."

Darwin John was watching the Cramer hearings only because Floyd Finch had talked him into it, and he knew Finch himself had been pressured by this Ames fart. But the Chief was not easily impressed by a mere congressman, and certainly not by his raggedy-ass TV coach. Even supplicative Presidents had found themselves blinking under Darwin John's pale gray stare, his lashless eyes seeming in his domelike head as unwavering as steel marbles embedded in cement.

Now, when he had hoped to be clearing paper work in preparation for eighteen holes that afternoon at Burning Tree, he was almost as resistant to Victor T. Donovan's appeal as was J. Conrad Cramer.

"I don't know how your staff could *ascertain*"—Cramer's voice, when he could be heard again, seemed to heap scorn on the idea—"any such thing, since that, sir, is an accusation you will have difficulty proving."

Victor T. Donovan appeared unintimidated. "That's not what I'd call a denial. If it's not true, Mister Chairman, why doesn't the witness just deny it?"

"Because I don't know as much about pornographic theaters as *you* seem to, Mister Congressman. And Mister Chairman, I suggest that all this has nothing to do with the supposed purpose of these hearings. I really must protest that these irrelevant questions are far afield—"

"Irrelevant!" Victor T. Donovan returned to the attack, and the camera caught Hartley G. Flander gazing at him as if at Frankenstein's monster. "The purity and morality of Americans are irrelevant to you? Is that right?"

Coming through the lens, thought Darwin John. *Finch hit that on the nose.*

"The degradation of innocent American girls is irrelevant. Is that what you're saying?"

"Innocent girls, my ass," said Darwin John, who doubted the existence of any such animal. But he sat up on the sofa, his heavy London shoes thudding on the carpet.

"Mister Congressman, you know very well I meant your inquiries are irrelevant to the acquisition of Allied Ventures by Cramer—"

"You think the God-given family values this country was built on are irrelevant, do you? You believe—"

"I didn't say that!"

Floyd Finch sat back in his chair, a look of rapture and vindication on his anorexic face. "You wanta bet *that* don't play in Peoria?"

Darwin John was careful to sound casual, unconcerned. "This Donovan gonzo. I remember right, that's a safe seat he's got?"

"Other Party ain't had it this century."

Hartley G. Flander cracked his gavel. "Of cose, the gemmun does not mean to imply the distinguish witness is delibritly tryin to conceal—"

"No, Mister Chairman, I didn't mean to *imply* it."

"Then what makes you think he'd go?" asked Darwin John.

"Go?" Floyd Finch shook his head in as near disbelief as it was wise to display in response to Darwin John. "Chief, who'd throw this kind of stuff in Cramer's face if he wouldn't *go*? On national TV?"

Darwin John could not imagine. He did not doubt what this pissant Donovan was up to. He was rolling the dice—trying in the good old, go-ahead American spirit to move up on Connie Cramer's back. Clearly the congressman would be willing to risk his safe seat for a call to higher service. Of course, he would make the sacrifice for the party, as the chairperson was sure he would be savvy enough to put it. Or well enough coached by this hot shit Ames.

But to Darwin John, a connoisseur of political tactics, the *means* of ascent were more interesting than the motive, which was always the same.

"Our research also shows," Victor T. Donovan was saying on-screen, "that the T and A Theater in North Beach was owned as a matter of record"—the congressman ostentatiously consulted notes—"by one Jan Konrad Kremenczsko." He spelled the last name aloud and held up an official-looking paper for the camera. "And I hold here in my hand, Mister

Chairman, a California court record, dated nineteen sixty-six, legally changing Kremenczsko's name to . . ." A pregnant pause. "John Conrad Cramer."

Again the hearing was interrupted by leaping and flashing stills, reporters heading for the door, excitement sweeping over the audience. The Takeover Tycoon suddenly slumped in his chair as if the steel had gone out of his spine. The blue and gray suits seemed, for once, to lean away from him.

"Who's digging up this shit?" asked Darwin John quietly, nonchalantly.

"Rafe Ames," Floyd Finch said, almost as casually. "He's got this ex-FBI bird dog that Ames says can find you a virgin in a whorehouse."

To Finch, Darwin John seemed little moved. But words were sweeping through the chairperson's gleaming head and massive brain, like searchlight beams in a dark sky: Porno. Smut. Family Values. Innocent American Girls.

Mileage in all that, thought Darwin John.

His lineup for the gubernatorial and congressional elections coming that fall was promising. Darwin John had personally recruited some photogenic new faces and seen to it that they were coached by the best television authorities money could buy, then drilled on the issues by the most reliable polltakers not already in the employ of the Other Party.

Most of his election team was or had been governors, attorneys general, congressmen—even one former three-star general who wore his paratrooper's wings prominently pinned to his civilian lapels. The lineup included a couple of women who had state legislative experience, had never been divorced or enrolled at the Betty Ford Clinic, and dressed in the style of Margaret Thatcher. All in all, a first-rate batting order that caused Darwin John to look forward optimistically to the first Tuesday after the first Monday in November.

But the only exception was grievous. Darwin John had no candidate at all—none, he reflected, zilch, *nada*—to oppose United States Senator O. Mack Bender, twelve years already in the world's most exclusive club, one of its Big Mules, the Other Party's leading spokesman on foreign affairs, a familiar on the evening news, a face to be seen on the front pages of the *Times* and the *Post*, eventually perhaps a *Time* or *Newsweek* cover.

"Mack Bender," the *Economist* had rhapsodized from London, "combines for some Americans the homely wisdom of Abe Lincoln and the political charm of FDR."

That kind of bullshit, fumed Darwin John, if duplicated in media that anybody read, could take a pol a long way. Even to a spot on a national ticket. Already, at the OP's last national convention, Mack Bender had been on the short list for Vice President—but also the "tall list." The inside scoop was that he had been passed over because the top of the ticket did not want to be towered over by a No. 2 standing four inches taller.

Not even the lure of a Senate seat, with its six sure years on the public payroll, followed by a generous federal pension, had smoked out anyone in Bender's state willing to take him on. In his extensive hunt, starting with a governor who had no balls at all, Darwin John had gone personally down the list of the state's members of Congress, concluding that they were a sorry lot—Victor T. Donovan no exception.

Now, as he watched the blue and gray suits recover themselves and again begin to pump up J. Conrad Cramer, or whoever he was, Darwin John was less startled by the exposure of a national icon than by the realization that a jerk-off congressman nobody outside his boondocks district ever had heard of might be the party's best shot at O. Mack Bender. And if this Charlie Hustle Ames came along as part of the package, maybe he'd even found himself a sleeper.

"Listen, Floyd . . . what's this boy genius got on you, you're so high on him?"

"Brightest guy on the party payroll in years, Chief. A real vid kid. Rafe Ames knows TV like Bo knows baseball. Like you know PACs. Took him just one look to spot what a knockout this Donovan is on the tube."

"I don't even remember any goddam Rafe Ames," said Darwin John. "Wouldn't I remember him, he's such hot stuff, working right here for the committee?" Which, of course, meant working for Darwin John.

"Got a lot on your plate, Chief. Can't be expected to . . . uh . . . mark the sparrow's fall."

Darwin John did not like the allusion since at once it suggested that he might consider himself God, while reminding him that he wasn't. He did remember Rafael Ames anyway, though not favorably—a smart-ass kid in cutesy-pie T-shirts, a glorified messenger boy always trying to rack up points. But Darwin John didn't want to give Floyd Finch grounds to think that maybe, even once, he had fucked up by letting Ames go, if Ames turned out to be usable goods.

"Mister Chairman . . ."

A resonant voice broke into the chairperson's concentration. Dimly, his mind on his lineup problem, he had been aware of J. Conrad Crimininsko pulling himself together on the screen. Now the schmuck was bouncing up and down in his seat, like a boxer ready for the next round. Darwin John fixed his attention on the hearings.

"Mister Chairman, I have never purposely concealed the fact that like many an offspring of those hardy souls who came to these shores seeking freedom and opportunity through hard work, I took a name more in keeping with . . . ah . . . my hopes. That a member of this committee would seize on that commonplace event in such a sensation-seeking manner, I consider—"

"But didn't changing your name purposely conceal"—Victor T. Donovan's voice was low and unexcited, but quite audible, pitched to the microphones; the camera zoomed in on his steady eye contact with America—"the fact that the Kremenczsko who owned"—the congressman's voice dripped with distaste—"the T and A Theater was the same man who became J. Conrad Cramer?"

"I don't know anything about any T and A Theater, Mister Congressman. I really don't see—"

"Bullshit," said Darwin John. "Looks to me like your man's got Crapinsko nailed to the wall."

"And wasn't it profits taken from the smut and filth onstage and on-screen at the T and A, before Kremenczsko became Cramer . . ."

Victor T. Donovan paused to shuffle through his notes, letting the silence of horrid anticipation hang over the committee and momentarily stilling the TV speakers. The working press stared expectantly—and the witness defiantly—at the congressman.

Show biz. And not too bad, thought Darwin John.

"That furnished the basic working capital for J. Conrad Cramer's later Wall Street career?"

"Good timing," said Darwin John.

This Ames jaybird, he told himself, *could not have given Donovan that. Like only God himself gave it to Jack Benny.*

"This is ludicrous, Mister Chairman! These hearings were supposed to be—"

"A career," Victor T. Donovan said calmly, "that included Cramer, Wentz, and Marbury's takeover of Allied Ventures."

Darwin John watched Crickinsko jump again to his feet. This time the blue and gray suits, clutching their briefcases, stood with him, each noticeably a head taller than the man in the middle. The latter spoke slowly, ominously.

"This muckraking colleague of yours, Mister Chairman, is on a fishing expedition. In extremely muddy waters. With due regard for the reputation of the great American firm I have the honor to head, I must bid you good day, sir."

As the three men turned to leave the witness table, and before Chairman Flander could respond, the TV director gave the full screen back to Victor T. Donovan.

"Mister Chairman, my inquiries obviously distress this witness. In deference to you, and without objection from my able and distinguished colleagues, I'll use the rest of my time not for further questions but for a brief conclusion that Mister . . . ah . . . Cramer and his lawyers probably would do well to hear even if they don't like it."

Right up the tailpipe, thought Darwin John. The Takeover Tycoon could hardly walk out after being so directly challenged. And that kind of fast footwork was something else no coaching from the sidelines could have given a two-bit congressman. Where had he been hiding all this time?

"Vrrumph," Hartley G. Flander said, cracking the gavel as if to smash it on Victor T. Donovan's fingers. "One minute fawty seconds, suh. And of cose, the distinguish witness is mo than welcome to change his mind."

The three men at the witness table, after a quick conference, sank reluctantly into their seats. On the rostrum Victor T. Donovan calmly perused his notes. In his luxurious office across Capitol Hill, Darwin John rose from the leather sofa and stretched, a hefty bull of a man in shirt and tie by Asser and Turnbull, with an expensive suit draped expertly on his fullback's body, almost concealing a paunch that was gaining on him.

His big frame and high polished head, not to mention the legendary wheeling and dealing of the political brain therein, had led a few daring cartoonists to depict Darwin John as Daddy Warbucks. Not even his friends, who could be counted on the fingers of one hand, called him that except behind his burly back. But Floyd Finch, from long and close observation, knew that Rafael Ames had made his point.

"You're liking what you're seeing, Chief. I can tell."

The chairperson nodded slowly, reluctantly.

"Only thing is," said Darwin John, "I wish he could of nailed that fucking Creepinsko in prime time."

2.

Milo Speed was less surprised by the unmasking of Jan Konrad Kremenczsko, in whose public pose as J. Conrad Cramer he had never put much stock, than at the more startling revelation of a Victor T. Donovan whose existence Speed had never even suspected. What had got into a go-along congressman to cause him to spring for the jugular of a hero of American business? Who had unearthed the material for his sensational charges?

Speed could not believe that Victor T. Donovan had done it all by himself. He watched in bemusement as the handsome congressman pondered some papers in front of him, then looked across the room at his wife. Speed was gratified to see that Josie did not notice; she was staring at something below and in front of her.

"I raise these serious questions, Mister Chairman," Victor T. Donovan began, in a hearing room suddenly so still that the scrape of a cameraman's foot sounded like a fingernail on a blackboard, "to show my concern at a profound threat to the moral and ethical values Americans cherish."

Speed thumbed quickly through the reliable index file in

his reporter's brain. The search turned up no suggestion, in what he knew of Victor T. Donovan, of Saul on the road to Damascus.

"Mister Chairman . . ." The congressman looked earnestly into the cameras. At the witness table J. Conrad Cramer-Kremenczsko seemed visibly to be compacting himself, his small form drawing up into something like a projectile. "Even as the biblical snake tempted Eve, innocent Americans are being tempted today by purveyors of smut and filth. In sinkholes like the T and A Theater! And in all these other festering dens of disgusting sex for sale that this witness helped to spawn."

J. Conrad Kremenczsko-Cramer, Speed saw, had to be restrained from leaping to his feet again.

"I apologize to this committee and to our national audience, Mister Chairman, for having to raise this distasteful subject. But I cannot sit silent when sex orgies and deviation and perversion are openly presented as entertainment in films and advertised on the marquees of theaters like the T and A. When depraved acts are used to lure decent young Americans from the paths of virtue and morality—even, Mister Chairman"—a pause for effect, a dropping voice—"even from the church."

Bound to get to the church, Speed thought. He put away his notebook and stole a glance at Josie. Surely, he thought, *she* could not be taking Victor T. Donovan's morality play seriously.

"Can anyone doubt a direct connection between the meteoric spread of repulsive pornography and the destruction of prayer in our schools? Both imposed on us, Mister Chairman, by the secular humanistic theorists and godless doctrines of the Supreme Court."

Bound to get to that, too.

"Now the witness tells us all this is irrelevant to the subject of this hearing. But I have evidence here—Victor T. Donovan waved papers at the cameras—"photocopies of original documents that I will, of course, provide to the subcommittee. Documents recording the acquisition of something called"—he consulted the papers—"Daisychain Screens. By Leisure Life Incorporated, of San Diego."

Gabby Lukes's hot whisper seared Speed's ear: "Are these hearings rated X?"

This time, he ignored her, as Victor T. Donovan continued.

"Leisure Life in turn was acquired, as a matter of public record, and is still operated by an entertainment conglomerate called Sunnyside Enterprises, of Phoenix, Arizona—"

J. Conrad Cramer-Kremenczsko jumped to his feet, breaking the restraining holds of blue and gray; his small stature made him seem no less menacing. But Victor T. Donovan never faltered.

"And just three years ago, Mister Chairman, in a takeover that was little noticed among many larger and more publicized transactions, Sunnyside became a wholly owned subsidiary of Cramer, Wentz, and—"

"A reputable business!" J. Conrad Kremenczsko-Cramer shouted from the witness table. "An organization built by risk-taking Americans in the best traditions of this country!"

"Do you really consider"—Victor T. Donovan broke in smoothly—"a film called . . . I'm sorry, Mister Chairman . . . *Eating Miss Daisy* in the best traditions of our country?"

"I never heard of it! I don't—"

"Well, isn't it currently running in all twelve theaters of Daisychain Screens? In a double feature with *Rear Entry*?"

"I don't know! And I can assure you, Mister Chairman, if there's a word of truth in these scurrilous allegations, Cramer, Wentz, and Marbury will immediately rid ourselves of any such sleazy activity anywhere in our operation!"

"But do you mean to tell this committee," said Victor T. Donovan, "that you don't *know* whether Cramer, Wentz, and Marbury is raking in profits from exposing America's youth to smut and corruption?"

Hartley G. Flander's gavel cracked imperiously.

"Time of the gemmun's expiahed. Reckanize next the able and distinguish gemmun from . . ."

Victor T. Donovan did not even hear the chairman out or glance again at the witness table. He gathered up his papers, enclosed them in a folder, and handed it to a hovering clerk. Then he stalked up the interior aisle, looking to neither right nor left. The cameras followed his march to the rear exit.

Gabriella Lukes again whispered in Speed's ear: "There but for the grace of God goes a candidate. Why don't you take me to lunch?"

"Call you next week," Speed lied over his shoulder.

He rose, pushed hurriedly past Frank V. Stratemeyer, stepped on the foot of Mona Garden, the head of a women's lobby demanding mandated wages for housewives, and headed for the huge oak doors. Victor T. Donovan had made *himself* the story that interested Speed; he aimed to find out why and how.

He reached the doors in a stride or two but had to pull up lest he charge into a woman hurrying across the front of the chamber. Almost too late Speed recognized Josie Donovan striding into the corridor.

He jumped to follow her past the uniformed guard holding open one of the doors, past the line of would-be spectators still waiting outside. Not slowing, paying no attention to gawkers from the line, Josie looked over her shoulder and spoke casually and conversationally, as if years and circumstance had not separated them as harshly as a wall.

"The whole country saw it, Speed. That featherweight's going to be famous."

So she remembered, too. Not only did the sudden knowledge, the quick glimpse of vivid remembered eyes break Speed's journalist's preoccupation with a story; but instantly, if irrationally, as if a fist had been punched through a window pane, awakening him from catalepsy, he knew that whatever else had happened that morning, the long silence in which he had wrapped his passion, his secret smothered life had been shattered.

Josie remembered.

★

She was moving past the curious, muttering queue of spectators, along the stone echoing corridor of the Rayburn Building, so fast that Speed had to run to catch up. She moved, as she always had, as if she knew where she was going and would not be deterred from getting there. Josie, Speed remembered, had never been a woman to hesitate.

"What's the rush?" he called. "Fire down the hall?"

Still not slowing, turning her head only a little, Josie gave him a smile that took him farther into the past.

"Don't have a heart attack. I'll meet you at Vic's office."

Breathing a little hard, Speed stepped up beside her, irritated at her suggestion that he was no longer young and fit, but also that she had known not only where she was going but where *he* was going. Milo Speed hated to be predicted.

"Even at this rate," he said vindictively, "we might be too late to save him. Connie Cramer was ready to fly over that table and get his hands on Vic's neck."

"Oh, Cramer's *finished,*" Josie said. "Nobody could stand that kind of debunking."

"His money's not finished. And you saw the way he looked at Vic."

"Not really. I wasn't watching him. I was *glued* to a television monitor they had under those cameras."

"All you had to do was turn your head. You could've seen the real thing."

Josie stopped so suddenly Speed went on two or three steps before he could turn back to face her.

"Speed, what the fuck do you think the real thing *is* in politics these days?"

No man I have to call Milo is going to take me to bed, she'd told him, the first time he did.

"You could call me Milo these days," Speed said. "I see you've still got your charming vocabulary."

"Mostly learned from you."

Josie walked on, and Speed wheeled to walk with her, exulting in the first moment in years that anything personal, anything that acknowledged what they'd once been, had passed openly between them.

"Speed, you really should have *seen* Vic on the tube. Not perched up on that rostrum with those silly old turkeys. It was mostly head and shoulders, and he came through that screen like—like—"

"Gangbusters?"

The cliché echoed in the long hallway, but Speed's intended irony seemed lost on Josie. She swung around a corner into another long corridor; in the Rayburn Building, which Speed avoided when he could, the halls were like railroad tunnels with lights, stretching on seemingly to infinity, he supposed in a vain architectural effort to influence members of Congress to dwell on the immensity of things, the distance of objectives.

"Like a President," Josie said. "Better than Reagan."

Speed barely made the turn after her, as if on the outer end of a game of pop-the-whip. She did not bother to look around as she walked on briskly but said: "Wasn't that one of your old girl friends whispering in your ear back there?"

Speed was thrilled again, to know that Josie *had* been aware of his presence in the hearing room and that somehow she had kept up, over the years, with what women he'd been seen with. And not from the gossip columns; he had been too fastidious to let himself and Gabby become an "item."

"One of the hundreds," Josie said.

"I can remember when there was only one."

Josie did not reply, and Speed retreated hastily.

"No matter who Vic *looked* like in there, what got into him, Josie? What caused *him*, of all people, to pop off like that?"

"I always wondered how you got to be such a famous know-it-all columnist," Josie said. "If you really can't see what was going on, they ought to run your stuff on the comics page."

Speed had been in no doubt that something *was* "going on," beyond the specifics of Victor T. Donovan's surprise attack on a formidable target. *There but for the grace of God goes a candidate.* Whatever else he thought of Gabriella Lukes, Speed knew she had a sharp eye for Washington's political folkways.

"Surely you didn't buy Vic's little lecture on morality," he said. "Not *you*."

Josie stopped again and glared at him.

"It doesn't matter whether I buy it, or you buy it. Lots of people will. Lots of people *did*. And like I said"—she turned and strode purposefully again along the corridor—"he'll be famous now."

Her throaty, arousing voice trailed away in the machine-gun tap of her heels on the stone floor. Speed hastened to follow; without warning, Josie veered left toward a massive door across which the name VICTOR T. DONOVAN sprawled above his state's great seal.

Josie put out her hand to open the door. Suddenly, desperately, urged by old perplexities, Speed seized her arm. "Is that what you wanted? Your husband to be famous?"

Her eyes flared. "I could have had *that* with you."

Even in this new acknowledgment, this tacit linkage to the past, Speed heard—he could not miss—the clear ring of dismissal, seeming even more final in his renewed sensitivity than any echo from long ago.

He released her arm, gave her a sweeping bow to the door, and with practiced flippancy denied the piercing hurt of this new spear in his side: "And you don't know what you've missed!"

Josie gave him back not even the satisfaction of an answer. She swept past the huge state shield with head held high; inside, a desk barred further entry. From behind it a red-haired receptionist peered at them through granny glasses, quickly rising when she recognized Josie.

"Oh, Miz Donovan."

The red hair was drawn back in a tight bun and a prim white blouse, to match the glasses, was buttoned to the neck. To Speed's automatic glance, there was nothing prim about the figure ill concealed by the blouse and the straight skirt.

"Wasn't he *won*derful?" the redhead said.

"You saw the TV?"

Josie managed simultaneously to smile at the redhead and to cut her eyes triumphantly at Speed. A television set stared blankly from a corner of the office, and the redhead nodded toward it.

"Rafe called me to turn it on at the exact right moment. I've never *seen* the congressman so—so—"

"Presidential?" Speed's urge to strike out overcame a quick flick of interest at the unfamiliar name. "Treasure the moment."

"Better than that! Miz Donovan, the congressman said for you to come right on in when you got here."

Beyond the receptionist, three desks were crammed into

the big outer room, reflecting the Washington staff rated by the Honorable Victor T. Donovan's unimpressive district. The desks were occupied by two young women and one middle-aged man of weary countenance.

"Hi, Mister Horn," Josie called to the tired-looking man as she started toward the closed door to the inner office. Speed followed, having learned that an assertive presence usually served a reporter better than a polite request. The redhead moved to get in his path.

"Your name, sir?" Correct but firm.

"Tell you mine if you'll tell me yours. I—"

"Oh, come on, Speed," Josie called. "You're too old to be flirting. It's all right, Lacy."

Speed suppressed a primal scream. He thought also that the redhead probably was not amused, and he cursed himself silently. She was not much more than a child, with a precocious body swathed in decorous clothing, and she obviously thought him an old fool.

I am *an old fool,* Speed thought, hating the idea, despising himself. *A* damned *old fool.*

★

He was not too chastened to pursue his calling—he seldom was—as he followed Josie into the presence of the Honorable Victor T. Donovan. The congressman was talking with two other men, the taller and thinner of whom apparently was asking him a question: ". . . making a prepared statement in there?"

As all congressmen did, Victor T. Donovan sat behind a massive desk, almost big enough for a Ping-Pong match; as all congressmen were, he was surrounded by a vast paneled cocoon of political memorabilia and men's club furnishings. His handsome head reclined against the leather back of a tall judge's chair—the kind members could scrounge out of government warehouses.

"No . . . I was mostly just winging it."

The glistening expanse of desk was bare of anything that resembled work, though a box on one corner was labeled "In" and one on another corner was marked "Out." Both were empty. These, and the shining mahogany, annoyed Speed; anyone who could keep a desk clear, he believed, was too orderly and disciplined to enjoy life.

"Milo . . . come in!"

The congressman acknowledged Josie only with a casual wave, and she edged to the side of the room with Speed following. The two inquisitors, though glancing around, offered no greeting; worse, Speed thought, they obviously failed to recognize him. Neither had the bosomy redhead. Speed liked to be anonymous only on his own terms.

"But you say you had all the documents and evidence," the tall man said. "What were you going to do with it?"

"Turn it over to the chairman. Let the subcommittee take it from there." Victor T. Donovan strutted a little in his chair. "I've always been a team player around here."

"Then what," asked the second man, a roly-poly fellow in a rumpled seersucker suit with legs and sleeves both an inch too short, "caused you to change your mind and sound off the way you did?"

The AP and the UPI, pads and pencils in hand, obviously had got there first. Speed wondered how, considering his race down the hall with Josie. He was not used to being second in line.

"I just got mad." Victor T. Donovan looked relaxed and anything but angry.

"At what?"

The thin reporter barely concealed an incredulity Speed shared. Getting mad in public—especially at a powerhouse like J. Conrad Cramer—was what most politicians learned early not to do.

Victor T. Donovan thrust himself forward, the leather chair squeaking under him, until his handsome face—now actually appearing angry—hovered over the bare reaches of his desk.

"At that bull Kremenczsko was spreading around in there." He suddenly clapped a hand over his mouth and took it away, looking rueful.

"Phil . . . Tom . . ." he said to the reporters. "Scratch the 'bull' for me, huh? And make it 'Cramer.' "

"Okay," Tom said, or maybe it was Phil. "But what bull was it that got you so mad?"

Victor T. Donovan twisted his hands together and looked up at the ceiling, seeming for a moment lost in thought. Then, still looking at the ceiling: "Take this down . . . and I'll stand by every word."

The two reporters had their pencils ready. The intensity Josie once had reserved for Milo Speed seemed suddenly to electrify the artificial air of the room, make it crackle like tissue paper; she leaned toward Victor T. Donovan's desk as if to touch and encourage him. Her redly reminiscent lips, the touch of which in delicate places once had sent Milo Speed spiraling into ecstasies, were open and glistening in anticipation. In a rage of longing and despair, Speed got out his pad and his fat Mont Blanc pen, focusing hard to be professional.

"I had heard just about enough . . . ah . . . self-serving clichés," Victor T. Donovan said, slowly, as if feeling his way, "about the American way of life . . . uh . . . from a man who has shown no real respect for it." Pausing judiciously, he put fingertips to fingertips. "I had heard too much about creating jobs . . . all that baloney . . . um, strike that, will you, guys? All that talk about management efficiencies and American know-how . . . from a man who made his fortune on sleaze and corruption and the tearing down of American moral fiber."

Jotting his own hieroglyphics, Speed noted a none-too-subtle exaggeration of J. Conrad Cramer's T and A profits. And he could not help wondering if the congressman mumbling with such apparent sincerity really was dredging up an extemporaneous statement he could stand by.

"I just thought somebody had . . . ah . . . to tell the American people about this . . . um, this deception. It was time for somebody to tell the *truth*, you know? No matter what the political risk . . . and ah . . . well . . . I decided it might as well be Vic Donovan."

The memory banks in Milo Speed's brain again whirred and blinked: Victor T. Donovan claiming outrage at self-serving clichés while producing a string of his own, pointedly citing his own courage, as if in America it took balls to denounce live sex acts onstage. And then that unmistakable touch of sanctimony, the shift at the end to the third person.

"You show me a politician uses the royal 'we,' " an older reporter had impressed upon Speed years before, after a turgid LBJ news conference, "I'll show you a man thinks he's hot stuff. Some pol actually refers to himself by the name his mother gave him, mark my words, kid, he's phonier than a three-dollar bill."

"Is that it?" one of the wires asked Victor T. Donovan.

It was an act, Speed thought. *Bet the farm.*

But he was honest enough to question his quick certainty. Was nothing but his reporter's antenna quivering? Might not anger and hurt and jealousy be equally at work?

"Isn't that *enough*?" Victor T. Donovan put his feet up on the uncluttered desk, laughing a little too loudly at his own remark. "You boys want Cramer coming after me with a tommy gun?"

Phil and Tom laughed, also too loudly, offered cursory working press thanks, and turned to leave just as redheaded Lacy opened the door from the outer office.

"Some television people are here, Mister Donovan. Can you see them now?"

"Television." Tom, or maybe it was Phil, turned back to Victor T. Donovan, contempt edgy in his voice. "You won't give 'em anything you didn't give us, will you?"

"Would I do that to the *wires*? After all these years on the Hill?" But the congressman sat up and adjusted his tie. Then, holding up a hand to Josie and Speed: "Send 'em on in, Lacy. You guys don't mind, do you?"

"A pleasure to watch you work." Speed could taste his own malice. "I like the part best where you get unexpectedly mad."

Lacy was lingering in the doorway. "Mister John is on the line, too."

"Darwin John?"

Victor T. Donovan's face quickly turned serious, but it was Josie's breathless voice that had spoken.

Can't be.

Darwin John—national chairman, fund-raising king,

maker of Presidents—surely had no time, Speed thought, for two-bit congressmen like Victor T. Donovan.

"That's the one," Lacy said. "Darwin John."

"You see, Speed? Didn't I tell you?" Josie's blue eyes shone with excitement. "Darwin John saw the TV, too."

Milo Speed did see. He saw, for sure, that Victor T. Donovan had not been merely "winging" his exchange with Cramer-Kremenczsko. The *decision*, moreover, to challenge such an apparent powerhouse could not have flashed up in a moment of heat. Nor could such a thorough ransacking of J. Conrad Cramer's subterranean history have been casual staff work.

So that explosion of righteous anger graphically detailed to gullible Phil and trusting Tom, complete with appropriate uhs, ahs, and ums, had been as deliberate and calculated as a commencement address. Perhaps only Victor T. Donovan's third-person reference to himself, the might-as-well-be-Vic bullshit, had been spontaneous.

That had been enough for Milo Speed, the giveaway to all the rest, needing only the confirmation of Darwin John on the line.

"Say to Mister John I'm doing television," Victor T. Donovan told Lacy. "But I'll get back to him right away."

No doubt about that, Speed thought.

None at all.

★

"Don't let them shoot till I get back." Josie moved quickly across the office toward the door to Victor T. Donovan's private bathroom. "I don't want to miss a thing."

"Hold them a minute or two, Lacy," she heard Vic say obediently as she closed the bathroom door.

Josie did not release or turn the doorknob. Carefully she eased the door a quarter inch back from the jamb; through the slitlike opening thus created, she had a narrow view across Vic's desk. She heard, but could not see, Lacy close the outer door.

Immediately, and just as Josie had expected, as soon as both women left the room, Milo Speed seized the moment. Every inch the bloodhound reporter—how well she remembered!—he strode across the congressional carpet into Josie's restricted view.

"Are you in debt, Vic?"

"Only my home mortgage."

She saw Speed brace himself with both hands on Vic's large, clean desk.

"Playing around? Getting into that gorgeous redhead out there?"

Hasn't changed a bit, Josie thought. Speed never had been able to keep his mind off sex.

"What is this, Milo?"

Vic sounded downright indignant; he was getting to be quite an actor. But she knew he would never have the nerve to move on a woman, and he was certainly too cautious politically to hit on some chickie who could take a sexual harassment charge to the Ethics Committee. So cautious that no matter what Rafael Ames had predicted, Josie had doubted—right up to the moment he did it—that Vic actually would go for J. Conrad Cramer's jugular.

Rafe.

Those knowing eyes of his, that prowling, youthful vitality—Rafe Ames made her strangely nervous. She was still dazzled, less at Vic's sudden daring than at Rafe's insight, sharper than her own—his ability to see what Vic's everyday blandness had concealed even from his wife. Or had she not looked closely enough?

"Better get used to questions like that," Speed said, "since you decided to play guardian of the national morals on Connie Cramer's TV time."

With her eye to the narrow opening, Josie saw Speed stand away from Vic's desk and fix him with what she supposed was his journalist's stare. *The only way to look at a politician,* Speed would say, *is down.*

"They'll be checking for any vulnerability," Speed said. "Money, booze, your zipper down too often."

Victor T. Donovan? Josie had to stifle a laugh.

"I don't even drink, Milo. Clean as a hound's tooth. Let me—"

And just as dull.

"—set the record straight, as long as you raise the question. I did *not* decide to play guardian of anything this morning. I just—"

"You just got mad enough to catch Darwin John's eye. And let *me* set the record straight. If Darwin John wants you, he'll go over you harder than I just did."

"Milo . . . what the hell would Darwin John want Vic Donovan for? He doesn't even *know* me."

Speed was silent for a moment. When he spoke, Josie thought there was a peculiar satisfaction in his tone: "He does now."

"Well . . . if he *did* look, Darwin John wouldn't find anything either. Vic Donovan has nothing to hide, Milo."

Josie had never heard Vic refer to himself by his own name like that. It was vaguely disturbing, as if somehow he were putting imagined distance between some newly assumed and his old familiar self. But it was surely true, she thought, that he had nothing damaging to hide. Vic was too careful, too calculating. Too unexciting.

Josie silently closed the door and applied herself in front of the mirror on the medicine chest. She fancied she saw a look of triumph on her face, and she *was* a little set up by her small but successful ruse. If eavesdropping was undignified, too bad; a woman needed any edge she could get. And she was glad to have put one over on two men who had claimed so much from her—Speed, for a time, her body and soul; Vic, the years she'd never get back. And not just the years.

"So much more," Josie whispered to the mirror.

She should have left him, she told herself for the thousandth time, after the miscarriage. Vic's disappointment then should have been all the signal she needed, because he had not grieved for her, or for their stillborn son, or for the other children the doctors said they could never have.

Victor T. Donovan had seen that terrible loss, that moment shattering to her life, as it should have been to his, only as a political setback, an unwanted stain on his image—the childlessness he feared someday would make him less attractive to voters.

She remembered exactly what he'd said to her, even as she

lay weeping in her hospital bed: "And where'll I be if I ever have to run against some guy that can show off a real American family?"

He had been no longer an AA but a member of Congress by then, Meldrim Hooks having gone to his dubious reward, his seat handed on almost by right of inheritance to young Victor T. Donovan, of whom such great things were expected. She couldn't just walk out, had told herself she would not as callously harm his career by desertion as he had damaged their life together by indifference to their loss and her pain.

So she had stayed with him for the moment, waiting her time—so she thought. The obvious escape, into love affairs, was difficult on the magnified screen of congressional life, and Josie's few flings had been short and rarely sweet, for she feared what she had learned too painfully from Milo Speed—how easily she could yield to the dark and the wild within herself. The less threatening confines of marriage to Victor T. Donovan had provided, as marriage does, a stability, even if resented, in her life.

"Dull, dull, *dull*," she said to the mirror, angered to recall how stability, slowly and reluctantly, had become acceptance and resignation.

Josie's image stared back at her; she was not sure what it saw or reflected. The morning's events had given her a nervous excitement, not unlike the strange edge Rafael Ames's predatory presence could cause. If Rafe was right again—and Darwin John's phone call suggested that he was—Victor T. Donovan might be about to realize what had been so often predicted for his public self, beginning in that dim past when he had seemed to her the embodiment of what their university classmates had voted him: Most Likely to Succeed.

But power was never what you *wanted*, she told the face in the mirror. *Or position. That was never what went wrong between you and Vic.*

Or was it?

Maybe she had been for so long accustomed to the sideline role of kibitzer that she had too nearly resigned herself to that, too. Even the suggestion that Vic might join the game at last—the Washington game, the power game—*had* picked up the beat a little, made her blood run faster. Ever since Rafe Ames had come to them with his confident ideas, she had to admit, life had seemed quicker, colors bolder, the air more bracing.

Hearing Speed's voice but not his words from the other room, she wondered if that new awareness was why an undeniable current had run between them that morning, recalling how he once could move her, virtually control her—carrying her back to a time—*the last time I swear*—when she had plunged into the fathomless pit of sensuality she felt always yawning beneath her.

"Bastards," Josie said aloud, staring at herself in the mirror. Victor T. Donovan and Speed together.

Bastards.

★

Thus buoyed by anger, at men, her life, the new excitement she felt somehow she should not enjoy, Josie came out of the bathroom freshly combed and lipsticked, and saw with pleasure that the men who had claimed her life thought her beautiful—Speed with an open hunger that gave her vengeful satisfaction, Vic with an objective appraisal that all but spoke itself aloud: She would do.

"Lights," Josie said, more brightly than she felt, "camera, action. Where are they?"

Victor T. Donovan touched a button beneath his desk, and Lacy appeared in the door.

"Send in the clowns," the congressman said. "And I expect you can show Mister Speed out."

"Oh, I'll hang around for the next show."

Josie was not surprised, though Vic clearly was. "None of your wise-ass remarks then." She was unwilling to see Speed score a total victory.

"Oh, I'd *never* interfere with television. Or Vic's opportunities."

Victor T. Donovan gave him a sour look that Josie watched turn into a broad smile as Lacy ushered in a television crew, led by a large Windsor knot under a well-sprayed hairdo and a broad ski instructor's smile. The hairdo vigorously introduced himself, and he and the congressman were immediately on first-name terms.

"You want me behind the desk, Joel?"

Joel adjusted his Windsor knot. Behind him, technicians were setting up; black cords began to writhe like snakes across the carpet.

"Tell you what, Vic. How's about we do it over by your wall of photos there?"

Victor T. Donovan began to stand up, but the cameraman, a surly-looking party with a dead cigar clamped in the corner of his mouth, waved him back down.

"No can do. Stills reflect too much light off the wall."

"Oh, right." Joel smoothed the blond hair that fitted his skull like a helmet. "Behind the desk'll be fine, Vic."

Victor T. Donovan sat down again. Speed tapped the cameraman on the shoulder.

"Frankie . . . you've come up in the world."

Frankie regarded Speed glumly. "You call this up?"

"Well, you used to be just one of the reels. The network's got to be better."

"Too fuckin' much work. 'Sides, this ain't network. How you comin', Speed?"

"Not often enough."

Behind the dead cigar, Frankie made a sound Josie supposed was a laugh. *I hope it's true,* she thought, even as she doubted it. *Since Speed never thinks of much else.*

"Otherwise okay," Speed said.

Frankie took the cigar stump out of his mouth, though some of it clung to his lower lip. "You use to get more'n any reporter in the White House press. Them days gone for good, ain't they?"

Lacy appeared to announce the arrival of more television, which caused Victor T. Donovan to remark to Joel: "I don't want to rush you guys, but I know you want your own interview. So we better get going."

"Right. No gang bang." Joel sat in front of the big bare desk. "Lemme tell you, Vic, the network wants a look at what we shoot. So make it good. All set, Frankie?"

"Get what?" Josie could not resist asking Speed. She looked

at him with eyes as innocent as she could make them. "When you were in the White House press?"

"I *been* set." Frankie pushed a light meter in Victor T. Donovan's face. "You set, Slats?" He looked over his shoulder at the sound person, a lanky girl in coveralls and a pigtail.

"News beats." Speed matched Josie's innocent expression. "But like Frankie said, them days gone for good." He could not quite, Josie noticed, keep a touch of melancholy out of his words.

"You mean you're not . . . ah . . . *up* to getting news beats anymore?"

Speed looked momentarily stricken, and Josie felt an unwanted pang of remorse. She felt, suddenly, as if she should say something comforting, maybe even touch his arm.

Before she could yield to impulse, if she would have, the lighting technician clapped his hands in front of Frankie's lens. Frankie bent to his eyepiece. Slats fiddled with knobs and dials. Victor T. Donovan, a tiny microphone clinging like an insect to his sober tie, lifted his chin and looked young for his years.

"Mister Congressman, let me ask you first . . ." Joel paused portentously. "What was the intent of your unexpected public attack on the financier . . . uh . . . J. Conrad Cramer?"

Victor T. Donovan drew a deep breath and stared straight into the camera's eye. "Well . . . I had heard just about enough self-serving clichés about the American way of life and the American dream from a man who doesn't really respect it. But I wouldn't say I made an *attack* on Mister . . . uh . . . Cramer. I just felt like somebody had to tell the American people the truth about the immoral foundation of his empire. And it seemed to me it might as well be Vic Donovan."

Josie heard a faint strangled sound escape Speed's throat.

"But what was the source of your surprising information about a man so many people admire—admired?"

Victor T. Donovan opened a drawer of his immaculate desk and took out a piece of paper. "An outraged and patriotic American came to us some time ago with this document. It set my staff investigators on a trail that nobody else seems to have followed or even imagined to exist."

Before Joel could reach for the paper, Victor T. Donovan held it up before Frankie's peering camera.

"It's a memo to J. Conrad . . . uh . . . Cramer, dated just after the buyout of Sunnyside Enterprises. It's unsigned, to protect the writer, but . . . that long ago . . . it urges the spin-off of Daisychain Screens to protect the image of Cramer, Wentz, and Marbury."

"And that was enough to start your inquiry?"

"That," said Victor T. Donovan directly into the camera, "was enough to make Vic Donovan's blood boil!"

Josie knew Rafe Ames had dictated the "blood boil" line. Vic had studied his lines well; the idea disconcerted her, even as her certainty of his new prospects mounted.

"So you're convinced," Joel concluded, "that J. Conrad . . . ah . . . Cramer knew all along that his company owned Daisychain Screens?"

"Joel, you can take that to the bank."

Another of Ames's answers; Vic had made it sound like his own, though Josie knew he seldom ventured into even mild colloquialism. He tended to say things like "The parameters of the problem may be more extensive than you think" rather than "That's too hot to handle." In bed, in the early days of their marriage, he had once spoken respectfully of her vulva, leading Josie to suggest that he call a spade a spade.

"Well, that's it from Joel Larch—"

Speed took out his notebook and a fat, pretentious fountain pen and jotted down something.

"—with Congressman Victor T. Donovan . . ."

The sight of the expensive pen took Josie back involuntarily to days and nights when Milo Speed, just getting by on a young reporter's salary, drove an ancient used car with broken springs in the back seat cushion.

"Livens up sex," he'd said one night while making love to her on that bristly and creaking seat, with cars whistling past the parking lot just off the George Washington Parkway.

"Since when," Josie had demanded, not breaking rhythm, "did sex need livening up?"

Imagine, she thought now, listening to Joel Larch, if one of those cars had stopped. Maybe the police. She was angered even to have recalled that night—to remember that then she really hadn't minded the broken springs or even noticed the passing cars. Now, she resented the fact that Speed, by his mere presence, brought back those long-ago times, made her recall the wild side of her nature she had worked hard, not always successfully, to contain.

Joel Larch wheeled to face Frankie's camera, expertly blocking Victor T. Donovan out of the frame. ". . . in the Sam Rayburn Building. Now back to you, Heidi."

Smiling at Josie, Vic relaxed in his high-backed chair. She smiled back. Rafe had been right about Vic on TV; Rafe somehow had seen a potential she never had: that Victor T. Donovan's bland manner appeared sincere but aggressive, almost tigerish, on the tube.

"Network'll find a coupla usable bites in there, Vic." Joel thrust his hairdo and his Windsor knot over Victor T. Donovan's gleaming desk and extended his hand.

"That part about the American Dream," Speed said to Josie, "Vic should set that sonnet to music."

"Smartass."

Josie threw the word back at him as she moved across the room. As soon as she had spoken, she regretted even that much renewed intimacy. Speed still had the infuriating ability to make her say things she wished she hadn't.

She took a compact from her shoulder bag and gently patted Vic's forehead with a powder puff; then she noticed, with a further stab of anger, how complacently he allowed her to do it. So before he could relax too much, think too well of himself, she whispered:

"Better call Darwin John before he forgets about you."

Frankie went out last, the cigar stump still in his mouth, a tripod over his shoulder. "Like I told you, Speed. Too fuckin' much work."

Lacy appeared in the door in time to hear this. Oblivious, Frankie pushed past her into the reception room.

"I'm sorry you had to hear that kind of language," Speed said to Lacy. "These cameramen are rather uncivilized sometimes."

He'll be in her pants, Josie thought, annoyed still further, *before she can get them off.*

"Lacy," Vic said, "you think you can stall those guys out there long enough for me to call back Darwin John?"

"They'll wait," Josie assured him. She knew—with Rafe calling the shots—this would not be the last time television crews besieged the offices of Victor T. Donovan. "They wouldn't be here if they wouldn't wait."

"I'll get him for you right away." Lacy started out of the office, then paused to hold out her hand to Speed. "I'm sorry I didn't realize who you were, Mister Speed. At first, I mean. It's really an honor to meet you."

Either Lacy had forgiven, Josie thought, or had not understood, the way Speed had looked her over in the outer office, measuring her tits and his prospects. Most likely Lacy was just a little fool; she seemed to think it really was an honor to meet Milo Speed, the well-known columnist.

With more scalps hanging from his belt than Sitting Bull.

"The honor is really mine," Speed said shamelessly.

That caused Josie to decide, as Lacy moved out of the office, that enough was more than enough.

"*Now,* Speed," she said briskly, decisively, "you can just get your ass out of here."

She came from behind Donovan's desk and leaned against its front, her arms crossed, letting her pleated skirt outline the long legs she considered her best feature, though in the old days, she well remembered, Speed often had said her breasts were more beautiful. "Glorious," he had liked to say.

"This is really going to be private business," she insisted.

"With Darwin John? But if *he*'s on the line, Josie, that's *news*. Could do Vic some good. Isn't that right, Vic?"

For the first time that morning a hint of indecision crossed Victor T. Donovan's handsome statesman's face.

"Well . . . the thing is, Milo, I don't know what this may be all about."

"Of course, you could *tell* me later . . . if we have lunch again."

Josie saw that Speed was reminding Vic of the lush expense account spread he'd already provided at Washington's best restaurant and suggesting that there might be more of the same. Or *no* more.

"But I've got a piece to write *today*," Speed went on. "And there's plenty of *other* stuff to write about—if you'd rather I didn't write about you, Vic."

"Oh, it's not *that*," Victor T. Donovan said. "You know it's not that, Milo. It's just that—" He was interrupted, from a table behind him, by the rattlesnake buzz of a desk phone the size and complexity of a computer keyboard. "Oh, hell . . ." He picked up the receiver. "Stick around if you want." He punched one among several rows of buttons.

"Pleasure to hear from you, Chief," Vic said. "Sorry I was a little while getting back."

Josie sat on a black leather sofa, grudgingly making room for Speed beside her, under an extensive photographic display of Presidents signing bills, with Victor T. Donovan unobtrusively among the other politicians clustered in the Oval Office or the East Room. There were other photos, too, of Vic on various rostrums and strutting in numerous parades, even a centerpiece of Josie herself, with outthrust rump, cracking a bottle of champagne on a ship's bow.

"I hate that picture," she'd told Vic. "Makes me look like I've got a fat ass, and I don't."

But Vic kept the picture on the wall because the ship was named for the only city of any size in his district. *Which was just like him*, she thought. *Not to give a damn what I think.*

"Well, thanks, Chief. I was really just winging it." Vic rotated his chair a little away from them.

A staccato crackle from the telephone sounded like a newspaper being crumpled. But Darwin John's words were not clear; Josie had to infer his end of the conversation from Vic's. Straining to hear, sensing Speed beside her straining, too, she was vaguely displeased to find herself hoping Rafe Ames's scheme had had its planned effect. She had to admit to herself that she *wanted* Rafe to have been right; *she* wanted the opportunity Rafe had opened to Vic. She had been a kibitzer too long.

"Tell you the truth," Vic said, "I don't know about you, Chief, but I'd heard just about enough self-serving clichés about the American way of life from somebody who really doesn't understand it."

"Let me get this down." Speed made a show of pulling out his notebook and the fat pen.

"Screw you," Josie breathed.

She hitched farther around on the sofa, showing Speed her shoulders and back. It was not just his physical presence she shunned; Josie had got used to that over the years, at cocktail parties, dinners where she and Vic were always below the salt and the famous columnist above, at inaugurations, receptions—any of the places where people saw each other in Washington, whether they wanted to or not.

She was accustomed to seeing Milo Speed in all those places, with his insolent eyes and no doubt his usual hard-on. But not until that very day had Josie realized how hard she'd run, not so much from Speed himself as from *the rest of it*, how desperately she had wanted to have been right that long-ago day when she had nerved herself to finish it.

"Well, I don't mind telling you, I'm glad to hear you say that, Chief. I had to get it all off my chest, but I did wonder a little bit if I was hitting one of your big contributors. I certainly didn't want to hurt the party."

Speed held up one arm and sawed the other hand slowly across it, mock playing a violin. He was impossible, Josie thought, shifting herself farther away from him.

"The party's been good to me," Vic said, "and I've always tried to be good for the party."

Finally, and really for the first time, Josie decided she *had* been right. That Speed could still affect her so forcefully, after so many years, told her again how nearly she had given herself up to him.

"Well, Chief, I have to tell you"—Victor T. Donovan's voice rang with pleasure—"that's about the most flattering thing anybody ever said to me."

Josie scarcely heard because she was trying vengefully to think of the worst thing that could befall Milo Speed, pay him back for his renewed presence in her life. Not losing his column and income and standing; he was cynical about journalism and politics, cared little for money, derided status. No, the worst thing that could possibly happen to Milo Speed had to be about his real life—his sex life. What would be the worst would be if he ever got Lacy into bed—no, *when* he got Lacy into bed—and couldn't get it up.

Josie hoped devoutly that it would happen soon. Lacy's virginity be damned. It was doubtful the little twit still had it anyway.

★

"Chief, I hope you know how much I appreciate what you're suggesting."

The crackle on the other end of the line resumed. Josie sat stiffly and straight up on the sofa, turned almost entirely away from Speed. It was obvious to him, and hurtful, that she was ignoring him, focusing her special intensity on Victor T. Donovan's conversation.

"One thing I ought to mention . . . before I could make any decision at all, I'd of course want to see some poll data. I never—"

The voice on the other end interrupted, in a staccato more rapid than before.

"Well, that'd answer a lot of questions for me, Chief."

So Darwin John had agreed to finance a poll, but of what? Only one office could be in question. Milo Speed already had considered that and dismissed it.

Impossible. Not a dim bulb like Victor T. Donovan.

More crackling on the receiver. The congressman leaned back in his impressive chair, looking at Josie with what Speed could only call a triumphant expression.

Impossible?

"All right, Chief, I'll look forward to that kind of data. And believe me, you and the committee should know that I'd *like* to take this on if that's what you decide and if I possibly can."

The rest of the conversation, as nearly as Speed could tell, was an exchange of the kind of meaningless pleasantries at which politicians excelled. He watched Victor T. Donovan replace the receiver on the computerlike control panel.

"Just like Rafe said!" Josie had jumped to her feet. "Rafe called it on the nose!"

Rafe again. Speed ran the unfamiliar name rapidly through the computer in his brain. Nothing printed out. But he had little doubt what that crackling voice on the line had proposed.

"Nothing's likely to come of it," said Victor T. Donovan, obviously for Milo Speed to hear. A tint of satisfaction lay on his face like pancake makeup.

"Oh, but it will." Speed crossed the room to the shining empty desk, his reporter's instinct moving with him. Josie stared at him defiantly. "You're going to accept, aren't you?"

Victor T. Donovan's face and voice were bland. "Accept what? The chairman was just talking a little local politics."

"Sure," Speed said. "Just a little local gossip about you taking on Mack Bender."

Victor T. Donovan laughed, a little hollowly. "That'd be sort of like running against George Washington, wouldn't it?"

"He's just guessing," Josie said.

At the malevolence he thought he heard in her voice, Speed could not help wincing.

"Josie . . . I make a living guessing."

Victor T. Donovan held up both hands. "The chairman was just kicking around some far-out ideas, Milo. Just blue-skying. Don't read too much into it."

Speed knew an evasion when he heard one; all Victor T. Donovan would have had to say was: "I'm not that crazy." Or "I wouldn't think of it." But nine times out of ten evasion was as good as confirmation.

"Not too much," Speed said. "I won't."

"Certainly nothing for you to *write* about. Mack Bender's been in the Senate . . . what? Twelve years? Some people even talk about him for the *top,* for Christ sake."

"If," Speed said, "he's reelected to the Senate."

The congressman's well-tended hands rose before him as if to fend off attack, and his words were as studied as a teacher's to a slow learner: "Do you really think Vic Donovan would be fool enough to give up a safe seat to take on somebody like *that*?"

This was close enough to a real denial to give Speed pause. But there was that third person again. Speed fell back on the political instinct he trusted more than anyone. He looked into Josie's defiant blue eyes and thought he would do anything to turn those eyes soft again, avid for him. Anything but go along with a sham.

"So why do you need a poll to tell you what you already know? And why put on that attack-dog show for TV? If Mack Bender would be so hard to beat?"

"Milo . . . I did *not* put on a show for anybody. I was flabbergasted Darwin John called me. I—"

"You're not fooling him, Vic." Josie spoke bitterly, knowingly. "He's too fucking cynical to fool."

Milo Speed took that gladly, and not just because he heard in it another distant note of personal recognition. The charge rang with the spirit of the old Josie, who had never deluded herself. In there somewhere, then, in the congressman's combed and apparently conniving wife, the old go-to-hell Josie lived and breathed. Speed was, for a moment, insanely happy.

"Cynical enough to tell you this." Speed was speaking to Victor T. Donovan, but he looked only at Josie. "You let Darwin John talk you into running, Mack Bender's going to frazzle your ass."

"Oh, I've had enough of this."

Josie marched past the desk, past Speed, chin high and eyes flaring. Halfway across the office, she flung over her shoulder: "Enough of *you*."

As if with flags flying, she went briskly on out of the room, slamming the door behind her.

"Josie's . . . uh . . . not used to dealing with the press," Victor T. Donovan said apologetically.

"Well, she'd better *get* used to it." Speed began to move toward the door, too.

Behind him, Victor T. Donovan asked mildly: "Are you going to write about Darwin John calling me? Get yourself out on a limb like that?"

"I might." Then he wondered if the apparently reluctant congressman was obliquely suggesting that he do so. He added: "Then again I might not."

Let him worry about it.

Just before leaving the room, Speed fired one more shot: "In my work, Vic, I live out on a limb."

When he opened the door, red-haired Lacy and a second Windsor knot rushed past him, tailed by a second set of technicians and equipment.

"Vic!" Speed heard the new Windsor cry. "How ya doing, Vic?"

Did he really, Speed wondered, want to lend the credibility of his by-line—one of the nation's most respected, which he was careful to protect—to what he was sure was a political scheme?

"Where do you want me, Ken?" he heard Victor T. Donovan inquire before the door closed.

His first Washington bureau chief had given Speed the best guidance. Never concern yourself with the *consequences* of a story, he had preached—only with whether or not you've got the facts or the sources to justify writing it.

"If you're going to worry about what happens *because* you write a story," he had told Speed, "better you should go into politics."

Josie stood by the reception desk, talking to a young man dressed casually in jeans and a sweat shirt blazoned with large red letters: "I NEVER VOTE." Smaller blue print proclaimed beneath: "THAT ONLY ENCOURAGES 'EM."

"Mister Speed . . ." Lacy had come out of the inner office and took his arm. "This is the congressman's new campaign consultant, Rafael Ames. Rafe, you ought to know Mister Speed."

"Milo Speed? I sure should," Rafael Ames said.

"I don't see why." Josie's voice now, Speed thought, was faintly derisive. "Speed still thinks television is a fad."

Rafael Ames chuckled, holding out his hand. "I doubt *that*. I thought that column you wrote the other day was a masterpiece, Mister Speed."

"Which one?"

Speed was pleased, in spite of a sudden conviction, based on little more than the juvenile sweat shirt, that he was going to dislike Rafael Ames when he really got to know him.

"You can call him Milo," Josie said brightly. "I certainly do and always will."

Ames shook hands firmly, vigorously. " 'The Old Dipsy-Doo.' The one about the spin doctors."

He had a sharp young face, piercing eyes beneath brows that almost grew together over his nose, a haircut rather more closely clipped than the network style. A fashionable hint of *Miami Vice* stubbled his hard jawline. Though not as tall as Speed, Ames looked fit, muscular—probably a runner, a goddam gazelle, Speed thought morosely. *Like all these hot dog yuppies today.*

"You probably haven't heard of me yet," Ames said, "but being one of the breed myself, I thought you nailed us on the head."

On second thought, Speed realized, there was more to dislike than the sweat shirt, more even than the hints he'd picked up that Victor T. Donovan's startling new personality and prospects were largely the fruit of this young man's calculations. False humility, in Speed's view, was the worst kind of arrogance.

"Oh, you'll hear about Rafe," Josie said. "Rafe's got ideas coming out the back of his head."

A tuft of black hair had crept above the loose collar of Ames's sweat shirt. Even standing still, Speed thought, Ames had a quality of nervous energy, of controlled motion, like a man who could do a black flip from a standing start. Or knee a mugger in the crotch before he could pull a knife.

"But you know how it is with ideas," Ames said. "Ten bad don't make one good."

"Same with columns," Speed said automatically, mechanically, out of his practiced skill at masking his feelings. "Looks like you turned up some pretty sensational stuff for your boss this morning."

"I didn't have a lot to do with that." Ames lowered his voice confidentially. "We got this tip, and this . . . ah . . . this investigator type that works with us sometimes, he managed to follow up the lead. But the congressman just sort of took off on his own this morning, and I got to tell you, I was glad to see him do it. That Cramer's a scumbag."

"I'll bet you were glad," Speed said.

He had not failed to see that Josie had focused on Ames, during this exchange, the laserlike intensity she once had turned on Speed himself. More than at any time since the sight of her in the hearing room had awakened the hibernating beast he had thought dead, Speed felt the full, shattering despair of loss.

"We got a lot to work with in this lady's husband," Ames said. "He's a TV natural. And we're going to make the most of what we've got."

Rafael Ames—the mere sight of him—made Speed feel old, tired, inadequate, his disguise penetrated, by the one person he could least allow to detect the reality beneath: himself. With harsh clarity Speed knew he needed what he seldom sought—support. Someone, something to cling to.

Red-haired Lacy's hand brushed Speed's, lingered. That had to be accidental, he knew. But desperate as he suddenly was for even feigned or inadvertent human connection, he moved his own hand against Lacy's, gently, gratefully.

Josie said warmly to Ames: "Vic's got confidence in you, too."

Lacy did not move her hand from Speed's. He supposed she had not even noticed their touch. It didn't matter; the warmth of her hand had given him the strength he had so abruptly needed.

"Lots of work to do," he announced cheerfully, in command of himself again, if only for the moment. "Share a taxi downtown, Josie?"

"No, thanks." She hardly looked at him. "I'm having lunch on the Hill."

Speed shook Rafael Ames's proffered hand again, reluctantly and as perfunctorily as he could, made a formal little bow to Lacy, gave Josie a nod of his head as painful as an hour on an exercise bike, and went alone into the empty and echoing corridor, his empty and echoing life.

One thing sure, he told himself, listening to his footsteps

on the stone floor, to his heart beating as hollowly in his chest. He would write no column about Darwin John and a Senate race for Victor T. Donovan. Some things asked too much, even of a reporter.

"They can damn well do their worst," he said out loud, to the silent corridor, "with no help from me."

As he spoke, a young man in an Atlanta Braves baseball cap had come out of a public men's room. A wide smile split his pudgy face.

"Mister Speed!" He seized Speed's hand, pumped it hard. "I seen you once on TV. My dad's been reading you—"

"Forever," Speed said. "Feels that way to me, too."

3.

Lacy Farnes could not remember a more exciting few days in all the months that she had been working on Capitol Hill—maybe in her whole life.

She turned off the power on her word processor, ready to leave the office, hardly believing that she actually was so nearly at the heart of the matter, the center of things. Back in Winooski, or later studying history at the University of Vermont, who could have imagined that little Lacy Farnes—daughter of a small-town dentist, Miss Congeniality in her high school class, scholarship student at college—would ever be in Washington, working in the Sam Rayburn Building? Working, at that, for a man who had stirred the nation with a single speech, of whom the television suddenly could not seem to get enough, and who was getting hundreds of telephone calls, including at least one a day from the national party chairperson? Not to mention what seemed like *every*body who was *any*body in his district.

Mr. Horn, the congressman's administrative assistant, paused by her desk on his way out. His eyes looked more tired than usual, after the hectic days they'd had, and his collar was wilted above an understated necktie.

"Looks like the fat's in the fire, Miss Farnes."

"Did you ever see anything like it? The *telegrams*."

Lacy mentioned the telegrams shrewdly because Mr. Horn had taken it upon himself to open and read them all—*stacks* of them—then personally carried the stacks in to show the congressman. Actually it had been the telephone that just about drove the rest of the office crazy. All those people from the district calling in to tell the congressman how much they admired the stand he'd taken for clean living and morality. How brave he'd been to expose that awful Cramer, or whoever he was.

An organized campaign, Mr. Horn said, with a wise look, from the *top*. But that didn't make all those phone calls any easier to handle. And all those press people asking for interviews, some even from the big eastern papers. One actually from *Time*.

"It's a mistake around here," Mr. Horn said, "to think they're not listening"—he swept his arm backward—"out there."

Lacy nodded in polite agreement, but she was still thinking of the phone calls. The congressman was always polite, of course, and always welcomed constituent contact, but the poor man had been able to talk to only a *fraction* of the callers. He had given only the most important interviews, though lots more were scheduled. Only so many hours in his day, even if he *was* a congressman. And the phone still ringing off the hook.

"I remember once I was a research assistant for old Senator Capps." Mr. Horn gazed solemnly down at her. "That they called the Sagebrush Solon? Wanted to go back to free coinage of silver at sixteen to one?"

Lacy had too much sense to admit that she had never heard of the Sagebrush Solon. She nodded brightly, as if her major in European history had taught her all about old congressional legends. Mr. Horn ran the congressman's office, after all, and Lacy had discovered quickly that in his tired eyes it was almost as important to appear knowledgeable about the Hill as it was to listen to his windbag stories.

"He could usually clear the Senate floor," Mr. Horn went on, satisfied that Lacy was following his account, "just by getting up and saying, 'Mister President.' But this one day, seems to me like it was no longer ago than last week, he shocked everybody. Being from the West, I mean."

Lacy had seen to it that Mister Horn liked her—especially since he was clearly too old and settled to make any of the usual moves men made. He was letting her go home, for instance, and making one of the other girls stay to answer the phone that kept ringing, just as it had ever since the congressman's famous speech.

"You maybe won't believe this, but old Capps actually came out for *handgun registration*." The shock of it was still in Mister Horn's voice.

The other girl had worked in the office longer, but Lacy had noticed that she sometimes acted impatient with Mr. Horn. Like keeping on with paper work while he was telling her something that happened during the Kennedy administration. Lacy was smart enough to see that the other girl wouldn't get ahead by slighting Mr. Horn that way, despite the way she crammed herself into her tacky skintight sweaters.

"Well!" Mr. Horn said. "There's more people in some cities than there was in Senator Capps's whole state, but the telegrams and phone calls just came flooding in. Near 'bout's many as we been seeing recently. Every one dead against him."

"I should *think* so."

Lacy could see that this was the right tack to take, though actually she thought that what had happened to President Reagan showed that Senator Capps had been right. But Mr. Horn probably was talking about before Reagan was shot.

"Senator had to climb down the next day, of course. I doubt he'd have got out on a limb like that if those Cubans hadn't shot up the House."

The phone rang again. *Never going to quit,* Lacy thought.

"Or maybe they were Porter Ricans." Mr. Horn tapped a long finger on the corner of Lacy's desk. "Point is, and you better believe it, young lady, a member wants to keep his head above water round here, he better never get too far out front of the voters."

On Mr. Horn's tongue, the word "voters" rang with veneration. He added: "Specially on guns."

Lacy tried to let admiration gleam through her granny glasses. "There's so much to *learn*, Mister Horn."

"Well, you never know." Mr. Horn paused, reflecting on this wisdom. "Like the boss the other day. Most people would have advised him against zinging that Cramer."

Including Mr. Horn, Lacy was sure. Except that she had reason to doubt he'd known in advance what the congressman intended to do. Even if he was the AA.

"Cramer's a bad man to cross, all right. But the boss had his facts straight, and he was shrewd enough to figger the voters were up to here"—Mr. Horn held the back of his hand under his chin—"with all these X-rated movies and four-letter words and public displays of immorality. The boss"—Mr. Horn tapped his forehead with a spindly finger and nodded confidentially—"knew what he was doing. And now the fat's in the fire."

Lacy had no idea what fat or which fire he was talking about, unless it was the phone ringing off the hook and all the telegrams. She *did* know that it had not been Mr. Horn but Rafael Ames who had given her the notes to put on the word processor and print out, the ones the congressman had used when he stripped the hide off that awful Cramer and made his wonderful statement about the threat to moral values. And later when he revised and extended.

This knowledge, Lacy suddenly realized, made her a little uncomfortable. She watched Mr. Horn open the door into the corridor; then he turned back. "Give you a lift home, Miss Farnes?"

The congressman, of course, had a perfect right to adapt someone else's ideas. No member could possibly keep up, by himself, with everything going on. The congressman *needed* help if he was going to do his job properly, and Lacy had no doubt that Victor T. Donovan wanted, above all, to do his job properly. Actually, she thought, not everyone could have taken somebody else's notes and turned them into a big hit on TV, the smooth way the congressman had.

"Oh, no, thanks anyway, Mister Horn. I have my own car."

As he surely knew, since he had pulled the right strings to get her a parking space. But he wasn't suggesting anything, not Mr. Horn; he was just being polite, the way—Lacy had quickly learned—an administrative career on Capitol Hill taught a person to be.

"That cooked the senator's goose, you know." Mr. Horn nodded solemnly, as if to confirm the voters' decision. "After four terms, too."

The phone rang again as the door closed behind him. Lacy dawdled a moment at her desk; though gratified to have heard the last of the Sagebrush Solon, she still felt unsettled about those notes. She was not, she assured herself, actually *worried*. How could she be, after the most exciting time of her life?

It was Rafael Ames who troubled her, she concluded, though she did not quite know why. Ames was certainly brilliant; even Mr. Horn said so. But he was so confident, so . . . Lacy searched for the right word. Ames was not actually pushy. But Lacy sensed that sooner or later he would try to take over the congressman, try to *influence* him, and it seemed to her that it ought to be the other way around. Ames wasn't even actually a member of the staff.

And that blowsy Mrs. Donovan. The way she hung on Ames's every word and looked as if she could eat him up, even if she was maybe twice his age. The congressman was too intelligent, too dignified to have a wife who acted like that. He must have outgrown her; they said Washington was full of important men and the women they had married in their youth.

The buzzer sounded on Lacy's desk. Even though she already had her coat on, she quickly dropped it on her chair and hurried to the congressman's inner office, hearing with a certain satisfaction the phone ringing behind her as she entered.

Victor T. Donovan was slouched in his high-backed chair, behind the desk he always kept clear. The congressman was as tidy a man as Lacy had ever seen; his shoes always gleamed like glass. He was lots tidier than Daddy or . . .

"Come in, Lacy. Sit down a minute."

If Daddy could see me now, Lacy thought, tucking her modest skirt neatly under her crossed legs. *If he could even* imagine me *sitting in Victor T. Donovan's office, actually talking with a congressman,* working *for him, I bet I'd hear a lot less about that stinkpot of a brother of mine he's so proud of.*

"Glad I caught you before you got away."

She was glad she'd got this job for herself, without *one word* of help from her father or anybody else, except the placement people at UVM. Even they'd been skeptical when she told them what she wanted to do.

"I'm glad to stay, sir. I'll stay as late as you need me."

That was one thing she had learned from her father, that if you wanted to get ahead, you had to be willing to work. But the way *he* lorded himself around, he probably never had realized you had to be nice, too.

Victor T. Donovan made deprecating gestures. "It's been a busy three days," he said. "I've never had so many calls and telegrams. Sorry if it's kept you people jumping in the outer office."

"Oh, we were glad to help, sir. Nobody minded at all."

Which was not strictly true, as the *other* girl—not the show-off in the tight sweaters—actually had gone out to the ladies' *five* times the first day, by Lacy's actual count. Ducking out on the job ever since, too, anytime she could. But Lacy knew better than to blow the whistle; she would look like a sorehead if she complained, particularly to the congressman himself.

"Did you read any of those telegrams, Lacy?"

"Oh, no, sir, Mister Horn handled the telegrams himself. I was mostly on the phone and with the TV people."

Victor T. Donovan put his hands behind his head and looked at the high ceiling of his office. Lacy had never seen him so relaxed. It was good, she thought, to see a busy man relax.

"Well, for your ears only," he said, "it's got to stay here in this office until I decide, but a lot of those telegrams were from folks back home urging me to run for the Senate."

"The phone calls," Lacy said. "A lot of them were about that, too. After your inspiring speech."

Which must have been what Mr. Horn meant by the fat being in the fire.

"Tell you the truth, I'm tempted to do it."

Lacy had learned from the calls she'd handled that the congressman would have to run against Senator Bender, if he did decide to run, and that apparently meant he'd be taking quite a risk. That increased her admiration for him.

"How marvelous," she breathed. "You'd be a great senator, sir."

The idea of an election campaign excited her. Lacy had never been in a campaign. Her high-and-mighty father would never believe she could handle such a job. Maybe she'd get a chance to show him. And they'd have more office space and more staff over on the Senate side. She might even get a better job, though a better one than she had was hard to imagine.

"But I don't know if I should risk it, Lacy. Lots of folks back there in the district count on me, you know? I'm not even sure I *want* to be in the Senate."

He took his hands from behind his head and gazed broodingly at something beyond her. Since she could not be sure what he might want to hear—urging him on or holding him back?—Lacy said nothing. Not that he needed *her* advice.

"But just the possibility," Victor T. Donovan said, "there's something I need to talk to you about."

Lacy sensed what was coming and wished it weren't.

"That night we were working late getting out the newsletter? And went out to dinner?" The congressman dropped his gaze to her granny glasses. Lacy let her eyes fall demurely.

"Of course, it was just dinner," Victor T. Donovan said, "but in this town there's plenty of people ready to make something out of nothing."

"I'm *sorry*, sir . . . if I'd thought for one minute there could ever be any trouble . . ." Actually she hadn't even taken a drink, only a Perrier, just in case.

"Not *trouble*, Lacy. It's just . . . well, it'd be better if we both just didn't say anything about that dinner to anybody."

"Oh, I wouldn't. I haven't."

She was thankful she had stopped herself from writing home about it. Her father might have bragged all over Winooski. Except that he probably would have thought— Of course, any sensible person ought to know that a man like the congressman wouldn't even dream of doing anything out of line. But there would always be people like her father to think nasty things.

"And if we don't do it again."

"I understand." But Lacy was disappointed. "I really do." When he had rung for her, she had hoped he might be going to ask her out to dinner again.

"Politics," Victor T. Donovan said. "You never know."

She stood up, eager to leave.

"After all"—he looked directly into her eyes—"you *are* a danm pretty girl, Lacy. Woman, I mean."

This time Lacy did not drop her eyes. She was used to being told she was pretty and to the way men looked at her. She was used to men. So the congressman's compliment did not quite surprise her. It soothed, instead, her disappointment, and it settled what she had been turning over in her mind since that night—whether even *he* might have had something in mind. Not *then*, of course, nothing so crude. He was always a perfect gentleman. But sooner or later.

She said: "Thank you," sounding quite proper—but filing away the knowledge that even a congressman was just a man and could think the way all the rest of them did.

"I'm sure you wouldn't have said anything anyway." Victor T. Donovan stood up, too. "But better have things clear, is why I mentioned it."

Lacy carefully controlled her face and manner, as—between her bossy father and slimebag brother—she had long ago learned to do. And anyway, probably, the congressman really meant what he said. Or thought he did.

"I'd better run along, sir."

"Get some rest." Victor T. Donovan looked at her kindly, benevolently. "Some tough days ahead, unless I miss my guess. People like that nosy Speed going over us with an X ray."

★

Lacy had been trying not to think about Milo Speed ever since she had found herself deliberately touching his hand in the office and had felt him touch hers in return. That had been a little forward, she thought, as she drove through downtown Washington toward her apartment building in Georgetown. Playing handsies with a man maybe as old as her father, and a man at that who had bedroom eyes and a bedroom reputation.

But even though she had been rude to him at first, Milo Speed had been *nice*. About the cameraman with the smelly cigar. And good-looking, too, in a kind of careless way, as if he were too busy to get his suit pressed or a good square meal. Sort of like James Mason in a midnight TV movie.

From several Milo Speed columns about the imperial presidency and a longer article of his in *Foreign Affairs*, Lacy had gleaned useful ideas for her senior thesis, which had compared presidential powers with the divine rights of the kings she had studied in European history. Speed had not seen much difference, which was not what Lacy had been conditioned to believe, so she had sent him a questionnaire. Naturally, he had not bothered to answer, busy as he must have been.

Lacy had written an A paper anyway, adapting Speed's thesis without actually borrowing it and never thinking *then* that someday she would be talking to the real Milo Speed in a congressman's office and finding him kind of cute. Though needing a haircut. And actually would have the nerve to—

"Make a pass," she said out loud, pulling up behind a car that was just leaving a parking space.

She actually had made a pass at Milo Speed. Not *much* of a pass, but what else could you call it? And since he was supposed to be a woman chaser, he was bound to have known what she was doing. In hindsight it was mortifying to think about. *Mor*tifying.

Except, Lacy thought, *I'd do it again*. Besides, he'd gone right along.

The car pulled out ahead of her, from the curb into traffic

on Twenty-eighth Street. Before Lacy could take the parking place, a convertible Volkswagen bug she had not even seen backed swiftly into it. Infuriated, Lacy hit the gas pedal and jerked her Honda to a halt beside the Volkswagen.

"That was my place," she yelled. "You took my parking place!"

A young man in blue jeans and an alligator shirt got out of the Volkswagen, slammed its door, and grinned at her.

He said, cheerfully: "Fuck you, sweetie."

Lacy had not been to college for nothing. "Asshole!" she shouted. An older woman on the sidewalk hurried past, mouth agape.

"Find another parking place somewhere," the young man said. "I'll buy you a drink."

Lacy put her fist out the window and raised her middle finger.

"Up yours, buster!"

She drove off with a squeal of tires, mad about the parking space but pleased with the exchange. Young guys were the pits. But a woman today didn't have to let some smart ass just out of short pants treat her like a pushover. Not anymore.

★

As Lacy was watching *L.A. Law* that night, the doorbell rang. She reminded herself to put the chain on before opening the door, since she had no idea who could be calling at that hour.

Through the crack of space the chain permitted, she saw Rafael Ames leaning against the doorjamb, wearing a sweat shirt that said "DIRTY YOUNG MAN." He was smiling confidently and balancing a large pizza box in one hand.

"Delivery boy."

Lacy had eaten only a container of banana-peach yogurt and was hungry; it was a woman's fate, she thought, to be hungry or fat, and she seemed always to be hungry. But Ames's manner annoyed her. He could have called.

"Wrong apartment," she said. "I didn't order pizza."

Ames's smile never wavered. "How about this?" He held up in his other hand a paper bag from which protruded the neck of a wine bottle. The movement was awkward because he clutched under that arm something that looked like a small cardboard box.

"I didn't order *any*thing."

"Certainly not me." Ames turned the smile down to low wattage. "I know you didn't, Red. But I was working late and needed dinner, and I thought you'd be nice to eat it with."

Lacy hated to be called Red. Her instinct was to slam the door. But she had to work with Rafael Ames. Not *for* but with. And he had to work with her, too. And it wasn't as if he were a total stranger.

She unhooked the chain. "You'll have to eat and run. Working girls get up early, you know."

Ames marched past her, a little too triumphantly, looked around the apartment perfunctorily, set the pizza and wine on the coffee table, and put the box from under his arm beside them.

"Aren't you going to ask me how I knew where you lived?" Without an invitation he sprawled on the sofa.

Mindful of her manners in her own house, Lacy turned off the television, although *L.A. Law* was going into a courtroom scene that she had been waiting for.

"That wouldn't be so hard to find out."

"Well, how hard would it be," Ames asked, "to find a corkscrew around here?" He took a bottle of red wine out of the paper bag.

"Tough luck. I don't have one."

"So I came prepared." Ames took a pocket corkscrew, the kind liquor stores gave away free, from the bag. "You don't drink wine?"

Lacy sat in her only easy chair, her knees tightly together in one of the short skirts she never wore to the office. She kept the coffee table between herself and the sofa, confident that a brassy type like Rafe Ames was not merely seeking someone nice to eat dinner with.

"I don't eat pizza either." But the hot odors from the box were causing her stomach to clinch.

Ames looked exasperated. "Why not cool it, Red? I'm not some damn rapist."

Lacy was not concerned about rape. She had managed,

even in her brief life, lots of grabbier men than she expected Ames to be. Men, experience had taught her, could usually be managed because they so badly wanted what she had. That gave her the necessary weapons—except, of course, with a raving lunatic. And whatever else, Rafe Ames was not a nut case.

"I don't care a whole lot for your manners," she said. "Not that you seem to have any."

It was Ames's blithe assumptions—that she would welcome him, that he could just barge in and eat pizza on her sofa—that had put her back up. Worst of all, calling her Red. And he was undoubtedly moving in on the congressman in just the same way. Without, Lacy was reasonably sure, any more of a by-your-leave in that case than in her own.

"All right," Ames said. "All *right*. I apologize. I should have called before I came. Now will you get off your high horse?" Before she could answer, he charged on. "Where're your fucking glasses?"

Hostility, she saw, was getting her nowhere. "Back there. But there aren't any wineglasses."

While he was blundering around in her kitchen, she called: "What were you working on?"

She didn't really care; she had only fallen automatically into the ancient woman's duty she had been brought up mindlessly to accept—playing hostess, keeping conversation going, maintaining the appearance of things. Second nature. If Ames *had* been a rapist, she thought, furious with herself, she probably would have done the same.

He came back into the living room with two juice glasses, put them on the coffee table, and tapped with a nail-bitten finger the little box he had been carrying under his arm.

"Cutting spots. Some real paint peelers."

Lacy recognized the box then as a carrying case for a videocassette. "TV spots?"

"That's what I *do*, Red. Among other nefarious things."

"Call me Red one more time," Lacy said, "you can take your pizza and your wine and shove 'em. Spots for the congressman?"

Apparently unmoved, Ames opened the pizza box. "With

that gorgeous head of hair of yours, how could anybody call you anything else? You think maybe he can beat Mack Bender *without* spots?"

Lacy was too amazed to protest further about her name. "But he hasn't even made up his mind to run."

"Bullshit." Ames put a gooey slice of pizza on the coffee table. "We made it up for him. Me and Darwin John." He poured two glasses of wine and pushed one across the table to her. "I just happened to see him in one of those TV reports these House guys make for free and sent back to their districts. I could hardly believe the way the camera loves the guy. He may be dishwater in person but, believe me—on the tube Victor T. Donovan knocks your socks off."

He sipped wine and grinned at her over the rim of the glass.

"Which is what swung Darwin John, when I set it up for him to see your hero ream Connie Cramer a new asshole."

Listening, impressed in spite of herself, Lacy was nevertheless angrier than ever. Exactly what she had feared. Ames was taking over the congressman the way he had taken over her living room; she liked *that* even less than pizza glop on her coffee table.

"What he told *me*," she said, with precision and dignity, trying to recover, "is that he doesn't even know if he *wants* to be in the Senate."

Ames pulled his pants legs up to his knees. He was wearing black Bass Weejuns with no socks.

"Got to be careful where you step," he said, "if the old boy's spreading that kind of shit around."

Lacy was shocked at such obvious disrespect for the congressman. Not even Ames, with all his assumptions, had any right to talk like that about Victor T. Donovan.

"You act as if *you're* the one in charge." Feeling the need of sustenance, she took a sip of wine. "But I expect you'll find out you *aren't*."

Ames chuckled and ate pizza. "You think"—he talked thickly, with his mouth full of cheese and pepperoni—"I could make Victor T. Donovan or anybody else do anything they don't really want to do?"

Lacy drank more wine. She saw no reason, with someone of her own generation, which was really all Rafael Ames was, to show the kind of deference she gave to Mr. Horn.

"I think you want him to run for the Senate so you can do what he pays you to do. Which you couldn't do if he didn't run, and then you wouldn't get paid."

"Damn right," Ames said. "But the money's nothing compared to what there'll be next election, and all the elections after that. If I can knock over a biggie like Mack Bender, with nothing to work with but a pretty face. Have some pizza, Red?"

"The congressman is *not*," Lacy said, "just a pretty face. And if you call me Red again, I'll throw—"

"You already drank it." Ames poured more wine in her glass. "You got a case on the guy, sounds like to me."

"I hold the congressman in deep respect, if that word means anything at all to you." Lacy took a slice of pizza from his hand, with the rationale that eating, like drinking, was good for relieving stress.

"Oh, it does, it does. But that's not exactly what I mean. You letting him have a little on the side?"

"That did it!" Lacy put down her pizza, as furious as she ever had been. "You can just take your dirty, evil mind and your smelly pizza and get out of here!" Her hand actually closed on the glass of wine, ready to throw it, except that it would stain the carpet and probably the sofa, too.

Ames picked up another slice of pizza, took a bite, and airily waved the rest at her. "Okay, so you're not. That's good. Guy running for Senate can't go round stepping on his cock."

Ames's language did not offend her, but Lacy hated the horrible image it evoked. With an effort, she brought her temper under control, as she so often had had to do at home in Winooski with her father and her fuckhead brother. Whom Rafael Ames kind of reminded her of.

"I hope . . ." Lacy paused to drink wine. "I hope he decides *not* to run and fires your ass."

"He won't." Ames wiped his lips with a paper napkin from the pizza box. "We won't let him."

It came to her then, in a burst of memory, that two could

play Ames's game. "And are *you* getting a little on the side? From Miz Donovan maybe?"

That, she saw with pleasure, almost made him spill his wine.

"Christ! You think I'm *that* hard up?"

"She looks at you"—Lacy's memory was distasteful but clear—"as if she could eat you for breakfast."

"Nice tits," Ames said. "But broads that age don't interest Rafe Ames. Not with all the young stuff around. And anyway, I'm not dumb enough to shtup the candidate's wife."

"The congressman is *not* a candidate," Lacy insisted, though these remarks left her as angered by his disrespect for women as by his disrespect for Victor T. Donovan. She wanted to say something in sisterly solidarity with Mrs. Donovan but could think of nothing apt.

"You think not? Then what the hell's this for?"

Ames picked up the cassette case and went over to Lacy's television, atop which perched the VCR she had bought with her MasterCard. He took a cassette from the case, punched it into the player, and turned on both machines.

Numbers flashed on the screen, counting down to zero. Then what Lacy recognized as a Concorde with its long needle nose appeared, racing along a runway into a smooth takeoff. A close-up of an airline logo, as if on the Concorde's side, filled the screen with large red letters: "BENDER GLOBAL TOURS."

"Jet-setting Mack," a portentous male voice intoned as the letters dissolved into a news show image of a smiling man waving from the top of airline steps, then turning to enter the open door of a plane.

"How does he find time to barnstorm the world?" the voice inquired.

The Eiffel Tower appeared, and the Parisian street scene surrounding it. They disappeared, and the man who had been entering the plane came on-screen again, this time with a pretty girl in a sarong draping a Hawaiian lei around his neck.

"Isn't that Senator Bender?" Lacy asked, unconsciously displaying her limited acquaintance with Capitol Hill.

Hawaii faded into a crowded urban vista identified with

superimposed letters as Mexico City. Then the same man strode briskly through an open door and past a sign proclaiming "Camino Real."

"Bet your sweet ass that's him." Ames voice was thicker, throatier, Lacy thought; he had a dreamy look on his face.

"And where does he get the money?" the sonorous voice wondered, as the Camino Real dissolved into an idyllic beach-and-yacht scene labeled "The Riviera." Then exotic Eastern bazaars appeared above the word "Cairo"; next, the same man stood smiling and waving, surrounded by Asians in Mao suits, atop the Great Wall of China.

"Globe-trotting Mack," the voice declared. "Everywhere but the place *you* sent him. Everywhere but the Senate."

The waving man was seen again about to enter the plane. The Concorde again raced down the runway.

"Isn't it time you had a senator in *Washington*"—the camera moved in to show again the huge red letters "BENDER GLOBAL TOURS"—"instead of living it up around the world?"

The Concorde was seen zooming into a blue sky; then, for an instant, almost subliminally, small letters appeared: "Paid for by Cleaning House Committee." And in even smaller letters, the name of the capital of Victor T. Donovan's state.

Ames clicked off the VCR, chuckling happily. "When we cut that one the other day, I damn near got off it's so cute. You still think he's not a candidate?"

"But it didn't say a *word* about the congressman." Even to Lacy, her protest sounded hollow.

As he put the cassette back in its case, Ames's face showed his impatience. "Who else do I *work* for, Red? It'd already be out in the open if old Speed wasn't so far over the hill," he said. "He got the hot leak from the horse's mouth and didn't even know he had it."

Lacy calmly finished her second glass of wine, proud of her self-control, though impressed in spite of herself with the evidence of Global Tours.

She said: "I received the *distinct* impression, when the congressman and I conferred on this matter, that he does not wish Mister Speed to write about it."

But what else could the spot mean, she thought, watching Ames sprawl again on her sofa, except that the congressman really was going to run?

"Speed could give a fuck *what* Donovan wants, Red. Speed may be a little thick this time, but he's so goddam independent"—Ames poured the last of the wine, most in his glass, a little in Lacy's—"he's been known to turn down an invitation to Camp David. Josie Baby told me herself Speed heard your boss kicking it around with Darwin John. So why he hasn't written it—"

Ames raised his brows and spread his arms.

Pensively, remembering the touch of Milo Speed's hand and his interested eyes, Lacy finished her slice of pizza. Thinking of Speed slightly cooled her anger at Ames, whose disrespect for his betters she had come to expect. Anyway, she could see no point in arguing with anybody as sure of things as he was.

"I can't get over it." Ames sipped wine. A drop stained his sweat shirt between "DIRTY" and "YOUNG." "You thinking I had it up for Josie Baby."

"Miz Donovan is a very handsome woman. For her age."

"I guess so." Ames looked interested. "If she's got an eye out for me, there's a little stroke there I can maybe use." He peered at Lacy over his juice glass. "Now you, Red . . . don't think I can't see through those old-lady glasses of yours."

Lacy could not resist wondering what he saw through her glasses, though she thought she knew. Disingenuously she said: "They're not hiding anything."

When she had opened her door and seen him standing there with his pizza and wine, Lacy believed she knew all she needed to know about why he had appeared. Why else would a man come to a woman's apartment at night? So she was unprepared for the shock Rafael Ames now gave her.

"Not from me," he said. "I look in those eyes, and I see somebody *like* me."

Lacy was speechless. Her mouth actually fell open.

"On the make, I mean. So you throw in with me, Red, and I'll take you everywhere you aim to go."

Lacy's teeth cracked together as she closed her mouth. She was not only surprised but insulted. She had done nothing, she thought, she *couldn't* do anything, to deserve such a conclusion.

I'm not *like you,* she wanted to cry out, but she was too shocked to get the words out.

"That's why I came over," Ames said. "As if a sharpie like you couldn't figure that out."

Lacy suddenly understood his remark about having stroke he could maybe use on Mrs. Donovan, which was what interested him rather than her nice tits. Nor was he interested, that way, in Lacy Farnes. Only in what she could do for him. But he had been blissed out by Global Tours. Almost got off on it. That was the way Rafael Ames got his kicks—not with women.

"You in the office, me the hand on the tiller. We could give each other lots of help managing your hero."

Loathing him, hating what he saw in her and what he suggested, Lacy found her voice. "Sounds as if *I'd* be doing all the dirty work."

She had no intention of helping Rafael Ames manage Victor T. Donovan. Even the idea was an insult to the congressman. Nevertheless, she felt a sense, not altogether unpleasant, of discovery. Ames had touched in her something she had not quite realized—certainly not admitted—about herself.

"No, you'd be on for the whole shmear," he said. "Tomorrow the world."

"Clean up that mess on the coffee table," Lacy said. "Then get your sleazy ass out of here."

She watched Ames stand up, grinning, the cassette case under his arm. He *was* like her ratfuck brother, the one she now knew she wanted to get so far away from, so far above, she'd never have to think of him again.

"Clean it up yourself," Ames said. "And I know what I'm seeing through those glasses, Red . . . if you don't."

★

Milo Speed contemplated the front page of the Washington *Post*'s Style section with distaste. It featured a two-column photo of the Honorable Victor T. Donovan, looking somewhat less like a President than usual, owing to what Speed considered a satisfied grin on the smooth, barbered face peering over a tall stack of letters and telegrams.

DONOVAN'S SPEECH LIGHTS DONOVAN'S FIRE said the typically flippant headline.

Speed did not need the Style section story to tell him what he knew already. Victor T. Donovan's defrocking of J. Conrad Cramer-Kremenczsko, witnessed by much of the country on daytime television, had turned an obscure congressman into a national phenomenon. Excerpted repeatedly on CNN, played back on C-Span, sound-bitten on all the network news shows, reprinted partially in both the Washington *Post* and *The New York Times*, discussed during the round table on *This Week with David Brinkley*, and favored by the momentary absence of war, earthquakes, scandals, or other competition for headlines, Victor T. Donovan's startling performance had caught the nation's ear, eye, imagination, deep-seated paranoia about big business, and profound conviction of its own moral righteousness.

Besides, in Speed's view, the only thing Americans liked better than a tough guy was an underdog, and Victor T. Donovan suddenly appeared to be both. That he apparently had come out of nowhere to take on and expose a famous Big Shot had whetted the national curiosity about a new star, and the media in their lemminglike fashion had hastened to fill in the blanks.

The Associated Press had moved on its national wire, for example, a detailed account of Victor T. Donovan's family and educational background, emphasizing the congressman's years as a triple threat back on his state university team, accompanied with a picture of his church wedding to "shapely Josephine Brett," and another of busty Josie as the college beauty queen, wearing Victor T. Donovan's letter sweater.

This florid account had appeared across the country on the first day after his confrontation with J. Conrad Cramer, and Speed had cursed and snorted unhappily through it—until one paragraph, near the end, stopped him: "One matter

Rep. Donovan is reluctant to talk about is the miscarriage his wife suffered during his early years in the House. The couple have no children."

Speed had dropped the paper. He put his face in his hands, feeling tears hot against his eyelids.

Ah, Josie, he thought. *My Josie. To go through something as terrible as that all by yourself . . .*

He stopped himself. Josie had not been, he forced himself to admit, all by herself.

But I wasn't there. I didn't even know.

"Goddammit," he had said out loud, crumpling the paper in his hands.

He *should* have been there. He *ought* to have known. Josie had needed him, Vic or no goddam Vic. Josie had needed him—somehow, he believed, she must have *wanted* him at her side—but he had not been there at a time in her life that must have been almost too terrible to bear.

After that painful discovery Speed had not been much interested in the other first-day stories, which made more of Victor T. Donovan's uneventful congressional service than Speed thought warranted. He did read, and was not surprised by, stories in *The New York Times* and other papers that established the truth of the sensational charges against J. Conrad Cramer.

In the days that followed, the tide of publicity mounted and moved to editorial pages and talk shows. "Capitalism at its best—but its ethical worst," thundered the Washington *Post*. The *Wall Street Journal*, though distressed at the blemished image of Cramer, Wentz, and Marbury, saw its own social views vindicated: "Now it can be seen, thanks to Mister Donovan's willingness to speak out, that something must be done to break the foul liberal cycle in which porn and permissiveness corrupt the weak and the strong alike."

"Donovan has both stimulated and exploited," a bearded panelist had pontificated on *Nightline*, "a tangible and growing national mood of antagonism toward the moral laxity becoming commonplace in a once-proud and settled society."

William Safire, in a column called "Porno-gate," had proclaimed Victor T. Donovan "the watchman on the wall." Evans and Novak reported that in a "hush-hush, closed-door, gloves-off session," the congressman had been berated by "ham-handed Chairman Flander" for failure to "tip his hand in advance, as demanded by all-important committee protocol" —though Chairman Flander was quoted as fully supporting "antivice legislation needed to keep America clean."

"Did you hear the latest Polish joke?" Johnny Carson had asked his midnight audience. "J. Conrad Cramer plans to open a nude pizza parlor. With sausage and pepperoni, you get a massage."

"At a time," the Chicago *Tribune* had asserted, "when the country seems to be falling apart from hedonism, salaciousness, political corruption, creeping socialism, crime, drugs, and AIDS, one man stood up like David against Goliath and spoke for traditional values."

The Boston *Globe*, however, did not see a biblical slingshot artist but a "self-righteous climber promising censorship and repression to promote his political career."

Even this assault, Speed supposed, had done Victor T. Donovan about as much good as harm. Criticism could only contribute to the rising curve of his fame; to keep that curve climbing was what a former unknown needed most.

"But he'll get no goddam help from me," Speed had mumbled, sipping bitter morning tea.

When a noted academic, in fifteen seconds of sound bite on the *Today* show, raised the possibility that Victor T. Donovan might have catapulted himself into a home state senatorial nomination against O. Mack Bender—"a dubious honor indeed"—the suggestion naturally had set off a further round of speculation in the political press.

DEFENDER BENDER? asked a New York *Daily News* headline. "Can Victor T. Donovan parlay a single courageous speech into the necessary moral crusade?" inquired New York *Newsday*.

Speed had not failed to detect, in the dramatic stories that quickly saturated all media—"a new conservative champion," announced the Manchester *Union Leader*—the leak technique of Darwin John. By the morning when the *Post*'s Style section featured DONOVAN'S FIRE, the nation had been widely exposed to the idea that Victor T. Donovan might launch a "crusade" in the fall campaign against Mack Bender.

That Senator Bender had not been accused of promoting pornography was only an incidental point in these stories, most of which pointed out ritually that it would take courage for an upstart congressman to give up a safe seat in the House in the face of almost certain defeat. "A momentous decision," suggested the Dallas *News*, "that even a man of such demonstrated courage can hardly take lightly."

But if you've got Darwin John and American morality in your corner, Speed thought, *who needs balls*?

He sorted through the numerous newspapers delivered to his door, and now scattered on his breakfast table, until he found in one of them—a scandal sheet, Speed liked to quip, "that ought to come in rolls"—the syndicated column of Lee Lestark, who was widely regarded as Milo Speed's prime ideological and circulation rival. That morning Speed was irritated more than usual by Lestark, who was writing, naturally, about Victor T. Donovan.

Lestark had taken a different tack: Congressman Donovan, he asserted—as usual, without authority—was "reported to be a willing tool" of unnamed executives at Allied Ventures who feared being ousted by "bottom-lining" Cramer, Wentz, and Marbury and who therefore had leaked the incriminating information to Victor T. Donovan.

Speed recognized this as a blatant counterleak from J. Conrad Cramer to Lestark—"that goddam tank artist," he said out loud.

Evangeline came in from the kitchen, carrying a pot of tea in one hand and his breakfast bowl in the other. She had been the keeper of Milo Speed's household ever since Nancy had left him, so long that Evangeline shared the secret with him that his reputation as a voracious lover had been vastly inflated—with some help from Speed himself, who had taken a certain wry pleasure in the overkill.

"Is there one in there this morning? Or can I go in to change the sheets?"

Evangeline never failed to ask this delicate question—

though rarely, if ever, was there one in Speed's bedroom anymore. His breakfast bowl, as always, contained raisin bran and a sliced banana in skim milk. Speed devoutly believed this regimen was the main reason his six-foot frame continued to weigh under two hundred pounds.

"I don't think so," he said, as he always did. "Better knock in case."

The phone rang, and Evangeline went across the room to answer. He resumed reading Lee Lestark, a professional necessity he deeply resented.

"But the betting here," Lestark's column concluded in what Speed considered its typically poisonous tone, "is that opportunist Donovan has done himself no real favor. An eager beaver congressman who lets himself be maneuvered into running against Mack Bender is actually heading straight into a buzz saw."

Speed also thought a campaign against Bender a fool's errand, but he saw with satisfaction that Lestark obviously did not know as much as he thought he did—not as much, certainly, as Milo Speed knew. Of course, Victor T. Donovan was going to run against Bender, and the maneuvering was mostly his and Rafael Ames's.

"Woman on the phone," Evangeline said. "You wanna speak to somebody name Donovan?"

Hope sprang wildly in Speed's heart. "Josie?"

Evangeline shrugged. "She call him a congressman."

"Oh." He might have known. Victor T. Donovan had good reason to call, but Josie very little. "I guess so."

He put down his spoon and went reluctantly across the room to the phone. Speed hated business before or at breakfast.

"Put him on."

"Oh, Mister Speed—right away."

He recognized the chesty redhead's voice, though he had heard it only on the one occasion, nearly a week earlier.

"Lacy . . . is that you?"

She sounded a little breathless. "Yes, but it's the congressman calling, Mister Speed—"

"I'd rather talk to you."

There was a silence Speed hoped was more cautionary than chilly.

"That'd be . . . interesting," Lacy finally said. "I'll put the congressman right on."

A click and a hum and a hearty voice: "Milo! I hope I didn't wake you up!"

"If you had, I wouldn't have taken the call. Seems to me I've been seeing your name in the papers."

Victor T. Donovan chuckled a pleased chuckle. "Tell you the truth, I'm floored by all this. Long as I've been in politics, I wouldn't have believed the telegrams, the letters, all this publicity. I just—"

"The hell you wouldn't," Speed said. "You didn't put the hit on Cramer just for the fun of it."

Another silence, different from that of Lacy.

"Milo, come have lunch with me. Got a little something to tell you."

It was Speed's turn to be silent.

"Here in the office," Victor T. Donovan said. "Just you and me."

"Lemme take a look . . ."

Thinking hard, Speed pretended to be checking his calendar. He knew he had no lunch date, since he had canceled one with a deputy secretary of state who wanted to talk about Cyprus. But he was not sure he wanted to hear Victor T. Donovan tell him that he had decided to run for the Senate. Undoubtedly, that was what had caused the congressman to call. Hearing it confidentially confirmed would make it hard for Speed not to write about it, which he did not want to do.

"Owe you a lunch anyway," Victor T. Donovan said.

Speed knew lunch *à deux* with the congressman would remind him that Josie, the sweet, renewed vision of his dim life, seemed to have fallen so low as to encourage the likes of her husband in his sudden pretensions. But Speed was a reporter; he thought he could not again resist, as he had once, even this rigged and cosmetic yarn; he could not resist being on top of a story, being first if he could, the best at his trade.

"Okay," he said. "Just so I don't meet Lee Lestark coming in when I'm going out. Or vice versa.

Victor T. Donovan took that seriously. "We don't play that kind of game around here, Milo. Twelve-thirty?"

And to hell with Josie, too, Speed thought. *The new model Josie anyway.* Not, of course, the Josie of his dreams, his past, his life.

He said, hoping the congressman would take it back to his wife: "Why don't you have that sexy redhead join us?"

★

What Victor T. Donovan thought of as lunch was, for Speed, a roast beef sandwich on a paper plate with potato chips. A green concoction from some federal salad bar lay limply in front of the congressman himself, on his immaculate desk.

"Down in the cafeteria," Victor T. Donovan said, "people would gawk. I thought we could chat better up here."

Speed found one compensation. Though Lacy Farnes had not been invited to join them, she served lunch, fussing over Victor T. Donovan's desk as if the canned Cokes were vintage wines. As she leaned above Speed to place a plastic cup by his paper plate, her green eyes behind the granny glasses glinted warmly at him.

"Enjoy your lunch, gentlemen," Lacy said. "And don't hesitate to call me if you need anything else."

"We're fine," Victor T. Donovan said. He and Speed watched the self-conscious swing of Lacy's hips until the door closed with a solid congressional clunk behind her.

"You know, Milo . . . when you asked me about that girl, I thought you were crazy. But she *is* sexy, isn't she?"

"You hadn't noticed?" Speed ate a potato chip, waiting for the expectable denial.

"Around here you don't even want to *look* at the girls in your office." The congressman shook his head wisely. "They'll scream sexual harassment to the Ethics Committee."

"Or worse. They'll blab to the press, and there goes your campaign down in flames."

Victor T. Donovan minutely adjusted the position of the Coke can beside his plastic cup.

"What campaign?" he said, a shade too innocently.

"But if I were you, I'd rather take a chance on getting in *there*"—Speed jerked his head over his shoulder, toward the door that had closed behind Lacy—"than over *there*." He pointed with half his roast beef sandwich toward the Senate office buildings beyond the Capitol.

The congressman closed his eyes and shook his head. "Milo, for God's sake. I've got better sense than to fiddle around with that girl. Or *any* girl."

Speed did not doubt it. "But looks to me like not enough to stay out of Mack Bender's way."

Victor T. Donovan put down his plastic fork and leaned back in his judge's chair, masticating salad and looking thoughtfully over templed fingers. When he spoke, it was deliberately and with emphasis. "Are you, even *you*, falling for all that bushwa that Bender can't be beaten?"

"What's worse than bushwa," Speed said, "is those bullshit spots you've got on the air in your state."

Victor T. Donovan raised his brows in innocence; he did it well. "Vic Donovan's not running any spots anywhere, Milo."

"More bullshit." Speed took a sip of Coke from his plastic cup. "Is that all you've got to tell me?"

"Those spots aren't mine. Something called the Cleaning House Committee put them on, not me. But I don't mind telling you, Milo, that crowd is bringing real pressure on Vic Donovan to run."

"Good sandwich. Nice rare roast beef." Speed pushed back his chair and stood up. "But I've got better things to do than listen to bullshit."

Donovan, suddenly appearing angry, threw his paper napkin beside his salad. "Oh, sit down, Speed. Ames *told* me you wouldn't hold still for this kind of fun and games. But you can't blame me for trying."

Politicians, Speed thought, never tired of the same old tricks. *Trying to get more speculation going.* He moved swiftly to the point. "Ames is handling your campaign?"

"And Darwin John's putting up the money."

Victor T. Donovan's anger had vanished swiftly—which

meant to Speed that it had not been real—and the congressman failed to keep satisfaction out of his voice or a smile from his face.

Speed sat down. "Vic, with the kind of money John can provide, you could get anybody you wanted. Roger Ailes. Bucky Overholt. Why this kid Ames?"

"You'll see. Take this Cleaning House business. They're the most effective campaign spots in my experience. Which goes back a long way. Have you actually *seen* them, Milo?"

Speed had not but had been given a graphic description by Theo Keller, the editor of the Capital City *Ledger* in Victor T. Donovan's home state and a link in Speed's nationwide network of trusty political sources. Theo had sounded troubled.

"The damn things aren't out-and-out *lies*, Milo. I mean, Mack *was* in China. Egypt, too, all over the place. Which is why he knows so much about the world. The film's the real stuff, see, but these goddam spots they've hoked up, you'd think Mack's only junketing around."

Dodging the congressman's direct question, Speed now said: "They make Bender look like Dick Nixon. Or Hugh Hefner. Or *both*."

Victor T. Donovan fixed him with a stare too earnest to be sincere. "There's not a frame in those spots that the Cleaning House Committee assures me they can't back up with good solid facts."

"You mean Rafe Ames? He cut those spots, didn't he?"

The earnest stare never wavered. "Well . . . tell you the truth, Ames *does* do some work for the committee. On the side."

"And Darwin John puts up the committee's money. Picks the members, probably."

"So as you've obviously guessed," Victor T. Donovan said amiably, "I *am* going to run against Bender. And I'll tell you something else, Milo. Whatever you and all those other genius reporters may say, it's Vic Donovan that's going to frazzle Bender's, uh . . . bottom."

"That's bullshit, too. But at least it's honest bullshit."

"You press guys." Victor T. Donovan spun to his constantly blinking telephone panel and punched a button, then turned back to Speed. "I told Josie, you're like a bunch of generals. Always fighting the last war."

Speed was startled. He had not credited Victor T. Donovan with that much understanding of the press; it was as if the congressman had spoken one of Speed's own judgments on his craft. For a moment, too, Speed wondered if mention of Josie and "the last war" in the same breath might possibly have referred to events in the history of Josie Donovan and Milo Speed—one particular war Speed now knew without doubt that he, at least, was still fighting.

Could Victor T. Donovan possibly know that? Was there something beyond that blandly handsome countenance that Milo Speed, for all his skepticism and experience, did not suspect? Was someone more calculating than Speed knew gazing out with deceptive eyes at an unsuspecting world?

"Take Reagan," Victor T. Donovan said. "Most of you guys thought he'd be another Goldwater."

The door opened behind Speed, just as he dismissed the sudden questions in his mind. In those long-ago times Victor T. Donovan had been too focused on himself, on getting his Washington career going, to have noticed or even suspected Josie and Speed's interest in each other. And one casual remark about the press, even if it happened to be right on target, was not enough to dissuade Speed from his long certainty that what you saw in Victor T. Donovan was what was there—even if malleable clay for Darwin John and Rafael Ames.

Ames came in grinning; he wore a suit jacket with mismatched trousers; his knit tie was pulled loose and askew from his open button-down collar. A videocassette case was clutched under his arm. Again, Speed sensed a restless vitality in the man and shied from it; having at one time realized a similar force in himself, he knew it could too easily turn predatory.

"You want to see some spots," Victor T. Donovan said, "Ames is going to show you some *real* spots."

Lacy Farnes came in and peered with distress at the

scarcely touched remains of Victor T. Donovan's salad and the uneaten half of Speed's roast beef sandwich.

"You ought to have let me send out," she told the congressman reproachfully. "The food in this building is just *horrible*. Can I anyway bring you some coffee or something?"

"Not for me," Victor T. Donovan said impatiently. "Unless Milo or Rafe wants it."

Lacy looked past Ames, as if she had not intended him to be included in her offer, and smiled at Milo Speed, showing dazzling teeth. Her red lips, her green eyes—flecked with brown behind the granny glasses—might have been smiling *for* him. He was seized by inspiration.

"Tell you what, Lacy. Why don't you stay and watch this stuff they want to show me? I'd like to see *your* reaction."

"Well, now." Victor T. Donovan failed to conceal his surprise.

"Oh, I don't know," Lacy said in a weak voice. "Maybe I—"

"Sit down, sit down." Ames, dismissing the matter, turned and strode toward a television set, topped with a VCR, at one side of the room. "It's not X-rated like Daisychain's stuff."

Lacy hesitated still, looking apprehensively at Victor T. Donovan. After a moment he shrugged.

"Of course . . . sit down, Lacy."

The congressman's virtual surrender to Ames was not lost upon Milo Speed. It tended to confirm his suspicion that Victor T. Donovan, despite his seeming confidence, was not so much managing as being managed and that Ames, beneath his casual manner, was as smoothly aggressive as a cat stalking a bird.

"Well . . . if it's all right."

Lacy sat down tentatively, in a leather chair that would have dwarfed her had she not remained on the edge of its ample seat cushion. She crossed her ankles and clutched her hands in her lap like a child in school. Speed smiled at her reassuringly, while noticing that she had nice legs, too. Speed held thick ankles in deep disdain.

"This is to follow the boss's announcement," Ames said. "Back in the state, of course. Starting tomorrow night."

A strange look, almost of chagrin, crossed Lacy's face as Speed glanced swiftly past her toward Victor T. Donovan. The congressman looked determinedly bland.

"You're announcing tomorrow night?"

Rafe Ames answered: "And you got a column going tomorrow morning. Right, Milo?"

Speed turned slowly in his chair. "Just in time to spread this leak you're dropping on me. Right . . . Mister Ames?"

"You got it." Ames grinned cheerfully. "And why not call me Rafe?"

Speed turned back to Victor T. Donovan, who now looked faintly embarrassed.

"I don't guarantee a goddam thing, Vic. I write what I please."

"We know you do, Milo. We're not asking you for anything."

The hell you're not, Speed thought. He had learned years before to recognize the signs.

"But this Bender," Ames said. "could be a presidential nominee. *If* he gets elected senator again." He pushed a cassette into the hinged maw of the VCR. "Somebody taking on maybe a presidential candidate, that's a *big story*. . . ."

Milo Speed did not have to be told. *A big story indeed.* And he knew, resentfully, that Ames thought he would not be able to resist it.

"Play your damn tape," Speed said.

Large numbers, counting down to zero, filled the screen; then, against a dark background, a scroll with ancient-looking writing appeared. On it, at the top, large, flourishing letters declared: "Constitution of the United States."

"America began in hope," an actor's voice proclaimed, from deep in the chest.

In living color, several red blobs dropped on the scroll. "Now it's awash," the voice announced, "in red ink."

Looking rather like blood, more red ink dripped on the Constitution, forming an expanding pool over the ancient script.

"And Mack Bender's votes in the Senate played a big part."

The Constitution and the ink pool disappeared, to be replaced by pictures of black men staggering out of a bar, with letters superimposed: "For Welfare."

A white man appeared in overalls, being turned away from a window labeled "Personnel." New letters rose on the screen: "For Quotas."

Three Arabs in headdresses and robes strode toward the audience. As the scruffily bearded one in the middle clearly became Yasir Arafat, the lettering changed again: "For Foreign Aid."

Then the Constitution reappeared, all but covered in red ink, with more blobs dripping steadily on it.

"Against Balanced Budget."

"Mack Bender," the actor boomed, as the words disappeared and the senator's familiar face appeared against the ink pool, smiling broadly. "Even his ink is red!"

Tiny letters, appearing subliminally fast, said the ad had been "Paid for by Clearing House Committee."

Ames flicked off the VCR. "Scrapes right down to the bone," he said.

Speed manfully concealed his reaction. "It didn't mention Vic. I thought it was an announcement spot."

"It'll come on right *after* I announce," Victor T. Donovan explained.

"It's . . . isn't it . . . *graphic*?" Lacy's voice was small, uncertain.

"You only got a few seconds to grab 'em by the balls," Ames said. "It's *got* to be graphic."

"And we can show you a vote Bender cast to back up *every single statement* in there." Victor T. Donovan lightly pounded a fist on his desk. "Vic Donovan's not going to deal in false charges. Never has, never will."

"Point is," Ames said, "Bender's such a big mother, all this presidential shit they're spreading . . ."

"I wish you'd watch your language in front of Miss Farnes." Speed thought he might subconsciously be protesting Ames's red-ink spot.

"Sorry. All this presidential talk, if the congressman here has to run against *that*, he'd look like small change. Anybody would. So first thing we have to do is raise Bender's negatives."

"And believe me . . ." Victor T. Donovan's voice rang with piety. "He's got 'em!"

"Like, for instance." Ames touched the VCR's play button. Again the big numbers counted down to zero.

Then an elderly woman appeared on the screen in an old-fashioned dress; she was somewhat stooped and walked with a cane along a sidewalk in what was obviously a small town. The camera cut to a close-up of a kindly, wrinkled old face, then back to the street scene of the woman walking.

"Effie Keene is eighty-four years old," the same actor's voice, this time in sepulchral tones, informed the audience. "She lives by herself in Beetville. She's walking to the post office to pick up her widow's check from Social Security."

Mrs. Keene made her way laboriously up the post office steps, passing two farmer types in checked shirts.

"But Effie Keene is worried," the actor confided. "She's afraid Senator Bender will vote against her Social Security benefits."

The post office dissolved into kindly Mrs. Keene rocking in a chair against the background of an old wood cooking stove.

"The way he did before," the actor said.

Mrs. Keene, looking apprehensive, opened an envelope with trembling hands and fumbled out a check. The camera zoomed in.

"Isn't it a shame?" the television voice inquired, "that our grandparents have to fear their own senator voting against them?"

Mrs. Keene's trembling hands and the check dissolved into a sleek limousine pulling to a curb. Mack Bender emerged, waving cheerily; a driver in a chauffeur's cap was visible behind him.

"Mack Bender," the actor said. "Is he really *our* senator?"

Speed exploded, even as the Cleaning House Committee message flashed on and disappeared. "Bender's not fool enough to try to cut Social Security. What the hell are you guys pulling here?"

Obviously having expected the question, the Honorable Victor T. Donovan leaned over his desk to hand Speed a long piece of paper. It was a photocopied Senate roll call sheet, dated five years earlier, recording a 63–32 nay vote. Beside the name Bender, a check mark was placed in the nay column.

"I told you Vic Donovan doesn't make false charges."

Staring at the roll call sheet, Speed clicked on his computer memory and sped rapidly through his lengthy inventory of congressional lore.

"Goddammit," he said. "That was that crazy amendment to *raise* benefits twenty percent. And damn near a two thirds vote to kill it."

Rafael Ames laughed out loud. "*You* know that. A few editorial writers may look it up. But a lot of voters, especially the old ones, they'll just *believe* that spot."

"Because it's true," Victor T. Donovan said righteously. "Even if Bender thought it'd be forgotten by the time another election came around."

Speed stood up. He was used to campaign chicanery. He held Mack Bender in little higher esteem than any other politician, though Bender's erudition in foreign affairs seemed genuine and he had been an able advocate for international responsibility. But Bender sometimes seemed too sure of himself for Speed's taste—too persuaded of his superiority to his colleagues, too willing to put himself forward as a statesman above politics. No politician, in Speed's view, was above politics, or should be.

"So it'll be a low-road campaign," he said.

Out of a lifelong fascination with the facile political arts, he felt a certain admiration for the skills with which Rafael Ames intended to raise Bender's negatives—even for the apparent innocence of the phrase itself. He was not sure, moreover, whether his dislike of Ames's manner and his low regard for Victor T. Donovan's talents might not be the real causes of the wrath he allowed to boil over.

"If that's what you want to call it." Ames gestured at the VCR. "Plenty more where those came from."

Speed held up his hand. "Don't show me. Vic . . . thanks for the lunch, if nothing else."

Victor T. Donovan rose from his judge's chair, looking

pained. "Not really *low* road, Milo. Maybe a little . . . ah . . . confrontational."

"If that's what you want to call it," Speed said.

"Aren't you going to wish me good luck?"

"That's one thing even Ames can't give you," Speed said. "Darwin John either. Why expect it from me?"

Something dark momentarily tinged the blue irises of Victor T. Donovan's bland eyes; then his lips pursed, and he shook his head as if in regret.

"Lacy, please show Mister Speed out."

★

When the door to the inner office had closed behind them, Speed gently took Lacy's upper arm, noting its firmness, and led her out into the echoing corridor of the Sam Rayburn Building.

"Just for my ears, Lacy . . . tell me what you really thought."

She stared solemnly at him through the granny glasses. "That Rafe Ames is a shit."

Speed blinked. So much, he thought, for protecting modern young women from rude talk.

"In the first degree," he said. "But I meant about the spots."

Lacy took a moment to consider. "I don't know much about Senator Bender," she said, rather as if reciting in class. "I was . . . surprised."

"But you heard your boss." Speed mimicked the mellifluous voice as best he could. "Vic Donovan doesn't deal in false charges."

"That's funny." Lacy gave him her broad smile again. "You sound just like him." Then she turned serious. "But don't blame the congressman, Mister Speed. He's really *nice*."

"He hired Ames, didn't he? And he's letting those spots run."

Lacy looked over her shoulder at the state seal on the closed door. Then she put her face close to Speed's and whispered: "Ames is moving in on him. I think that's why the congressman's running for the Senate . . . when he doesn't really want to."

Like hell he doesn't. But Speed was not too preoccupied with what Lacy was saying to notice her full lips, to sense her close, warm presence.

Lacy whispered again: "He just doesn't realize what Ames is doing to him. Not yet." She glanced a second time at the closed door and spoke normally: "I'm not really supposed to talk to the press, Mister Speed."

He saw that she was worried that Ames or perhaps even Victor T. Donovan himself might come out.

"Oh, I'm not exactly the *press,* Lacy." Though he knew ruefully that he was. "Let's go down to the cafeteria, get a cup of tea or something."

Lacy shook her head, the red hair shimmering beautifully about her white neck. "I've got to get back to work. Besides, *they* think you're the press."

Speed was too male not to sense the attraction flowing between him and a pretty young woman. He savored the brilliant smiles Lacy had given him, remembered the touch of her hand the day they had met. And he was too assiduous a reporter not to recognize and seek to cultivate a strategically situated source. Before she turned away to Victor T. Donovan's office door, Speed had to suppress the painful thought of how much older he was than she.

"You'd better watch your boss make his announcement tomorrow night," Speed said. "At my place maybe?" The moment he said it—ancient instincts disastrously at work—he expected rejection, and he was horrified to have opened himself to it.

Lacy opened the office door an inch, then pulled it to without letting the latch catch or click.

"I've got my own TV, Mister Speed."

The granny glasses flashed in the harsh overhead light, concealing her eyes as she looked at him over her shoulder without a trace of a smile, as seriously as if he were an insurance salesman or a job counselor.

"You come over and watch it with me," Lacy said.

★

As it turned out, they had to listen on Lacy's clock-radio because Victor T. Donovan's announcement of his candidacy for the U.S. Senate was televised only in his home state.

"If I'd done what Ames wanted"—Speed turned the radio dial in search of the speech—"your boss might be on all the networks. If I'd written my column about it for this morning's papers, I mean."

Lacy looked at him with large green eyes. In her apartment, she had explained, she did not always wear her granny glasses.

"Are you all that important?"

"Some people *think* I am, because my pieces appear in a lot of newspapers. But if what I write really *meant* anything, this old world would be a very different place."

He laughed somewhat bitterly, knowing his own futility, how little things ever changed. Lacy started to reply, but just then he found the right station, and her words were drowned by Victor T. Donovan's resounding voice.

". . . undertake this campaign out of no personal ambition. In fact, I could stay in the House, where I believe I've earned the confidence of my district and I'd be chairman of an important committee before long. No, my fellow Americans, I run for the Senate because it's time this state had a *real* senator, a senator who represents the good people who sent him to Washington—not a jet set junketeer trying to high-roll himself into higher office!"

There was a burst of applause, cheers, and whistles. A little tentatively Speed put his feet up on Lacy's bed and leaned back against the headboard.

"Ten to one Darwin John bused in the crowd," he said.

Speed was acutely aware of the young woman beside him on the bed, of her slender legs stretched beside his own. Her bedside radio was the only one in the apartment, so it probably meant nothing. Still, she had made no fuss at all about leading him into her bedroom.

"So let's get one thing straight, folks, right here tonight . . . Vic Donovan doesn't think there *is* any higher office than a seat in the United States Senate . . . representing *this great state*!"

More cheers and applause.

"I don't really see why he needs to be a senator," Lacy said. "There's lots of important state stuff we handle in the office we've got now."

"He doesn't *need* to be a senator," Speed said. "But if he wins, he gets six years at the public trough." *Fat chance,* he thought.

Lacy slapped lightly at his hip. "That's mean." The immemorial girl's gesture signaling reproof without anger seemed to him startlingly intimate. "The congressman doesn't think like that."

"And I say to the great people of this state," Victor T. Donovan declared, "when *you* send *me* to the Senate, my friends and neighbors, you can be sure you'll have a senator—at last—who's *against* these tax and tax, spend and spend programs that drain good Americans dry! Who's *against* the permissiveness and moral emptiness undermining this great nation!"

Victor T. Donovan was getting wound up, and Speed put aside his awareness of Lacy long enough to imagine his earnest face, his steady eye contact, in the television version that would be going out to his state's voters. Speed pictured them listening solemnly, nodding their heads, gaunt Grant Wood figures holding pitchforks.

"Then you'll have a senator—at last—who'll fight to the bitter end to protect *your* Social Security rights and *your* Medicare. Who won't tolerate—at *long* last!—all these welfare queens and quota kings that'll never do an honest day's work while they've got *you* to do it for 'em!"

"I never heard him *mention* welfare before," Lacy said. "I always thought welfare just fed a lot of poor people."

"In his state, Lacy, poor people don't get fed. They're lucky they don't get shot."

"So I say to you tonight," Victor T. Donovan intoned, in the sad but clarion voice of a minister predicting doom, "isn't it time for a change, ladies and gentlemen? Isn't it time *you* had a senator—instead of a globe-trotter? Isn't it time somebody paid attention to *you*—instead of feeding freeloaders, coddling criminals, and tolerating all this immoral vice and pornography?"

A suspenseful pause while cheers and whistles began to build. Then, timed just before the crescendo: "I say it's *high time* for a change!"

There was more; Speed and Lacy listened to the end, including the long final ovation Darwin John no doubt considered well worth his money. But Speed finally turned off the bedside radio, a little shaken by what he had heard. If Mack Bender could be beaten, he thought, Ames and John obviously believed the way to do it was to tear him down. Raise his negatives indeed. And in Victor T. Donovan, Speed had to admit, they might have found—unlikely as it once would have seemed—a willing tool for the job.

"I've known your boss a long time," he told Lacy, "and I never would've believed he had it in him to do anything like this."

Either the guts or the gall.

"It was such an uplifting message." Lacy looked inspired. "And his voice sounded wonderful. Doesn't he have a great voice?"

A political innocent.

At the moment it hardly mattered. He looked her over—the slender neck, the face no longer made serious by the granny glasses, the gray sweater outlining the large breasts that in office hours she sought vainly to camouflage beneath sedate clothes.

"The voice was the voice of Jacob. . . ." Speed did his imitation of Victor T. Donovan. "But the hand was the hand of Esau."

Lacy laughed out loud, throwing up her arms. "You're really *funny*. I thought all famous men were serious. And I didn't guess you were religious."

"Not religious," Speed said, "biblical." *Now or never,* he thought, readying himself for the ritual moves.

Curiously he wanted it to be never. He had no real desire to go through motions once so familiar and exciting that now would be so lacking in spontaneity as to be false—and in their falseness, though not in themselves, shameful. Still, the controlling fact, he knew, was that he did not want to be alone anymore. He feared to bypass a possible opportunity;

he hoped one more time—against hope—to find something beyond momentary comfort.

"I hear," Lacy said, just as he was about to roll toward her, "that you're the most famous womanizer in Washington."

For years this reputation had been sustained mostly by rumor and assumption. On Lacy's lips its repetition made him shrink, as if she had said he had bad teeth.

"Someone's been telling you things."

"They say you're bad," Lacy said. "They say you sleep with anybody who wears a skirt."

"It's better," Speed said, with sarcasm, "when they take off the skirt."

"They say you're *real* bad. The only thing you want from a woman is below the waist."

"A lie." *That,* he thought, was only what he got, not what he wanted. "I *like* women. Most women."

"A bad dude," Lacy said. "Love 'em and leave 'em. That's what they say, anyway."

Speed felt checkmated. If he moved, he confirmed her matter-of-fact statements. Immediately he made up his mind to do nothing; then he retreated into flippancy, his all-purpose camouflage.

"Another lie. Sometimes I don't even love 'em first."

Only Josie. But it was she who had done the leaving.

Lacy had turned a little on the bed, propping herself on an elbow. Her face was close to his.

"Didn't it even occur to you," she said, "that I could have moved the radio into the other room?"

Faint warning signals went off somewhere in Speed's head. Before he could heed them, Lacy lowered her mouth to his. Her red hair against his skin seemed to spark, like static electricity. She kissed him for a long time, hard. At first he did not resist. Then he responded instinctively, hungrily.

After a while Lacy wriggled more comfortably against him, before she lifted her lips an inch and looked with avid green eyes directly into his.

"I knew it'd be easy to get you into bed, Mister Speed. But I didn't think it'd be *this* easy."

4.

By midsummer Rafael Ames had concluded that Senator O. Mack Bender did not yet know what had hit him. Or maybe he was too interested in famine relief for Ethiopia and separatism in Estonia to keep his eye peeled on his home state. How else, Ames asked himself, to explain the fact that, so far, the campaign was going all Victor T. Donovan's way?

Wearing clodhopper shoes and a checked shirt, Bender had visited the state for a few lousy speeches, full of abstract propositions about the winds of change and the emerging peoples of the third world. He was being careful, however, Ames had noted gleefully, to stay put in the good old US of A after the Bender Global Tours spots had jangled his balls a little. In Washington the senator had even taken to answering all roll calls, a boring ritual he once had disdained.

But the real tip-off, in Ames's opinion, was that Bender had set up only one campaign headquarters in his home state and had put not so much as one spot on the air.

No TV! To Ames, that was like playing baseball without spikes or fishing in catch-and-return waters; it was like sitting down to a steak dinner with no teeth. That was why, as the campaign unfolded—or as Victor T. Donovan's did—Ames began referring to Mack Bender as the Gummer.

"This goddam Gummer," he said to Floyd Finch one fine summer night, after they had put in a hard day's work on the complex and expensive state phone network that linked the campaign volunteers Darwin John had bribed into the service of Victor T. Donovan. "How'd that toothless windbag ever get to play with the big boys?"

" 'Considered by his colleagues a man of principle.' That's what these liberal media finks always call him. *That's* what puts Bender up with the biggies."

They were in Floyd Finch's rather bare room in the Lewis & Clark, the best hotel in Capital City—which was not saying much. Ames was monitoring local television for any spots Bender might have sneaked on the air—"though my high-priced information," Finch had disclosed over their spaghetti dinners at the Pony Express Café, after he had consulted his spy at a local network affiliate, "if it's worth a fuck, is there's nothing booked. Not even reserved till after Labor Day."

Rafael Ames had asked a rhetorical question, designed only to show his disdain for O. Mack Bender. He knew Bender did it with image—not exactly with mirrors, of course, but once a pol had a favorable image, he could go a long way. Image could clear the track, as it certainly had for O. Mack Bender.

Up to now, Ames thought.

"What I'd say, Floyd, the Gummer's maybe got principles, but he's never had a real shit-kicking opponent. Practically a free ride in two straight elections."

From the television set flickering in a sand-colored armoire facing the bed, the sounds of screeching tires, automatic gunfire, a woman's scream rang through the room.

"That piece in the *Atlantic,*" Floyd Finch said. "You know what it said?"

Ames was more interested in the poll data he had in his pocket, from Darwin John's first-string number cruncher. Naturally the data had the Honorable Victor T. Donovan running way back, just barely ahead of "Undecided." But Ames had expected nothing else, with the national press rating Bender a sure thing for his party and the campaign not even half finished. The number that really signified for Ames was the Gummer's changing favorable-unfavorable.

"Maybe three eggheads from Harvard read the *Atlantic*, my man. And nobody from this state went to Harvard except the Gummer. What's it matter what the *Atlantic* said?"

What *did* matter was that the data showed one thing clearly: From the day the Honorable had announced his candidacy, O. Mack Bender's favorable rating with the voters had declined seven points. His image. Unfavorable had gone up only two, but that told Ames something else he liked almost as well: Quite a few Bender voters had gone undecided. Up for grabs.

Floyd Finch struck a pose, puffing himself up in his chair. " 'A man who reasons with the people—and always listens to reason.' That's what the *Atlantic* said, and that's the kind of stuff gives Bender this straight-arrow reputation he's got. Why they always mention him for the brass ring."

Ames did not dispute it. But he dismissed the *Atlantic* and Bender's image with a sweep of his arm. "Not for long, they won't. Not when I get all his negs on the air."

Rafael Ames's faith in television was almost genetic. He was a child of the tube. As boy and man he had watched TV far more than even the astronomical national average; TV had shaped his barefoot days, replaced baseball, dogs, apple pie, even comic books. TV had become his life. One of his earliest memories was Elvis Presley, from the waist up, on the *Ed Sullivan Show*. Ames could identify old theme songs, forgotten game shows, obscure character players, sit-coms long dead, Richard Nixon getting it socked to 'im on *Laugh-In*.

In his mind, after so much viewing, the ads—particularly political commercials—were compelling, convincing, irresistible. Ames had studied campaign spots back to the fifties, even an old singing commercial for Eisenhower—primitive stuff now, probably a grabber back then. To him, campaign spots *were* politics; television and political campaigns provided the same empty canvas. Filling in form and color was Rafael Ames's art.

Practicing it, seeing that art become life, sometimes more

than life—on the screen, in voters' perceptions—was his religion. It was only an incidental, though one he was happily aware of, that he could take 15 percent off the top of Darwin John's extensive television buys for Victor T. Donovan. That was standard in the consultant community.

"Time I'm finished with the Gummer," he said to Floyd Finch, "his mother might vote for our guy, she's still living."

Finch had seen them come and go, candidates, officeholders, kingmakers, the good, the bad, and the indifferent. Ames had learned that Floyd Finch had not endured those uncounted years of faithful service to all three without absorbing a certain elemental wisdom.

"Rafe," Finch now said, "you got all the talent in the world. Maybe the sharpest operator the party's had in my experience and I go back past *Sputnik*. Even Darwin John kind of sees it now. But one thing you still maybe got to learn is this: You don't ever want to underestimate the other guy."

Ames was relieved to hear no more than these conventional words. He drained the last of the one bottle of Carta Blanca he had decided to allow himself and said: "You got it one hundred eighty degrees back-asswards, my man."

He doubted, in fact, if the Gummer—who was too busy reforming NATO and glasnosting with Gorbachev—had even paid attention to the *other* interesting fact in the poll data. Assuming Bender had some poll data of his own, which was maybe a big assumption the way things were going. But there it was, from Darwin John's polling honcho, in black and white: The Honorable Victor T. Donovan's name recognition had *doubled* overall and was up like ten points even in the vast sugar beet field he called his district.

"It's the Gummer," Ames said, "that's underestimating *us*."

"Yeah, well, maybe," Finch looked skeptical, as he usually did. "But I seen some tough campaigns didn't even start till Labor Day."

Ames took aim and clunked his beer bottle into a tin wastebasket. He was wearing unpressed chinos, unlaced Nikes without socks, and a green T-shirt with the slogan "ALMOST HEAVEN—FOOTHILL COUNTY JAIL."

"So has the Gummer. He thinks this is still the good old

days. But what hasn't dawned on him yet, every day that passes, our spots are *defining* him. Chewing up his image. And you can bet the family jewels: Come Labor Day, the Gummer won't be getting away with this man of principle shit anymore."

Someone rapped on the door, and Floyd Finch rose to answer.

"Even now," Ames said to Finch's back, "the Gummer's going down and the Honorable's moving up, and we're even getting a little free TV on the local news shows. Thanks to you."

"Can't offset Bender's weekly show from the Senate." Finch put his hand on the doorknob. "These incumbents fix themselves up pretty good."

He opened the door a crack, then wider, to admit a short, stout man, looking not unlike Edward G. Robinson—rumpled in a dark pipe rack suit, slicked-back hair, a jowly red face. He carried a once-white Panama hat, dingy with years.

"Oh, Cal." Ames waved a languid hand. "Glad you could drop by. You know Cal Kyle, don't you, Floyd?"

"Sure. Want a beer, Cal?"

"No, thanks, Mister Finch."

"Cal never drinks on duty," Ames said. "And Cal's always *on* duty, that right, Cal?"

"Try to do my job, Mister Ames."

"Look at that hat, Floyd. You see anybody else wears one of those these days?"

Floyd Finch popped open another beer for himself. "Hardly see anybody wearing *any* kind of hat anymore."

"It's Cal's training. The FBI. J. Edgar himself always wore one of those things in summertime. Switched to the fedora in winter. Right, Cal?"

"Mister Hoover," Calvin Kyle said reverently, "had a great influence on all his agents." He looked at Floyd Finch with protuberant eyes, as if daring him to deny it.

Ames said: "That's why Cal's the best investigator money can buy. FBI training. J. Conrad Cramer found it out the hard way."

Calvin Kyle accepted the compliment without acknowledging it. The Panama slowly rotated in his meaty hands. "Mister Hoover took a personal interest. He wanted things done right."

"Like me," Ames said. "You get the whole nine yards on that little item you told me about the other day?"

Leaving the Panama in one hand, Calvin Kyle reached with the other into the inside pocket of his jacket and brought out several sheets of folded paper.

"Hot stuff, Mister Ames."

"Will it stand up?"

Calvin Kyle pursed thick lips. "Not maybe in court."

"We're not going to court. With . . . say . . ." Ames slumped back in his chair, tapping the papers against his knee, and looked at the ceiling. "With Lee Lestark?"

"Up to you." The Panama moved infinitesimally toward the papers in Ames's hand. "What's there is in there."

"Lee Lestark?" Floyd Finch laughed. "Anything that gets him a headline stands up with that dirtbag."

"I hear he's AC-DC." Ames folded the papers again and put them in his pocket. "Goes whichever way pays off the most. Now, another little job, Cal, in addition to all the great stuff you're already doing for me. Check out the candidate, will you? Right back to the womb."

"For Christ sake," Floyd Finch said, "how much more can he find on Bender?"

"The candidate, I said. Not the Gummer. *Our* candidate."

Finch's mouth fell open, but Calvin Kyle took the assignment like any other.

"Check out the Honorable Victor T. Donovan," he said. "Back to the womb. Right, Mister Ames."

"Just as if you were running a check on Senator Bender. Or Martin Luther King. I want everything from his toothpaste brand to his date of circumcision, if he had one. Anything *you* might think is unimportant, put it in anyway. Let me decide if I need it."

"Put it in," Calvin Kyle said. "How much time I got?"

"Well, the sooner the better, but the main thing is a good, thorough job. You're pretty well cleaned up on Bender, aren't you? After this?" Ames tapped his pocket.

"Except you don't ever have *every*thing there is, Mister Ames. There's always some little something, you keep looking, you'll find it." Calvin Kyle looked from Ames to Finch and back again, his red face suddenly lit with the fires of heady experience.

Ames, slumped in his chair, solemnly nodded his head, shadowed by its usual beard stubble. "You can get back on the Gummer when you polish off the Honorable. And Cal . . . a bloodhound like you don't need advice from me. But there's one little thing."

Calvin Kyle placed the Panama on his head, produced a notebook from one pocket, a pencil from another, and stood more or less at attention, his red face glistening with interest.

"Take a look at Speed," Ames said.

Alarm flashed across the weary face of Floyd Finch. "What's Speed got to do with anything?"

"Floyd." Ames spoke like a father admonishing a child. "That's what I want Cal to find out."

"But Milo Speed writes in *hundreds* of newspapers. And he's not Lestark. You don't want to mess around with Speed."

Ames nodded. "That's right, Cal. Be extra-careful, you nose into Speed's business. He could cause a stink."

"Right." Calvin Kyle put away the notebook and the pencil. "Mister Hoover use to say some reporter called Milo Speed was a Communist. This the same one?"

"Could be, but that's not . . . ah . . . quite what I'm looking for. More like something in the past that links Speed with the Honorable. Just a hunch I've got." Ames touched his chest. "Inside. You'll know what it is if you find it."

"If it's there," Calvin Kyle said, "I'll find it."

He offered something that might have been a nod to Ames, something less than that to Finch, turned to the door, and left, the Panama perched squarely on his head.

"Having that slimeball around," Floyd Finch said when the door had closed, "feels like maybe you should send your laundry out."

Ames looked surprised. "Cal brings the laundry *in*, my man." He pulled the folded papers from his pocket and handed them to Finch. "Like this."

Finch read quickly, looking up only once. "Who'd have thought it?" he said. Then he read on to the end and handed the papers back to Ames.

"Gabriella Lukes. I wouldn't mind getting in *there* myself."

"Might be a little crowded." Ames put the papers back in his pocket. "But you see what I mean. Cal delivers the dirty linen."

"Including maybe yours someday. To the OP, you don't watch your step."

"Not as long as we pay Cal's salary. And say nice things about J. Edgar."

Floyd Finch pulled at his beer and gazed moodily over the bottle at Ames. "Like he said. That stuff wouldn't stand up in court."

Ames shrugged. "It'll cost the Gummer the church ladies' vote."

"So let me get this straight. Now you're turning your gumshoe loose on *our* candidate? What'll the Chief say when he finds out he's forking out a wad to investigate his own man?"

Ames raised his legs and examined the loose Nikes. "I don't go behind the moneyman's back, Floyd. It's cleared with John. He and I agreed, if there's anything there the Gummer's people might come up with, we want to know it first." He giggled, almost girlishly. "If the Gummer's *got* any people."

"And *if* the Honorable ever did anything in his Boy Scout life he wouldn't want his mother to know about."

Ames lowered the Nikes with a thump. "Everybody has, my man. Everybody's got a secret life. Don't you?"

Floyd Finch nodded gloomily and took another swig of Carta Blanca. "Milo Speed could be real trouble, though."

"Ahhh . . . Speed's been out there so long, a good story bites him on the ass, he can't spot it anymore."

A voice from the armoire described in soulful tones the overwhelming advantages of a Japanese automobile. On the screen it zoomed along a mountain road, looking as if it might never need maintenance.

"Tell you one thing about Speed," Floyd Finch said. "He won't whore like Lestark. Not for us, not for the OP. Not for *any*body, that I know of."

Ames got up and moved restlessly to the window of the Lewis & Clark. He peered out into a downtown street on which, at that hour, nothing moved save a drooping overhead banner, stirred by the hot summer wind. It proclaimed: CAPITAL CITY COMMUNITY PICNIC—PIONEER PARK—COME ONE, COME ALL—BARBECUE—MUSIC—FUN FOR THE KIDS!

"Or can he?" Ames said to the windowpane, on which a frosted arc rose above the air conditioner. "That's what keeps sticking in my throat."

The Community Picnic was to be held the next day, with the Honorable Victor T. Donovan as featured speaker. Not, Ames thought, that even the Gettysburg Address live in Pioneer Park would be worth as much as even one of his TV spots, but the Honorable had insisted. In *his* experience, the Community Picnic was a big deal.

"Can he what?" Finch asked. "You want another beer?"

"Can Speed still recognize a story, somebody drops one on 'im? Nah, no more beer. You swill down that stuff too much, Floyd."

Floyd Finch popped the fourth beer from the six-pack he'd brought from the 7-Eleven.

"Man's too old to get it up, he might's well pour it down."

Ames shrugged and returned to his own thoughts.

"I mean, Speed had a big one handed to him, and he either didn't know it or didn't bite. I got to wonder which."

"Wha'd you give 'im?"

"Me? I wouldn't give that broken-down stud a kick in the ass. It was the candidate himself. He let Speed stand right in his office—can you imagine?—and listen to Darwin John pumping up his tires about the Senate. And Speed never wrote a fucking word."

Just then a sound from the television caused Ames to spin toward it, holding up a hand toward Floyd Finch. "The Schoolhouse is coming on."

A little red country schoolhouse appeared on the screen, with happy children cavorting on the playground. The camera moved swiftly forward, peered through a window, and disclosed a motherly gray-haired schoolteacher behind her desk.

"It's my job to help those kids out there—" a close-up and

a gesture toward the schoolyard with a pencil—"become good citizens of our beloved country. But how much do *you* know about the great issues facing us all?"

The teacher held up a tablet, the camera closed in, and the pencil pointed to questions inscribed on the tablet, each followed by two boxes.

"How did this state's senior senator vote on each of the following?" the teacher asked. She read the top question, as her pencil followed the words.

"Constitutional amendment to require a balanced budget?" The pencil checked a box under "Against."

"Handgun control?" The pencil checked a box under "For."

"Cut funds for water projects?" A check in the "For" box.

"Prayer in the schools?" The pencil firmly checked off "Against."

The camera held on the tablet with the check marks. Then the picture dissolved into film of Senator O. Mack Bender in black tie at the head table of an elegant dinner. Superimposed letters read: "The Waldorf, New York."

A strong male voice supplanted the gray-haired teacher's soft tones: "Does this man *really* represent our state?"

Successive closing frames quickly declared. "Donovan for Senate . . . For America" and lingered on "Vic for Victory!"

Music blared for a woman's shampoo ad, and someone cooed: "No more split ends . . ."

"That's sharp stuff," Floyd Finch said, "but we need a better slogan. I don't much like that Vic for Victory."

"Slogans and bumper stickers. That's all you old-timers think of." Ames pointed at the TV set. "Get it through your head once and for all, my man: The votes are in *there*."

Finch looked hurt and drank beer. "A better slogan wouldn't hurt," he insisted. "How'd you know about Speed listening in when the Chief was talking to the Honorable?"

"Josie Baby. Just like me, she wondered why Speed didn't write the story."

A dreamy look that could not be accounted for by four bottles of Carta Blanca suffused Floyd Finch's face. "Rafe . . . you think the Honorable gets much"—Finch made a bottle-shaped motion with his hands, while holding his beer in one of them—"from that honeysuckle rose of his?"

"You mean Josie Baby? Why not?" Ames had started to pace the floor. "Then after that we showed Speed both the Ink Spot and Mrs. Keene. He already knew what was up, so we leaked the *timing*, for Christ sake. And still he never wrote a word."

"I was the Honorable," Floyd Finch said, "I'd get in here tonight, pick that honeysuckle rose while the pickin's good."

Ames threw up his hands in disgust. "You're getting pissed, Floyd. Better watch it. He'll be in too early for you to sleep it off."

★

Ames slammed the door to Finch's room. He was not amused by the fact that a man he had to work with was on the sauce every night. Not that Floyd Finch ever showed it in the morning; Ames had to admit that. He had to admit, too, that Finch knew his stuff, knew his way around, even out here in the asshole of the nation. Finch knew somebody everywhere, it seemed, having been around practically since the original Lewis and Clark.

Still, mixing booze and politics was not a good idea, and Rafael Ames had no time and little patience for anything but politics.

He walked to the elevator bank, the loose Nikes flopping in the silence of the hall, and pushed the down button, feeling uncharacteristically purposeless. He did not want to go, just yet, to his own sparse cubbyhole, a neomotel space on an upper floor of the Lewis & Clark, with dirty movies on TV. He stayed out of bars, it was still too early for the morning paper, and the night was too hot to walk outdoors.

Maybe there would be a paperback worth buying at the newsstand, maybe an Ed McBain. Ames loved procedure, any kind of procedure. What was politics, he often thought, but procedure? And Ed McBain had police procedure down pat; he would have made a good political consultant.

But the newsstand was closed. Ames turned back toward

the elevators and was startled to see Milo Speed at a table in the lobby bar, in earnest conversation with another man.

Ames wondered immediately why a media bigfoot like Speed would have come all the way west to Capital City—Armpit City, as Ames thought of it—at this early stage of a supposedly one-sided Senate campaign. The hairs on the back of his neck tingled with interest. At least the high-nosed asshole would be someone besides pie-eyed Floyd Finch to talk politics with.

Ames made his way through the nearly empty bar area, shrugging off a titsy blonde giving him the once-over and staring down a bozo in a red shirt who was eyeing the loose Nikes with elaborate disdain. When Ames was halfway to Speed's table, Speed saw him coming. He did not wave or rise.

Ames said affably: "Milo. Getting on the big story, huh?"

"I've been following it . . . from afar."

Ames did not think he had imagined a faint wrinkle of Speed's nose. "What was it Red Smith wrote? Biggest upset since Serutan. That's what we got out here."

The other man at the table rose and held out his hand. "I'm Theo Keller."

"I'm sorry." Speed did not sound the least bit sorry. "Theo, this is Rafael Ames, Vic Donovan's mastermind."

Ames was secretly pleased by Speed's description. There was irony in it, of course, but Ames took it as he wanted, at face value.

"Theo writes the editorials for the *Ledger*, Ames."

"So you're for Bender." Ames presented his most agreeable smile, though he despised all newspaper people. None were to be trusted to stay bought or stroked.

"All the way," Theo Keller said. "Did they give you that T-shirt as an inmate?"

Ames chuckled amiably. "My father sent it to me for Christmas. He just got out."

Speed had not asked Ames to sit down, but Keller politely indicated an empty chair. Ames took it and said: "You make about as good a case for your man, Theo, as anybody could."

Theo Keller was not amused. "That's more than I can say for you, if you're responsible for Vic Donovan's TV. When'll you guys get around to airing what he's *for*? Other than getting elected."

Ames never took offense when talking politics. He liked the old Lyndon Johnson story, about LBJ being interviewed by a school board that asked if he taught that the earth was round or flat. I can teach it round *or* flat, Johnson claimed to have replied, and got the job. LBJ was before Ames's time, and the story was a Texas whopper, but Ames liked it anyway; he thought he might have answered that school board the same way, and he *knew* he could teach it round or flat.

"But getting elected's the first thing, Theo. Right?"

"Not always. You want a drink?"

Ames did not mistake Theo Keller's elaborate courtesy for liking. He saw at once that the man was too committed to the Gummer to have an open mind or take a relaxed view.

"No, thanks," Ames said. "Ask your senator. Ask what he could do back there in Washington if he didn't get elected out here."

Theo Keller did not acknowledge Ames's advice.

"Two more of these," he said, indicating his and Speed's glasses to a waitress wearing what Lewis & Clark management apparently thought was Indian dress—beaded doeskin up to her ass and down to her cleavage. Ames was not surprised to see Speed's gaze travel up and down the woman's bare legs.

That superannuated stud.

But Speed apparently had paid less attention to the doeskin waitress than to what the other two men were saying.

"I've heard that song a thousand times, Ames. You got to get elected to do anything, so anything you do to get elected is okay. You need some new lyrics."

Ames was totally at ease, fully in his element. "You media guys don't run for office, Milo. You can afford to hold your noses. But you and I both know what makes Sammy run. *And* the Honorable Victor T. Donovan. *And* the Gum . . . Mack Bender, too."

"So what makes Mack run? In your exalted opinion?"

Theo Keller's voice was quiet, controlled; but he had been drinking, and his eyes told Ames he was a little scorched under the collar. Drinkers always lost control, sooner or later.

Ames started to answer, then delayed while the fake Sacajawea put down the new drinks. She was about the same age as Josie Baby and showed it twice as clearly. Her fat boobs bulged almost out of her top when she leaned over the table. No doubt interesting Speed, Ames thought, since the creep was supposed to freak on women.

"What makes Mack run?" Theo said again, when the waitress had gone away, her long pigtail swinging. "You know so much."

"Winning."

Theo Keller laughed, drank, put his glass down. "That's what I'd expect from anybody makes those shitty spots of yours." Theo sat up, his voice still quiet but his eyes flashing. "That one tonight we saw on the bar TV over there. I think that's the first outright lie I've caught you in . . . that Mack voted for handgun control. From *this* state?"

Ames smiled again. "Check it out, my man."

"No need, Theo." Milo Speed sipped what looked to Ames like water with lemon peel. "Bender cast a yea vote ten years ago on a bill to make it a crime in the District of Columbia for a bus driver to carry a handgun."

"See?" Ames said. "Milo's done his homework. Like I always do."

Theo Keller sat back in his chair and drained his glass. "If *that*'s handgun control, I'm in the wrong business."

"We both are," Speed said. "We ought to be spin doctors, Theo, like Ames here. No more of this *informing* the public. The thing now is to *bullshit* the public."

Ames raised a glass of water the doeskin waitress had set out for him. His restlessness was gone. He felt gratified, happy, in tune. "To the public, gents. You inform it your way, I'll bullshit it mine."

"And never the twain shall meet." Theo Keller set his glass down, refusing the toast.

The man was positively a goddamned goo-goo, Ames thought.

"Fact is, that vote Speed says Mack cast, that had to be a *brave* vote, goddammit. Considering guns in this state sit at the right hand of God."

"Theo." Speed waggled a finger at the editor. "You make that argument in front of a crowd around here, you better be wearing a suit of armor."

"Don't I know it? Listen, Ames"—Theo Keller straightened belligerently in his chair—"I'm going to give your man a hard time tomorrow, when he comes by the paper. He *is* coming, isn't he?"

"It's on the schedule."

Ames was piqued by the question. He had advised against the visit to the *Ledger*, considering it a waste of time to talk with the editors of a rag already out for the Gummer. Almost any editors, for that matter. Those *Ledger* bastards wouldn't give the Honorable the time of day, much less a fair shake. Anyway, who read the fucking *Ledger*? Voters were too busy watching TV.

"A hard time," Theo said, and Ames saw to his disdain that the editor was getting smashed. "Bout your spots. Bout what Donovan stands for 'f anything. Bout why this state ought to trade in a pres'dential contender for a goddam know-nothing congressman."

"Victor T. Donovan"—Ames rose gallantly, if none too enthusiastically, to the defense of the Honorable—"is not a know-nothing. As you'll see tomorrow."

"Won't even be a goddam congressman soon. Be out of office wishing he'd stayed put."

Speed was looking over Ames's shoulder with sudden, almost fervent interest. Ames glanced back and saw Josie Baby coming toward their table. She'd been out among the natives, doing the kaffeeklatsch circuit for the Honorable's campaign. As if such stuff really mattered anymore. But it gave her a part to play.

Speed all but leaped to his feet. "Josie . . . I heard you were out here."

"Why not?" Her voice was cool. "Vic's coming in in the morning."

Theo and Ames rose, too, and Speed introduced Theo. Josie looked him over icily.

"Don't you think your editorials are a little biased, Mister Keller?"

She was dressed conservatively, as befitted the appearances she was making, and to Ames she looked a little pneumatic around the pelvis. But he had to admit that she carried herself like a queen. Like a senator's wife in the movies.

"Considering those poison dart TV ads your husband's running, Miz Donovan"—Theo Keller stared at her defiantly—"I think we've been rather generous."

Josie Baby chilled him, Ames was happy to see; her glance swept past the editor as if he were not there, and she did not respond to his words.

"Rafe, I need a chat with you. Do you have a minute?"

Her manner, plainly suggesting that of course he did, irritated Ames; this queen stuff could get old in a hurry. For the moment he only nodded assent.

But Speed said, a little plaintively: "I was hoping you'd sit down, Josie. Have a drink."

Speed sounded disappointed, and Ames had to wonder if the old billy goat was so pussy-whipped he'd even try to score off the Honorable's wife, on the Honorable's turf.

"Long day," Josie said. "I'm afraid I'm worn out. Rafe?"

"I'll walk you up." Ames stood and winked at Theo Keller. "You won't be *really* rough on my man tomorrow, will you?"

He waved to Speed, enjoying the sour look on his face, and touched Josie Baby's elbow. They walked toward the elevators.

"I don't see why Vic would want to give the *Ledger* anything but the back of his hand," she said. "They're so strong for Bender."

"You got to give the press a little stroking here and there. You don't, they just get worse." *Besides,* Ames wanted to say, *what the* Ledger*'s been handing out, the Gummer's getting back in spades. From me.*

Josie Baby turned suddenly playful. "Caught you drinking with the enemy, didn't I?"

That irritated Ames, too. Usually she was all politics, the way a candidate's wife ought to be. It bothered him when she seemed to get more personal, and he remembered with discomfort Lacy's suggestion that Josie Baby had a case on him. If so, she'd done nothing about it; he devoutly hoped she never would.

"I wasn't drinking," he said. "What'd you want to talk about?"

Just then they reached the elevators. One of them opened, and a bellman came out carrying a tray. Still in her playful mode, Josie Baby said: "Come on up, Rafe . . . *I'll* give you a drink."

Ames did not want to offend the Honorable's wife, especially in public. And it was sort of a kick to force Speed to see them going upstairs together when he looked like maybe he had his horny eye on Josie Baby. So he followed her obediently into the elevator, but as the doors slid shut and she punched seven, he pointedly let her know where they stood.

"I don't drink. What's on your mind?"

"Those old bitches I spend the day talking to, I'm so sick and tired of their chatter and all that goddam coffee I could scream. I need a *real* drink."

"Well, somebody's got to do it." Ames did not really think so but considered it best to humor her along. "And you're good at it . . . ah . . . Miz Donovan." He had just stopped himself from calling her Josie Baby.

"That makes me sound like Vic's mother. And she's dead."

The remark alarmed Ames. It sounded maybe as if she were going to hit him up for a bigger gig than swigging down coffee with the local bridge clubs.

"But *I'm* not dead. I like that T-shirt." She plucked at it, smiling, and he felt her fingers touch his nipple and fall away. The implication thoroughly frightened him; it suggested she might get *really* personal. But surely . . .

The elevator stopped at seven, and Josie Baby walked out, swinging her hips. A nice ass, Ames had to admit. He followed her down the hall to the door of her room, eyeing her swivel hips with hostility, wondering how best to get her back in line and keep her there. Maybe, he thought, he should just tell her to shut the fuck up.

"Tell you the truth"—Josie Baby fumbled in her bag for her key—"I really just wanted somebody to have a drink with." She found the key and unlocked the door. "Maybe get a little drunk, the day I've had."

"Oh, well, now . . ." Ames could not bring himself, after

all, to lower the boom on the Honorable's wife. "I—I really don't drink, you know. This late at night hardly ever."

She turned to face him, smiling. "You don't have to drink. Just keep me company awhile."

Ames was repelled. He had, at best, little time for women, or for anyone or anything but the path he followed, the track stretching infinitely in front of him, into the misty distances of politics, power, politics, and more politics. Ad infinitum.

"I better not, uh, Josie." *Enough of this queen-for-a-night shit,* he thought. "Got to be up early, y'know, with the candidate coming. There'll be lots to do."

He saw Josie Baby's eyebrows rise a little, whether in anger or just in surprise Ames could not tell and did not care. He did not intend to sit around a hotel room in the middle of the night watching a bored cunt get sloshed. Even if she was the Honorable's wife.

A faint, strange smile touched Josie Baby's full mouth. "I'm not going to drag you into bed, Rafe . . . if that's what you're worried about."

"Good God, no!"

Rafael Ames was genuinely shocked. Not only was the candidate's wife a furrow he knew better than to plow, but the idea itself was repugnant. It violated his every instinct to have to deal openly with it and with her.

"That never occurred to me . . . a lady like you? It's just, y'know, it's late and—"

"Never *occurred*? Not at all?"

The playful tone had turned sharp. Ames noticed again, unhappily, the queen's carriage, the queen's voice. It would not be easy, it came to him, ever again to think of the Honorable's wife as Josie Baby.

"Never mind," she said. "Like Vic would say, scratch that for me, will you?"

"I only thought . . ." Ames felt himself floundering. He was not accustomed to that and tried to steer back to firmer ground. "You said you had something you wanted to talk to me about."

Josie stared at him, but her face and eyes were blank, as if she were seeing nothing. An agonizing moment passed.

Suddenly Ames wanted desperately to get away; he had to stop himself from running back up the hall to the elevators. But he couldn't just leave, he told himself, while the candidate's wife was standing there with her face hanging out.

Another moment dragged by.

"Politics," Josie said at last. "Those ball-breaking spots of yours. Vic's campaign. My goddam kaffeeklatsches. That's the kind of thing I wanted to talk about. Nothing special."

Ames felt, with relief, that the danger was past, if there'd been any. Surely she couldn't actually have had the hots for him. Or thought he had for her. That kind of thing was pure trouble, no good, out of place in a campaign. Disruptive. In a campaign everybody had better things to do.

"That's all I figured it was," Ames said. "But it's so late, and anyway, we can talk tomorrow."

He added hastily, hoping to smooth down any rough edges he might have left: "Always like to know what you're thinking, Josie."

"Of course you do." Josie began to close the door, the strange smile back on her face. "But you just run along now. Sleep tight."

It sounded almost as if *she* were dismissing *him*, Ames thought, when *he* was the one who'd kept the lid on. He had started toward the elevators and could see her no longer when, just before the door latch clicked behind him, he heard her say:

"And don't forget to pull the covers up."

★

In the rapidly emptying lobby of the Lewis & Clark, Milo Speed sat glumly over his vodka. He was so depressed by the sight of the elevator doors closing behind Josie and Rafael Ames that he scarcely heard Theo Keller's rambling denunciation of modern American politics.

"Use to be a man could shake a few hands, kiss a baby, maybe stick a sign on somebody's lawn. Didn' have a jail record, he was in like Flynn."

Speed imagined what had happened as soon as the elevator had arrived upstairs. Ames had youth, vitality, a flat stomach, no doubt perfect pecs, and Josie, even cast as the candidate's wife, wouldn't have changed much. Josie still would be a steam locomotive racing down her own inimitable track.

"Nowadays got to get up maybe a million bucks for TV, an' prove he *don't* get it up for some chick onna side. *Then* prove he ain't a goddam daisy sniffer."

The only question in Speed's mind was whether they'd gone to Ames's room or Josie's. *Your place or mine?* He could hear Josie laughing as she said it, knew just the way her hands would tug expertly at Ames's belt buckle.

"Like these shoppin malls ruinin' downtown." Theo spoke like a man discovering truth. "Campaigns're like shoppin' malls, y'know? All glass and parkin' space, things to buy. No place to sit inna shade."

Speed could not long bear to think of what was transpiring in either her place or his. Though in his loneliness he had become a virtuoso of erotic fantasies, he saw nothing erotic in lurid visions of Ames and Josie that left no garment unshed. Fury gradually fueled his imagination, as rage rather than sex drives a rapist.

If Josie—upon whose remembered glories (Speed saw too late) he had expended the last of his best years in fruitlessly suppressed desire—if Josie could not see beyond Ames's smart-ass manner and college boy exterior, if she could take a public elevator up to bed beside a snakelike yuppie sleazoid with white teeth and the ethical sensibility of Joseph R. McCarthy, then . . .

"To hell with Josie," he thought he muttered, standing up abruptly.

His voice in the cavernous lobby bar was louder than he'd intended; the words echoed and seemed to mock him from the saloon atmosphere Lewis & Clark management had worked hard to create. A gaping face between a spreading hat and a sheriff's uniform stared at him from the bar; from nearby tables a few inquiring heads turned. Theo Keller looked up at him with faintly bleared eyes.

"I signed the check," Speed said. "See you in the morning, Theo."

Steady blasts from the air conditioning carried his anger swiftly away. The air was no chillier, he thought miserably, than the voice in which Josie had cut him down in front of the unspeakable Ames. And it was one thing to say to hell with her but quite another to get her out of his head, his heart, his fervent longing.

Christ, he thought. *I'm far gone.*

"Damn time zone," Theo said. "Gets ev'rybody from back East."

Nodding vaguely, Speed strode toward the elevators, hoping he would not have to ride in the car that had taken Josie upstairs with Ames. He would be able, he thought, to sense her recent presence, even though he had no memory of what perfume she had used, tonight or in the past.

Thoughts of Josie had preoccupied him nevertheless, kept him in a state of anxiety bordering on despair, since the fatal day of the Cramer hearing, which, to Speed, was more significantly the day he had realized that life without Josie, the life he had thought so controlled, was, in fact, a snare and a delusion, a fraud he had concealed from himself with work, cynicism, and—for a while—other women.

"Good night, sir."

The doeskin waitress, turning from an outer table, gave him a bright, fake smile. Speed could hardly help looking down at her upturned breasts, most of which were exposed by the supposedly Indian outfit. But he was not really interested; rather, egged on by the waitress's flesh, he was wondering if his preoccupation really was with Josie's marvelous body, his painfully remembered awareness of those lush treasures that once had yielded him indescribable delights. Was he merely hoping for another chance to fuck Josie's eyes out?

"Have a good evening," the waitress called after him.

Speed went on toward the elevators, telling himself it was more than sex; his agony *had* to be more than sex—though the thought of Josie in bed was a particular torment. But nothing pained him more deeply than the knowledge that he had not even known, had been able to offer her nothing, when she had to live with the ordeal of her miscarriage. And he had known too many women to concede that what he had had with Josie was mere lust. He knew lust, all right, but he knew love, too, he assured himself.

And I can tell the difference.

Certainly, he had never felt with another woman, not even in the early years with Nancy, the obsession that had gripped him in his time with Josie, the desire to *know* her, know everything about her, past, present, body no more than soul, to penetrate every memory, every possibility, every mystery, to the heart of what Josie was, what *they* were together, and could be.

And Ames or no goddam Ames, I still want all that.

An elevator's doors slid open before him; he could not remember if it was the one they had used, but he got on anyway and punched nine. If it was the same elevator, Josie—as if to spare him—had left no scent of perfume, no tangible trace of herself. But she was there anyway, Speed knew in real anguish; Josie was *always* there, in his fatal consciousness, his acute sensibility.

Even when he was with Lacy, as he had been a good deal lately, Josie had rarely been out of his head. Speed now knew she never really had been, not in all the long years since the rainy afternoon he once had persuaded himself was forgotten.

As the car went smoothly up, he focused upon a poster on the side wall that pictured a steaming stack of pancakes in the Lewis & Clark's Chuck Wagon Grill. "Real Cowboy Grub!" But the mocking image of Josie and Ames writhing together, whether in her place or in his, soon replaced the pancakes.

At the seventh floor the car braked itself, and the doors opened. Rafael Ames stood outside in his flapping shoes and Foothill County Jail T-shirt. He looked startled to see Speed.

Struck out, Speed thought immediately. His spirits lifted as swiftly as had the Lewis & Clark elevator.

Ames stepped in and punched ten. "Seems like a candidate's wife *always* wants to do more than the kaffeeklatsch bit."

"I'll bet." Josie must have seen through Ames like a pane of glass, Speed thought. Plexiglas.

"Women." Ames spat the word at the elevator door. "Never know *what* they want."

Well, it certainly wasn't you, Speed thought happily. But as the elevator braked itself for his own floor, his mood slowed with it. And as the doors opened, this time on an empty hallway leading to his empty room, he remembered sadly: *It's not me either.*

★

A half hour later Josie Donovan was still sitting upright against the headboard of an overly soft Lewis & Clark bed, her shoulders bare in the light of a reading lamp. Her paperbound copy of *Northanger Abbey* had been cast on the bed beside her. Josie had found herself in no mood for Jane Austen's gentle heroines, forever in want of a husband.

She was tired, for one thing, of her part in the campaign. *Bor-ing!* And at that on old and depressing home grounds she'd long ago thought were far behind her. But the kaffeeklatsches and the homebody women and the God-ridden cowboy atmosphere were the least of it.

As that editor downstairs had suggested, the campaign itself seemed unworthy, even mean, not at all what she'd anticipated. She wasn't sure exactly *what* she'd expected, what had so excited her at first; but a higher plane had seemed somehow to be opening to her, and—Josie conceded ruefully—she had been eager to move up to it and on it.

"Should have known better." The words were loud, mocking in the silence of the room.

There had been, she recognized all too plainly in hindsight, no higher plane—only the hope of escape from the old, familiar level, the stability that gradually had imprisoned her. But as leopards did not change their spots, grown men seldom exceeded their established limits. Victor T. Donovan, placid congressman become hard-hitting Senate candidate, certainly had not—not, at least, in her eyes.

He seemed, if possible, even more calculating than before, more concerned with himself, with the expansion of his career. His pious antiporn spiel now repelled her, she had heard it so often and found it so practiced. His public outrage at immorality was too hot, in a cold man, to be more than contrived. And his celebrated TV sincerity, Josie knew from experience, was as projected as a hooker's smile.

Victor T. Donovan, she saw with sudden, hard clarity, was as aimed and as dangerously tipped as what the editor had called Ames's "poison dart" spots.

Ames. That juvenile slug.

That was what had really upset her. Josie picked up *Northanger Abbey* and slammed it down on the mattress; in the glow of the reading lamp, she saw the paperbound volume bounce to the floor and made no move to pick it up. She could hardly believe the anger that surged in her, that Rafael Ames had set off. She was angrier, she knew, than she ever had been with Vic. Not hotly furious, as she sometimes had been at Speed, and still could be. At Ames she was just coldly angry.

Never occurred to him.

He's got to be queer, she thought. But Josie was too fair-minded to believe it. Besides, all the gay men she knew were likable.

"Which that snotnose certainly isn't," she said out loud, the echo mocking her.

She decided then that she really hadn't *liked* Rafael Ames all along, even before his revealing performance at her door. He was too sharp, too clever, too sure of himself, of everyone and everything else.

A real snake.

This realization only forced her to admit, however, what then seemed doubly hurtful: that she nonetheless had been foolishly, physically attracted to Ames, more than she had known—to his slim, hard-looking body, his youthful vigor, his penetrating eyes. It had been a long time since she had been with a man, and perhaps she had been needier than she'd known. She'd been fascinated, moreover, by a sense that Ames was always about to leap, make a daring move, take a risk.

The way I used to be.

She tried to insist to herself that she'd meant what she'd told Ames, she really had; she had *not* invited him into her room to drag him into bed. She had not been that needy or that foolish.

Or was I?

The inescapable fact, she reluctantly conceded, was that she *had* been willing to let nature take its course. If Ames had dragged *her* . . . She shuddered a little, not entirely in revulsion. She wasn't really sure what she would have done, in that case. But after so many years of Vic Donovan—*dull dull dull*—it would have been nice, it would have been *exciting* to have had that kind of decision to make. Instead . . .

"The little wimp chickened out."

Listening to her own words, she understood that *that* had been the trouble with Rafe Ames. Not that he was gay, not that she was the candidate's wife. He just didn't have the gumption to take on a woman. Ames would have acted the same way with a *Playboy* centerfold. Or a hundred-dollar whore. None of his nerve, none of his barely leashed eagerness was for living. Not *real* living, which was men and women—searching, loving.

It must be all for politics, Josie thought, in sheer contempt. A man who was not interested in women, in love, she believed, might as well be *dead*—as Speed used to say. She thought suddenly and with vague regret of her chilly response to him in the lobby bar. Speed had been like an eager pet, anxious for approval, and she had dashed cold water on him.

Speed, she well remembered, was of a different breed from the bloodless Rafael Ames. Speed had loved just to *look* at her; he had never tired of telling her she was beautiful. Josie twisted her head to peer down at her bare shoulders, the rise of her breasts from the low neck of her nightgown. Then she lifted one of her long legs, letting her nightgown slip above her knee. Speed had even liked to watch her take off her stockings. Or put them on.

No one else ever had looked at her, loved to look at her, the way Speed had; certainly not dishwater Vic Donovan. And now not Ames. Speed actually had cried once, real tears, because he said she was so beautiful.

Josie had touched his cheek. "I thought men weren't supposed to cry."

"If something's beautiful enough, they can."

"I only cry when I'm sad."

Speed had buried his face in her hair, muffling his whisper: "There's not much difference, is there?"

In that time Speed had been full of odd twists, strange dark places to be discovered. But he had been demanding, too, controlling, pulling her down—she was not sure to where, only that his power over her finally had seemed threatening. Maybe her chance meeting with him in the lobby, she thought, had led her to the momentary foolishness with Ames; maybe it had set off in her what Speed so often had excited in the past.

Strange to think of him in the same hotel, probably imagining—if she knew him—that she and Ames were making love. Was he perhaps a little jealous? she was surprised to find herself wondering. He had seen her go up in the elevator with Ames, and it would have taken no more than that to set his imagination going, preoccupied as he always had been with sex—with what, he'd told her, had been made in his youth to seem forbidden and therefore infinitely desirable.

"I want more than sex out of life," she'd had to say to him, that last afternoon, the rain slithery on the window of the Georgetown café.

"Maybe there isn't any more," he'd said, their hands hotly clasping.

She'd denied it—knowing, even as she did, that what she really wanted was to be lying with him in the oblivious ecstasy she had known with no other man. But she had believed then that desire, like the moment, would pass, would have to pass.

Josie reached to switch off the reading lamp by her bed. She had pulled the draperies across the window, and in the sudden, total dark of her room, oppressive as the years, she not only knew with sharp pain that the desire, unlike the moment, never really had passed; she wondered if Speed had been right after all.

Maybe there really *wasn't* any more than that.

★

After breakfast in the Chuck Wagon Grill, where the menus were shaped like tepees, Milo Speed checked out of the Lewis & Clark and stowed his bag in the trunk of a rented car. Through the morning hours he clocked more than fifty miles on surrounding highways, counting seven large billboards from which the handsome face of Victor T. Donovan peered out at the sugar beet fields and the cattle on the range. But there were *no* billboards for O. Mack Bender, unless he counted one that must have been paid for by Darwin John.

It depicted a large and recognizable Senator Bender sleeping peacefully in a reclining chair by a swimming pool, his hands crossed on a slight senatorial paunch. In the chair beside him a young woman barely confined to a bikini sipped a cooling drink. A single line asked passersby: "Our Man in Washington?"

The billboard—no doubt a photographic fraud—did not startle Speed; by then he could recognize Ames's style—the style of Victor T. Donovan's campaign. But he was amazed that Mack Bender apparently had failed to lock up his state's billboard space long in advance. Not that billboards would make much difference in modern politics, but Bender's neglect, more particularly the absence of television spots on his behalf, suggested that he was not yet taking the campaign seriously.

In the small town of Bedrock Speed followed Theo Keller's suggestion and dropped in on J. Carson Ritch, owner and editor of the Bedrock *Crusher*.

"Vic Donovan?" The editor did not take his dusty boots off his desk. "Spending a shitpot full of money, is all I can say."

"But you don't think it'll do 'im any good?"

"Doin' *me* some good. Full-page ad ev'ry week."

Speed reflected on the virtues of a free press. Then he said: "But you're for Bender anyway, I understand."

"Put it this way: I don't see any reason *not* to be for Bender."

Speed's interest perked up at this odd formulation. "That sounds to me like something might change your mind, Mister Ritch."

"If it got to look like a race, maybe," the editor said. "Which I don't yet see any signs that it will."

"Not even that shitpot full of money they're throwing around the state?"

J. Carson Ritch contemplated his boots. "Talks as loud round here as anywheres else, I reckon."

Especially, Speed could not help thinking, *if it pays for a full-page ad every week.*

In Flint Hill, a community slightly larger than Bedrock, Speed asked directions from a service station operator to the office of Raymond Goodwood, the sheriff of Buckboard County.

"As Goodwood goes," in Theo Keller's knowing words, "so goes Buckboard."

The sheriff turned out to be enthusiastic about Victor T. Donovan, causing Speed's sensitive nose to pick up the scent of Darwin John's shitpot full of money.

"That speech he made, y'know? Bout that goddam fat cat ruinin' our kids with all this fuckin' smut? Lots of folks round here liked that speech."

"You figure Donovan could do anything about that, he was to get elected?"

"Leastways," Goodwood said, "he don't think immorality's *good* for us, like the fuckin' ACLU."

"But, Sheriff . . . I thought Mack Bender was your party's candidate."

"My party." Goodwood's words dripped with disdain. "It ain't me that's left my party, y'know? It's the fuckin' party that's left *me*."

"But you don't really think Vic Donovan can beat anybody well known as Mack Bender, do you?"

Goodwood looked him up and down. "Well known back East, you mean?"

"Well, this state's elected him twice. Must be pretty well known out here, too."

"Can't beat a horse with no horse . . . uh . . . Speed, wadden it? Speed. But this time around we got another horse runnin'. And I tell you what. You out-of-state media come out here spreadin your liberal fuckin' bullshit, y'know, us home folks just might get on that other horse and *ride*."

On the way back to Capital City Speed accidentally tuned his car radio to an appearance by Victor T. Donovan with Rudolph "Country" Rhodes, the host of *Your Turn!*, a local call-in show.

"Folks round here been won'drin', Vic . . . you don't mind ol' Country callin' you Vic, do you?"

"I'd be honored, uh, Country."

"No side to this man," Country Rhodes informed his audience, as if speaking privately to a friend. "They told me they wa'nt no side to 'im like they is to some a these politicians get back there to Washin'ton, then can't recollect where they come from. But they ain't no side to Vic Donovan, folks, take it from Country Rhodes. Now I been wantin to ast 'im: What was it that caused 'im to tee off on this here immoral fariner, Kremenskoff or Cramer or somethin', like our guest here done on TV last spring?"

"Well, Country . . . I'd heard just about enough . . . ah . . . self-serving clichés," Victor T. Donovan said, "about the American way of life . . . uh . . . from a man who didn't really respect it—"

Speed listened in spite of himself to the familiar lines. Victor T. Donovan sounded knowledgeable, confident, *convincing*; Speed was struck again by the change that seemed to have been worked in this man he had known so long—a ninety-pound weakling suddenly become muscular Charles Atlas.

"—defiling American womanhood."

Victor T. Donovan's words rang with sincerity, obviously impressing Country Rhodes, who passed it on to the airwaves:

"See what ol' Country told you? No side to the man, none a-tall. Now, Vic, we got a call comin in from Larry, way out 'n Cottonwood County. Larry's been waitin awhile to speak to you. Hi, Larry, you there? You're on the air, Larry . . . it's your turn! On five-five-five-four-four-three-three!"

"Yeah, well, what I wanted to ast the congressman, uh, Country, I got this card in the mail, y'know? I couldn't hardly bleeve my eyes, but this card I got in the mail, it just flat-out said the gov'ment wants to take our *guns* away from us and I—"

"Glad you asked that question, Larry." Victor T. Donovan broke in smoothly. "Just so happens Vic Donovan's got a hundred percent unbroken perfect voting record against every one of these un-American so-called gun control propositions that keep coming down the pike. But I regret to have to tell you that your *senior senator* voted . . ."

Victor T. Donovan went on to make a compelling case that if O. Mack Bender were to have his way, every handgun, hunting rifle, target pistol, and child's B-B in every patriotic American home would be confiscated and carted off to Washington.

"But I'm here to tell you folks one thing. When you send *Vic Donovan* to the Senate—now you can count on this, you can take this to the bank—Vic Donovan will represent *you* back there in Washington, *you*, the good people of this great state. . . ."

Speed listened with reluctant admiration. Neither Darwin John's money nor Rafe Ames's slick tutelage could have given Victor T. Donovan the confident voice, the semantic ease with which he had hung gun control around Mack Bender's unsuspecting neck. John could buy the time and Ames could supply the research and the skulduggery, but neither could provide the skill Victor T. Donovan was displaying for Country Rhodes's audience.

The talk show host responded with deep concern: "Now ol' Country never heard the beat o' *that* in all his cotton-pickin' *life*. I bet you never did neither, Larry."

Speed's still-grudging revision of his long-held view of Josie's husband suddenly combined with other events of his morning into a piercing thought:

Maybe this campaign's not so far-out after all.

"Now all you other good folks out there in God's country, just waitin' your turn! You gonna get it, I kid you not . . . just soon's we hear this good word from Tucker's Feed 'n' Supply over 'n Tulaville. . . ."

Maybe that smooth congressional voice conning the public on 555-4433 *could* give Mack Bender a race. Not the old Victor T. Donovan whom Speed had thought he knew, but that voice on the air, that image on the screen, the presence emerging from Rafe Ames's carefully calculated themes to raise Bender's negatives.

". . . for greener grass," a hearty voice proclaimed, "use Lawn Gro!"

Milo Speed prided himself on a keen eye for fakery and bamboozle. He had made a reputation for exposing those numerous politicians who won or retained public office primarily by their use.

But "Which came first?" he had once been asked in a newsroom bull session Speed had never forgotten. "Men or politicians?"

That question caused Speed ultimately to understand that politics could not always be successful *and* straightforward—and necessarily was sometimes devious indeed. Men had to be persuaded by politicians, but the thin line between deception and persuasion could not, with honor, be deliberately crossed. Speed believed, however, that politicians who tiptoed along that line were less to be flayed for their means than judged by their ends.

As the man with no side took leave of Country Rhodes, amid mutual effusions of admiration for each other and the listening audience, Speed had to acknowledge that Victor T. Donovan and Rafael Ames were *creating* a vulnerability where none had appeared to exist. But as he reluctantly credited the *act* of creation, Speed deplored the creation itself. That thin but vital line was being repeatedly crossed—certainly by Ames. And only by willed determination could Victor T. Donovan still consider his campaign merely confrontational.

"Now all you good folks out there that wants your turn!" Country Rhodes announced, "pick up that phone right now!"

Speed clicked off the radio. The Donovan campaign's effectiveness, he thought, might be admitted—but not *accepted* because a candidate financed by Darwin John, operating by Rafe Ames's ethics, and showing himself unexpectedly adept at the broadcast smear was not likely to redeem himself by desirable deeds if elected. Still . . .

"The bastard's *not* just a featherweight after all."

Speed could hear a note of surprise in his own voice, loud in the closed and air-conditioned car. Josie had tried to tell him as much, in their last rainy hour together, he remembered painfully, but he hadn't been able to believe it or to focus on anything but the terrible decision she was announcing.

Now, years later, Victor T. Donovan was surprising him every day; maybe, just maybe, therefore, he might surprise O. Mack Bender, too. And if *that* was possible, he might even someday surprise Rafael Ames. Even Darwin John.

Maybe, Speed thought, everybody had underestimated Victor T. Donovan. *Not just me.*

But he had committed, he knew, the journalist's unforgivable sin: He had let his personal feelings, his personal disdain for Josie's husband, color his professional judgment.

★

As Speed was listening to *Your Turn*! and driving toward Capital City, Josie and Floyd Finch drove past him in the other direction. No one in either car noticed anyone in the other.

Josie, indifferent to the drab countryside she had seen too often as she was growing to maturity, was listening politely as Finch regaled her with old campaign stories. He was peeking, when he thought he could, at her legs, unusually exposed in a short skirt.

". . . so the other candidate's up there making this long-winded speech he made at every stop, y'know, all about the beauties of Texas. And we got this old boy planted in the audience, y'know? So the other candidate he goes like 'from Lubbock on the High Plains down to Brownsville in the Rio Grande . . . from the beaches of Padre Island through the piney woods of East Texas—' "

At least, Josie thought, Finch was *interested* in her. He wanted to talk to her, make an impression on her, as well as look at her legs. Not like Ames. Floyd Finch not only knew she was the candidate's wife but knew she was a woman.

" '—from Austin to Dallas, Fort Worth to San Antone . . .' and like that, on and on, till my guy in the audience gets the nod from me. So he stands up, then, y'know, and goes like this." Finch took his hands off the wheel, cupped them around his mouth, and yelled: " 'Next time you pass Lubbock, how 'bout lettin' me off?' "

He grabbed the wheel again, chortling at his own story, his cadaverous body shaking all over, just before the tires left the pavement.

"Now I just plain don't believe that," Josie said. "You're putting me on, aren't you?"

She watched Finch steal a glance at her crossed legs—slim, she knew, as any young girl's. Slimmer than some.

"Would I do that to a pretty lady like you?" Finch looked arch. "I might of dressed it up a little maybe. Anyway, our man won going away." He shook his head. "Not cause of *that*. Fact is, y'know, what happened, I think the Chief prob'ly bought more votes in South Texas than the OP."

He chuckled again, looking less guardedly at Josie's legs.

"You mean Darwin John?" Josie was not shocked at the fact but was surprised that Finch spoke openly of it. "He *bought* votes?"

"Course in South Texas," Floyd Finch said, "it don't cost a hell of a lot."

They were on their way to a coffee in the town of Chalk Cliff, where, Josie knew, the usual array of housewives, schoolteachers, and a few unmarried hopefuls would have been rounded up by Darwin John's advance man in somebody's living room by the promise of refreshments and by the chance to eye the eastern clothes they hoped the candidate's wife would be wearing.

John's hand, Josie thought, was in everything. She said: "How much does it cost to buy votes in this state?"

Upon waking in her room at the Lewis & Clark, she had been galled anew by the memory of Rafe Ames's dismal performance and had decided to compensate herself by shocking the Chalk Cliff ladies with a skirt shorter than they probably would approve. Shorter, too, than Floyd Finch was used to.

"Oh, now, Miz Donovan, no question bout that kind of stuff in *this* campaign. Anyway, the Chief, he only does something like that if he *has* to, y'know, fight fire with fire."

The short skirt was halfway up her thighs as she rode along with Floyd Finch. He had been pressed into service after Josie's regular driver, a clerk from Victor T. Donovan's local office, had begged off with a summer cold.

"Besides," Josie said with a certainty she hardly felt, "my husband wouldn't stand for vote buying."

Finch nodded vigorously. "Not from what *I've* seen of the Honorable Victor T. Donovan."

Which probably was less, Josie thought, than Finch was seeing of *her* at the moment. But the skirt would come down no nearer her knees, and besides, she *did* have good legs.

"Now Rafe Ames," Finch said, "he's a pistol, that boy."

In politics maybe.

"What's that mean, Floyd? What're you suggesting?"

Floyd Finch drove awhile in silence. Josie could see in his laconic face that he was wondering whether he should say anything more, whether he might not already have said too much. She made a bet with herself that he would want to keep her attention.

"Yeah, well . . . I only meant, push comes to shove, Ames'd prob'ly do whatever it took to win."

Finch had said precisely about Ames what Josie had been thinking, without being able quite to put her finger on it. *That* was what had been troubling her about Ames, building up inside her, even before the fiasco outside her room.

"You don't like Rafe?"

"Oh, I *like* 'im all right. See, I'm kind of the same sort of guy myself. Do what it takes to win, I mean."

"I'll bet you'd know, too." Josie gently stroked his ego; in her experience, men preferred that even to having more personal parts stroked. "You've been in so many campaigns, I mean."

This led Floyd Finch to admire her legs quite openly.

"Seen a few, all right." He sighed wearily. "Way I figure it, y'know, whatever you do, chances are the other side's doing it, too. I mean, like the man said, politics ain't beanbag."

"I'm seeing *that* pretty clearly. But, Floyd"—again she spoke with more certainty than she felt—"Vic won't stand for anything really underhanded. I mean from Ames."

"Well, underhand," Floyd Finch said. "Depends what you mean by underhand. This stuff he's giving Lestark, I wouldn't call *that* underhand. Hardball, maybe."

Josie restrained herself from asking "What stuff?" Her instinct, sharply honed about men, was that Floyd Finch needed to be led along, not pushed.

"The Hon . . . I mean, the congressman. *He* cleared this one himself, so he must think it's on the up-and-up."

"Cleared it for Lee Lestark?"

From her old association with Milo Speed, Josie was conditioned to think of Lestark as something from under a rock. That Rafe Ames was leaking to him, even leaking something Vic himself had cleared, alarmed her. She had not imagined that such "hardball" would be a part of running for the Senate or that cautious, upright Vic Donovan could possibly be involved in it.

"Just a little dirt on Bender, is all. Kind of thing he'd most likely use on us, he got the chance. Rafe says it'll cost 'im the church ladies' vote."

She thought immediately: *Must be about sex*. What else would trouble church ladies?

Josie was surprised less that a front-page, highly respectable figure like Mack Bender might have dabbled in sex—*everyone does*, she thought, *except lately me*—than she was astounded that Vic would have the nerve to use such stuff against an opponent. Rafe Ames, of course, would have planned it all, no doubt eagerly.

"You got to get up early in the morning, Miz Donovan, you want to get ahead of Rafe Ames."

Josie's temper flared intensely. Ames suddenly seemed even more despicable than she had awakened believing. Ames had wormed his way into Vic's confidence, and now he had Vic doing just what Ames wanted him to do. She was angry at Vic, too, for being such Silly Putty in Ames's hands. Vic's big chance had come around at last, but he hadn't had the courage and self-reliance to play it straight. Raging, Josie forgot her instinct not to push Floyd Finch.

"What's the story then? What're they leaking to Lestark?"

"Now don't you worry your pretty head about it." Finch beamed at her, then dropped his eyes to her legs. "Rafe's got everything under control."

Josie was further angered by his patronizing manner and decided to give him a jolt. "Goddammit, Floyd, what's Bender *done*? Screwed a page boy?"

Floyd Finch looked shocked, as she had known he would. The car sped up a little, and he cut his eyes at her furtively, this time not looking at her legs.

"Well, I guess . . ." His prominent Adam's apple went up and down. "You'll read it in Lestark's column anyway."

Josie listened in rising indignation as—with several starts and stops, many "ums" and "ahs" and not a few euphemisms—Finch filled her in on the Bender story.

"What in *hell*," she demanded when he lapsed gratefully into silence, "has that kind of thing got to do with running for the Senate?"

Floyd Finch's Adam's apple bobbed again. "Well, uh, y'know . . . Rafe says this thing'll cost him—"

"The church ladies' vote," Josie said. "Maybe so. But *I'll* tell *you* something, Floyd."

He was only too eager to hear. "What's that, Miz Donovan?"

"Rafe Ames doesn't know shit about women."

A few minutes later they passed the city limits of Chalk Cliff. By then, Josie could see, Floyd Finch had not yet recovered, and she herself was wondering if after so many years of marriage she knew any more about Victor T. Donovan than Rafael Ames knew about women.

★

Just after noon Speed was back in Capital City, managing to find a parking place near Pioneer Park. A crowd already had gathered, smoke and odors rose from the barbecue pit, and from a flatbed truck trailer a country and western band twanged away at "On the Road Again."

Speed was making his way through the crowd toward the trailer when someone touched his arm. Grinning at him from under a snowy western hat, wide-brimmed and tall-crowned, was Darwin John's number one advance man.

"You like the lid?"

"Last time I saw one of those, Mingo, LBJ was wearing it."

"His was smaller. The candidate handed me this when he got off the plane this morning."

"On you," Speed said, "it reminds me what they say about western politicians: all hat and no cattle."

Mingo laughed. "I didn't expect to see you out 'n these wide open spaces, Speed. Not so early in the year anyway."

"Darwin John's assigned *you* to this one, he must think he's got a hotshot out here."

Mingo accepted the compliment without objection as they made their way nearer the trailer platform. "Most ev'rywhere else all we got are landslides and garden parties. Here . . ." He shrugged and pulled the hat down on his forehead. "My candidate's got a ways to go."

Speed stopped, and the Pioneer Park crowd swirled around them. Off to one side children in burlap bags bounced along in a gunnysack race. Cheers and screams filled the air.

"I see spots before my eyes, Mingo. Your candidate's spots. I see billboards lined up like Burma-Shave. Your man's billboards. I see Raymond Goodwood's palm outstretched. But there's one thing I *don't* see."

Mingo took off his ten-gallon hat and fanned himself with it, looking weary and overweight, like a heart attack waiting to happen.

"Who's Goodwood?" he said.

Speed was not deceived. Art Mingo had had an effective hand in more Darwin John victories than Speed could count; Mingo was a human encyclopedia of practical politics. If the Bedrock *Crusher* was getting a full-page ad every week, it was Mingo who had arranged it, who had *known* that it should be arranged.

"Your bagman in Buckboard County."

Mingo sighed heavily. "So what is it you don't see?"

"Any sign of Mack Bender. No footprints even."

Mingo knew how to commandeer a school auditorium or a state university stadium even if the law forbade it to partisan uses. He knew exactly why a given county or precinct or ward had gone to the OP in the previous election, or had not. He could handle it if a candidate—Mingo's own or the "other guy"—had a weakness for "booze or broads," and he instinctively knew whether the "bloc vote," as he called it, was best swung in a particular election by paying off black preachers or black politicians or both.

"The other guy's not up *there*, of course"—Mingo pointed at the trailer—"but he's around all right. I *feel* him, Speed. He's tough."

Watching Mingo fit the huge hat back into the crease it had worn in his brow, Speed rather liked the man. *Enjoyed* him. Art Mingo was undeceived and undismayed by human nature.

"Bender's not here *enough*, Mingo. While you guys're making hay."

"On the Road Again" had come to a merciful end, as had the gunnysack race. A procession of booted men wearing hats like Mingo's, together with two short-haired women in print dresses, were making their way up a set of steps to the flatbed of the trailer. Speed spotted the Honorable Victor T. Donovan, fourth in the procession and looking uncomfortable under an overwhelming hat, like Mingo's.

"Lucky you," Mingo said. "You get to listen to my candidate."

"Not for the first time." Speed was disappointed that Josie was not with her husband. "And tell you the truth, I've heard just about enough self-serving clichés about the American way of life—"

"Smartass." Mingo did not take his eyes off the truck bed platform.

"—from a man who doesn't really respect it."

"Who does?" Mingo said.

Mayor Chet Blade introduced platform guests, including ancient Chief Sam Runninglegs, whom the mayor acknowledged as a true city father, since his tribe once had owned the ground on which the city stood. The chief gazed from under his paleface hat with animosity he did not bother to conceal from his unwanted heirs.

"Need your help," a man in overalls said to Speed, handing him a card, another to Mingo, and moving on into the crowd.

Colonel Jennings B. Larue, the beribboned commandant of the local Air Force base, was presented. He twisted his cowboy hat in his hands while speaking a few impassioned words on behalf of the B-2 bomber.

Speed read the card the man in overalls had handed him: "No More Lightning Fires! Sam Stennis for Pinto County Commissioner."

Up on the flatbed several other candidates were presented—one for alderman, one for Water District Control Board, two for the state legislature. One of the bareheaded women turned out to be the state superintendent of public instruction, running for reelection to a seventh term.

Mingo took Sam Stennis's card out of Speed's hand, turned it over, and handed it back. Speed read:

> 'Tis the sticker who wins in the battle of life
> While the quitter is laid on the shelf.
> You are never defeated, remember this,
> Until you lose faith in yourself.

Mingo muttered: "Darwin John's philosophy, too."

Mayor Blade announced that the governor had sent regrets at the press of business, which had him inspecting a grasshopper blight in Saddlehorn County. The lieutenant governor was laid up in hospital with a slipped disk. Speed surmised that neither wanted to appear on the platform with Victor T. Donovan—not yet anyway.

Senator O. Mack Bender offered telegraphed felicitations, which the mayor read in their entirety, on "this festive occasion," at which the senator assured the audience he certainly would have been present had it not been for a pending Senate vote on extending the debt limit.

"Which he better damn well be against," Speed told Mingo, "or your guy will blame him for the whole federal deficit."

"He might anyway," Mingo said.

Then Mayor Blade turned to the introduction of the day's main speaker, the Honorable Victor T. Donovan. The mayor concluded with remarkable informality:

"Down his way, folks, they think the world of good old Vic. They think so much of 'im they's some that figger he ought to stay in the House sted of reachin' for the Senate. Vic . . . come up here and tell 'em why you're fool enough not to take good advice."

"Jesus." Speed watched Victor T. Donovan rise, doff his tall hat, and acknowledge polite applause. "Friends like that, your guy hardly needs enemies."

Art Mingo nodded sadly. "The mayor use to be Bender's AA. Not what you'd call impartial."

Victor T. Donovan put his hat back on his head and strode to the microphone.

"Mister Mayor . . . I thank you for that . . . ah . . . warm introduction. Mack Bender must've written it for you."

This evoked much laughter and applause, the audience apparently understanding the mayor's political loyalties. Speed was impressed; Victor T. Donovan had taken a chance by using his opponent's name, but it had paid off with a cheerful crowd reception.

"Telegraphed it out, I s'pose." An amused murmur from the crowd. "But I was glad to hear, Mister Mayor, that the senator's staying in Washington to vote . . . at least this once."

Only a few in the crowd laughed. Stretching the joke, Speed thought; any live audience in Bender's state was likely still to be mostly a Bender audience—though not perhaps for long, with Rafe Ames poisoning the airwaves every night.

"Like the senator, folks, my wife, Josie, sends her regrets for not being on this platform today. But *unlike* him, she's right here in our state, right this minute, working her head off, talking and meeting with good people like you, sitting right down on your porches and in your kitchens and *listening*."

"And hating every minute," Speed murmured to Mingo.

"And she'll be doing the same thing, folks, when *I'm* your senator, which with *your* help, if you'll give me *your* hand, I *will* be when the votes get counted on election night."

"Mileage in that hand stuff," Mingo observed in Speed's ear. "Makes 'em feel needed."

But Speed noted that Victor T. Donovan had to pause for only brief applause.

"She'll be out here listening to you good people, and so will I, folks, cause when I'm your senator, we're not going to be in Tokyo all the time. We're not going to be in Moscow soft-soaping those Communists in the Kremlin. We're not going to be living it up down in Florida or the Caribbean."

He pronounced it CRIBBY-un, his voice rising and one hand sawing the air for emphasis.

"We're going to be right here in this great state *listening* to you ev'ry minute we're not back in Washington *working* for you!"

That could hardly be what Josie wanted, Speed thought. Just then Mingo nudged him and whispered: "I better work the crowd a little. You'll be around?"

"Leaving today."

"Come back soon." Mingo tipped his incongruous hat. "Best is yet to be."

Victor T. Donovan's address was not as convincing as good old Vic Donovan, the man with no side, had seemed on *Your Turn!* with Rudolph "Country" Rhodes; evidently the broadcast media provided a more natural habitat for the congressman than a live audience. For the most part, however, the crowd in Pioneer Park listened quietly, and Speed thought Victor T. Donovan landed some effective jabs at Mack Bender's unprotected chin.

Speed knew that Bender was not a habitual absentee from his Senate duties. Nor was he a crusader for gun control; as a westerner he usually voted against it. Neither did he hobnob with Communists, foreign or domestic. By most standards Bender was not even a big spender. He had voted for some foreign aid programs but not for any obvious "big giveaways." He had too much political savvy to support a real assault on Social Security or to oppose any but the most outlandish water projects for the parched West.

The Honorable Victor T. Donovan nevertheless managed rather adroitly to indict Senator Bender on each of those counts. And Speed was sure that he and Rafe Ames could produce some bit of evidence—like the D.C. bus driver bill—to be twisted and tortured into support for every charge. Shrewdly the attack was aimed as much to inflame the most cherished prejudices of the state's voters as at Bender himself.

"And I'm frank to tell you," Victor T. Donovan proclaimed in a fist-thumping peroration, "that I don't believe for one single second in taking God out of our public schools. No matter what the Supreme Court says, this day 'n' time with all these X-rated movies and drugs and this gay liberation and immorality everywhere you look, our children need the guidance and the *responsibility* they get from religion and the Bible. Vic Donovan wants our sweet little girls and boys to grow up God-fearing, hardworking Americans—like you good people! We don't need any more addicts and prostitutes and porn stars!"

Speed wanted to get ahead of the crush so he could catch his plane; he began to make his way through the crowd before the speech was finished. As he moved along, he saw that the faces turned toward the speaker on the truck bed were unexcited but focused; Victor T. Donovan had them listening. So some would believe, while few would head for the public library to verify the charges he was making.

"Anybody like my opponent, that the way he votes as good as says God has no place in our schools . . . anybody that says a thing like that, Vic Donovan says there's *no place for him* in the Senate of the United States!"

Speed pushed through the last ranks of listeners and turned back for a final look at Victor T. Donovan on the platform. Suddenly, from that distance, the big hat no longer looked incongruous; the figure at the microphone seemed commanding, as he thundered:

"Not from this state! Not from God's country!"

5.

By prearrangement, Lacy met Speed at National Airport. They drove in her car to a late supper at a restaurant he knew in Old Town, Alexandria, a quiet place where he would not be bothered by publicity seekers. He seldom was anyway, but he liked Lacy to think that he might be and was too modest to risk it.

"I'm glad you called last night," Lacy said after they'd been seated and had ordered. "But I still want to know why you did. What was wrong?"

He had telephoned from the Lewis & Clark, picking up the phone immediately after leaving Rafael Ames in the elevator. Seeing Ames rejected had given him only a momentary elation because Josie could not have sent Ames packing any more bluntly than she had already dismissed Milo Speed in the lobby bar. So, Speed told himself, he *needed* the reassurance of talking to someone who wanted to talk to *him*, someone who cared about him.

On the fourth ring he heard a click and a mumble he could not decipher; then he remembered that in Washington the hour was much later.

"Sorry to wake you up . . . I forgot the time zone break."

Lacy seemed instantly to come awake. "What's wrong?"

"Nothing," he lied. "I just wanted to hear your voice."

"You never called me on a trip before."

"Lacy . . . this is the first time I've been on a trip since I've known you."

"You hardly ever call me just to talk even when you're *not* on a trip."

He did not know whether to be put off by her insistence or moved by her apparent concern.

"I could pretend I had some papers or something the congressman needs to sign." Lacy's words tumbled out in a rush. "I mean, if you want me to come out there."

Speed did not and momentarily wondered why she sounded eager to come. But then he was strangely happy, nearly as uplifted as he had been to see Ames standing forlornly outside the elevator. Happiness, no matter how induced, was a feeling, he thought, to which he was not much accustomed. He decided he would like to get to know it better. Talking to Lacy, he could almost forget Josie, his age, the empty room in which he stood. But not quite.

"What've you got on?" He knew but told himself he wanted to hear her say it.

"The bedclothes. If you were here, you could see for yourself."

He did not even have to close his eyes to envision Lacy's red hair falling over her shoulders and breasts, her long legs and slim flanks white in the darkness of her bedroom. It was a compelling but oddly lustless vision—aesthetic, not passionate.

"Or if I was out there with you."

As quickly as happiness had flooded him, another change of mood overtook him; the sour taste of deceit rose in his mouth.

"I'll be back tomorrow night."

Vision and disdain mingled in his head, incompatible as fire and water. He felt demeaned, and demeaning, to think of Lacy lying naked in the dark so that he need *not* think of Josie dismissing him on a rainy afternoon in a Georgetown café and again in the lobby bar.

"I'll take you for a late dinner."

"Don't think that'll get you out of telling me what's wrong. Why you called."

Lacy's perceptiveness only reminded him painfully that something *was* wrong: all the years of delusion and waste. But since he was calling her mostly to ease his pain, how could he tell her his real trouble, the trouble she seemed to want to share? Maybe, he thought, Lacy had not seen through him. Not yet anyway. She still seemed to think he was worth her concern.

"Nothing," Speed forced himself to say, firmly, treacherously, "is wrong with me."

Now, in Old Town, over clams on the half shell, he tried to ignore her insistence by giving her a detailed report on Victor T. Donovan's surprising campaign.

"You wouldn't believe it," he said of the speech in Pioneer Park. "That he was the same man you work for, I mean."

"*I'd* believe it."

"You really think he's a hell of a guy, don't you?"

Lacy put down her fork and sipped wine. "Are we going to argue about that again?"

"Not after I flew halfway across the continent to see you. I just don't share your reverence for the great man."

They finished the clams before she responded.

"Reverence is not a word I associate with you, Milo. And I don't flatter myself you flew halfway across the continent just to *see* me."

"Why else?"

She looked at him coolly. "You're planning to sleep alone maybe?"

Speed delayed response while a waiter removed their plates. He had not settled in his own mind whether he would sleep with Lacy that night. Sometimes he sensed a hardness in her; she could be too assertive, uncomfortably so. That was not Speed's style in personal relations; he preferred circumlocution, the little white lie, even on occasion a genteel duplicity.

When the waiter moved away, he said: "You don't have to be so up front."

Lacy paid no attention. "I just happen to think that the congressman is an honest, decent man. I know you don't think so. But you don't think *anybody* is."

"Oh, Lacy . . . your precious congressman's so honest and decent he's trying to convince people out in God's country that Mack Bender beats his wife and screws his mother."

The waiter placed lobsters in front of them and tied paper bibs around their necks. When he withdrew, Lacy said: "That's Rafe Ames. That's not the congressman doing that."

"But Donovan *wants* him to do it. Lets him do it."

"I thought you weren't going to argue." Lacy picked at her lobster, then looked at him with challenging green eyes. "But I'll make a bet with you. By the time this campaign's over, the congressman's going to fire Ames."

Speed sat back in his chair, startled. "Have you been listening in on Vic's phone calls?"

"I don't eavesdrop, and I don't *know* anything." Lacy assumed a frosty dignity that went well with green eyes. "It's just my feeling that in the long run the congressman won't put up with anybody like Ames."

"Who you believe, if I remember correctly, is a shit."

Lacy nodded solemnly. "The congressman will see through him sooner or later and get rid of him. He may look like he's just putty in Ames's hands, but I happen to believe he's a lot stronger than you give him credit for."

For the first time it crossed Speed's mind that maybe Victor T. Donovan, too, had something going with Lacy Farnes. It would not be the first time, after all, that he and Speed had shared a desirable woman. Still, not only was the thought distasteful, but it quickly seemed ridiculous. The congressman, now the candidate, would never risk his prospects by hitting on a girl in his own office, a few doors away from the Ethics Committee.

"And a lot smarter than you *or* Ames think."

Speed was about to make a sarcastic reply when he remembered the compelling figure on the flatbed trailer in Pioneer Park.

"So . . . I'll make you a bet the congressman fires him."

Maybe, he thought. Lacy was a bright girl, quick and observant. A good head atop a spectacular body. Even if she didn't listen in on her boss's calls, she still saw him at close range. Maybe sometimes from the same pillow; stranger things had happened—though not much stranger. Speed had underestimated Victor T. Donovan before; he was determined not to do it again.

"What you like best in bed," Lacy said, matter-of-factly. "You win the bet, that's what you get, whenever you want it."

Speed responded automatically, instinctively, to intimate talk with a woman. "I like it *all*, my dear."

Lacy pulled off a lobster claw. "You like this best." She put the end of the claw in her mouth.

Speed was at once repelled and aroused—repelled by a gesture too blatant for his current sensibility but aroused because it evoked Josie's well-remembered sexuality.

"What if I lose?" he managed to say. "What do *you* get?"

"Satisfaction. Ames out and you wrong—for a change."

"Not much of a payoff. I'm often wrong."

"Winning then," Lacy said. "That would be enough for me. I like to win."

"All right, I'll call your bet. Since I've got so little to lose."

They ate lobster and drank wine, mostly in silence. The waiter brought finger bowls, then coffee.

"One reason *you*'ll lose," Speed told Lacy. "Ames has a hell of a campaign going for Donovan. Bender doesn't get moving soon, your hero's going to give him a run for his money."

In the echoes of his remark Speed knew what he'd write for his next article. He had to let Bender know his danger. But he could not actually collaborate with a politician, advise him on his campaign; he was independent of them all and aimed to remain so. The only ethical way he could send the message was to send it to everyone, Bender included.

"Of course he will," Lacy said. "Otherwise the congressman wouldn't be in the race. But he'll fire Ames anyway." She looked at him over her coffee cup, with eyes he now saw were less green than sharp and knowing. "And don't think I don't realize you've chickened out on telling me what made you call me last night."

Speed took Lacy's hand, wishing he could tell her, tell somebody, how empty he had come to know his life to be.

"I just wanted to talk to you," he lied. "Wasn't that reason enough?"

Lacy squeezed his hand. "For such a great lover, Milo, you're a terrible liar."

★

Later that night, in the cool drafts of the air conditioner humming in Lacy's bedroom window, Speed said: "Not even such a great lover, I guess."

He was lying on his back. Lacy turned on her side, facing him.

"I *knew* something was wrong," she said.

Speed took her wrist and kissed the palm of her hand. Now, he thought, he had betrayed her in more ways than one.

"I'm sorry, Lacy."

"Don't be—not about *that*."

"It just never happened before."

"Bullshit," Lacy said.

"Well, hardly ever. Not with anyone I really cared about."

"Men always say that. Men worry too much."

Speed was astonished. His eyes were accustomed to the darkness, and he saw her, propped on an elbow, looking down at him, her hair falling partly across her face.

"About *performing*," Lacy said. "Guys think they're supposed to be like track stars in bed."

"You mean you've had that happen before? With some other man?"

He knew so little of her, he thought, of the years she had lived before he knew her, even knew she existed. He was offended at the thought, as if Lacy had deliberately kept important information to herself.

"Milo, do you think that never happened to anybody but you?"

"That wasn't . . . ah . . . what I meant."

Lacy was silent for a moment. Then she rolled away, on her back, kicked her bare legs in the air, and let them fall with a thump on the mattress.

"Why, you arrogant SOB. Did you really think you were the only man I ever got it on with?"

"Well, no . . . no, of course not." But to have had the fact thrust in his face had startled him. Annoyed him, too. *When*

I'm not even in love with her, he thought. "I just . . . I hadn't *thought* of you with anybody else, is all."

Except Victor T. Donovan. And that had been just a passing speculation. Speed thought now of other men in Lacy's life, other men holding her soft breasts in their hands, kissing their wide brown tips.

"The first time I ever did it," Lacy said, "I was fifteen. One Sunday night after Youth for Christ. How old were you?"

Speed was newly taken aback. *Lacy deflowered at fifteen.* He saw her spread-eagled in some back seat, skirts about her hips, a pimply ass between her thighs. It was as if he were seeing his own daughter, if he had had one.

"Christ," he said, squeezing his eyes closed but not banishing the vision. He wondered what he had expected. "I must have been . . . let's see, that would be what . . . ten years ago?"

"I don't mean *then,* stupid. I mean when *you* first did it."

Speed did not like to remember that far back into his life. For his professional career, his memory was long and precise, a computer in his head; but he had tried to shut much of his earlier life out of his conscious mind. Now he tried again.

"I can't remember."

"Bullshit." Lacy was undeterred. "Everybody remembers their first screw. Like mine played trombone in the school band and the rubber broke inside me. Scared me to death."

"No . . . I really don't remember." But he was suffering painful glimpses of his youth, like the leg cramps that sometimes awakened him in the soundless night.

"Oh, come on, Milo. I didn't hold out on you, so don't hold out on me."

He had no faith in confession. But he saw that Lacy was determined to unearth the shards of truth he had tried to bury, wanted to hide even from himself.

"My mother . . ." He found that from long disuse, his memory *was* rusty, like an unused machine tool. "She was difficult."

"I hear most mothers are," Lacy moved back against him, warm and soft in the darkness. "Mine died so young I hardly even remember what she was like."

Something—Josie's continuing coldness, his inability to put her out of his mind, Lacy's youth and candor, his own falseness—perhaps all of that caused him at last to want to explain himself, to himself. But Lacy spoke before he could.

"After the trombone player I just sort of kept going. I did so many other kids it was getting kind of gruesome. But then this older guy, my social studies teacher, told me to get smart. After that he was the only one until I went off to college."

But Speed was no longer much interested in Lacy's sexual history, startling though it seemed. Instead, she had forced him to face his own.

"You see . . ." His words came swiftly, in a rush. "My dad worked in tobacco warehouses down South. He had to keep moving from market town to market town in four states, so he was out of the house most of the time."

"And your mother ran the family." Lacy leaned over him so that her lush breasts swayed against his rib cage. "Ran *you*, too, I'll bet."

Her soft touch more nearly frightened than aroused him. But he was carried along by escaping memory and heard himself saying what he had said only once before, to Josie:

"Watched me like a hawk. Told me I had to do bigger things than my dad had done in the warehouses. That if I didn't go on to . . . something . . . whatever it was she wanted for me, I'd break her heart."

"Well, you made it." Lacy's warm hand found him. "We had to study you in college." She stroked smoothly.

Too late. By then his mother had been dead for years.

"Those days, if I showed the least bit of interest in a girl, she could always find enough wrong with her to turn me off. And believe me, she always did."

"My father was kind of like that," Lacy said. "Bossy. But most of the time I managed to do about what I wanted."

"Not me. But finally . . ."

He shuddered slightly, remembering the long ordeal of gathering his nerve. Lacy must have thought it a shiver of feeling; she began to stroke more rapidly. But he could not respond for remembering, and he spat words into the chill darkness: "I was twenty-six years old the first time."

Lacy tensed beside him, and he felt her surprise, the near-disdainful surprise of a generation that had routinely made love at fifteen, as casually as if smoking pot at a slumber party or shoplifting in a mall. She lifted her head from his shoulder and took her hand away.

"But . . . that's older than I am now."

He felt himself flaccid, withered. He had, he knew, made himself in Lacy's eyes suddenly older than the social studies teacher. He had become a creature out of another time, an object of anthropology. He felt compelled to complete his abjection.

"Twenty-six," he said. "When Nancy and I ran away to get married."

He remembered Nancy's pleasure in the discovery of what, even in those days of sexual repression, she could hardly have dreamed: that she would be his first woman as he was her first man. But her pleasure had been brief.

"I couldn't get it up that night either."

The room was quiet for a while; only the air conditioner whispered icily in the window.

"No wonder . . ." Lacy put her head on his shoulder again, her breasts soft against his arm. "No wonder you want it so much."

"Not as much as I used to," he murmured into her hair, thinking: *Not what I need now.*

"Like I said . . ." Lacy's voice again was confident, full of a kind of wisdom he thought he would never know. "Guys get too uptight about it. When it's just what people do."

He hardly heard, in the eager necessity to expose the last of his buried truths:

"After we ran away, I dropped out of grad school, got a job and never . . . I never could go back home. Being just a crummy reporter on a weekly down South . . . that wasn't exactly what my mother had in mind for her son."

The pain of ancient wounds was not salved even by so much acknowledgment, and he realized that he had not expected that it would be. He was a scarred veteran of suppression, never to be redeemed by confession.

"Broke her heart," he said. "So she told me."

★

Before Speed stumbled out of bed the next morning, Lacy was long gone to Victor T. Donovan's office. He found teabags in her kitchen, burned his fingers lighting the stove, and blearily boiled water. Until he tasted the tea he brewed, he had not realized it was camomile. Speed poured the stuff into the sink, and went home to Evangeline and a proper breakfast, then sat down at the old-fashioned typewriter he still used and rolled in a clean sheet of paper.

He worked steadily for nearly three hours, consulting occasionally the notes he had taken in Pioneer Park and on the previous morning's swing through Bedrock and Flint Hill. He X-ed out a word or a line here and there, but for the most part he wrote his article—though slowly—without much change.

He was halfway finished when Evangeline called from the front door: "You don't need me anymore, I'm going."

"See you tomorrow." Speed did not look up from his work.

"This girl," Evangeline said.

"What girl?"

"She's too good to come over here, you got to do it at her place?"

"Saves you changing the sheets." Writhing mentally at the memory of his failures the night before, Speed felt uncomfortable even talking about Lacy.

"Didn't even give you a decent breakfast."

Evangeline slammed the door, but he remained hard at work. When he had finished his draft, Speed took out his thick fountain pen and went carefully over his copy, crossing out and interlining. Then he made a clean version, changing a few words as he typed. It was his regular column-day routine, comforting in its familiarity.

Speed could have afforded a secretary; in fact, he retained both a researcher, who was on call, and an expensive service that prepared and mailed the voluminous correspondence he dictated by phone, in reply to his readers. But he told himself it would look pretentious for a man who worked at home to have a secretary. Speed hated being thought pretentious.

Anyway, he had told himself, *with my reputation, she'd be ruined. They'd be sure to say I was banging her*. (Like most men of his generation, Speed had not considered hiring a male secretary or even realized it was possible.)

When his article was cleanly typed, he took it to the fax

machine that his syndicate had installed and that he had laboriously learned to operate. He hand-lettered a cover sheet addressed to the syndicate and fed his pages in delicately, fearful—as always—that something electronic and unspeakable would chew them up and spit them back at him. But as always, after he dialed the syndicate's number, the last page, like its predecessors, went through intact.

Watching the pages go, thinking of Rafael Ames, Speed recalled a famous movie line. It made him feel muscular and lethal, and he said aloud in a thick Germanic accent, wishing Ames could hear:

"Fuck you, asshole."

★

When his telephone rang the following morning, Speed was still in bed, sleeping off the effects of an excruciating dinner party at the British Embassy, which in a moment of weakness he had agreed to attend.

Speed groped on his bedside table for the raucous instrument. "Rumm-umph," he said.

"Mister Speed?" An obnoxiously cheerful female voice.

"I guess."

"Senator Bender is calling."

"Does he know what time it is?"

"Oh, sir, the senator's been in the office for an hour at least."

"Jesus Christ." Speed renewed his determination never to have a secretary. "Put him on."

After a properly senatorial lag, calculated to show he had better things to do than talk on the phone, O. Mack Bender came on the line heartily, his deep politician's voice vibrating.

"You're a cheeky bastard, Speed. It says here in the morning paper that you think I'm nonchalanting my campaign."

"Well, aren't you?"

Bender paused perceptibly. "You don't know the half of it."

"What I *do* know is pretty bad. I just came back from out there."

"I know you did. Theo Keller briefed me on what you'd probably write. He agrees with you."

Speed was awake enough by then to pick up Bender's earlier remark, obviously offered on purpose. "But you say that's not the half of it?"

"Not even what I called about. You're not the only columnist giving me a stomach ache this morning. Have you seen the papers?"

"I'm used to working nights, not mornings, Senator. I'm not out of bed yet."

"Your colleague Lestark," Bender said. "He's—"

"Don't call that mudslinger a colleague of mine."

"Beg your pardon. I thought you reporters stuck together."

"Mostly we have to. But Lestark's not what *I* call a reporter. He's a garbage collector."

The senator chuckled. "I can believe *that* after his column this morning."

Bender was one of the few politicians Speed knew who could laugh at themselves. Annually, while brandishing a sugar beet on the Senate floor, he introduced a resolution to make it the national tuber. This gesture apparently was taken so seriously in his home state that Theo Keller's *Ledger* solemnly reported each year that more yea votes had been cast than the year before. Passage, though remote, was getting closer.

"Lestark's got me in bed with Gabriella Lukes," Bender said. "Ten years ago, for God's sake. And I don't even let that bitch in my office."

"But ten years ago," Speed said, "did *she* let *you* in?"

"Are you nuts?" Bender roared. "Hellfire, man . . . I knew better even then than play around with that kind of stuff."

Speed took this vehemence with a large grain of salt, owing only partially to his reporter's cynicism. Listening to Bender's denial reminded him of his own weekend in New York with Gabriella Lukes—an enticing package that had proved disappointing when unwrapped. The weekend had been more exhausting than exciting, not memorable enough to override his later self-criticism.

In rueful counterpoint to Evangeline's scorn, he had confided: "She's had everything lifted but her mind."

But Gabby knew well enough how to exploit her blond good looks and prominent bust. And ten years earlier she had not appeared at all faded, at least to the male eye. More than one pol and—to Speed's knowledge—at least two Cabinet officers had fallen prey to Gabby Lukes. That made a link to Mack Bender not only plausible but just Rafe Ames's kind of thing.

"So what's Lestark got? Not that the bastard *needs* much to smear somebody."

"Thin stuff," Bender said. "Somehow Lestark found out about this trip I made down South for a golf weekend with three other senators. No wives, no girl friends. We were even paying our airfare, but of course *that*'s not part of Lestark's junk."

"Nobody'd believe it anyway."

"You're a real barrel of laughs, Speed. What I didn't know was, through one of the other guys, that blond slut had invited us to stay at some villa owned or leased or something by this outfit she represented. The asshole accepted for all of us, like a damn fool."

"So Lestark's got you for accepting a corporate favor, too?"

"Hell, no. I sent them a check as soon as I got back, and I've got a record to prove it. He only suggests I was humping her. Maybe that creep that got us into the whole mess *was*, for all I know, but his name's not in Lestark's column either. Just mine."

"And of course Gabby *was* there in the house with you that weekend, wasn't she?"

Bender sounded almost sincere enough to be believed: "Speed, honest to God . . . I didn't pay much attention. We played golf all day and went out to eat at night, and ten years later this son of a bitch Lestark makes an orgy out of it."

Speed was impressed by Bender's apparent sincerity but found it hard to believe that any man had paid so little attention to a woman like Gabriella Lukes.

"Even my wife doesn't believe this garbage, Speed. She knows me too well, thank God."

Bender's wife was a large, motherly-looking woman often

pictured in aprons or holding little black children on her lap. Speed thought of Effie Keene worrying about her Social Security. He thought about Country Rhodes and gun control.

"I shouldn't have to tell you, Senator . . . it's not your wife that matters. Out there in God's country *they*'ll believe it."

Bender was silent for a long time. Then: "Theo says it looks kind of bad."

Speed was sitting up in bed by then, hearing Evangeline rattling around in the kitchen. He felt a certain satisfaction at his prescient article, warning that Bender had better start running hard. But rather to his surprise, he was angry, too, about Lestark's column.

Got to be Ames's work.

"I already decided," Bender said, "even before this, they want to play these kinds of games, it'll have to be fire against fire. Know what I mean?"

Speed was used to clever and ruthless men; in politics most were. He despised Ames, not just for that but for further cheapening the already debased politics of the country—the politics and the country in which, despite his cynicism about both, he profoundly wished to believe. It was getting no easier.

"I'm afraid I do," he said.

"Listen, Speed . . . come up and see me this afternoon. Got something to show you."

"All right, but one thing, Senator. I'm not Lestark. I haven't carried any water for Vic Donovan, and I won't carry any for you."

His words echoed from the walls, sounding hollower than they were. Speed was surprised anew; he had fallen back on another faith—this time in his calling and its often derided honor. That wasn't getting easier either.

"The difference," Bender said, "is that I won't ask you to. And listen, Speed . . . you probably won't believe it, but I never touched that woman."

★

On his way to Capitol Hill Speed decided on impulse to settle that question for himself. He stopped his taxi on L Street near Connecticut Avenue, before an ugly glass structure that resembled a block of frozen black coffee. A red-faced guard, his rumpled uniform representing Washington's mania for "security" in the era of terrorism, barred the path to the elevator. He demanded that Speed sign a log sheet.

Speed took the proffered ball-point and wrote in a flourishing hand: "Abou Ben Adhem."

The guard turned the log sheet, read the name, and eyed him nervously. "That's an A-rab name."

"Not at all. It's Palestinian."

The guard peered at him with narrowed eyes, at the log sheet, back at Speed. "You sure it's not A-rab?"

"Do I *look* like an A-rab?"

Behind the red face and the slit eyes, a decision gradually took shape. "Kind of like an American, I'd say."

"Us Palestinians," Speed said, "have to take what we can get."

He went on to the elevator bank, torn between impatience with pervasive security and a nervous nation, on the one hand, and regrets on the other. He had mocked the well-meaning guard, and he wondered if he would have done it had the man been black. He knew he should not have done it at all.

On the wall listing, he found what he was looking for: "Modern Images—4th Floor." Gabriella Lukes was in, and only too happy to see him. She came out from behind a desk littered enough to meet Speed's approval and seated herself—showing much nylon-shimmering leg—beside him on a wide flowered sofa beneath a a large print of Monet lilies. A tray of bottles and an ice bucket stood on the coffee table.

"I might have known Lestark's column would bring you around, Milo, an old swordsman like you. How's about a drink?"

"Too early for me."

Gabriella was low-cut and cinched at the waist; she had, Speed saw without surprise, a high-maintenance body. He detected, nevertheless, a faint sag beneath the once-clean line of her jaw. As if to deny it, Gabby held her chin a little too high.

"I didn't know," she said, with insinuation, "that *anything* was *ever* too early for Milo Speed. Or too late."

"Well . . . I'm getting to be an elderly gentleman these days. Now it's early to bed, early to—"

"With a certain stacked-up redhead?"

"Gabby . . ." Speed was horrified at her knowledge, which he was sure was not a guess. "I'm not here to gossip. Did you spill that Bender shit to Lestark?"

Gabriella Lukes lifted her chin higher and assumed an ethereal look. "Please don't spoil my wonderful memories with your evil mind. Oh, Milo . . . it was lovely, romantic . . . so-o-o romantic, I—"

"Bender says he never touched you. He says he can hardly remember if you were even there."

Gabriella Lukes laughed, lowered her head, and looked Speed in the eye. Her own were blue and hard.

"If you were a presidential candidate, what would you say?"

"If I were a presidential candidate, I wouldn't get caught playing around with . . ." He remembered Bender's description but finished lamely. "With anybody like you."

"You wouldn't anyway." Her manner was no longer playful. "Not since you got the only thing you wanted from me. Anyway, Mack wasn't a presidential candidate then."

"He may not be *now*. After Lestark's trash."

Gabriella Lukes's eyebrows went up. Speed remembered, too late, the sharp political instincts Gabby numbered among her more evident assets.

"What do you care whether he is or not?"

"All I care about is whether that *was* a piece of shit Lestark put out."

She shrugged, exaggerating well-displayed cleavage. "You won't find out from me."

He believed he just had and rose from the flowered sofa, starting for the door; then he stopped and asked: "How much did they pay you for Lestark's column?"

Gabriella Lukes laughed again, with a sound like glass breaking. She swayed slowly to her desk, giving him the full effect of her expensive hips and bottom.

"You know the business I'm in, Speed. Do you think Lestark's little item will hurt it?"

Speed gestured toward the sofa and said meanly: "Not the kind you do over there."

He regretted the mean words before she could whirl to face him, her face flushed with anger.

"Most people in this town know I do my work *here*. . . ." She banged a beringed fist on her desk. "And do it damn well, too. Except when some hard-up prick takes me to New York."

He opened the door. *That guard downstairs. Now this.*

"Ah, hell, Gabby," Speed said, "I hope Darwin John throws so much business your way you won't have any time to waste on a guy like that."

★

O. Mack Bender was waiting for Speed in a small room on the east side of the Capitol; it opened from a corridor along which tourists were not permitted to wander. Such hideaways were among the perks of seniority and party position, but Bender's was Spartan for a congressional office—only a television set, a desk on which sat the ubiquitous Washington telephone console, its myriad lights winking like a jukebox, and two huge black leather visitors' chairs, hulking like grizzly bears.

Bender took Speed's light summer jacket and hung it on an old-fashioned hatrack in one corner.

"If it's any consolation to you," Speed said, "I think Gabby's lying."

The senator was burly, broad-shouldered, with a lined and genial face and a mass of brown hair, about which critics said unkindly that he had to work hard to keep it looking uncombed. Bender had been known to appear on the Senate floor in a checked western shirt and boots; he never wore a tie for his weekly TV report to home state voters.

"She told you so?"

"No. But if her story was true, she *would* have."

Gabriella Lukes, Speed was sure, would not have been able to resist telling him in detail how even a famously upstanding senator had succumbed to her charms, if he had.

Bender obviously was disappointed. "Not the kind of evidence I can use, Milo." He shook his head glumly. "Theo called again. That Lestark column is all over the state."

"I saw you denying it on CNN. You sounded pretty convincing to me."

Bender moved behind his desk. "That thing's going to follow me like a horse's tail. I was *supposed* to be talking about the situation in Moscow. But the only thing they wanted to ask me about was that damned woman."

"Out there in your state, Senator . . . seems to me that talking about Moscow may not be just the right way to win the voters' hearts and minds."

"Or any state," Bender said. "You got to give the voters some flag and mother, maybe some farm price supports, so you can slip in a little Third World. You talk about jobs you've landed for the state. Stand up and salute national defense. Kick a little ass on big government. *Then* maybe a word or two about global warming and the ozone layer. Give 'em some red meat"—Bender punched the air with his right fist—"then some real world." He punched with his left. "Anyway, that's what I aim to do if I get a chance. Which I may not after Lestark hung this Gabriella Lukes around my neck."

He leaned over his desk, then looked up and winked. "Not exactly what I ought to say about that slut, I reckon."

Speed laughed. "I see you're not quite ready to put your head in the oven, Senator."

"Hell, no." Bender took a videocassette from a desk drawer. "Listen, Speed, I've been paying more attention to the campaign than you think. Which is what I wanted to show you."

Speed sank deeply into one of the grizzly chairs. "The fire," he said.

"What fire?"

Bender was dressed casually in slacks and a sport shirt, with the sleeves rolled to his elbows. Speed noted that his wristwatch was a Timex.

"The fire you're going to fight the other guy's fire with."

Bender pushed the cassette into a VCR on top of the television. "Vic Donovan started it, didn't he?"

Some snow and a few numerals flickered across the screen; then a watch face appeared in close-up, a hand set at one minute to noon, another audibly ticking around the watch's numerals. Speed recognized a good imitation of the familiar opening trademark of *Sixty Minutes*.

"Time is running out," a doom-filled voice announced, "on Victor T. Donovan!" The second hand ticktocked on.

"So far he's got away with"—a furtive-looking photo of Victor T. Donovan appeared in the center of the watch face—"his false charges"—ticktock—"his distortions"—ticktock—"his hit-and-run ads." Ticktock.

The watch face and photo disappeared. Film of Senator O. Mack Bender's face, looking grimmer than usual, replaced them. The unseen watch ticked on.

"His outright *lies* about me," Bender declared, in his own well-modulated politician's voice.

He leaned closer to the camera then, the grimness easing from his face, his voice confiding. He wore a checked shirt, open-necked to disclose hair on his chest.

"Funny that Donovan hasn't told you anything about himself. About his votes for beef imports . . . against highway funds for our state . . . to tax video games."

The watch continued ticktocking. Bender smiled at his constituency. "But you'll hear a *lot* about Vic Donovan from now on. Mack Bender guarantees it."

His smiling face disappeared, and the watch replaced it. The doom-laden voice returned: "It's time to put a *stop*"—just then both watch hands came to rest at high noon; the loud ticktocking ceased—"to Tricky Vic Donovan's low-road politics!"

Bender pressed a button, and the screen went dark. "That goes on right after I make my formal announcement. How'd you like them apples, Speed?"

"Deserves an Oscar. In one ad you manage to steal the *Sixty Minutes* theme and hang Nixon's nickname on Donovan. Couldn't you get the Stars and Stripes in there somewhere?"

Bender chuckled. "That's in some of the others."

"But what was that about highway money? I never thought Vic was *that* stupid."

"He isn't. He made himself some points in the House a year or so ago by voting to build a road the Speaker wanted in *his* state, enough to twist some arms for it. But the money came out of the general pool, so it left that much less for the other states, including ours."

Speed sighed. "Senator, that's exactly the kind of nothing ball stuff Rafe Ames is slinging at you."

Bender clenched his fist and shook it at nothing. "Damn right it is. That's the *point*, Milo. They started this shit . . . but *I'm* going to finish it!"

Speed had deduced, from Bender's morning call, what he was likely to see and hear, but he had hoped to the last that perhaps Mack Bender might find a better answer than fighting fire with fire. Wasn't Bender supposed to be a man of principle? Speed did not bother to hide his chagrin.

"Right down there in the gutter with Donovan, huh, Senator?"

Bender's lips tightened, and his eyes flashed. "Like you said this morning about this Gabby Lukes baloney. People will *believe* it if I don't answer."

"Some'll believe it," Speed said, "if you *do* answer."

"Which is exactly why it's necessary for me to throw out some charges of my own. Keep *him* busy answering, instead of spreading horseshit on me."

Bender slumped in the other leather chair, put his head back wearily and looked up at the ceiling.

"I hate it like sin, Speed. I'd rather go out there and make speeches about the new world we'll have with communism collapsed. Environmental hazards. Nuclear proliferation. Stuff that *matters*. But Vic Donovan's left me no choice."

Probably not, Speed conceded—not if Bender wanted to win. And as Ames had observed, they all did. Maybe it had been too much to hope that Mack Bender might prove an exception. Was anything really to be gained by losing nobly rather than winning meanly?

And I don't have to do either. I don't have to choose.

Bender reached for the VCR again. "This one really flicks the scab off."

Before he could press Play, however, a light tap sounded at the door. Bender rose and opened it. A slight man in a wrinkled poplin suit came in and immediately pulled down the knot of a subdued tie, then opened his white shirt collar.

"Hotter'n hell," he said. "Sorry I'm late, Senator."

Speed was astounded. At once he knew who had made the *Sixty Minutes* commercial for Bender.

"Bucky . . . you know Milo Speed." Bender hung the newcomer's coat on the hatrack.

"Yes, unfortunately," Bucky said. "You're kind of careless the company you keep, Senator."

Speed laughed. "I was just thinking the same thing."

Over the years Bucky Overholt had made little secret of his disdain for journalists. In return, Speed regarded Overholt as one of the less savory of the fast characters who were taking over politics. Oddly, the two got along by means of insults neither took seriously, and each grudgingly respected the other as a professional, if at a disreputable trade.

"Personally," Bender said, "I wouldn't hit a hog in the ass with either of you guys. But in my business beggars can't be choosers."

Speed's sensitive ear instantly picked up the suggestion that Bender needed *both* his visitors. *Maybe Overholt,* he thought.

"I warned you, Senator. I don't play games with politicians."

"Aren't we high-and-mighty today?" Bucky Overholt said to Mack Bender. Without invitation he had seated himself in the other black chair. "Speed had a high horse, he'd be up on it all the time."

Bender wheeled the desk chair around between them. "The only reason you're here, Speed, I figured Bucky's stuff would knock the notion right out of your head I'm taking Vic Donovan too lightly."

"But, Bucky"—Speed was still curious—"I thought you worked for Darwin John?"

"This gun for hire, Speed. As you damn well know."

Bucky Overholt was thin, wiry, intense, with hot eyes set deep in bony sockets. A mustache hung raggedly on an ascetic profile; the mustache had tended to collect food flecks on the one occasion when Speed had warily taken Overholt to an expense account lunch.

"So if John thinks this smartass Ames yuppie can put Donovan over, that's John's business. Leaves me free to make a buck off the senator here."

Not only to make a buck, Speed thought, *but to cream Ames* and *John, while he's at it*. Like a woman scorned.

"A *lot* of bucks," Bender said. "This campaign'll cost me twice my first two put together."

Bucky Overholt shrugged. "You want the best, you pay for the best. What've you shown 'im so far?"

Speed had no quarrel with Overholt's self-description. He was *the* campaign consultant without peer and without scruple—unless Rafael Ames could manage to capture both titles. As Darwin John's hired hand Bucky Overholt had handled winning campaigns in a dozen states. He had cut spots and advised on tactics for the last two Presidents. He was best known to Milo Speed for having said on *Good Morning America* that "in football and politics the name of the game is 'get the quarterback.' " Which, in football and politics, no one was supposed to say.

"Just the *Sixty Minutes* spot," Bender said. "Gets better every time I see it."

Overholt's greatest coup, in the opinion of political students, was a spot lampooning the challenger in the most recent presidential campaign. The man had unwisely allowed himself to be photographed in military headgear, peering out of the turret of an Army tank.

Within the week Bucky Overholt had on the air a spoof in which a look-alike of the challenger appeared first in an engineer's cap gazing as solemnly as Buster Keaton from an old steam locomotive—which was promptly shown in borrowed movie footage plunging head-on into another locomotive, a terrific explosion resulting. Quickly the look-alike reappeared helmeted and deadpan as Keaton, this time at the wheel of an Indianapolis race car, just before newsreel clips of a horrifying three-car crack-up. Finally, in earflaps and goggles, the grim-faced look-alike piloted a World War I Spad—which, in old silent film, flew straight into the side of a barn. The only caption needed came at the end:

"Whose Hands Do You Want on the Wheel?"

"I was just about to screen the Lemons when you came in," Bender said.

"Good." Overholt pressed Play. "It'll frost Ames's . . . I mean Donovan's balls."

Lemons came rolling yellowly across the screen, dozens and dozens of them. One came to a stop in close-up; it was labeled "1982 Farm Bill."

"The corporate farmers conned Vic Donovan into buying *this* lemon," said a strong male voice.

More dozens of lemons rolled past on a conveyor belt.

"But Tricky Vic didn't learn a thing." Another lemon came to a stop, the words "1985 Farm Bill" on its side. "He bought this one, too."

The smiling face of O. Mack Bender, under a farmer's straw hat, flashed on the screen.

"Those two lemons would have sent most of our farmers to the poorhouse," he said, conversationally. "Good thing this state had a senator whose vote helped defeat *both* of 'em."

The camera tracked down his extended arm to disclose, first, a rolled-up sleeve, then a big hand resting on an open case of lemons. Bender pulled his hand away, and a lid was fitted over the lemons. It bore a shipping label addressed to "Tricky Vic Donovan, House of Representatives, Washington, D.C."

"He'll scream bloody murder when he sees that," Bucky Overholt said. "He made a record voting against the final bills, but we've got the slippery bastard dead to rights voting in committee to send them both to the floor."

Bender spun the desk chair toward Speed, who was sunk in black leather and deep thought.

"You still think I'm not running hard enough?"

Rafael Ames versus Bucky Overholt, Speed reflected. Quite a match. They would put on a dazzling show. New versus old, fresh blood versus experience, challenger pitted against champion. And like a brace of fighting cocks or a pair of pit bulls, neither would know restraint or limit.

"Not with Bucky giving you the goose," Speed said.

But the race, he thought sadly, was supposed to be between Victor T. Donovan and O. Mack Bender, a campaign between flesh-and-blood candidates, about voters' concerns. Instead, the work of Ames and Overholt would make it a contest between the sharpest slogans, the cleverest sound bites, the most persuasive television images—and, worse, the slickest deceptions. It would be a campaign about winning—nothing else.

Speed stood up slowly, painfully, the deep chair tacitly reminding him that he was not as spry as he had been or as hopeful.

"I know I'm old-fashioned," he said, "and of course Vic did start the rough stuff. But you're the good guy, Senator. A lot of people believe in you, in what you stand for. I hate to see Bucky take you down in the gutter, too."

Bender looked for a moment as if he had been slapped. Then he sat up straight and looked Speed in the eye.

"What choice do I have?"

"None," said Bucky Overholt. "These days you show me a candidate sticking to the high road, I'll show you a loser."

★

Owing to Theo Keller's journalistic sensibilities, the Capital City *Ledger* did not carry the columns of Lee Lestark, but Keller was fair enough to publish a wire service account of Lestark's exclusive about Gabriella Lukes and Senator O. Mack Bender. Owing to Theo Keller's political loyalties, however, he had buried the wire story on a page carrying mostly classified and patent medicine ads; he had cut it, moreover, to a few paragraphs.

While being driven by Floyd Finch to the airport that morning, Josie Donovan read what remained. She was infuriated—not just at the story itself but also at the fact that Vic had done nothing to stop it. Or not enough.

"Dammit, Floyd—that cheesy scandal yarn about Bender. Here it is, after all."

She held up the paper and pointed with a finger:

> WASHINGTON—Senator O. Mack Bender, the potential presidential candidate who is considered a man of principle by many of his colleagues, spent a weekend at a southern resort with a shapely blond lobbyist in a

> house leased by one of her clients, the columnist Lee Lestark has reported.

"Only that's not the whole thing in there, Miz Donovan." Finch carefully kept his eyes on the car ahead. "The *Ledger*'s in the tank for Bender, y'know. So you think *that's* tough, wait'll you see Lestark's whole column."

In the first car the Honorable Victor T. Donovan and Rafael Ames also were being driven to the airport, by a local recipient of Darwin John's generosity. Ames and the Donovans were to return to Washington on a corporate jet made available by a multinational whose CEO had been assured by the Chief that he could see the President on demand.

"Will you tell me what in the *hell* a man playing around ten years ago has got to do with *this* campaign?" Josie glared defiantly at Finch, who continued to look straight ahead. "As long as it wasn't with some underage schoolboy?"

Finch shifted uncomfortably in his seat. "She looks like a movie star," he finally said. "I saw her picture in *USA Today*."

Josie had discovered from hours of driving alone with Floyd Finch that he had an eager and overripe appreciation for women—the younger, the better—sharpened, she guessed, by too little regard *from* women. She decided to take some of the gleam out of his eye.

"Gabby Lukes might have looked like a movie star *then*, Floyd. But today she looks like she's been driven too far and left out in the rain too often."

Finch nodded sadly. "I see her around Washington, y'know? A little over the hill, I guess, but all they'll see out here is that cheesecake picture. What she looked like when Bender was bang— I mean back when . . ."

"But we really don't know from this *Ledger* item that he *was* banging her." Josie was pleased to see again that Finch could be shocked by the candidate's wife's language. "Does the Lestark column say so for sure?"

Floyd Finch followed the front car into the airport entrance and around a curving drive to the small terminal. "He didn't really have to, Miz Donovan. Anybody could guess what must of happened."

And anybody would, Josie had to admit, as both cars came to a stop. *Just like that snake Ames calculated.*

Finch opened the door on the driver's side. Before he could step out, Josie touched his arm. "You think it was worth it, Floyd? Just to cost Bender the church ladies' vote?"

Finch shuddered a little, whether at her touch or her question Josie could not tell. He was a sad man, she thought, an old retainer who knew his place, a dry husk sustained by lecherous fantasies.

"Church ladies might make the difference, Miz Donovan. That'd be worth it, wouldn't it?"

Finch and the other driver hustled luggage from the first car through the terminal and out to the waiting jet. The Honorable Victor T. Donovan and Rafael Ames—both looking ridiculous, Josie thought, in cowboy hats that seemed about to take wing—carried briefcases only. She lugged her own dress bag through the terminal until the other driver hurried to take it from her.

At the steps of the plane she shook hands with him, then with Floyd Finch. She pulled Finch closer and kissed his cheek. He smelled of last night's beer.

"Driving around with you was an education, Floyd."

"Pleasure for me, Miz Donovan." She was glad he had been able to look his fill at her legs.

Ames followed her up the steps, while the Honorable Victor T. Donovan—ever polite—also stopped to shake hands with Floyd Finch and the other driver.

"What kind of an education?" Ames said. "Beer guzzling?"

There were only four seats in the cabin, two facing each other on either side of the aisle.

"Political." She resented Ames's implied contempt for an older, less fortunate man. Purposely, she took the seat facing forward on the left, knowing very well that Vic always preferred that seat.

Ames sat across the aisle from her, in the other forward-facing seat, tossing his giant hat into the one facing him. He wore faded blue jeans and a sweater too big for him, over an open-necked shirt. Stubble lined his jaw as usual, but he had abandoned the flapping Nikes for a pair of pointed-toe cowboy boots in black leather with elaborate stitching.

"For a *real* political education," he said, "you only need to listen to me."

Josie saw no reason to restrain herself. "For you, buster, I don't have any need at all."

Ames had the sensitivity, or the facility, to look startled and sound plaintive. "But what have I done to you?"

Victor T. Donovan was coming heavily up the steps, the light plane lurching under his weight. On the tarmac Josie could see Floyd Finch backing away and waving at the windows, his smile fixed on his thin face—a man, she thought, who would usually be left behind.

"I mean, I know you don't like doing all those coffees every day, but there's not much I—"

"It's not the coffees, Rafe. I can do coffees standing on my head."

Nor was it, she told herself, their exchange at the door of her room. Not entirely, anyway. She said, bluntly: "You want to know, I think you're a cheap political hit man."

Ames looked wounded, but he was faking it, Josie decided. Her directness had only surprised him.

"You didn't think so when I put Darwin John on your husband's track."

Vic was in the front of the plane, speaking jovially to the pilots. He had been a pilot himself during his military days and prominently featured in his campaign bio a youthful picture of himself in a floppy fly-boy cap.

"I didn't really see you then," Josie said. "Not for the cheap-shot artist you are. I didn't imagine the sleazy influence you'd have on Vic."

Ames stopped faking. His stubbled face turned hard; his lips tightened. His eyes were cold; Josie realized they always were.

"My influence is making a winner out of that—"

He stopped abruptly, as the Honorable Victor T. Donovan came into the cabin.

"That what?" Vic asked. He looked unhappily from Josie

to Ames, each sitting in a forward-facing seat. But Josie had no intention of offering him hers.

"That natural talent you've been wasting all these years."

Victor T. Donovan made a show of studying the empty backward-facing seats. Josie knew he hated to face backward in planes or trains.

"Oh, I learned a thing or two"—the congressman dropped his own huge hat over Ames's and reluctantly sat in the seat facing Josie, his legs crowding hers—"in all those . . . uh . . . wasted years."

If he had real balls, Josie thought, he'd tell Ames to get his ass out of that seat and take it for himself. Or if Ames had any common courtesy, he wouldn't have to be told. The candidate was supposedly the boss. If Vic put up with that kind of insolence, it showed how Ames dominated him.

"Is this the kind of thing you learned?" Josie tossed her copy of the *Ledger*, folded open to the patent medicine page, in her husband's lap.

By then the plane was moving toward the runway, the jets whining. Victor T. Donovan picked up the paper and looked it over, showing no expression.

"Surprised that crummy Keller ran this much."

He turned the paper so that Ames could see the headline. Josie could read it, too: OLD CHARGE RAISED AGAINST SENATOR.

"They'd look like idiots if they didn't run something," Ames said. "Every other paper in the country played the story."

"Still, the way they slant everything for Bender, I expected them just to ignore it."

"Cheated on the headline, though. They make it look like old stuff. Actually that yarn never made the papers before Lestark."

"Before *you* leaked it to him," Josie said to Ames. Then she turned to Victor T. Donovan. "Before *you* let him leak it."

He continued to read, still without expression, as the plane swung into the runway and raced toward takeoff. The jet engines screamed. But when they were well airborne and the engine noise had abated, Victor T. Donovan leaned forward and gently dropped the folded paper in Josie's lap.

"It was too late, my dear," he said. "I couldn't stop it."

From the corner of her eye Josie saw Ames's mouth tighten again. In that movement she read quite clearly that Victor T. Donovan had not even *tried* to kill the leak to Lestark—whatever he'd promised her, whatever he was saying now. She wondered again if she really knew her husband, despite their long familiarity, and she wondered, too, if she had only been willing . . . but of course, Vic was used to *that* by now. At least he hardly ever made the effort anymore.

Which was why she'd been so surprised when he did.

★

Josie had returned to the Lewis & Clark late in the evening of the day Floyd Finch had told her about the Bender scandal story. She went straight to her husband's room, down the hall from her own; he had insisted he needed a private place to meet with important locals, and she had been only too willing to have a room to herself.

Vic answered her knock in shirt sleeves but still wore a tie tightly knotted—his idea, she thought in exasperation, of casual dressing.

"I didn't expect you, my dear." He held the door open. "You must be exhausted."

Josie went past him purposefully, toward the coffee table where he kept liquor for those important locals. She poured a stiff drink of vodka—a taste acquired from Milo Speed and never lost—then dropped in a handful of tiny ice cubes from the plastic Lewis & Clark bucket.

"I'm beat, too," Vic went on, as if she had answered his first remark. "I get a real kick out of campaigning, but today was about as much as I could take. I only got back here ten minutes ago."

Josie flopped in an armchair, letting her short skirt ride well up above her knees. Unlike Floyd Finch, she saw without surprise as she sipped vodka, her husband showed no interest in her legs.

"Wish you'd heard my speech at the picnic, Josie. Seemed to go over pretty well."

"Ames wrote it, I suppose."

"Just suggested some themes." He shrugged. "I winged it

mostly. Kind of let myself go. I'm sort of getting the hang of it."

That would have been worth seeing, she thought, feeling the slight burn of vodka in her chest—a welcome counter to the coldness farther inside.

"Were you just winging it with that leak to Lestark?"

Victor T. Donovan did not openly react. He crossed to the coffee table and studiously examined the makeshift bar.

"What leak?"

Josie never had been able to break him out of his calculated calm. Now, as she often had, she tried to shake him, shock him—anything to liberate some genuine emotion from his blandness.

"About Bender fucking that Lukes woman."

Victor T. Donovan selected a bottle of club soda and poured himself a glass, careful not to let it fizz over the rim.

"Ames mentioned something about her and Bender. Nothing about sex, though."

Josie set her glass on the coffee table with a sharp crack. She leaned forward intently, elbows on her exposed knees. "Don't bullshit me, Vic Donovan. Ames cleared that story with you before he dropped it on Lee Lestark."

Victor T. Donovan put ice in his club soda and said, still with maddening calm: "I wouldn't try that on *you,* my dear. Rafe Ames didn't clear *any*thing with me. Oh, he ran the story past me, all right." He swirled his glass and took a swallow of club soda. "But I let Ames have a lot of leeway, you know. He's darn good at what he does."

Which is just the damn trouble, Josie thought. *All that leeway to let Ames do what he does so well.*

"That's lawyer talk, Vic. Hairsplitting. If he ran it past you, you could have stopped it."

His smooth face assumed a practiced look of puzzlement. "It seemed legitimate. Bender should have known better than to—"

"Fuck some woman besides his wife? Maybe so, but what's something he shouldn't have done ten years ago got to do with *this* campaign? Even if he did do it?"

Victor T. Donovan sat down on the end of the king-size

bed, holding his glass carefully, so as not to spill club soda on his trousers. "I told you, Josie, I didn't know that part of it."

Josie picked up her own glass and glared at him. "Oh, Vic, dammit, you've been around long enough to spot a killer story when you see one. You're bullshitting me again."

"And you're going to slip up someday, my dear, and embarrass yourself with that kind of language in public. Now listen to me." His face and voice were earnest but little more than they usually were. "Ames told me Bender mooched a weekend on some corporation that owned this house he stayed in. I saw nothing wrong with exposing something like that, considering the high-and-mighty airs Bender likes to put on."

She drained the vodka, rose, and poured herself another, stiffer this time. "Nothing about Gabby Lukes?"

"Just that she arranged things for him."

"Not that she was staying in that house, too?"

"If Ames mentioned that," Victor T. Donovan said, "and I'm not sure he did, I guess I just somehow didn't put it all together."

Could he really be that innocent? Josie wondered. Or stupid? Not to see the implications, which were what really mattered? Or was Ames that clever and Victor T. Donovan that dumb that such a story could be slipped past his scrutiny?

"Besides, Bender's so well known out here I'm not sure even a yarn like that could hurt him much."

Or was Vic lying to her now? Which would mean not only that he had been a willing accomplice in a sleazy scandal story of uncertain validity, but worse—that he, under Ames's tutelage, was ready to do anything to win. And liked his own pretensions too much to admit it even to his wife.

"You think the church ladies won't believe it, Vic? Those old bitches I'm having coffee and cookies with every day, you think they're going to vote for somebody cheats on his wife?"

"If *that's* the story," Victor T. Donovan said, "Bender cheating on his wife, I'll try to stop it. Vic Donovan's not going down the low road."

In the beginning she had believed he never would. Not that he was so pure in heart but that he was too unimaginative, too conventional, too concerned for appearances. She had thought that with Victor T. Donovan, what you saw in office was what you'd get in a campaign. Now . . .

I don't know. I'm not so sure.

"It's a cheap shot, Vic. When half the people in this country, in this *state* probably, are out there getting a little on the side."

"Maybe they are," Vic said. "Maybe Bender does. But not Vic Donovan. He's trying to set a good moral example, and always has."

And not me either, she thought regretfully, almost bitterly. *Not anymore.* It had been a long time since she had been able to live her life to the hilt, the fullest, the richest way—the way she once had thought was the *only* way.

"People like Mack Bender ought not to be playing around," Victor T. Donovan said. "It's just not—not *right*."

He sat calmly on the end of the bed, swirling his club soda, his face as bland and innocent as a baby's. Watching him, Josie realized again what she had known for years: that Victor T. Donovan bored her. His precisely knotted ties, his sobriety and clean living, his care for his career, his interest in sugar beets, and his pale, safe years in the House. He bored her.

"I thought this campaign would be fun, Vic."

"It *is* fun. For me, it's as much fun as I've ever had."

"Taking on Bender, I mean. Taking a chance like that. Risking everything. I wouldn't even mind losing, Vic. Not as long as I know you grabbed for the brass ring, at least this once."

For the first time in their life together, she saw that she had broken his detachment. His stare was as near malevolence as she ever had known him to allow himself.

"*I'd* damn well mind," he said. "Vic Donovan's not in this race to lose."

Josie drank vodka. His words seemed to confirm what she feared.

"Neither is Rafe Ames. Or Darwin John. I tell you, Josie, we're not *going* to lose."

The intensity in his voice, in the figure hunched on the bed was as strange to Josie as the emphasis in his words. Victor T. Donovan always had seemed a man to take things more or less as they came. Which, she had to concede, was one good reason he had bored her. So maybe she was only getting, at last, the passion, the daring she had hoped for.

"It's not like I expected, Vic."

Josie rose, holding her vodka, and started toward the closed window, feeling suddenly smothered by the air conditioning. She had wanted excitement, all right, to shed boredom, dare the odds, feel again the once-familiar rush of living recklessly. Instead, she felt herself battered by the grim realities of what Floyd Finch called hardball.

"Not as much fun?"

Victor T. Donovan reached for her hand as she passed the foot of the bed. That was strange, too, so unlike the unemotional Vic of her experience that she resented what she took as a clumsy effort to placate her.

Which he doesn't even know how to do.

Josie pulled her hand free and went on past him. Maybe the window would open, let in some fresh air.

"Not as much fun," she said, "and I don't like what the campaign seems to be doing to you." *Not,* she thought in wry contempt for her own misplaced hopes, *that I liked what you* were *either.*

She set her glass on the sill and tested the window. It was fixed in place, of course, to avoid wasting the air conditioning. If only, she thought, even in her irritation at the window and the dry, cold air, everything could be so fixed.

"What it's doing," Victor T. Donovan said, "is what Vic Donovan waited for all his life. Until the time was ripe." His voice came from right behind her, though she had not heard him move from the bed.

A long wait, she thought. *And not just for you.*

"I didn't know that, Vic. You never showed it."

"Maybe I didn't know it either." He did not sound as if he meant it.

"But Ames knew," Josie said. "Ames saw he could make you do anything to win."

"You think I can't handle Rafe Ames?"

She remembered guiltily that she had wanted Ames to come to her room. No use telling herself that was *all* she had wanted. No use denying she had been ready to go where it might have led. But at least one good thing had come from a bad moment: Now she saw Rafe Ames clearly for what he was.

"Get rid of him, Vic. Before it's too late."

He put his arms around her from behind, taking her breasts in his hands, lifting them.

"Ames can't *make* me do anything, Josie."

She was too surprised to answer, clasping his hands in hers, trying to pull his away. But he was strong; he jerked one hand free and pulled the hem of her blouse out of her skirt. He got both hands up under the blouse, and she felt his fingers fumbling for her nipples, through the lace of her bra. His breath was hot on her ear and neck, smelling of spearmint.

"*I* don't cheat on my wife," Victor T. Donovan whispered. "So what do I get in return?"

It was like him to put it that way. Tit for tat, so to speak. He squeezed her breasts rhythmically. That was like him, too—methodical, even in sex.

"I'm having fun these days, even if you're not."

Though her breasts had not been touched by a man in a long time—certainly not by Victor T. Donovan—his hands did not arouse her; his fumblings were clumsy, demanding, an affront to her sex and self.

Spearmint breath whispery on her skin.

"I like winning, Josie. Winning turns me on."

She remembered how Milo Speed had touched her almost reverently. Speed always had wanted her to slip off her bra last. He would watch as she dropped it along her arms, his eyes warm with pleasure as she disclosed to him what he thought the loveliest part of her body.

"You have the most beautiful breasts," Speed had murmured once, during this ritual, and she had almost laughed as he had caught himself before saying, "I've ever seen," amending adeptly: "of any woman in the world."

But it was not her body—it was *winning* that turned on Victor T. Donovan. Even as her anger rose at this realization, and at his determined gropings under her blouse, she wondered: *How can he be sure he's winning*?

Then, with strength she had not known she had, she

clutched his wrists and dragged his hands away from her breasts.

"That's *over,* Vic. You know it's been over a long time."

Victor T. Donovan took his arms from around her and turned away to the coffee table bar.

"If it ever *was,*" he murmured.

"Well, if it wasn't"—Josie stared out the window, aching for fresh air, for something—"you never seemed to care."

Behind her, she heard only the splash and fizz of club soda.

★

For most of the long flight to Washington Victor T. Donovan and Rafael Ames desultorily discussed the campaign.

"Next trip, we'll probably have some press along," Ames said.

"Sooner or later I guess we have to."

"Word's getting around you're moving up. Not to mention this new trouble the Gummer's in. You'll need a bigger plane, you go out there again."

"Tell John. Planes are his worry."

Josie again had been trying to read *Northanger Abbey* but had not been able to keep her mind on Jane Austen's amorous pirouettes. She could not help thinking, instead, of the *Ledger,* crumpled against her hip in the narrow seat and of the shabby wire story Theo Keller had tried to bury on the patent medicine page. How much worse could Lestark's original article be?

"We'll have Mingo lay on a bus for road trips."

She felt dirtied by the *Ledger* story, not so much because she was morally certain Victor T. Donovan was complicitous in leaking it—though she was—and certainly not because of what two human beings like herself, like anyone, might have done in bed years before, but because she felt she had no right to *know* about them, their private world and selves, that it was a transgression on her part to know—and worse for someone else to have told.

Ames said: "Maybe John can charter a seven-twenty-seven or something like that. Make the goddam reporters pay for it."

Josie felt as if she had peeped in a window and seen two

people entwined, with no idea they were being watched by prying eyes. Of all the moments in life, Josie thought, none was more private, more *personal.* No one had a right, or a need great enough, to violate such intimacy—to profane life itself, of which the desperate needs of lovers, however momentary, were the essence.

"I guess reporters got to be good for something," said Victor T. Donovan.

"Just to pay for campaign planes, far as I'm concerned. Take that goddam Speed. Ten to one, sooner or later he'll give us the shaft."

"One time when I was in high school"—Josie closed *Northanger Abbey* with a snap; the two men, startled, looked at her as if she had only just then appeared in her seat—"I was going out with this boy I thought was dreamy. But you know what? The basketball coach caught him and two other creeps peeping in the girls' locker room through a ventilating grille."

"Can't blame 'im," Ames said, "long as *you* were in there."

She turned a cold face on his lame effort at gallantry. "I was there all right. In my birthday suit. Right in front of where they got caught."

"Josie"—Victor T. Donovan looked and sounded disapproving at these disclosures—"what's this got to do with anything?"

"Maybe you think I was ashamed he saw me naked," Josie said. "But I just decided he was some kind of slug"—she looked her husband in the eye—"to break into a private place where he had no right."

"Ah . . ." Victor T. Donovan leaned back in his seat. "I see. We're back to the Bender story, aren't we?"

"We're not likely," Josie said, "to get away from it."

The plane was flying just above the clouds, hurtling over a vast, fluffy layer of white fleece—cleaner by far, she thought, than the world below. How nice it would be to sink peacefully into that vast softness.

"You didn't like that story?"

Ames had turned in his seat, so that he almost faced Josie. He sounded interested, as if he really wanted to know what she thought.

"I don't like anybody peeping at what they're not supposed to see. And I particularly don't like the way that slimy Lestark got hold of it."

She saw that Ames was no longer the embarrassed, flummoxed boy last seen outside her room at the Lewis & Clark. He was back on familiar turf. His face was animated; his eyes shone eagerly. He spoke rapidly—happily, Josie thought.

"Bender goes around dipping his wick, Miz Donovan, the voters got a right to know."

"If he did," Josie said, "which only he and Gabby Lukes can say for sure, *nobody* else has a right to know."

"You think immorality like that's not a political issue? It doesn't go to character?"

"I can think of things a lot more immoral than sex, if sex *is* immoral. Things that *really* go to character, like lying. So no . . . I *don't* think Bender's sex life ought to be an issue. Or yours. Or mine."

Ames grinned, he probably thought disarmingly; Josie thought wolfishly.

"What say we let the voters decide that?"

"You already did, didn't you? You and Vic."

"Well, you know what Harry Truman said. If Bender can't stand the heat, he should stay out of the kitchen."

Josie's eyes locked with his. "That boy the coach caught peeping. The difference with you is, you get your rocks off on hardball."

Ames took it without blinking. "It's better than anything," he said. "Better than money."

Better than sex, she started to say. *For you.*

But Victor T. Donovan, who had been listening intently, moved smoothly into the exchange, like a referee coming between boxers. "Well, ah, of course, you're right about the kitchen, Ames. I'm not sure Bender's got a valid complaint. Or that he wouldn't have done the same thing to us if he could have. On the other hand . . ."

This sounded more like the Victor T. Donovan Josie once had been sure she knew. With *that* Vic, there was always an other hand.

"Josie's right, too. It's kind of an unsavory story."

"Which is why we leaked it, for Christ sake." Ames sounded as if explaining the obvious to the obtuse.

"I *know* that's why you leaked it." Victor T. Donovan did not emphasize the change of person, but it did not escape Josie or—she thought, watching across the aisle—Rafael Ames. "But what I mean, it's kind of unsavory for us to be linked to it, isn't it?"

"Who can prove we leaked it?" Ames spread his hands expressively. "And who gives a shit if we did?"

Victor T. Donovan glared pompously. "I'd prefer you didn't say things like that in front of Josie."

"Oh, don't be such a nerd," Josie said. "*I* say things like that in front of *him*."

"All *right* then." Vic seemed genuinely angry, she thought, though she wondered if he was genuine about anything anymore. Maybe about being called a nerd. "Why should *I* give a shit if you don't?"

In all their years of marriage she had never heard him use the word. Immediately, however, the old Victor T. Donovan reasserted himself. "Just so neither of you talks like that where the press might hear you."

Ames flipped a hand impatiently. "What's this unsavory you're bothering about?"

Vic carefully—transparently, Josie thought—chose his words. "Well, I know my state. I guess I ought to. This story could hurt Bender, people out there think he's, ah, fiddling around. But what worries me . . ."

His earnest eyes sought Josie's; she stared back, trying to penetrate to whatever reality there might be.

"It could hurt us, too. If the word gets out that you leaked it to Lestark."

Ames shook his head. "Plenty of people, like Theo Keller, maybe the Gummer himself, probably can guess we leaked it." He put no special emphasis on the "we," but again Josie caught the change. "How's that going to hurt us, they can't prove it?"

"Because it looks sleazy," Victor T. Donovan said. "So sleazy they might not think it's just hardball. They might think it's low road. And I won't have anybody even *thinking* Vic Donovan takes the low road."

Rafael Ames leaned into the aisle, and Josie noticed again the leanness of his body, his barely restrained vitality, and felt again for a fleeting moment the sheer physical appeal that had attracted her. Now she saw that it was not sexuality that animated him but a kind of rapacity. Above the raveled sweater and the open neck of his shirt, the stubble on his jawline seemed to bristle with aggression.

"You worry so much about that, my man, why'd you go along with it?"

Victor T. Donovan was silent for a long moment. "If you'd explained the whole thing to me," he finally said, "I'd have stopped you."

"Get off my case." Ames spoke evenly, clearly. "You heard the whole fucking thing. *Before* you signed on."

Josie was surprised only by his directness. But Victor T. Donovan, facing backward, was apparently undisturbed, impervious. He responded without emotion.

"Not that *I* remember. Anyway, Ames, what you do when we get to D.C., I want you to call a news conference for me."

He spoke calmly, Josie thought—as if Ames had only described the gray-green landscape occasionally visible through sudden gaps in the layer of cloud.

Ames was clearly surprised. "A news conference? What—" he started to ask.

But Victor T. Donovan held up his hand. "I'm going to fire Kyle."

★

Josie's first thought was woman's vanity: that by getting rid of the man she supposed had dug up the old scandal, Vic wanted to get back in *her* good graces. Then, watching his bland face, recalling what he'd said with his hands fumbling under her bra *winning turns me on*, she realized her good graces meant little to him. Even if it was her reaction that had caused him to see the "unsavory" side of the leak to Lestark, Victor T. Donovan did not really care what the candidate's wife might think. It was not she with whom he was concerned.

"You're off your goddam rocker," Ames said.

"I told you, Ames . . . I know my state. When Vic Donovan

pins that leak on Kyle and publicly dumps him, we'll get the credit for doing the decent thing, not the blame for taking the low road."

Ames's whole body seemed to shake in protest. "All you'll be doing is *admitting* we leaked the story."

"You said yourself they'd guess it anyway."

"That's different. That'd be just speculation."

"If I remember correctly," said Victor T. Donovan coldly, "your philosophy is that speculation can hurt as much as facts."

Ames stared at him. "I don't believe this. I really don't. We drop a blockbuster on the Gummer, and you're worried it'll hurt *you*?"

It was Victor T. Donovan's turn to speak as if explaining the obvious. "Look at it like this, Ames. Your way, Bender gets hurt and we get the blame. My way, we get some credit and Bender *still* gets hurt."

Neither man, Josie noticed, seemed to feel any concern for the one to be thrown to the wolves. She had never liked Calvin Kyle; she sensed something threatening in his obsequiousness. But that was no reason for him to be sacrificed to the same gods of hardball he no doubt had believed he was serving.

"Because whatever Vic Donovan does *now*, a lot of people will *still* believe Bender had his little fling with Gabby Lukes."

"I don't buy it," Ames said. "What I see, you'll just be topping a good headline with a bad one."

Victor T. Donovan sat back in his seat and looked up at the cabin roof, as if thinking over Ames's objection. The jet bumped erratically through a patch of turbulence, shaking *Northanger Abbey* off Josie's lap. She leaned against her seat belt to pick it up, astounded—in spite of what she had believed was her political sophistication—at the cold ease with which the men on either side of her were calculating the practical pluses and minuses of action, with no regard for right or wrong, good or bad. Such abstractions obviously had no place in hardball.

The plane emerged into smooth air. As if that had resolved any question in his mind, Victor T. Donovan held up his left hand, fingers extended.

"We'll hold it in my office." He folded down his index finger and held it with his thumb. "Phone Lacy from the airport to set it up." He folded his middle finger into his palm. "Five P.M., and we can still make the evening news shows."

"Listen, my man. You're going off half cocked here."

Victor T. Donovan bent down his ring finger. "Make sure Lestark's not there. Don't want him screwing up our story." The little finger went down last, leaving a fist he was not quite shaking. "Get me a short statement to read, right to the point. And don't call me your man."

"Write your own damn statement," Ames said.

That should have been enough, Josie thought, to get him fired on the spot. As if he hadn't *already* said enough. But Victor T. Donovan seemed not even to hear.

"Make three points, Ames. One, an underling dug up that story and leaked it on his own. Two, Vic Donovan won't stand for that kind of low-road stuff. So, three, the guy no longer works for Vic Donovan's campaign."

A pilot's voice, full of metallic cheer, grated through the sound system: "Landing in about ten minutes, folks. When the sign comes on, seat backs up and make sure your belts are fastened."

"Darwin John won't like this," Ames said. "He won't like a fucking thing you're doing, and he particularly won't like it you didn't clear with him."

"What's he going to do about it, this late date? Let Bender walk into the White House?"

For the first time Ames sounded uncertain. "He could cut off the money."

Victor T. Donovan smiled, coolly, confidently. "What I like about Darwin John, he likes to win, too. He reads the polls, sees how things are going. Darwin John's smart."

Josie had been sensing, across the aisle, Ames's rising anger, his gathering intensity. She shrank away from him, as if he were dangerous, expecting his explosion before it came:

"Goddammit, I'm smart, too! *I* found you, *I* brought John in, I *made* you. You can't—"

"So what are *you* going to do, Ames? Find another candidate to make your name for you?"

Ames collapsed back in his seat, as if he literally had been exploded, like a balloon with a pin. A confident smile played across the smoothly handsome face of Victor T. Donovan. But Josie had never seen his eyes so steely.

"This is Vic Donovan's campaign," he said, so softly that the words hardly could be heard above the whine of the engines. "You might as well get it into that smart head of yours, Rafe."

Josie was sure, then, that she never really had understood her husband. She never really had seen the burning will that underlay the bland surface. "Winning turns me on," he'd told her. Winning, the apparent taste of it on his tongue, the rising sense of it in the air around him, had made of Victor T. Donovan something she liked even less than the man whose seemingly easy ride through life she once had held in unspoken contempt.

"Since when," Milo Speed had demanded to know, one rainy day in an obscure café in Georgetown, "does that damn featherweight come between you and me?"

So even Speed, with his knowledge of politics, his insight into politicians, had not seen the real Victor T. Donovan.

"That's not fair," she had replied, that long-ago day, in automatic defense of the man she thought her husband was. "Vic's not a featherweight."

But she had not known then, had not even conceived, what he could become. Now the remembered words made her shudder within herself. Oddly, she wished she could talk to Speed, in the old wholehearted way. Whatever his manner, his deceptive presentation of himself to the world, his cynicism about that world, Speed would listen. He would *care*.

"One thing you may not have thought about . . ."

As the plane lowered along the Potomac, past Georgetown University and the Key Bridge, heading for National Airport, Rafael Ames finally brought himself to speak—but only, as it seemed to Josie, in the monotone of defeat.

"Kyle won't take this lying down."

Victor T. Donovan shrugged. "I'll run that risk. Anyway, he's not much good to us anymore."

6.

The Honorable Victor T. Donovan moved quickly. Lacy Farnes set up the office and prepared the machine with which he had taken to taping his telephone calls and other conversations. Rafael Ames, his survivor's instinct working overtime, not only drummed up good press attendance for the afternoon news conference but also produced a statement that imparted exactly the desired ring of innocence and outrage.

"While I have many policy differences with Senator Bender," Victor T. Donovan thus had been able to intone across the empty expanse of his desk, to an attentive circle of reporters and cameras, "I have always had the greatest respect for his office. My intent in this campaign has been only to emphasize the differences—not to engage in personalities or vituperation—"

"Then why," interrupted Phil, from one of the wire services, "did your campaign leak this story that he shacked up with Gabriella Lukes?"

Victor T. Donovan had been around long enough to know that Phil was taking a shot in the dark. Phil didn't *know* who had leaked the story but had guessed, as everyone else had done, that it must have been Bender's opponent.

"The Donovan campaign," the congressman replied with unruffled dignity, "did no such thing." Then, gently rebuking the unruly press for the interruption, he spoke directly into the television lenses.

"If I may go on with my statement . . . I had hoped I might fight it out with Senator Bender strictly on the issues. Indeed, that is the course I have enjoined upon my staff, both here in Washington and in the state. I have not been the one to depart from that course and engage in personalities.

"It is with the greatest regret that I must inform you, however, that one low-level campaign employee failed to heed these explicit directions. He has been discharged and will have no further connection with the Donovan campaign."

"You mean," said Tom, from the other wire service, "somebody on your staff *did* leak the Bender story?"

Victor T. Donovan looked angry and thumped his desk with a clenched fist, in full view of the TV cameras.

"And as soon as I found it out, I fired him!"

"Are you saying *you* had no part in leaking that story?" *U.S. News & World Report* sounded faintly incredulous.

"I don't know how I could say it any more clearly." Victor T. Donovan looked *U.S. News* squarely in the eye. "If I had known the man's intention, I wouldn't have had that kind of person on the staff in the first place."

"Wasn't he trying to help you?" asked the Washington *Post*.

The congressman turned a manly face to the lens. "But Vic Donovan won't go down the low road. Never has, never will."

"Who is this individual?" the New York *Times* wanted to know.

"Well . . . I told you he'd been discharged. As of today. I see no need to embarrass him further."

"Well, he embarrassed Bender, didn't he?" NBC News demanded. "Why can't we interview him?"

"I suppose he did, in your words . . . ah . . . embarrass the senator—but against my precise instructions. And just as I didn't, and don't, want to get into personalities in this campaign, I don't want to hold up even this"—Victor T. Donovan hesitated, distaste plain on his countenance—"this person to the scorn and contempt he deserves."

"Does that mean," the Los Angeles *Times* promptly inquired, "that you think Senator Bender has been held up to scorn and contempt?"

"The voters of my state will have to decide that. And they're perfectly capable of doing so."

"Are you apologizing for the leak?" the Baltimore *Sun* persisted.

Victor T. Donovan looked steadily into the cameras. "It seems to me that what Vic Donovan has done in so promptly punishing a disloyal and unethical employee speaks for itself."

"An admirable example of political decency," the Chicago *Tribune* declared the next day. And in the view of the Richmond *News Leader*, "Congressman Donovan did his best to do the impossible—get American politics out of the mud."

On the MacNeil/Lehrer *NewsHour* a clutch of editorial writers from around the country concluded that Victor T. Donovan had risked his chance to win a Senate seat by coming clean about the source of the Bender leak.

"Showed guts," they agreed.

"A cynical attempt to evade his clear responsibility for this despicable smear," grumbled New York *Newsday*.

"Didn't I tell you folks out there they just flat out wan't no side to this old Donovan boy?" Country Rhodes asked his listeners. "Kicked a little butt when he found out it was his man got the goods on Bender, didn't he? Myself, I like a man'll kick a little butt ever now and then. Okay . . . you're on the air from Flat Rock, Earline."

"You think up that dodge all by yourself?" inquired Darwin John. He had phoned Victor T. Donovan after the evening news shows, but Rafael Ames came on the line instead.

"Uh, well . . . not entirely." Ames sounded properly modest.

"Risky," said Darwin John. "A long shot. In this business, though, you always play it safe, you might's well go home to Peoria, practice some law."

"You got *that* right, Mister John."

"Tell Vic he's coming on strong," said Darwin John. "Tell 'im I got an eye on 'im."

Art Mingo was an early caller, the next day, at the offices of the Bedrock *Crusher*. "What I hear," he said to J. Carson Ritch, "folks I talk to think it was mighty white of Vic to stand up like a man and do what he did."

"Yeah, but the fact still is, Bender got caught with his pants down."

"Begins to look like we got us a campaign," Mingo said. "Wouldn't you say so, Mister Ritch?"

Josie Donovan, at breakfast across from Victor T. Donovan, put the Washington *Post* aside and said: "What happens to Kyle now?"

The congressman shrugged but did not look up from his section of the *Post*. "Ames has a big check all written out for him. More than Kyle's ever been worth."

Josie sipped coffee, thinking: *I never* dreamed *how hard he could be*.

"I'm not going out there anymore, Vic."

"Out where?" He still did not look up from the *Post*.

"To campaign."

He glanced up then, almost casually. "Ames said you were kind of fed up with the coffee business. We'll have to find something more interesting. Maybe . . ."

"No," Josie said. "I'm not going out there at all."

Victor T. Donovan carefully folded the *Post* and placed it beside his plate of dry toast and sugar-free jam.

"Don't you think that would look odd? Back in the state, I mean."

"I don't give a shit how it looks," Josie said.

She had decided on the spot that she would make no more campaign appearances for Victor T. Donovan—just as, after the miscarriage, she had moved into her own bedroom and kept him out of it.

"You'll find some way to explain it, Vic. The way you explained the Bender smear."

"Leak. Josie . . . I *told* you . . . we made it worth Kyle's time. More than worth it."

"He did the dirty work and took the fall, and you paid him off. Is that what you mean by worth his time?" She could hear, and did nothing to conceal, the contempt in her voice.

"Kyle's kind"—Victor T. Donovan picked up the *Post* again—"can always be paid off."

"But not me," Josie said. "I'm through, Vic."

She tried to make her stare as hard and cold as his and thought she had succeeded when his eyes wavered. He snapped open the *Post*, looking annoyed—but perhaps resigned, too.

"If that's how you feel, Josie, you'll do what you want anyway. I suppose"—his momentary resignation, if that was what it had been, gave way to sarcasm—"I can manage without you. I've been doing it for years."

Later that morning Lacy Farnes came quietly into her boss's office, careful not to interrupt him during one of his many telephone calls. He looked at her across his bare, gleaming desk with what she thought was a rueful smile.

"I just wanted to tell you . . ." Lacy folded her arms under breasts more prominent than she usually allowed, lifting them beautifully. "It's a privilege I never thought I'd have, to work for a man like you."

"Why, Lacy." Victor T. Donovan relaxed in his high-backed chair, his handsome face turning a bit red. "I don't deserve anything like that. But how nice of you to say it anyway."

"To risk everything like everybody says you did. To do the right thing, I mean. When I know how much going to the Senate means to you."

"Well, one thing it means . . . when the campaign's over, maybe I can take you out to dinner again sometime." She did not miss his quick glance at her upthrust breasts. "If you've got any time left over from Milo Speed."

"Oh, no," Lacy said. "I mean . . . I just see Mister Speed now and then, that's all. Nothing special. I've got lots of time, sir . . . I really do."

Across Capitol Hill, Senator O. Mack Bender at that moment was saying to Bucky Overholt: "That mealymouthed four-flusher Donovan. Let's shoot a few rockets up *his* ass."

Calvin Kyle's identity quickly became known since Victor T. Donovan had instructed Rafael Ames to provide it to selected reporters on a not-for-attribution basis. In his furnished apartment in Southeast Washington, therefore, on the day following the congressman's news conference, Kyle finally had to take his telephone off the hook.

To the four callers from the press who reached him before he did, he allowed himself only "no comment." Calvin Kyle had learned from Mr. Hoover always to be a good soldier. But to Rafael Ames, he listened a minute or two before saying: "Fuck your big check. Fuck you, too."

Then Calvin Kyle hung up. By 10:00 A.M. TV cameras were stationed in front of his building. An hour later he slipped out the back way—an unobtrusive, rather anonymous-looking man in a Panama hat and a pipe rack suit. That afternoon he resumed certain inquiries he had begun earlier, at Rafael Ames's instruction.

Milo Speed, who had spurned Ames's invitation to attend the afternoon news conference, was annoyed primarily that it had produced even more publicity for Lee Lestark. And he did not believe for a moment that Victor T. Donovan had known nothing of the Bender leak.

But publicly firing the leaker, Speed had to admit, as he read the story the next day, was an interesting ploy. Mack Bender was going to need Bucky Overholt on his side because the unspeakable Ames—give the devil his due—was delivering some innovative moves for Victor T. Donovan. And Vic himself had shown once again that he was not, after all, the featherweight Speed once had thought him.

Should've listened to Josie.

But he hadn't believed her when she'd tried to tell him he was wrong. He'd hardly even listened to her insistence, on that dark and drizzly spring afternoon that had turned out to be a fit occasion for their last meeting. He had come back, a few weeks earlier, from a solid month of travel in various states where primaries were being held. In the weeks since his return, he had been able to arrange only one or two meetings with Josie. He was desperate to see her, even in a public place.

Speed tried to concentrate on his newspaper to deflect the chill memory of that long-ago afternoon, but as so often before, he could not. It was as if, he thought, the record of that day had been branded on his forehead: *F* for "Finis."

"Vic . . . he kind of . . . needs me," Josie had said, after a stiff vodka she had seemed to need more than usual. "But you . . . a team of wild horses couldn't keep *you* from getting where you're going."

Which had been true, he remembered. *But merely true.* And not enough of a reason, then or now.

"What the hell does that mean?" Speed had demanded. "Since when does that featherweight come between you and me?"

Outside the obscure Georgetown café where they had met in the late afternoon, dark forms huddled under umbrellas and spread newspapers hastened past the window, in which hung a single flickering neon sign: *Good Eats and Booze*. The sign was still in the same window, but Speed never let himself look at it.

"That's not so." Josie had put her hand on his, causing him to flinch as if burned; he had never known her hands to be cold. "Vic's a lot of things, but not a featherweight."

"Don't change the subject, Josie. The subject's you and me, not Vic."

"You and me," Josie said. "That's nice, Speed, the nicest thing I've ever known. But it's mostly sex."

Speed stared at her, not believing, not *willing* to believe what he was hearing.

"And I want more than sex out of life."

"The hell you do," Speed said. "Not when you're in bed with me, you don't."

Josie's eyes—blue-black that day—seemed to glaze over. He had seen those eyes roll up in the lunatic transports of love, and he knew what she was feeling—*oh, I knew all right*—because he was feeling it, too. He had picked up her hand and formed it into a tight, hot fist around his extended forefinger. He said:

"You want it right now, don't you?"

Josie closed her telltale eyes. Someone peered in the window behind her and moved on. Glasses rattled at the bar. Her burning hand clasped and unclasped Speed's finger.

"So do I," he said.

"All right then. Neither of us is dead. But I want *more* than sex."

He was infuriated that she could dismiss what they had had as less than anything else she might want.

"Maybe there isn't any more. For anybody."

"Even *you* can't believe that." Josie had let go of his finger then; it felt limp from her clutch. "And anyway, I'm not going where you're going, Speed." She hesitated, and he hunched his shoulders against what he could no longer doubt was coming. "I'm sticking with Vic."

★

The first spot for Senator O. Mack Bender—Bucky Overholt's takeoff on *Sixty Minutes*—appeared on the state network the next weekend. It followed Bender's formal announcement that he would seek a third term in the U.S. Senate.

"Because," the senator had proclaimed in a canned speech Overholt had provided to all the local news shows, "I've got our state here"—he tapped his head—"and more important"—he tapped his heart—"I've got our state *here*."

Rafael Ames and Floyd Finch were watching in a room at the Lewis & Clark.

"Mushy," Ames announced at the end. He had flown out to see what Bucky Overholt, whom he envied and admired, might be up to.

Floyd Finch opened another bottle of Carta Blanca. "Mush goes down easy."

Later that same evening, however, Overholt aired one of his specialty numbers, a parody of one of those late-evening TV ads for recorded collections of old hit tunes, in which the names of the songs roll up over the screen while a well-known singer belts out a few of the lyrics.

"Tricky Vic's greatest hits!" cried the breathless voice of a huckster. "Cheap at the price—just for your vote!"

Song names began to crawl across the screen:

Two-Face Blues
Tricky Vicky Voo
My Sticky Fingers

"You can't afford to pass up this once-in-a-lifetime bargain!" the huckster shrieked. "Tricky Vic's whole song and dance . . . all those never-to-be-forgotten sour notes!"

On rolled the song titles:

How Many Times Can a Man Change His Mind?
Baby, He's Cold Inside
Down on the Old Low Road
Vic the Knife

"Just for a vote!" the huckster screamed. "Tricky Vic will dance on your grave!"

And the titles crawled on:

Just a Flip-Flop-Floppin' Man
Payoff Saturday Night
You Made Me Con You (I really love to do it)

"Available for a limited time only! Election day special!" The huckster's voice abruptly calmed down: "After that, folks . . . Tricky Vic Donovan's song and dance comes to an abrupt end."

"Now that ticks me off," Victor T. Donovan later complained to Rafael Ames, after Ames had shipped a cassette of Overholt's spots to Washington. "That line in there about the low road, I mean."

At the time, after the huckster and the song titles had disappeared into an ad for incontinent women's underwear, Floyd Finch swallowed a large mouthful of Carta Blanca and observed: "Bender won't think it's so funny, he reads the latest polls."

"Get your head out of your ass, Floyd." A slight tone of admiration—for Overholt—underlay the irritation—at Finch—in Ames's voice. "They get voters laughing at the Honorable, the joke'll be on us. The Gummer's getting a move on."

Finch nodded wisely. "Didn't I tell you not to sell 'im short?"

Ames had time reserved to fire back almost immediately. By the next evening, just before a Bill Cosby rerun on local stations, he aired a spot that began with thick smoke billowing and swirling across the tube.

"Ever seen a smoke screen?" Victor T. Donovan—appearing in an upper corner inset—inquired in a conversational voice.

FARM PRICES DOWN came out of the smoke in bold letters.

"This one's not thick enough to hide Mack Bender's failure to bring farmers a decent income."

NATIONAL DEFENSE CUT.

"Or to cover up his votes to weaken our nation."

FEDERAL DEFICIT UP.

"And there's not enough smoke in the universe to hide . . ."

BIG SPENDER BENDER!

The corner inset expanded to fill the screen with Victor T. Donovan's smiling face, over billowing smoke in the background.

"But some people just keep blowin' smoke, don't they?"

As the end of summer brought congressional recess, both candidates left Washington to roam in shirt sleeves through the sugar beet fields, past the Air Force bases and the rolling pastures, along the endless highways and into the sunbaked towns and cities of their contested state.

Just after Labor Day a poll published by the *Ledger* showed O. Mack Bender running well ahead. Art Mingo knew, however, that the polltaker—at Theo Keller's direction—had been careful to ask his questions mostly in precincts known to favor the senator. Mingo's private observation was that Victor T. Donovan was moving up.

Through the early fall both candidates—as Bryce Powers, the *Ledger*'s political columnist, put it—"stepped on the gas." In sweltering heat they roamed the state by bus, sometimes by helicopter, with throngs of local and visiting reporters at their heels; at any crossroads or small-town traffic light, wherever as many as two voters might be found to listen, they spoke confidently through hand-held amplifiers.

"Waste of goddam time," Rafael Ames complained. "The Honorable ought to be cutting spots instead of scratching a few votes out where the buffalo roam."

Ames was particularly annoyed that Victor T. Donovan

warmed up his listeners with the same country and western band that had played before his speech in Pioneer Park.

"Those assholes can't even play 'Welfare Cadillac,' " Ames lamented.

Since the musicians could pick out a reasonable facsimile of Willie Nelson's "On the Road Again," that became the Donovan campaign song. Senator Bender had planned to feature a troupe of dancing beauties clad in imitation of the Dallas Cowgirls but dropped the scheme after being blindsided by Gabby Lukes.

He switched then to an all-male jazz band clad in spangled suits and derby hats. Bender insisted they open all his appearances with a rollicking version of "Happy Days Are Here Again," though Bucky Overholt objected that the song brought bad vibes.

"Reminds 'em of the New Deal," Overholt grumbled. "Plowing under the pigs."

Each campaigner repeatedly challenged the other to debate; each ritually refused on obscure procedural grounds. Their real reasons, Theo Keller theorized in a telephone conversation with Milo Speed, were that Bender had no intention of allowing Victor T. Donovan to appear on the same platform as an equal, while the congressman realized that "face-to-face Mack wouldn't let him get away with all this hit-and-run bullshit."

The debate question appeared to Art Mingo to favor neither candidate; "a wash," he told Ames. But Mingo did see an edge for Bender on a matter of considerably more interest—the contrasting roles of the two campaign wives.

Mrs. Bender was a popular and effective campaigner who liked to wear an apron and hand out recipes for best uses of the state's farm produce. Mingo considered her motherly presence a helpful response to "the Gabby Lukes affair" (as all state papers except the *Ledger* referred to it; the *Ledger* called it "the Lukes smear").

"A wife that looks like Martha Washington," Mingo observed. "If she can live with a dish like Gabby, why should anybody else give a damn?"

Victor T. Donovan, on the other hand, frequently had to

explain why Josie, after her summer foray into the state's living rooms and breakfast nooks, had made no further appearances in what was, after all, her home state, too. Her absence quickly became a sensation, though her earlier presence had not been widely noticed.

"Whole state's wondering why she's not out here," Mingo conceded, and Ames raged in private: "That cunt's costing us votes." Floyd Finch loyally insisted to Bryce Powers that Miz Donovan surely would be on hand "when the campaign peaks."

The candidate himself offered numerous excuses for her; they ranged from vague health references to vaguer remarks about "volunteer work" and finally boiled down to the jovial admission—grudgingly crafted by Rafael Ames—that "my wife cares more about her charitable work in Washington than my political chances out here."

★

Milo Speed was mildly gratified when the national press—attracted by Mack Bender's fame and alerted by his late-starting campaign—took a post-Labor Day interest in an election Speed had written about weeks earlier. Even network television offered occasional reports to a suddenly, if only faintly, interested nation, and Senator Bender and his challenger were invited to visit a local network affiliate to appear, on consecutive days, on *Good Morning America*.

After interviewing both, Charles Gibson told his viewers the Bender-Donovan contest was "a bloodletting." Not to be outdone, Bryant Gumbel then brought Bucky Overholt to the *Today* show.

"Tricky Vic," Overholt told Gumbel and the nation, "is a throwback to Joe McCarthy."

It may have been this view, as well as national television exposure for Victor T. Donovan, that roused the New York *Times* to inform its editorial page readers that Mack Bender should be returned to the Senate "for the good of the nation and the world." The Philadelphia *Inquirer* called him "a national resource." These Bender endorsements reduced Bender's lead by several percentage points, Raymond Goodwood estimated to Art Mingo.

"Anything we hate out here," Goodwood insisted, "it's the goddam pinko eastern press telling folks what's good for us. When it was us, not them, that knew Castro was a Communist from day one."

As election day ceased to be far in the future and the state's voters became more attentive, even a poll Theo Keller permitted to appear in the *Ledger* reflected a gain for Victor T. Donovan. An important reason was what Bryce Powers had identified in his *Ledger* column as Senator Bender's "handshake gap."

Mack Bender, Powers had discovered, had offended a lot of his constituents by appearing to them more interested in foreign and national matters than in the problems of his home state. The voters generally were impressed by his celebrity and respected a local boy who had made good in the outside world, but too many stories circulated about his neglect of mail from the people who had elected him, his failure to attend hallowed local events, his greater attention to affairs in London and Bonn than to those in his own state.

"He comes out here and leans on the fence," Art Mingo said when Milo Speed phoned to talk about the campaign. "Asks some cowboy, 'How you feel about those Cubans in Angola?' The cowboy couldn't tell Angola from Arizona on a four-color map. 'I'd nuke 'em,' he says, but what he really wants is higher wholesale prices on beef."

Obstinately, and to Bucky Overholt's ire, Bender widened the handshake gap with a few campaign speeches about issues he thought the voters *should* be interested in—such as nuclear arms control and Palestine—even when opinion polls and focus groups showed they weren't.

"Trouble with the Gummer," Ames remarked, after the senator had addressed himself on statewide television to pressing problems in Southeast Asia, "all those Bangladeshis he wants to feed don't vote over here."

The press, local and national, ever ready to repeat a catchy phrase, quickly picked up the "handshake gap." This caused a certain reconsideration among voters who had not previously thought much about their accustomed support for O. Mack Bender. Reporters—often primed by Mingo or Floyd Finch—repeatedly quoted "political observers" to the effect that Victor T. Donovan provided the plausible alternative the state's voters had not had in Bender's earlier races.

Several of Ames's commercials played shrewdly to local pride and propagated the suddenly fashionable idea that Mack Bender had become a world figure who—as Country Rhodes put it—had "got beyond his raisin'."

"America is being overrun by beef imports!" an Ames spot proclaimed, over a spectacular Hollywood version of stampeding longhorn cattle. The scene shifted to Victor T. Donovan in his big white hat, rather nervously eyeing a vicious-looking bull.

"Vic Donovan stands up for American beef!" the sound track asserted.

The bull shot was replaced by a still of the challenger, youthful-looking in an Air Force uniform.

"Vic Donovan stands up for America!"

Hands were seen dropping ballots into the box, quickly followed by an American flag and a state flag, proudly waving side by side.

"Vic Donovan stands up for this state! Isn't it time this state stood up for Vic Donovan!"

"Not my kind of campaign," Bucky Overholt grumbled to Ernest Fulton, the "issues man" for O. Mack Bender. "Not even my kind of state."

"Why not?"

"No ghettos. No minorities to hate."

Ernest Fulton thought this over and replied: "Plenty of Indians, though."

Bucky Overholt made a face. "Native Americans? Even Hollywood's scared to shoot the bastards anymore."

Overholt nevertheless aired a number of what Ames called "real kick-assers." His spot headlined "The Great Debates" caused tongues to wag when it appeared on the set hanging over the lobby bar at the Lewis & Clark.

Still pictures appeared, side by side, of Lincoln and Douglas. Then Kennedy and Nixon. They gave way to Reagan and Carter frozen at their podiums. Next came identical pictures, again side by side, of Victor T. Donovan.

"The greatest debate of all," the sound track announced. "Tricky Vic versus Tricky Vic. Talking one way, voting the other. On toxic waste. Nicaragua. The MX. Acid rain."

A Vic Donovan bumper sticker flashed on the screen, over the twinned pictures. It flipped upside down. Then it flipped upright again.

"Tricky Vic." The bumper sticker turned over again, righted itself once more. "More flip-flops than the eye can see." The bumper sticker began to whirl, too rapidly to read.

Then the screen divided itself again. On one side was a photo of O. Mack Bender. The other half was blank.

"You'll always know," the senator said, "where *I* stand. With the other guy"—he gestured at the empty half of the screen—"you'd have to fill in the blank."

"Now that is just the most outrageous lie," Victor T. Donovan said, upon viewing this. "I never in my life voted for acid rain."

"Bucky could figure you did," Ames replied, "since you never actually voted *against* it. I already checked."

Theo Keller had excised a reference, in another Bryce Powers column, to the state as a "stepping-stone for Senator Bender's presidential ambitions." But with much whispered help from the Donovan campaign, this suspicion also became barroom and barbershop currency. In a jealous state many voters already peeved at the handshake gap were further irritated to think that Mack Bender might represent them in the Senate only two more years before "he grabs for the brass ring" (as a widely seen Ames spot suggested he would).

"A State or a Stepladder?" bumper stickers (paid for by Darwin John) appeared, the query flanked by crossed state flags. With timing nicely calculated by Art Mingo, the Honorable Victor T. Donovan—in his positive television manner—pledged fulsomely to serve a full six-year term and demanded equal honesty from his opponent.

In vain, the senator issued numerous statements repeating that he had "no plans to seek higher office and no plans to make plans." These hedges only fed suspicion. Exasperated, Bender, in response to a question shouted at him as he worked a mall in Elk Ridge, huffed the widely reported retort: "The office seeks the man!"

That inspired Ames to a spot in which pictures of Washington, Lincoln, Eisenhower, and Reagan followed one another across the screen, accompanied by strains of "Hail to the Chief." O. Mack Bender's face abruptly appeared, looking startled.

"The office seeks *him*?" a voice inquired in tones of incredulity.

"Our great state is not just another whistle-stop on the road to the White House," Victor T. Donovan took to saying in every speech. "That may be what my opponent thinks, since before this campaign he spent so little time out here. But he'll have another think coming after election day!"

Victor T. Donovan's campaign, however, was based less on such "issues," whether real or created, than on making the home screen the campaign battleground. As originally recognized by Rafael Ames, the congressman's natural reserve and calculated modesty, together with his statesmanlike physical appearance, resulted in a persuasive presence on the tube. That presence was in sharp contrast with the television image of O. Mack Bender.

On the screen—as Rafael Ames also had foreseen—the senator's outgoing and gregarious manner produced a "busy" image, too hot for a cool medium. His volatility and quick emotions became distracting, sometimes seeming blustery; he had also an unfortunate propensity to sweat under studio lights, great drops gleaming on his broad forehead as he repeatedly wiped his brow and under his nose.

Ames had Floyd Finch spread the rumor that before his every TV appearance Bender used a makeup man with a spray can of refrigerant to freeze his upper lip and stave off perspiration.

"You really expect anybody to believe that?" Finch asked.

"I could care less," Ames said. "If they laugh at the story, they laugh at the Gummer."

Victor T. Donovan's early splurge of television spots, moreover, had "defined" Mack Bender effectively—and adversely, true to Ames's intention. Numerous voters had known the senator mostly through the usual self-serving senatorial press releases and his weekly television "reports" to the state (on which the sweating had first been discerned by eagle-eyed Rafael Ames). Laudatory articles about Bender had appeared, too, in the eastern press.

"Those puff jobs may've made the guy look like Henry Kissinger," Mingo said. "But how many votes would Doctor K get out here in the boonies?"

Ames's spots therefore found an audience which, for the first time, was getting a searching look at Bender's "negatives"—forcefully presented, though many were as obscure as his vote on the D.C. bus driver bill. The press, meanwhile, seldom let a day pass without some reminder of the senator's supposed liaison with "blond and shapely" Gabriella Lukes, sometimes called "sultry" and occasionally "notorious." In Washington, the *Ledger* reported in a piece that hinted darkly at her motives, her lobbying business had picked up nicely.

"That Lukes yarn was the key that opened the lock," Mingo told Floyd Finch. "Nobody ever lost an election overestimating the moral hypocrisy of the American voter."

As October and somewhat cooler weather arrived, the nearly unanimous view of the omnipresent political observers was that a monumental upset had become possible. It was, Milo Speed thought as he watched from Washington, an old, familiar story: a well-known senator had failed to take a little-known (but suddenly formidable) opponent seriously, had paid insufficient attention to his constituents, and had only belatedly got his own campaign rolling.

"But once aroused," *Newsweek* reported, in a piece that labeled the senator still a narrow favorite, "Mack Bender has shown himself no slouch at catch-up football."

Time observed, however, that "at the heart of the strategy that may propel little-known Vic Donovan into the world's most exclusive club is what political soothsayers have long known: that in America, all politics is local."

"Bullshit," Rafael Ames retorted when he read this. At the *real* heart of the winning strategy, he had no doubt, were the TV spots that had highlighted Bender's "negs" and "defined" him for the voters as a man far different from the one they had thought they knew.

Ames had taken a sort of visceral pleasure in his television contest with Bucky Overholt. Even before the Honorable had asserted unwelcome dominance by firing Calvin Kyle, Ames had found his real stimulation in creating his spots; more than ever, as the campaign and his rivalry with Overholt developed, he wanted not just to win but to win in such a way as to make himself known as the new and most formidable star of the consultant community.

Ames got perhaps his most electric charge from a spot that began with a jowly man smoking a long cigar at a cluttered desk in what looked like a sleazy office.

"If this straight-arrow Donovan character gets elected," the man confided to the camera, around the cigar cocked in his mouth, "he'll crack down on our stuff. No more skin flicks. No more peep shows. No girlie mags."

He looked around furtively, as if to make sure no one was listening, and leaned closer to the camera.

"If Donovan wins, he'll try to clean things up. No way *he'll* play ball. We're better off with the guy we got."

He sat back and took the cigar out of his jowls, looking even more worried.

"Yep . . . if Vic Donovan wins, the good old days are finished. And *so are we*."

He put the cigar in his mouth, his elbows on the desk, and his head in his hands. The camera pulled back slightly to reveal a nameplate on the desk: "SMUT, INC."

"That sneaky goddam line about better off with the guy we got," Theo Keller called Milo Speed to complain. "Makes it look like Mack helps out these porno kingpins."

Speed decided wearily to change the subject; he had long since concluded that Rafael Ames had *no* scruples, and Victor T. Donovan little—if any—more.

"How's it looking overall, Theo?"

A heavy sigh whispered along the cable that spanned most

of a continent. "Mack can pull it out, I think. But it'll be tight as Dick's hatband."

"That's how I read it from here. I'm told Darwin John thinks he's maybe got a new star on his hands."

"I never would have believed," Theo said, "that an airhead like Vic Donovan could spend a lot of money on TV and tell the voters a pack of lies and they'd choose him over a man of real principle like Mack Bender."

Out of respect for Theo's loyalties, Speed did not point out that Bender's principles seemed in the crucial final weeks less essential to his campaign than Bucky Overholt.

"Theo," he only said, "if you still think Vic Donovan's an airhead, you haven't been paying close attention."

★

As the World Series came to an end—that traditional October moment when political campaigns are supposed to take the central place in public attention—the Honorable Victor T. Donovan returned briefly to Washington. He had been summoned—or invited, as he told himself—to have lunch in Darwin John's private dining room.

On arrival at National Airport the congressman briefly considered calling Josie. But when she was being so bitchy about the campaign, he thought, why should he even be polite? If she wouldn't act like a wife, he certainly didn't have to act like a husband. When no press was watching anyway.

As Darwin John's car took him across the Fourteenth Street Bridge, Victor T. Donovan reminded himself bitterly that Josie had not *really* acted like a wife for years. Off there in her own bedroom, guarding it like a diamond. From him, at least.

On impulse, he picked up Darwin John's mobile phone and called his office. He was disappointed that one of the other girls answered.

"Be in for a few minutes after lunch," he told her, thinking of Lacy Farnes's red hair and green eyes. Boobs bigger than Josie's.

Lacy had seemed to think he was worth a little attention even before he became a candidate. So when he went to the

Senate side, there was certainly going to be a cushy job over there for a certain little cupcake. See how Milo Speed liked *that*.

"Here's the latest," said Darwin John, over lamb chops and *nouvelle cuisine*. He took a folded sheet from his pocket and tossed it across the table.

Victor T. Donovan studied the poll with care. He was gratified, though not much surprised, at the numbers he saw. But he was careful to maintain an air of deference and humility.

"Looks pretty good, Chief." He refolded the paper and put it beside his plate.

"Goddam right it does. Six months ago somebody told me I'd have a candidate only three points down to Mack Bender in October, I'd have had his head shrunk."

"Still . . ." Victor T. Donovan thought it best to appear cautious, calm, controlled. "There *are* three weeks to go."

"And we're within the margin of error," said Darwin John. "That's straight goods, too. Not like those bullshit polls in the newspapers out there."

He refilled their wineglasses with Grgich Hills cabernet and lifted his in tribute. "Vic, I got to hand it to you. I never really was sure you could do it. Or anybody else, for that matter. I was about to give Bender a free ride when you came into the frame."

Victor T. Donovan felt himself rewarded, though no more than fairly, for the long years through which he had waited patiently, confidently, for his chance. He felt himself vindicated, confirmed in his certainty that his time would come, sooner or later, if he stayed ready to seize the moment. He smiled modestly and lifted his glass in return.

"I had plenty of help, Chief."

"Ames," said Darwin John. "That boy's showed me a thing or two, and I never thought anybody in this business could do that."

With practiced ease, Victor T. Donovan kept his distaste from showing on his face.

"I wasn't thinking *just* of Ames, Chief. I mean, without *you* and all you've done, even with Ames's good work, I couldn't have pulled it off." The congressman could not quite help emphasizing the "I." He had almost said "even I." So he hastened to add: "Not that we *have* pulled it off yet, with three weeks to go."

"You will," said Darwin John. "Less Bender catches you in the men's room with a page boy."

Victor T. Donovan was jolted. "There's nothing like that for him to find."

Darwin John waved a hand in dismissal. "I didn't say there was. I just meant you're coming on so strong Bender's down the tube unless he pulls something out of his hat."

"Well, there's nothing he can pull."

Nothing at all.

Victor T. Donovan ruefully recalled his one evening with Lacy Farnes, when she had managed to give him the idea, without ever being less than ladylike, that she could be had. But he'd been too careful to respond, much less to *do* anything. He'd always been careful. Paid his dues in full. But maybe when he could relax a little with a six-year term in front of him . . .

"One thing bothers me a little," said Darwin John.

Here it comes.

Victor T. Donovan was not surprised. After a lifetime of subordination to party and public and his secret aspiration, he had not for a moment believed that he had been summoned to Darwin John's presence merely to discuss the latest poll numbers or to exchange compliments.

"I wish maybe the last week out there you could show the voters that good-looking wife of yours."

So it was Josie—Josie sulking over the Gabby Lukes business. As if she were some kind of saint herself. Holding herself back, just like she held back what she had between her legs. Hurting his chances. He'd maybe be ahead by now, even in the *Ledger*'s phony polls, if Josie had only done what any real wife ought to do.

"Well"—he shook his head doubtfully—"I don't think she'll be able to get away from all this charity work of hers."

"Fuck her charity work," said Darwin John. "I don't bullshit you, Vic, you don't bullshit me. What's wrong with that bitch?"

Victor T. Donovan wondered if, for appearance's sake, he ought to make a show of resenting this description of his wife. But Darwin John, he knew, could not have intended a mere insult, and the Chief never used words he didn't mean to use. Therefore, it actually had been something of a compliment, one politician to another, dealing on equal terms, that he had been willing to speak so frankly about Josie's behavior. Which Darwin John certainly had every right to resent. After all, he was putting up the money.

"My wife doesn't exactly, ah, enjoy campaigning, Chief. The kind of campaigning we've had to do out there, I mean. So she's being . . . a little contrary."

Darwin John sipped Grgich Hills. "She doesn't like the low road. That what you're saying?"

"Oh, we're not exactly on the low road. I'd say . . ."

"She better *learn* to like it," said Darwin John, "she wants to play in this league."

Which was exactly the trouble, in Victor T. Donovan's opinion. Josie, having gone one time around that league, wanted no more of it. And he knew her well enough to be sure—*all the years I've spent with the bitch*—that she had no intention of learning to like it. Josie went her own way, and damn the torpedoes.

"Well . . ." He had no trouble sounding reluctant. "I'll talk to her again."

He savored, he realized, having thought of Josie as a bitch. Having let Darwin John call her a bitch. She *was* a bitch. With her track record, to get hot and bothered over the way he'd handled the Lukes thing . . . what else could you call her?

"Talk some sense into her," said Darwin John, "and while you're at it, you can tell her a little something from yours truly."

He rang a silver bell by his plate, and Victor T. Donovan saw with well-concealed irritation that he was going to be kept in suspense about what he could tell Josie from Darwin John. A black waiter in a white jacket came in, poured coffee, and took their plates. A consummate actor enjoying his moment, Darwin John waited until the door closed again.

"Tell—it's Josie, isn't it?—tell Josie I think you're going to win out there. Tell her I see great things ahead for you."

Victor T. Donovan kept his face calm, though a surge of electrical excitement seemed to stiffen his body. *Great things ahead.* But he was too astute to spoil the Chief's moment.

"A giant killer. With six safe years in the Senate," said Darwin John. "Pick one or two good issues over there to be an expert on. Make a few speeches we got top people to write for you." He spread his arms and beamed across the table, his bald head glistening above its gray fringe of hair. "Who knows what might come next?"

Victor T. Donovan knew. In recent days he had had the same vision but had hardly dared entertain it.

"I haven't thought that far ahead," he lied. "With three weeks still to go."

Darwin John waved away the three weeks. "But, Vic, you know and I know . . . a man can't, ah, reach his potential in politics if he's got a wife that—that holds 'im back. Know what I'm saying?"

Victor T. Donovan did know. He nodded, slowly and judiciously, but his mind was racing and his blood pounding.

God damn Josie.

She could spoil everything, he thought. *If I let her.*

"But Josie'll see the possibilities," said Darwin John. "Smart girl like her, that married above herself. She'll want to help you, she sees the possibilities."

The Chief winked broadly and lowered his voice to a conspiratorial whisper.

"Josie gives you any guff, buy her a silk nightgown. Stroke her ass a little. That brings 'em all around."

★

Milo Speed was working away at his typewriter, with Evangeline banging dishes around in the kitchen, when the phone rang. He was expecting a call from Arlington Stangler, the chairman of a subcommittee intricately involved in what the Senate grandly termed "oversight" of the CIA. Its oversight, in Speed's view, was less supervision than a blind eye, but Stangler was an honest leaker, whose information was usually straight and who demanded in return only that his name be spelled right.

"One goddamn *R*," he insisted.

But Senator Arlington Stangler was not on the line.

"Hey, man," a high-pitched voice said, "this Robbie."

For a moment Speed could not place the name or the voice.

"Robbie who?" Even as he spoke, with a stab of guilt, he remembered.

"You gettin' mighty uppity, seem like."

Speed tried to recover. "I didn't know you were out of the slam yet."

"Shit, man," Robbie said. "Fuckin' respectable these days."

When Speed had last seen Robbie Beechum, he had been leading a sit-in at the Lincoln Memorial, at the height of a long-ago summer tourist season. His ragged followers had prevented droves of white sightseers—the Man, as Robbie Beechum called them en masse—from catching more than a glimpse of the Emancipator's great brooding stone face.

"Robbie's like, y'know, a biiig mutha," one of the earnest Vassar or Sarah Lawrence or Barnard girls tagging along with the sit-inners had told Speed. "A reeel baaad dude."

At the time Speed had been able to decipher street talk well enough to know that "reeel baaad" meant "good." Having made his way into the midst of a not entirely friendly demonstration, he spoke diplomatically to the Smithie, or whatever she was, though he knew what Robbie Beechum thought of these wide-eyed, high-breasted groupies, in their tie-dyed T-shirts and blue jean cutoffs. Robbie called them "white chicks" and availed himself of their eager services interchangeably.

Like most of the sit-inners, Robbie Beechum had worn overalls and sported a red bandanna around a sinewy neck; his bristly Afro enclosed his skull as roundly as a bowling ball. Periodically that day, as Speed took notes, Robbie had leaped onto a rickety box to lead his disciples in a chorus of "We Shall Overcome" or to exhort them to fear no evil—especially the Park Police encircling the Lincoln Memorial like a blue picket fence.

"Nowadays that kinda shit don't get it, man," Robbie

Beechum explained to Speed, to whom Robbie's unexpected call seemed not unlike a dunning note from an old and forgotten creditor.

"So what've you been doing with yourself all these years?" As far as Speed knew, Robbie Beechum had dropped completely out of the news.

"Mindin' my own business, man. Gettin' smart, gettin' rich, gettin' pussy."

"Nothing new in that, except getting rich."

"Man," Robbie said, "money you can't even count in the promotion bidness. Y'know? I ain't bashful 'bout makin' it neither."

To Speed's astonishment, Robbie Beechum invited him to lunch, any place he wanted to go—"but maybe some Frenchy joint?" To his greater astonishment, when they met at the Sans Souci, no trace of the Lincoln Memorial sit-in could be discerned in an emphatic jacket, gleaming chains, exuberant hair. Entering the restaurant with flamboyant and very black Robbie, Speed wavered between embarrassment and defiance of the stares of more sedate patrons.

Jean-Marie, the maître d', looked askance at Robbie Beechum, radical leader turned rap and gospel music promoter and recording entrepreneur; Jean-Marie was used to seeing Milo Speed only with the buttoned-down Washington establishment. He led the two men hurriedly to a cramped table near the kitchen door.

"Want to wait 'alf an hour," he murmured discouragingly, "something better open up."

But Speed considered it beneath him to quibble about tables, and Robbie confided over onion soup that he was used to Siberian seating in white restaurants. He had, he said, enough money to salve the wounds—" 'cept, I was you, I'd bust that French fucker in the snout."

They were almost finished with steaks au poivre when Jean-Marie returned, looking apologetic, to announce a phone call for Speed. He knew Speed disliked being disturbed at lunch.

"But ee insist."

Though he usually shrank from being conspicuous, Speed

took a certain satisfaction, as he strode toward the telephone on the reception desk, in turning heads and curious faces, in the whispers he sensed behind him like the sibilant exhaust of an expensive automobile. Sophisticated Washington onlookers, he knew, Robbie or no Robbie, were imagining the well-known columnist on his way to take a call from the President, or the secretary of defense, or maybe the Speaker of the House.

"Hello?"

He tried to sound gruff and irritated, expecting the voice on the other end of the line to be that of an editor demanding to know what he planned to write about next or complaining about some obscure error in what he'd written last or perhaps some political apparatchik who would try to peddle him a self-serving story. Speed was quite sure, however, that the President was not calling, whatever the luncheon crowd might think. This knowledge converted his satisfaction into his more accustomed sense of fraudulence—of being less than he was assumed to be.

"The senator will be right with you, Mister Speed," cooed the phone in his ear.

So Arlington Stangler had tracked him down. Speed waited, looking across the room at Robbie Beechum in his vivid threads and gold chains, the hair that sprang wildly from his head like a dark, hanging fern.

"That you, Speed?"

Speed knew at once that the voice was not that of Arlington Stangler.

"It is, and I'm wondering what's so damn important you had to interrupt a good lunch?"

What, he wondered, was Mack Bender doing in Washington, instead of out West locking horns with Victor T. Donovan?

"Did I do that? I just told the girl to see if she could find you."

"She did, in the middle of dessert."

Eyeing, across the room, Robbie Beechum in his striking attire, Speed was ashamed to feel a new wave of embarrassment.

"Sorry. Listen, can you come up right away, meet me at that little office I keep in the Capitol?"

"Busy afternoon," Speed said. "Can it keep till tomorrow?"

"You can't make it, I'll come to you. Where'll you be?"

Speed was amazed. In all his years in Washington he had never heard a senator offer to leave his natural habitat on Capitol Hill. Maybe a congressman. And no doubt senators volunteered to visit the White House. But a journalist?

"Must be a hot story, Senator."

Bender spoke carefully. "You could say that. Your apartment okay?"

"Could be bugged."

Speed was wary of people he dealt with professionally coming familiarly to where he lived and worked. Such people were better kept at arm's length or formally entertained in restaurants. But Bender's urgency was apparent.

"I'll come up there. Give me thirty minutes, considering traffic. And it better be good."

"Well . . ." Bender hesitated. "Important. I wouldn't say *good*."

When Speed got back to their table, Robbie Beechum had consumed his dessert and most of a brandy.

"Breaking story," Speed explained. "Sorry to eat and run, Robbie. Let's split the check."

Robbie Beechum waved him away. "I ain't on food stamps, man. You ever on the Coast"—he fished a red and yellow business card out of a pocket of his neon jacket—"give us a call."

Speed took the card, feeling the engraving with his fingers, lifted a hand in farewell, and started to turn away. It was like taking leave of a woman he had once thought beautiful.

"Hey, man," Robbie Beechum said. "That time at the Lincoln? Pigs broke up the show?"

Speed suddenly paid no attention to stares from adjoining tables; he was no longer embarrassed by the jacket, the chains, the glistening gusher of hair.

"They broke your head, too. You were a biiig mutha, Robbie."

He remembered the white chick maybe from Wellesley but stopped himself from adding "back then."

"Good old days," Robbie Beechum said. "See you round, man."

★

Mack Bender was alone in the hideaway office. He pointed Speed to one of the grizzly bear chairs, took a bottle of scotch from a desk drawer, and held it up.

"Vodka for me, Senator."

Bender took another bottle from the desk, set out two plastic glasses side by side, and poured a drink in each. He handed the vodka to Speed, sat down in another of the grizzlies, and peered over his scotch.

"Looks like you're still in trouble out there," Speed said.

Bender downed scotch. "Deep shit is more like it. You were right, Speed. I started too late. Took it too lightly."

"But now you've got Overholt."

"If I didn't," Bender said, "my ass would be in a sling."

Which, Speed thought, was a judgment on the age of television. Bender no doubt had paid too much attention to Mikhail Gorbachev and not enough to Raymond Goodwood. The handshake gap was real. But before the tube had taken the place of the kissed baby, the grasped hand, and the poster on the tree, the likes of Rafael Ames could not so easily have exploited Bender's local inattention.

"The only reason I'm here in Washington even one day, less than two weeks before election, is that goddam Kyle."

Nor would a reasonably diligent and public-minded senator have had to rely on the likes of Bucky Overholt to keep his ass out of a sling. Television had made American politics more fraudulent than a magic show; now, when the pretty lady was sawed in half, the rubes never saw her put together again, smiling and bowing, hand in hand with the trickster. Instead, they took the trickster's work for gospel, and the only defense against him was a trickster of your own.

"Who?" Speed said.

"The fall guy Vic Donovan set up on the Gabby Lukes garbage. Some old G-man type."

Speed had not recalled Calvin Kyle's name, but he did remember the man Victor T. Donovan had fired so publicly.

"Kyle's knocking on my door now."

"I told you Gabby was lying," Speed said.

Bender sipped the last of his scotch. "Not about that. Since he got fired, Kyle's got a real hard-on for Tricky Vic."

"Good." Speed noted, not for the first time, that in the emotions of battle politicians usually came to believe their own charges, no matter how wild—even their slogans and derisive nicknames. "If he can prove his boss knew about that story and approved the leak, then you can blow Vic out of the water for the sanctimonious bastard he is."

"Not about that either. Kyle says he only dealt with Rafe Ames on the Lukes story. He's got something else this time."

Speed's newspaper-trained brain immediately connected whatever Kyle had with Bender's urgent call to the Sans Souci.

"And you want me to do a Lee Lestark for you? Not a chance, Senator."

Bender went to his desk, refilled his glass with scotch, and held up the vodka bottle to Speed, who shook his head. Bender sat down again.

"Don't be so prickly, Speed. I may not even use Kyle's stuff."

"Why not, if it's any good?"

Bender drank more scotch, this time like a man bracing himself to his task.

"It's about Donovan's wife."

Speed's first reaction was anger, which he struggled to keep off his face; it rapidly turned to grief. Josie might have slammed the door on Ames at the Lewis & Clark, but that hardly meant she only stayed home knitting. He'd heard she wasn't campaigning with Vic anymore; he guessed bitterly that Kyle had found out why she was staying in Washington, whom she was seeing on the sly.

"Josie?" he managed to say. "I never heard any, ah, gossip about her."

Whoever's getting in there, he thought jealously, *I'd like to throttle the lucky bastard.*

"No wonder," Bender said. "You'd have been the last person anybody would have told Kyle's story to."

The truth dawned on Speed, not slowly but as if the sun had leaped above the horizon. After all these years of silence and concealment, denial even, after all the misery . . .

"Don't you think so?"

Speed recovered rapidly from surprise and began to think procedurally. A long-experienced interviewer himself, he saw at once that Bender was not so much making an accusation as angling for a confirmation, which perhaps meant that Bender was not sure of what he had. What Kyle had.

"I don't know what you're talking about, Senator." Speed drank vodka, trying not to look desperate.

Bender stared at him in the quiet room. High heels rapped down the stone corridor outside and faded into the distance.

"You want me to tell you?"

So he did know. And Kyle knew.

In Speed's rapidly developing thought the full consequences were becoming clear. He cared little that he might be suddenly the subject of public prurience; his existing reputation as a womanizer, however exaggerated, had accustomed him to a measure of that. Sometimes he even enjoyed it.

Having so little regard for Victor T. Donovan, Speed cared even less about the congressman's political fate—though if this Kyle, hence Bender, had the real goods, they could certainly ruin the congressman's upstart campaign. Bender's supposed fling with Gabby Lukes was one thing, but no candidate could survive *his wife*'s infidelity, his own cuckoldry. Not in macho America. Not in God's country.

The ingrained instincts of Milo Speed, the reporter, were violated, however, by the possibility that he might become, even involuntarily, a factor in a political campaign. And it was revolting that his time with Josie—looking back on it, Speed knew it had been his time of true happiness, the only time in his life when he could feel he was *somebody*, a man worth a woman's love—it was nauseating to think of concupiscent snickers from people who had no right even to *know*, much less to lift hypocritical voices in criticism of, what they had no standing to judge.

But most of all, Speed was infuriated to imagine what such people would say and think of Josie.

My Josie. Then and forever.

"I won't go into detail," Bender said. "Let me just say that Kyle has got you cold." He went to the desk and picked up a blue folder. "Four pages of testimony. Five eyewitnesses. Times and places. Looks like you were careful, but a lady that looks like this particular lady looks . . . I guess you couldn't be careful enough to be invisible."

Speed wondered briefly from whom the unknown Kyle had gotten the necessary tip. He did not doubt that a determined investigator, who knew what he was looking for, could have turned up five witnesses to long-ago happenings, even supposedly private events. The bartender or the waiter at the Georgetown café, for instance. Or both. Maybe the clerk at some now-forgotten motel had seen a newspaper picture of Victor T. Donovan's wife and remembered her, even years later. Men remembered Josie.

"If you're so sure of what you've got"—Speed chose his words carefully—"why'd you say you might not use it?"

Bender looked disgusted. "You won't play Lee Lestark. What makes you think I'd play Donovan?"

"*I'm* not running for office, Senator. And you said yourself, you're in deep shit out there."

Bender nodded. "I hired Overholt in self-defense and because I couldn't just lie down and take what they're dishing out. But do you really think Mack Bender would stoop to *anything* to win?"

Speed heard the words sadly. "Somebody running for office," he said, "might convince himself he didn't really *stoop*. Just did what he had to do not to let a bad guy win. So a *good* guy would get elected."

Bender nodded slowly. "I've seen that. I suppose it might happen to me."

Speed held out his glass for more vodka. Bender took it and went to the desk.

"Hand me that folder while you're there, Senator."

Bender gave him the refilled glass and the folder. "I don't plan to use that story, Speed. I've kept it from Overholt." He looked earnest, convincing. "I just don't want to get reelected that badly. That *way*."

Kyle's folder lay heavily in Speed's hands. But he realized that he did not want to look at it after all. Even the neatly typed label jolted him: "Activities, Mrs. Victor T. Donovan."

He did not want Josie described that way or to think of anything they'd done together as "activities." That sounded like archery and beadwork in summer camp. But he said:

"Can I keep this?"

Bender hesitated. He looked at the folder, looked up at the ceiling, down at his scotch.

He doesn't want to win that way now, Speed thought. *He doesn't think he'll* have *to win that way. Yet. But of course, even Mack Bender won't give away the evidence.*

Just in case . . .

"It wouldn't do you any good to keep the stuff," Bender finally said. "Kyle must have another copy."

Speed dropped the folder on the floor, without having examined or even opened it. Professionally, he had suffered for years the terrible sense that someday he would be found out. At such a moment, as when the Sans Souci crowd had believed he must be talking to the President while *he* knew the President could not be bothered, that even a well-known columnist did not have the intimate connections they assumed, at such moments, the fraud and deceit upon which his professional life sometimes seemed to have been built sagged under him like a rotten foundation. He felt termites of doubt and fear boring toward his inner truth.

"If he didn't keep a copy," Bender said, "he's still got his notes, his witnesses."

But now, with so much of his *personal* life about to be exposed, Speed knew no doubt, no fear—only outrage and disgust. He felt befouled, as if he had stumbled into a compost pit, by spying witnesses who had recorded the most valued, intimate moments of his life. Josie would feel the same sense of desecration—or she would, he thought gloomily, if she had ever felt as he had about their time together. On the evidence of recent years, she at least would hate being publicly linked to him.

"Thanks for letting me know, Senator."

As he said it, he realized that Mack Bender also had put him in debt—a situation Speed had tried always to avoid. Someday any due bill, the common currency of politics, might be called.

Bender looked at the folder on the floor as if reluctant to be associated with it. "What'll you do about Kyle?"

Speed rose with difficulty from the grizzly chair and put his glass on Bender's desk. "Nothing I can do."

With either *of you,* he thought as he went out into the echoing Capitol corridor. But as he walked despondently toward the Senate side, he suddenly realized that he would have to warn Josie.

Immediately he felt better for the idea; he would have to see her alone to do it.

★

On the third ring Josie put down *Mansfield Park* and picked up the phone. She was reluctant to answer any call, fearing that Vic might be on the line imploring her to return to the campaign. *Or* forcing *me,* she thought, in newfound recognition of his long-hidden hardness.

"I need to talk to you, Josie. Right away."

She was only momentarily surprised to hear Milo Speed's voice. Josie missed Victor T. Donovan not at all and frequently wondered how she could have been so blind to his true qualities for so long. But she was not a woman accustomed to being alone or without a man's attentions, however uninspired—as, in her experience, most men's were.

Speed had made it quite plain that *he* still paid attention to her, at least wanted to, though their last encounter at the Lewis & Clark could not have encouraged him. Since her return from Capital City Josie had had the instinct that he would call, and she was gratified by the sound of his voice. But she only said, cautiously:

"Is that a good idea?"

"I'm not trying to play games," Speed said. "It's important or I wouldn't call."

Josie actually had been busy with volunteer work among

the street children of Washington's less savory areas, many of whom led lives akin to those of wild animals. Dealing with these waste materials of urban society exhausted, exasperated, and exhilarated her. It quelled unpleasant memories and reflections, but it left her too often depressed and too seldom relieved of the loneliness that had long haunted her—interrupted only momentarily by brief and misleading euphoria at Vic's sudden prospects.

"I guess I know how you feel about me these days, Josie. I've still got to talk to you."

Josie suspected she knew *what* Speed was mostly interested in, as he always had been; that didn't so much offend her as put her on her guard against some new wound. Besides, with Vic so much in the news, she could never be sure whether the TV bastards were staked out somewhere on her block.

"Then not here," she said.

She heard what seemed plainly to be a sigh of relief.

"You name it, I'll be there."

With hardly a thought, Josie answered as she might have years earlier: "What about that little place in Georgetown? You know, where . . ."

"Not there either."

She understood at once that he did not want to return to the place where she had rejected him, though she herself thought of the little café rather romantically, as the place where they'd last seen each other.

"I could pick you up, Josie. Drive to Virginia, maybe talk in the car."

She remembered the lights of the cars going by on the George Washington Parkway as they clung together in the back seat with the broken spring, another time when in broad daylight, somewhere among the ghosts of the Manassas battlefield, they had made love on the grass, taking turns on top of each other, in the hot and elemental sun of July.

Josie shuddered a little, not in revulsion, and said defiantly: "You *could* say what you've got to say right now."

"Josie . . . I told you I'm not playing games." Speed sounded infinitely patient—and, she thought, infinitely sad. There always had been something sad about Speed. "It'd be better if I could meet you somewhere."

"All right."

She had made up her mind what to do, and it was as if she had broken some intangible barrier; as it fell, she knew she *wanted* to see Speed, no matter what he might really have on his mind. She was tired of being alone, of Jane Austen's upstairs intrigues, even of the feral children who needed so much help.

She said, almost gaily: "I'll be walking in Montrose Park in an hour. Near the tennis court. Put on your walking shoes and meet me by accident."

That was the kind of tryst, she thought, that Speed always had loved.

★

Speed had no walking shoes. "I'll be the one in the black loafers," he said, and hung up.

He floated out of the downtown phone booth, all but forgetting his basically unpleasant mission. He cared only that he was about to see Josie again, that they would meet as they so often had before—apparently by accident, innocently to any onlooker. That could not be happenstance, he told himself; Josie could not have been unaware of what she was suggesting.

"Quarter for some food," a shambling derelict mumbled, thrusting a paper cup at him.

Speed dropped a dollar in the cup and stepped into the street for a taxi, quelling the thought that his money probably would go into a bottle of Thunderbird.

Got to change my shirt.

That seemed only appropriate to the moment. Even after he had reached home and put on a fresh button-down, retrieved his car from its basement garage, and started for Montrose Park, elation filled and lifted him, like the gas that wafts away fear of the dentist's drill.

In that airy mood, as Speed drove past one of the more elaborate foreign embassies, he was easily reminded of another "accidental" meeting with Josie, years before. Embassy guests were leaving after dinner, violins were bouncing out "Good Night, Ladies," and Speed had made a show of politely inquiring, loudly enough for the ambassador's faintly mustachioed wife to hear, if he might drive Mrs. Donovan home. Since she was unaccompanied. Since it was raining. Since taxis were so hard to get.

A half hour later he'd said, rather nervously: "What if Vic comes in?"

"He won't."

Josie was undressing slowly. She knew he liked her to give him the full effect of her beautiful body slowly emerging from its clothing.

"He's back in the district, making some speeches for that old fart of a congressman of his. Nothing's more important to Vic than that."

Speed was stretched out in Victor T. Donovan's bed, in Victor T. Donovan's undistinguished apartment on P Street in Georgetown. He clutched connubial Donovan sheets to his chest.

"He might finish early. Catch a red-eye flight."

Josie rolled a stocking halfway down her calf and pulled it gracefully from her leg. "He's got a breakfast speech. If you're going to be nervous about Vic, you'll give yourself problems."

Under the sheets Speed tested the state of his manhood.

"I'm not *nervous*. It's just sort of funny being *here*."

"Here isn't really any different, Speed. From anywhere."

He watched her hungrily, as she took off the other stocking, let it fall filmily to the floor by the first, and stretched a newly bare leg straight out for approval—whether his or hers, the familiar, feminine movement always left him unsure.

"What about the Girl Next Door?" Josie said. "Won't she expect you home?"

"Knocking out a bout of flu with booze and pills, lucky for us. That's why she didn't go to the dinner."

"She drinks too much, Speed. Not that I wouldn't, too, in her place."

"If you were married to me, you mean?"

Instead of answering, Josie rose and with a small, graceful roll of her hips and an inward lift of one leg, then the other stepped out of something pink that seemed to him no larger than a handkerchief.

Watching her movements, Speed overlooked her edged remark. He thought instead of the only time he had been to the Uffizi; he had stayed so long to look at "Venus Rising from the Sea," impatient with the crowds of gawkers who interrupted his view, that Nancy had had to pull him out of the Botticelli room.

Josie stood above the bed, arms behind her back to unhook the bra he had persuaded her always to remove last, her vivid blue eyes shining in the amber light from a shaded bedside lamp. Speed watched in wonderment as she let one perfect breast slip magically free.

I'm in heaven. I'm going to be in heaven.

Josie pulled her shoulders slightly forward, stretched her arms, and let the bra slip along them until it, too, drifted to the floor. Speed had never seen anything, anyone so beautiful. Not even the Venus in the Botticelli Room, rising from the sea. Something like hurt welled in his chest; amazed, he felt tears salty in his eyes.

Josie sat on the edge of the bed and touched his cheek. "I thought men weren't supposed to cry."

Her eyes were shadowed, a darker blue than usual. Josie's eyes changed with the light.

"If something's beautiful enough, they can."

"I only cry when I'm sad."

Speed buried his face in her hair, muffling his whisper: "There's not much difference."

The truth of this idea, new to him, was like a dull blow to hopes he had scarcely known he had. He moved his hands and pulled her down until her long, hot body lay close against his.

A car honked fiercely. Speed had slowed almost to a halt, staring at the embassy in the hard grip of memory; he had not been in it since that evening. Or ever could be again, he thought.

The car honked again and sped past, a Jaguar or something foreign, the gloved young man at the wheel casting a look of disdain at Speed in his sedate sedan.

"Goddam yuppie," Speed muttered, into the Jaguar's unmuffled roar.

But it was not the honking horn or the young man's glare that had broken his mood. He stepped down on the accelerator, thinking of Josie, of the pitiless unmaskings of the years, the harsh boundaries of his existence without her, the false consolation of his work that meant so little.

★

Autumn leaves lay red and yellow on the grass. Lovers nuzzled on a bench. An old man fussed among the shrubs, carrying a stick with a metal point on which he impaled stray bits of paper and stuffed them into a sack hanging around his waist. From the tennis court behind her, near the R Street entrance to Montrose Park, Josie could hear the thunk of strings on ball, the occasional shouts of the players. She turned off the path a few steps and sat on a boulder under an oak from which nearly all the leaves had fallen. Pale sunlight dropped through its dark branches.

Josie had dressed carefully, in jeans and a long, enfolding black sweater, before making the short walk from her house to the park. She wanted to appear to be taking only a casual stroll, and she particularly did not wish to give Milo Speed the idea that meeting him was an occasion for special dress or attention.

"Because it isn't," she told the mirror in the hall, while taking a last look at herself. "I'm just going because he insisted."

Still, she had admitted to herself that she *was* rather looking forward to seeing Speed alone. She could not help wondering, after all, about that very insistence, the urgency she'd heard in his voice. She could not help wondering, either, how she would feel to see him again—not with Vic, or in a public place like the Rayburn Building or the lobby bar at the Lewis & Clark, but privately, in the quiet and shadowed park.

It would not, of course, be like meeting him in the old days.

Nothing could ever be like that again—the reckless desire, the hot, frantic rush to possess and be possessed, the imbecile eagerness with which they all but tore each other's clothes off, and sometimes did. When some things were over, like the flaring passions of youth, they were *really* over.

She discovered, nevertheless, that she was filled with curiosity, long suppressed. What had Milo Speed been doing all these years? *Really* doing, besides becoming famous? What would time and notoriety have done *to* him?

Oh, she'd seen him often enough, as the years passed; she'd watched the great professional success she'd always known he would have, observed with no surprise the departure of the Girl Next Door, and followed many of his other doings through Washington's knowing gossip. All that, however, was no more than she might have done in the case of anyone she'd known well—say, an old college classmate.

But through it all—Josie had conceded to herself as she strolled into the park past the tennis court—another level of wonder, of interest, had lain repressed under the conventional surface of her life with the Honorable Victor T. Donovan: the congressional receptions, the embassy dinners, the endless fund-raising parties for colleagues and for Vic himself, the boring visits back to his sedate and unchanging district, the required entertainment of constituents and contributors—particularly contributors, buyers of time and privilege.

"If one more fat cowboy with a thousand dollars to burn tries to feel me up under the table," she had fumed to Victor T. Donovan after one of these obligatory evenings, "I'm going to stick a fork right through his hand."

Vic, of course, had not believed a rich and respected cattleman could have been so raunchy.

"He's a Baptist deacon, Josie. A grandfather. You must be imagining things."

"I haven't got to be my age," Josie insisted, "without being able to tell when some asshole's got his hand up my skirt."

Through such evenings, through all the excruciating years, Josie now realized—though she had not admitted or perhaps known it—she never had ceased to watch Milo Speed with possessive eyes, with an unconscious jealousy not so much of what and who he was, or what he did or didn't do, as of what he had meant at a certain time in her life, a time and a meaning she feared she never would know again, perhaps feared, more terribly, that Speed *would* find again, with some other woman.

Remembering, Josie even understood, as she perched on the boulder in the wan sunlight, why she had briefly, foolishly thought that time might be lived again with Rafael Ames. She had fantasized another headlong, heedless flight out of the safe confines of the expected into the terrors and transports of passion.

She laughed out loud—uncomfortably at the thought of how nearly she had made a fool of herself, disdainfully as she recalled Ames's dismayed face imagining what uncontrollable fate might await him in her room at the Lewis & Clark.

Ames and Victor T. Donovan deserved each other. Men did, people did, who found politics *or anything* more vital than love. As for Speed and herself, as they once had been, love and being in love had been the only realities—life itself.

And I miss that, Josie thought. *God, how I miss it—the wanting, the caring, the madness*—the life.

Especially, she could at last admit to herself—she sat up, not even glancing around—and defiantly said it aloud: "Especially the fucking."

Which was what it had been—nothing held back, nothing pretended, nothing so genteel as "making love" or so clinical as "intercourse" or so biblical as "knowing." Oh, how they'd loved it! Loved each other, what they gave and what they took. Anywhere, anytime, any few moments alone, any bed, any patch of grass, once on the staircase in Speed's house, with the Girl Next Door out shopping.

That broken spring sticking me on one side and Speed on the other.

Lounging back on the cool boulder, her face upturned to the tree-filtered light, Josie wondered if she actually had been still in love with Speed during those years when she had forced herself hardly to think of him—consciously, at least—when at times, as on the day of Vic's clash with J. Conrad Cramer, she had thought she might hate the cynic Speed seemed to have become? Or had she only been in love with what they'd had, and been, together?

Memory, wonder drove her thoughts relentlessly. Just as she'd known for a long time—except for the brief, misguided excitement when Darwin John had tapped Vic for the Senate race—that she had been mistaken to stay with Victor T. Donovan, might she not also have come to know, somewhere in her unadmitted depths, at some bleak point, that she had been equally misguided to leave Milo Speed?

She saw him come into the park just then, walking along the path beside the tennis court. She would have known it was Speed, even if she had not been expecting him, even if he had been twice as far away. She would have known his stride, the set of his shoulders, the alert carriage of his head.

Dammit, she thought. *Damn* him.

Speed's undiminished familiarity angered her unexpectedly. She was irrationally furious to find herself so aware of him, so much still in linkage to him.

As she watched him coming along the path, passing the tennis court, the nuzzling lovers, her hostility rose. Why had he forced this meeting? Why did he have to rake up the past when it was over and done? Why had she consented? What good could it do? Better to limp on through the years than to be constantly reminded of a real life, impossible to regain. She wanted to snap her ties to him, as if they were made of string.

"This better be good," Josie called, fiercely, as soon as she thought he could hear. "You interrupted a terrific book I was reading when you called."

He walked across the grass toward the boulder; a starling ranted at them from the tree.

"I wouldn't say good, Josie."

She hardly heard, for watching his eyes. No other man had ever looked at her as Speed had, as he looked at her then—as if she were beautiful, not just sexy or smart or well dressed or socially important. Speed's eyes made Josie *feel* beautiful, in a way she had all but forgotten. Her anger faded, as illogically as it had come, and she was startled to hear herself asking what she learned only from the words that she most wanted to know:

"Did you really fuck all those women they say you did?"

"Not all," Speed said. "Not many."

"I thought not."

Hoped not. It didn't occur to Josie to question his word.

"Sex used to mean too much to you."

"*You* meant too much to me."

Josie leaned back on the boulder, both elbows against it. She was not trying to be suggestive; she was hardly conscious of her body, which was swathed anyway in the voluminous black sweater. She could not remember when she had felt so relieved, unburdened, at ease.

He could ask me, she thought, *with as much right*. From some compelling sense of fairness, she did not wait for him to do so.

"I tried it a few times myself," she said. "But it always seemed too much like trying."

She detected Speed's effort to look impassive; he often had tried to conceal his feelings, though never at times when they really mattered. She had seldom been deceived then, and she was not now. A glint of what she was sure was gladness flashed in his eyes and disappeared.

"If that's out of the way," Speed said, "I've got . . . kind of bad news."

To Josie, it did not much matter. She had not expected, from his urgency and insistence, that he would bring good news. But now that she had seen him, now that she *knew* what she realized she had agonized over for years, whatever else he had to say seemed oddly insignificant.

"Bender knows about you and me," Speed said. "Everything."

Her first reaction was: *Not everything. Not how it really was.*

"He's got witnesses, statements. He says he's got it cold."

Then she realized what he'd said. *Bender* knew. Vic's opponent, the man Vic had smeared, who would surely try to repay him in kind.

"Then it'll come out," she said.

"Not from Bender. Not yet anyway. Maybe not at all."

"Why not? It would blow Vic away, wouldn't it?"

"Probably. But . . . you know, I think *maybe* Bender's got a shred of decency left in him. Even after everything."

"Unlike Vic."

Speed seemed to choose his words. "If you say so."

Josie sat up, as the full meaning of Speed's news began to hit her. The TV people would be all over the block, day and night, ghouls feasting on her privacy. She would be spread out in the headlines like a naked whore, like Gabby Lukes. The press would rake up the most precious part of her life—she conceded, without real surprise, that that was what it had been—and turn it into smirks and sneers.

"Vic used the Lukes story," she said. "Vic would do anything to win that lousy campaign. Anything." He had violated others' private lives. Now he would pay for that, and she along with him.

"There won't be much he *can* do if Bender or somebody puts out this story about you and me." He told her about Kyle, the investigator, and the report Kyle had given to Bender.

"Calvin Kyle," Josie said. "The way Vic treated that man, no wonder he's hitting back."

"So if it does come out, it'll probably be from Kyle, not Bender. Kyle must have kept a copy of that report. And I doubt he's got even a *shred* of decency."

"It'll come out." Josie had no doubt. That was the way things went. "One way or another."

She felt as if she were watching a storm approach, lightning flashing, winds swirling dust into a funnel. Speed looked at her with his kind eyes; for a moment Josie thought he was going to take her hand. She wished he would.

"What about . . . I mean . . . won't it be hard on you?"

Josie knew a period of her life was coming to a close. Probably her marriage, too. Not that it had been much of a period or much of a marriage, but all endings brought change. She would be uprooted, forced out of familiar patterns. She took Speed's hand.

"Tell you the truth, Speed, now I know I'm not just one of the scalps on your belt, I don't really care a hell of a lot about anything else."

He looked down at her hand in his, turned it over, examined her palm. When he looked up at her, he was making no effort to conceal the wild joy in his eyes.

"I suppose," she said, "I'd rather not have . . . lovely things dragged in the mud. But I don't regret a single moment."

"Regret?" Speed said. "I *loved* every moment of it. I loved *you*, Josie."

She did not miss the past tense or make too much of it. There would be time to explore such things. But first . . .

"Speed, if Vic's going to be blindsided, maybe ruined, by something I did, I'll have to warn him it's coming."

Speed looked alarmed. "But you don't *know* it's coming."

"Yes, I do," Josie said. "Vic shouldn't have done what he did, even to Calvin Kyle."

Speed took her other hand. "But how do you think Vic'll take it when you tell him? I mean, not just the campaign but . . . the rest of it."

"He'll mostly care about the campaign."

Josie let her hands lie quietly in his. Their dry palms seemed to mean protection, care. *I am going to need this*, she thought, *this concern*.

"I really don't know how Vic will take it," she said. "But I'm not like him. Whatever he does, however he feels, I have to warn him."

7.

The Honorable Victor T. Donovan took the call from his Washington office in a public booth at the rear of the Buck and Doe Café in Riverbend. He had dropped in to shake hands with Buck and Doe patrons and to have a cup of coffee, sandwiching the stop between a radio conversation with Elton Adler of Station KPEP, the Voice of the Pioneer West, and a luncheon address to the Riverbend Sertoma Club at the Ramada Inn.

The call from Washington was prearranged with Mr. Horn, who found on his desk every morning a faxed copy of the campaign schedule Art Mingo had arranged for the congressman that day. But this morning the caller was not Mr. Horn.

"He's down with the flu," Lacy Farnes said. "He says he won't be out but a day or two."

Victor T. Donovan, envisioning her red hair and lush young body, was delighted to hear Lacy's voice. He took a sip of powerful coffee, a Styrofoam cup of which he had brought to the booth with him, holding it precariously in his left hand while with his right he had exchanged vigorous shakes with the check-shirted, red-necked men seated at the Buck and Doe's Formica tables.

"He said to tell you there's nothing to worry about here," Lacy said. "A package of letters you need to sign, but I'm Fed-Exing them out to the Lewis & Clark today. How's everything out there?"

"Getting better all the time. I think we've got the other guy on the run, Lacy. He's sounding a little panicky."

Through the glass front of the phone booth, he watched Mingo in animated conversation with the Buck and Doe's counterman and with a straw-hatted rancher on a neighboring stool. Mingo never missed a chance to massage a voter, and Victor T. Donovan never missed a chance to study Mingo's technique and absorb it into his own.

"People back here are talking about an upset," Lacy said. "I hear it everywhere. There was an article in the *Post*, too."

Listening with pleasure, basking in her evident admiration, Victor T. Donovan sipped his coffee. Gathering courage from its afterburn, he said daringly: "Things'd be even better if *you* were here."

In the pause that followed he feared he had gone too far. Not, of course, that he'd intended anything more than to give her a taste of campaigning, liven things up with her presence. Maybe get Speed's goat a little.

Then Lacy said, cheerfully enough: "I'd love to be out on the campaign trail. But with Mister Horn down sick, there's an awful lot to do in the office."

Victor T. Donovan thought that *that* could be managed. But before he could say so, Lacy spoke quickly and apologetically: "Oh, I'm sorry, I almost forgot. Miz Donovan called to say she's taking the plane out to see you."

He almost choked on the hot coffee. "Today?"

"She should be in the air right now. She said she'd see you tonight."

Victor T. Donovan did not know whether to feel triumphant that the bitch—he readily thought of Josie, these days, as Darwin John had described her—was at last ready to do her part or annoyed that she was coming around just when he had worked up his nerve to bring Lacy Farnes from Washington to spruce up the campaign team.

"I know"—even with most of a continent between them, he could hear the diplomatic tone in Lacy's voice—"you'll be glad to have her with you these last days. On the campaign trail."

Darwin John would be pleased anyway. Victor T. Donovan, while he supposed Josie drinking coffee and eating cookies with the local housewives might be worth a few votes, felt himself well able to do without her cold indifference, her accusing presence. He was used to the indifference, even in some ways preferred it to the *clinginess* of some wives he had observed, but the accusing presence—coming from Josie anyway—was a little much.

Besides, what he had told Lacy was what he really felt. The election was moving his way, more definitely every day. Ames's lethal barrage of TV spots had had an effect—and still did—that even Bucky Overholt's return fire could not overcome. The Lukes story had been devastating. Darwin John was optimistic. Victor T. Donovan, consequently, had little doubt that he would win, Josie or no Josie.

"I guess she can't hurt," he said.

Actually Josie worried him more for the future than for this campaign. He did not know what he would do about her after he won—just that *something* would have to be done. He wondered if Darwin John had talked her into returning to the campaign, maybe twisted her arm a little. Be just like him to protect his investment.

"Maybe she'll bring you good luck." Lacy sounded a little tentative, following his unenthusiastic remark.

Just as well, he thought, to let Lacy draw her own conclusions. For even if Josie's surprise presence had frustrated his hopes to bring Lacy out for the last days, lend a little tone to the campaign, there would be lots of possibilities later on, when he'd be in the Senate with a six-year term for cover. To get to know her better.

"Lacy, my dear," he said, "one thing Vic Donovan never depends on is luck."

★

Art Mingo was pleased to hear the news. By late afternoon he had Josie scheduled for the next three days and was at work on coffees and other appearances for the rest of the campaign.

"With Bender's wife handing out those goddam recipes," he told Floyd Finch, "we need a little kitchen help ourselves."

Finch was delighted. He had had several warm dreams about Josie Donovan, and he remembered her frank language with a sort of guilty pleasure. Finch felt confided in, a little more than befriended, rather illicitly *knowing*.

"All the candidates' wives I've been around," he told Ames, "that little honeysuckle rose has got to be *número uno*."

Ames only looked sour. *He* had had no sweet dreams of Josie Donovan and thought of her as a hot-pants broad whom he had had to turn off. He was sure he could do it again, if he had to, but the candidate's wife had a tongue on her like a double-edged Gillette, and Ames was not eager to feel more of its slash.

"What we really need," he grumbled, "is some mother-looking old babe in an apron with a basket of doughnuts."

★

After taking the call from Lacy, Victor T. Donovan flew in one of Darwin John's freebie planes to Denver, where he spent the afternoon cutting spots with Ames. They returned early, because that night at nine they were staging a statewide TV talkathon, during which the candidate would be asked a lot of softball questions, most of them planted, by callers Art Mingo had handpicked.

Victor T. Donovan looked forward to the impression he expected to make in this event, but as he disembarked in Capital City from the plane lent to the campaign by a Chicago bank, his mood was jaundiced by the forthcoming meeting with Josie. He had himself driven directly to the Lewis & Clark, where he found, as he had expected, that the bitch had registered herself in a separate room.

He took the elevator immediately, with a copy of Mingo's thrown-together schedule in his pocket. Better to let her know right away that if she'd come all the way out here thinking she could just hang around the hotel and make dog-in-the-manger remarks about the Lukes business, she could turn right around and go home. Better to let her know what Darwin John expected of Vic Donovan's wife. Not to mention what Vic Donovan himself expected.

"A pleasant surprise," he said when Josie opened the door to his knock.

She was holding a glass of vodka and wearing a loose gray sweat shirt above a straight dark blue skirt. "Falls Church Horse Show" read the slogan that crossed her barely outlined breasts; the words semicircled a jumper taking a fence. Riding was Josie's favorite exercise.

"I'll just bet you're pleased," she said. "I can see in your eyes how pleased you are."

So it was to be no holds barred. He was rather glad of it; he was tired of playing games with her. Years and years of game playing with a bitchy woman could wear down even a patient man.

"All right then. Just surprised."

She gestured at the room with her glass. "No use standing out in the hall, though."

He came in warily, almost expecting a trap to fall on his head or some other setup. He saw immediately that the vodka bottle on the coffee table was not full.

"There's club soda, too."

"Nothing for me. Did Darwin John talk you into this?"

"Into what?"

"Coming out here to help in the campaign."

Josie laughed and picked up the vodka bottle. "I don't take orders from Darwin John, Vic. And I'm not here to help."

Victor T. Donovan's hand, in his side pocket, crumpled Mingo's schedule sheet. He was momentarily baffled. He could not imagine what the bitch was doing in the Lewis & Clark if she hadn't come to help his campaign. He knew better than to think it was anything about him, anything personal, that had brought her. Not Josie.

"Mingo's got you scheduled." He took the paper from his pocket and handed it to her. "You can't let us down again."

She dropped the paper on the coffee table without looking at it.

"Mingo got ahead of himself then. I just told your office I was coming out to *see* you. I never said I was going to campaign for you."

"Josie . . . you don't give a hoot about seeing me. What're you up to?"

Josie drank vodka, sat on the sofa, and tucked her bare legs sideways beneath her. "Bender's got a story."

Victor T. Donovan felt a hard, sickening pull in his stomach; he felt as if he were plummeting, as he supposed passengers must feel when an airliner begins to plunge out of the sky. So the waiting, he thought—all those years of waiting—would come to naught.

"About me," Josie said.

He had understood *that* at her first words. Somehow, he realized, even as his campaign had seemed to take off—somehow he had *known* all along that the waiting would come to nothing. Because of Josie. That everything would come crashing down at the last minute. Because of Josie. The knowledge—as if of one of those terrible sights the shrinks said might be suppressed but never really forgotten—had been there in his head, just waiting, like the story itself, to come out.

"About you and Speed."

He tried to spit the words at her, and it pleased him to see the shock on her face. It would have pleased him more to see his finger marks vivid on her rouged whore's cheek.

"You knew about us?"

"You both thought I was a fool." His calm voice amazed him, even as he was proud of it. "But Vic Donovan was *never* a fool."

Josie put her vodka glass on the coffee table, staring at him as if she'd never seen him before. Which, he thought, she never really had. He'd been too careful.

"How long . . . when did you find out?"

"From the start. I could smell it—like something rotten, when you'd come back from fucking that stud. The sex on you."

Silence fell like a heavy frost on the room. He saw Josie actually shiver. He was glad to have shocked her, glad at last to have hit her in the face—if not with his fist, at least with the word, to show he knew her for a common slut.

Then he remembered, as if himself absorbing a blow, the true import of what she had said: *Bender knew.*

Desperately he thought: *Maybe she only* thinks *he knows.*

"What makes you think Bender's got the story?"

"He told Speed. Speed told me."

Victor T. Donovan had to restrain himself from actually hitting her. He saw with satisfaction the fear that flashed on her face at the jerk of his arm.

"So you're back in bed with your old stud? Didn't get enough the first time?"

"Think what you want." Josie was cool again, hateful, recovered from shock. "Speed warned me, and I"—she shook her head ruefully—"I thought I should warn you. I thought it would be a shock to you."

He would not give her the satisfaction of seeing that it had been—not the story itself but that it was coming out at last, as he had always feared.

"How'd Bender find out? Did Speed tell him?"

Josie poured more vodka. "To spite you? Don't be such an ass, Vic. Speed wouldn't do that to me *or* you. That man you fired dug it all up and took it to Bender."

"Kyle?" *But we paid him off.*

"Ames warned you that day on the plane. Kyle didn't take it lying down."

"But Ames *paid* him."

Josie put both elbows on the back of the sofa, thrusting out her big breasts beneath the jumping horse. Watching, Victor T. Donovan thought: *Disgusting*. The bitch was all body, all sex. Except with her own husband, of course.

"If he did," Josie said, "it must not have been enough. And if it's any comfort to you, Speed doesn't think Bender will use the story."

Victor T. Donovan saw no comfort anywhere. "The hell he won't," he said.

"Speed says"—he caught the edge of malice in Josie's voice—"*Bender* may have a shred of decency left in him." He noted the emphasis, understood, and did not care.

"He'll use it. Bender wants to win, too, don't kid yourself about that. And he probably will, after he puts out that story."

"Even if *he* doesn't," Josie said, "don't forget Kyle has it too."

"That nobody. That *nothing*." Victor T. Donovan's face screwed itself into a mask of disgust and resentment. "Kyle won't get away with this, and neither will Bender." He heard the hollow echo of his words and tried to banish it with repetition. "They *won't* get away with it!"

Josie looked as if she knew the threat was empty. He hated the way she sometimes looked as if she knew all about him when she'd never really known the first thing, never even tried to know him.

"When the story comes out . . . it'll ruin your chances, won't it?"

Which would suit the bitch just fine, he thought. He thrust his face at her savagely, furiously, and held his index fingers up beside his ears.

"These horns you and Speed stuck on me? Of *course* it'll ruin me!"

But even as he spoke, as Josie shrank slightly from his contorted face and accusing hornlike fingers, a way out came into his head.

"If I let it."

He remained for a moment with his face close to hers, his fingers beside his ears, thinking fast, instructing himself firmly: *Get hold of yourself; figure this out.*

"I wish I could say I'm sorry," Josie said.

Victor T. Donovan straightened, pulled away, paced toward the window, in control of himself again. The bitch didn't matter anymore, he thought. Let her say what she wanted. That didn't matter either.

But the story—how to handle it, get on top of it—*before* it came out. That was what mattered. That was the only way to win. Because the story *would* come out.

"But I'm not sorry, Vic. I'd do it all again."

Something clicked over in his mind, like digital clockwork going from A.M. to P.M. He saw how he could do it, how he *would* do it. Get on top of the story. Salvage the campaign. The future. But he had to think it through carefully. That was Vic Donovan's way. To be sure what he was doing.

"I'm only sorry I didn't see you sooner," Josie said, "for what you really are."

He paced back across the room, shutting out her words. They didn't matter. He looked at his watch and saw that it was after eight-thirty. He came again to the coffee table. Josie sat still on the sofa, looking up at him snottily, her insolent goddamned tits jutting like a whore's under the horse on her sweatshirt. For Speed to slobber over, Victor T. Donovan told himself venomously.

He snatched Mingo's schedule sheet from the coffee table, tore it into strips, and let them fall to the Lewis & Clark's thin carpet.

"I want you on tomorrow's plane out." He turned and strode toward the door. "I want you out of here before Bryce Powers or that stinking Keller can get hold of you. Understand?"

"Can't be too soon for me. But . . . one last thing."

He had his hand on the doorknob before he looked back.

"Make it quick."

"Are you thinking about *anything* except yourself and your campaign? Do you care the least bit how *I* might feel if Kyle spreads that story?"

Victor T. Donovan opened the door. "About as much," he said, "as you and Speed used to care about me."

He felt immense satisfaction with his answer, his dismissal. He did not bother to close the door, much less slam it, as he hurried to meet Rafael Ames for the statewide talkathon.

★

The questions were easy, the answers rehearsed, and the show went well. But as he performed, Victor T. Donovan's mind ran ahead to the next day, toward what he was thinking of doing.

Afterward Art Mingo gave him a thumbs-up sign. "Nixon

used to do that kind of show, but you're better at it than he was."

The candidate nodded curtly and went on to the car. As they returned to the Lewis & Clark, he said to Ames: "Sounds like Mingo's been listening to Bender's Tricky Vic crap."

"No, no," Ames protested. "Art just meant you're as good at the talkathon as Nixon was."

"That *better* be all he meant."

Victor T. Donovan was irritated at more than Mingo's remark. Mingo was too close to Darwin John to be told where to get off. Besides, this damnable Josie business . . .

In silence the candidate glowered out the window, angry at Mingo, hating Josie. In the few minutes of the drive to the Lewis & Clark, he decided he had no alternative. It would have to be done.

In the lobby he seized Ames's arm. "Buy you a drink."

"You must be feeling good about the talkathon," Ames said.

In the lobby bar they looked for a table where they would not be overheard. When they had seated themselves, the waitress in the doeskin outfit came to take their orders. She had even bigger ones than Josie, Victor T. Donovan decided. Another whore. But not bigger than Lacy's, what he'd been able to tell through her prissy office clothes.

"Ginger ale," he said.

Ames ordered the same, and the doeskin twisted away.

"Listen, Rafe, I thought you took care of Kyle."

Ames looked uncomfortable. He was wearing a letter sweater from Brigham Young University.

"I tried. He wouldn't take the check."

"Well, why didn't you *tell* me?"

"Ah . . . you see . . . I kept trying to get to him, talk some sense into him. I figured he'd come round."

Victor T. Donovan glared at him. "He came around, all right. All the way to Bender."

Ames did not look surprised. "I warned you Cal wouldn't take it lying down."

"But you were supposed to take care of him."

"I'm not a miracle man. I did my best."

"That wasn't good enough, Ames. Now Bender's getting ready to dump a load on *us*."

"Bucky Overholt, you mean. The Gummer wouldn't know how."

"I hardly see"—Victor T. Donovan gritted the words through his teeth—"that it makes a dime's worth of difference."

Ames was not intimidated. "What'd Kyle dig up? You used to cut school? Put turpentine up a cat's ass?"

"You won't think it's so funny when you hear—"

The doeskin came back just then with the ginger ale, leaning over much farther than necessary to put the drinks on the table.

"Those things ever fall out?" Ames asked sharply, his face darkening above the Brigham Young sweater.

"Only in front of my husband," the doeskin said. "That big guy sitting over there at the bar in the deputy sheriff's uniform."

When she went away, Victor T. Donovan said: "I don't like to be embarrassed like that, Ames. Don't do it again in front of me."

"I just hate a damn woman throwing it around like she's got something somebody wants. What's Bender unloading on you?"

"Nothing on *me*. I've seen to that."

Over his ginger ale Ames looked quizzical.

"It's about my wife."

Quickly, without visible emotion, Victor T. Donovan related that Calvin Kyle had found evidence of Josie's involvement in a past love affair and had turned the evidence over to Bender. He did not say how he had learned this, nor did he mention Milo Speed.

"Bender will use it, of course. But even if he doesn't, we have to figure that Kyle will."

Since you fell down on the job, he did not say to Ames, letting his tone of voice imply it.

"That's dynamite," Ames said. "Maybe even a nuke." Remembering Josie Baby practically inviting him into bed, he added: "Who was she banging?"

Victor T. Donovan eyed him icily. "I'm not here to discuss

my wife with you, Ames. I only want your professional opinion on what I propose to do."

"Like you wanted my opinion on firing Kyle?"

"That was a good move. It was only *your* part that backfired."

"Well, frankly"—Ames set down his glass with a sharp crack—"I don't see a hell of a lot you *can* do. Right here at the end of the campaign, this kind of a state, Bucky Overholt will blow us out of the water with stuff like that."

"Or Kyle."

"And after we came so close to pulling it off." Ames seemed suddenly to realize something else. "Goddammit," he said, surprise tinging his voice, "I guess I'll go down with you."

"Not," said Victor T. Donovan, "if I move first."

He watched Ames closely while he outlined his plan. He watched the incredulity in Ames's eyes and face change slowly to doubt, to grudging comprehension, finally to something he could not quite define. When he finished, Ames sat quietly for a while, staring at the table. Then he finished his ginger ale.

"That just might work."

"It *will* work." Victor T. Donovan no longer allowed himself to entertain doubt. "I've thought it all through."

Ames fell silent again. Then: "You'd really do a thing like *that*?"

"Vic Donovan hasn't come this far just to lie down and die, Ames." *And you can take that to the bank,* he thought. "Vic Donovan set out to *win*, and he's damn well *going* to win."

Ames shook his head slowly, sadly, pensively. "First time I watched one of those TV reports you used to send back to your district, I saw something I could work with. You got star quality on the box. Which is what started all this. But"—he sighed heavily—"even I didn't see what was *really* inside you."

Victor T. Donovan no longer remembered that it was Rafael Ames who had "started all this." He did not care for the idea. And he had no interest in what the likes of Rafael Ames might see inside him.

"Ice," Ames said.

He might as well have said iron and steel or milk and honey. Except for his state's voters and Darwin John and the few others who might help or hinder Victor T. Donovan—among whom the crass Ames need not long be numbered—Victor T. Donovan no longer cared what *anyone* thought.

"Just clear the time for me, Ames, tomorrow night. And keep your mouth shut about what I'm doing. Pull some spots if you have to."

The look on Ames's face suggested that he would rather pull his own teeth. Victor T. Donovan did not care about that either.

"Dry ice," Ames said, as if watching a master headsman at his craft.

★

Rafael Ames had booked five minutes between syndicated showings of *Wheel of Fortune* and *Perry Mason* for the next night on the state's most watched TV channel. It was a good time slot—too good, Ames thought, for most of it to be used, as planned, for a dullsville campaign bio, replete with old home movie film of Victor T. Donovan in college football regalia, a still of the candidate as a dashing jet pilot, staged scenes of him riding a horse and decked out in hunting gear with a shotgun over his shoulder, and a few obligatory frames from the famous denunciation of smut, filth, and J. Conrad Cramer.

Ames felt no regret at pulling the plug on the bio, especially since it featured a scene of the Honorable with one arm around Josie and the other waving at the voters. Awkward in the circumstances. It hurt him, however, to pull the lead-in spot—admittedly not one of his real barnburners, but still a torpedo below Bender's waterline. Ames had been eager for Bucky Overholt to see that one.

It began with stock footage of a beautiful movie actress, famed for her political activity, doing exercises in a bathing suit that went up as far as possible and down as far as possible. An overline described her as "Hanoi's Honey."

The sexy stuff segued into more sedate film of the actress, modestly clad and testifying before a congressional committee. "Americans eat too much beef," she was heard to say, before the camera swiveled to Senator O. Mack Bender, listening gravely from the committee chair.

Back to the star, full face: "Too much marbled beef on the backyard grill is a major reason American men are too fat."

A shot of Senator Bender making notes, head bent in concentration.

"Mack Bender's radical friends," a voice-over said. "They don't like red-blooded American food . . . *or* red-blooded American men." The movie star had married a long-haired Italian film director with openly leftist views.

Scenes of a cattle herd, sides of beef hanging in a warehouse, laughing men and women at a backyard cookout, thick steaks sizzling on the grill:

"Mack Bender's radical friends don't like beef."

Senator Bender again, smiling and shaking hands with the famous actress.

A final voice-over, low and insinuating: "Maybe they don't even like America."

Ames killed the VCR, by which he had been gloomily viewing his handiwork.

"I got to squeeze that one on the air somehow," he told Floyd Finch. "Too hot to keep in the can."

"What's the Honorable gonna *say*?" Finch asked. "That'd be better, I mean, than the stuff you're having to pull?"

Finch had been devastated by Josie Donovan's quick return to Washington and not just because he and Mingo had had to make some fast explanations to irate hostesses all over the state.

"She didn't even say *hello*," he lamented.

Ames had listened to Finch's bleary recitals, after the third or fourth Carta Blanca of the night, often enough to have heard all about Josie Donovan's legs. He personally thought they were nothing special but said anyway: "You're just pissed you didn't get another peep up her skirt."

"I didn't *peep*." Floyd Finch had been indignant. "I *stared*."

Now he was in a state of high curiosity, at Josie's unexpected arrival and sudden departure, not to mention Victor T. Donovan's even more sudden decision to go on the air for a speech to the voters.

"I don't *know* what he's gonna say, Floyd."

Which was true enough because Ames couldn't quite believe that even a fish-eyed gambler like the Honorable, who'd risked his whole campaign when he sank the shiv into Calvin Kyle, actually could go through with his latest butcher boy scheme.

"I could of got him some ink," Finch complained. "Worked up the ratings a little. If he'd given me some time, some idea what's up."

You don't know the half of it, Ames thought.

But he only said: "You want to find out what's up, Floyd, you got to do what I'm doing. Tune in at six fifty-five P.M."

★

"Fellow citizens of our beloved state," Victor T. Donovan began. "I beg your indulgence tonight for a personal statement."

"Shit," said Carl Fulk, a weather-stripping salesman in Crater City. He turned his set to another channel, remarking to his wife: "These political creeps make me want to puke."

But Steve Burd, an up-and-coming attorney in Black Ankle, decided to stay tuned for *Perry Mason,* from which he kept hoping he might derive some useful tricks of the trade. So he stopped his wife, Penny, from changing channels.

"Grab us a coupla beers, Pen, help us sit through this."

"I've based my campaign for the United States Senate from the start, my friends, on fostering and protecting certain values—good old American *family* values and traditions of hard work, churchgoing, children, community, and charity—"

"Charity!" snorted Slim Chance, who weighed 290 pounds bone dry and had been watching *Wheel of Fortune* with pinochle buddies on an old black-and-white set at his Exxon station in Yellowtail. "You was dying of hunger in the desert, one a them political bloodsuckers wooden give you doodly squat."

"—and I'm proud to say that no hint of scandal of any kind has ever touched the name of Victor T. Donovan—unlike, I might add, my opponent's recent misadventures in the headlines."

"That dirty old Bender, he's talking about," Penny Burd

said. "Running around with some blond bimbo young enough to be his daughter."

"All my political career I've tried to stand for the same values the people of this state stand for—values I learned right here *in* this state: the sanctity of the family, religion and morality for our young people, rugged American individualism, opportunity for everybody to get to the top—"

"This guy reely grabs me." Deputy Sheriff Blanton F. Hollis turned on his stool at the lobby bar of the Lewis & Clark and spoke seriously to his wife. "Lays it on the line, y'know?"

She pulled her sagging doeskin well up on her cleavage and lifted a tray with two Coors, a Seagram Seven and ginger, and a Kahlúa for the tourist party in the corner. Remembering Victor T. Donovan's mouthy friend from the night before, she said over her bare shoulder:

"I don't trust *any* of 'em."

"So if there's any one thing I want to do *for* this state, it's to represent you in the Senate with clean hands, to set a moral example our youth can look up to—"

Jehue Branch, star tackle for Granite Pass High, six-two, 235 pounds, 4.7 in the 40-yard dash, recruited by UCLA, Colorado, and Oregon State, among others, looked up at the TV from the couch in his girl friend Didi's living room. Her naked legs were wrapped around his naked waist.

"Only moral example"—Jehue lowered his lineman's shoulders and began pumping again—"I need . . . 'sides four-year tuition . . . is a four-door Caddy . . ."

Didi, shivering, cold, and worried sick that her parents would come home early, wished Jehue would hurry and get himself off. Doing it in his pickup was safer and better.

"—until today, my friends, I had no doubt that if you gave me your confidence and your votes on election day, I could return your trust with plenty of hard work on your behalf and that moral example I was determined to set—"

"Why's he keep running off 'is mouth?" asked Bart Goings, a driver for Yellowtail Cleaning and Pressing, as he watched with Slim Chance at the Exxon station.

"—but today, to my shock and sorrow—"

"Case of oral dyree-er," Slim said. "Ever see a goddam politician 'thout one?"

"—I learned something that made me question—not whether I can provide the service you deserve from your senator and that you've been failing so obviously to get—I learned something that made me ask myself whether I can really set that shining moral example that means more to me, and I know to you, than anything else."

Floyd Finch, already on his third Carta Blanca, stared openmouthed at the set in his room, the political wisdom of a lifetime confounded.

Downbeat. Too downbeat for the last few days . . .

"So, my friends, I've spent the afternoon wrestling with my conscience. I don't mind telling you that I got right down on my knees and sought my maker's guidance—"

"If he was on his knees," Bucky Overholt said to O. Mack Bender as they watched TV in a back room at the Robert G. Merkle Community Building in Meriwether, "he was either rolling dice or eating pussy."

"—and the overriding question I sought an answer to, my friends, was this: Could I really be the kind of senator I wanted to be . . . for *you*? Knowing what I'm sorry to say I had just learned, could I serve you and stand up for you the way you deserve? Make you proud of your senator, for a change?"

"Is he going to pull out of the race?" Penny Burd cried in alarm. "Leave us with that dirty old man?"

"Listen to 'im!" Steve made shushing gestures with his hands. "What was it he found out?"

"At first I thought: 'Now Vic Donovan can't do what he wants to do for the good people of the state he loves so much.' But then, and I do believe the good Lord reminded me, then I thought: "Vic Donovan wants to *serve*. Vic Donovan *lives* to serve.' And those two thoughts had me in a flat-out tug-of-war, folks—pulled me this way, pulled me that—"

Rafael Ames, in a Taos Valley ski parka, watched from the studio control room. He was glad he had not written such cornball shit. At the same time, turning his gaze from the studio desk at which Victor T. Donovan sat to the several monitors flickering before him, he had to admit that the Honorable, as usual, was coming through the tube like a ballistic missile.

Eye contact. Sincerity. *Believable,* like Cronkite. Even though Victor T. Donovan happened to be a world-class turd.

"—and then," said the handsome face on the screen, gazing solemnly at the unseen audience, "the answer came to me. And I don't have a doubt in the world that it came straight from the Man Upstairs."

"You know something?" Slim Chance proclaimed. "I didn't know better, I could almost believe this bozo's leveling with us."

Floyd Finch opened another Carta Blanca. Penny Burd wiped a tear from her left eye, the weak one, hoping the more cynical Steve had not seen her do it. Rafael Ames, his gaze fixed on Victor T. Donovan's sincere screen image, realized the moment had come.

He's really going to do it.

"I concluded that I *could* go to the Senate with clean hands and an honorable name—"

"The suspense," said O. Mack Bender to Bucky Overholt, "was killing me."

"—to serve you as I wanted and as you expect. But *only,* my friends, only if"—the smooth voice seemed about to crack—"I made the most painful decision of my life—"

"Get on with it!" Steve Burd cried. "Only if *what?*"

Ames, unable to sit out a ballsy political gambit, tried hard to ESP his advice to the Honorable: *Don't milk it too long.*

"I could serve you and our great state as I would wish *only* if I came before you like a man and a Christian, a right-thinking American—"

"Of which"—Deputy Sheriff Blanton F. Hollis gazed belligerently left, then right along the Lewis & Clark bar—"ain't none too many round here."

"—to tell you straight out—no excuses, no ifs, ands, or buts—that if I'm going to continue my crusade to serve you in the Senate—"

Victor T. Donovan appeared to find it necessary to stop, draw a deep breath, shake his head a little sadly, before he could go on.

"—then I find it necessary . . . I have no real choice . . . to separate from my wife, Josephine."

"I knew it!" Bart Goings shouted to the boys at the Exxon station. "Had to be a nigger in the woodpile somewhere, her back East 'stead of out here helping 'im out!"

"Skirts." Slim Chance sounded almost happy. "Ain't I always said a skirt'll shaft a man ever time?"

Victor T. Donovan, like a hiker who had crested a steep hill, began to pick up speed: "Words, I assure you, cannot express the pain and sorrow this decision has brought me. But I feel as if a great burden has been lifted from me."

"Me too," Jehue Branch said to the face on the screen, reckoning as he pulled on his Jockey shorts that it had been more than a week since the last time Didi had been willing to put out.

"Now I can again come to you with clean hands, my friends, confident that I can uphold, that I've *stood for* those family values, those moral beliefs, that you and I know are the bedrock upon which our beloved state and nation were built—"

"Josie most of been fucking around," Bucky Overholt said. "She's built for it."

O. Mack Bender did not reply. *Beat me to the punch,* he thought. *Not that I'd have used it, but still . . .*

Then he realized: *Beat Kyle to the punch, too.*

"—and tonight, my friends, having come to you as candidly as I know how—"

Penny Burd was weeping openly. She had been to one of the few kaffeeklatsches at which Josie Donovan had appeared the summer before, and as she told Steve brokenly, "I knew right away . . . something about her . . . I just *knew* she was a slut! Steve, I could *tell*!"

"—tonight I can only rely on your goodness and your understanding. I can only ask your forbearance. *Not* your forgiveness, because *I* have done nothing . . . I repeat, *nothing* . . . of which I need be ashamed. Nothing to sully my good name or that of this state."

Floyd Finch threw a Carta Blanca bottle at the TV. It missed and bounced off the wall, spraying beer on the carpet.

Finch rose and stumbled across the room. He leaned down to the screen, shook his fist at it, and ground words through clenched, yellowing teeth:

"Too good for your Honorable son of a bitching ass!"

The solemn image on the screen paid Finch no attention and went steadily on: "I ask your help . . . just as, in my sorrow and travail, I asked the help of Him who serves us all—"

"But tell us what she did!" Steve Burd was unmoved by Penny's sobs. He wanted the real lowdown.

"—and I believe with all my heart that *your* answer, my friends, will be as loving and true as His. And now . . . good night . . . and may God bless you all."

Carl Fulk was just switching back to catch *Perry Mason* as Victor T. Donovan looked up from the paper he had been reading from and gazed into the camera in soulful farewell.

"Prob'ly promising more pie in the goddam sky," Carl said to his wife.

But Senator O. Mack Bender, breaking the silence in the back room of the Merkle Building, told Bucky Overholt: "Greater love hath no man than this, that he lay down his wife for a vote."

"For a *lot* of votes," Overholt said, "you want my best guess."

At the lobby bar of the Lewis & Clark, as *Perry Mason* finally came on-screen, Deputy Sheriff Blanton F. Hollis pronounced judgment:

"Now there's a man that's *really* above politics."

★

Victor T. Donovan, his face contorted in anger, strode into the control room and threw his script in Ames's lap.

"I screwed it up. You don't have to tell me."

"I wasn't going to say that. I—"

"Just, goddammit, let's get out of here! I don't want to talk about it."

He was angry at Ames, angry at himself, but above all angry at Josie. If she hadn't cheated on him, if she hadn't been such an irrational bitch, none of this would have had to happen. He wouldn't have had to make a fool of himself, the way he just had.

"Why're you're so upset?" Ames asked.

Because, Victor T. Donovan stopped himself from shouting, that bitch beat me again!

All those years I went along quietly, knowing she'd made a fool of me once. Now she's done it again.

Josie's bitchery had forced him to go out there and plead for his life. Forced him to let the whole state know how she'd humiliated him—*him*, Vic Donovan, who'd had the Senate seat he'd coveted all his life right there in the palm of his hand, the unlimited future his for the taking—until at the last minute his whore of a wife had grabbed it all away.

One of the two cameramen who'd filmed the speech hurried into the control room. Victor T. Donovan was startled to see the man's eyes were slightly red and moist.

"I just want you to know," the cameraman said, "I been in this business a long time and I seen a lot of fast talkers come and go. But Mister Congressman, I never seen anything as—as *honest* as that in my life. I just want you to know."

Another control-room worker had risen from his knobs and dials and joined them. He seized Victor T. Donovan's hand.

"You got my vote, Mister Donovan. All this immorality going around . . . I got kids to raise, so you got my vote."

"You see?" Ames said. "You knocked the ball out of the park."

Victor T. Donovan was not persuaded. The cameraman's red eyes and the other man's fervent grip seemed genuine enough, and Ames certainly knew his television. Still, maybe there in the studio they'd been more affected than the home audience was. He still had the feeling he'd had all the time he was on the air. Like a man in a deep ditch, trying to dig his way out; the more he dug, the more the dirt walls caved in on him.

"What I liked the most," the cameraman said, "was the part about setting a moral example. This country reely needs that."

A wall phone rang impatiently, and the control-room worker answered. He listened a moment, said, "He's right here," and held out the phone to the congressman. "Says he's J. Carson Ritch of the Bedrock *Crusher*."

Victor T. Donovan seized the receiver. "Good to hear from you, Mister Ritch."

Art Mingo had been trying for weeks to swing Ritch and the *Crusher* over to the Donovan campaign; the editor pulled a lot of weight in his part of the state.

"That was a gutsy speech just now," said the voice on the line.

Victor T. Donovan reverted to its solemn tone. "It wasn't easy to make."

"I could see that." A momentary silence. "But tell the truth, I expect it made you a lot of votes in these parts."

Now that, Victor T. Donovan thought, *was worth a ton of Ames's bull bleep*. But he kept his voice carefully solemn.

"That wasn't . . . I didn't . . . really have that uppermost in mind, Mister Ritch. I just wanted . . . well, I thought . . ."

He hesitated expertly, and J. Carson Ritch took the bait.

"Sounded to me like you just wanted to get square with us folks out here."

"Right. That was exactly it. No false colors."

"I admire that," said J. Carson Ritch. "I like a man that's not afraid to come clean, and I think the voters will, too."

"All I can do is hope they understand." Cannily Victor T. Donovan added: "Maybe pray a little."

"Always helps. And so will the *Crusher* coming out for you."

Victor T. Donovan managed, during the rest of the conversation, to sound abjectly grateful. He hung up to find his anger gone, replaced by a giddy sense of elation. When he and Ames reached the reception lobby, they found Art Mingo—who'd watched on the lobby monitor—taking down names and numbers from a frantic telephone operator; the switchboard was blinking redly.

"Ten-strike," Mingo said. "Not a dry seat in the state. Folks calling in from all over to say they're with you."

Despite this message, Mingo looked to Victor T. Donovan as if he had smelled something bad. The congressman carefully noted the sour expression in his mental futures book.

"And they're . . . uh . . . calling Miz Donovan names."

Well, then Mingo could smell what he smelled. If all the phone calls meant what he said they did, *that* was what mattered; that was what would matter, most of all, to Darwin John and, therefore, sooner or later, to Art Mingo.

Ames held open the car door, deferentially enough that Victor T. Donovan, trying to control his giddiness, decided to let him stand there a moment in his silly ski parka. Let him know how things stood.

"I got to admit I had my doubts," Ames said. "But I'll bet Bender's holding his head about right now."

Victor T. Donovan took a deep breath of the cool autumn air, stretched, and looked up at the stars. *Ad astra.* He was on his way.

Something rubbed his leg, and he looked down. A stray cat, its back hunched, was shivering against his trousers. He kicked it aside and got in the car, remarking to Ames:

"Looks like even the cat vote's with me tonight."

★

Speed arrived promptly at 7:30 P.M., and Lacy met him at the door. She knew she looked adorable, in a little white apron, heart-shaped and just slightly shorter than her short skirt, with a dab or two of flour applied just so on her face, prettily flushed from the kitchen.

With a flourish, Speed handed her a bottle of Quail Ridge Merlot, and she took it with appropriate cries of delight. Speed looked amused.

"I know you well enough by now." He followed her into the apartment. "It could just as well have been a jug of Gallo."

"Well, I'm learning." Lacy put the wine on the table she'd taken nearly a half hour to set, in imitation of a picture in *Connoisseur*. "Will this red go all right with spaghetti?"

"If it has to. But I *said* I'd be happy to take you out to dinner."

"Oh, don't look so frightened, Milo. Spaghetti's the one thing I know how to do really well."

Lacy had cooked spaghetti, in fact, only twice before. But she was a quick learner and had observed that it was better to undercook the stuff than to boil it into a soggy mess.

"I'm just kidding, Lacy. I don't have all that many pretty girls offering to cook for me."

He didn't have to know the sauce came in jars at the supermarket down the block, Lacy thought. And spaghetti had been her only choice, once she'd decided it would be better to say what she had to say in privacy rather than risk a scene in some restaurant. Not that Milo Speed was likely to make a scene anywhere, much less in public. He had too much pride to make a spectacle of himself.

"The way I hear it"—from the kitchen door Lacy looked at him over her shoulder, which she knew was one of her better effects—"women flock to your place in the middle of the night with pots of caviar."

"If they did, it'd better not be cooked."

"Don't try to tell me," Lacy called back from the kitchen as the swinging door closed behind her, "it's the caviar you're *really* interested in."

She lifted the lid to see whether the pasta water had come to a boil. All the talk about Speed and women, she had decided, had to be exaggerated. It was something to tease him about, but she had reason to know he was hardly the world's greatest lover. But at least Speed was considerate—not zip-zam, thank you ma'am, like the hard-breathing males she'd mostly known.

"Vodka and ice on the shelf by the TV," she called.

Speed stuck his head in the kitchen door and held up a glass. "Did you think I couldn't find a drink for myself? Fix you one?"

"Not before wine." She made a show of stirring the bubbling sauce, and he went back into the living room.

Speed was nice. He even seemed to like talking to her; he actually listened to what she had to say in return, making him a man virtually unique in Lacy's experience. Except the congressman, of course. So, she thought, it wasn't going to be easy to talk to Speed; nevertheless, it had to be done.

Maybe I can take you out to dinner again sometime. She

knew the congressman's words by heart. *If you've got any time left over from Milo Speed.*

Lacy was pretty sure he hadn't meant just that he'd heard she had gone out with Speed. In Washington it was assumed that if a woman was going out with Milo Speed, she was having an affair with him. Lacy didn't mind most people thinking that—it sort of set her up to have grabbed off a man as well known as Speed when she was just a nobody; she had even hoped that rumors might get back to Winooski—but Lacy felt she should appear to the congressman to be above that sort of thing.

More important, his remark had suggested that if she *did* have any time left over, maybe he himself was at least a teeny-weeny bit interested. Which, of course, a man like that might not have meant to suggest, but if a woman heard only what men *meant* to say, she'd practically never hear anything but sports talk and chest thumping.

Like when she'd quoted word for word some of the suggestive things her fuckface brother used to say to her on the sly, her stupid father had just kept insisting:

"What's wrong with that? He didn't mean anything."

"But he *did*," she'd argued, until she realized it was no use. The little shitbird's actual words couldn't convey his tone of voice or the look on his smirky face—what he had *meant*.

"Anyway," her father had told her once, "you ought not to be wearing a skirt like that, up to your fanny."

Like it was her fault. So no matter what her jerk-off brother might have said, it wouldn't have mattered. He could not possibly do anything wrong, as far as her father was concerned, especially after he'd made Eagle Scout and all-state basketball, and certainly not with his own sister. Not in her father's family.

Thank God that was all in the past: the nasty little whispers—"puttin' it out for ever'body else, ain't you?"—and the nastier grins, the times she *knew* he'd been fumbling around in her underwear drawer. Thank God she'd got away to Bennington before anything worse had happened than having to run downstairs when he'd try to make her touch his weasely thing in the upstairs hall.

Speed brought a glass of wine to the kitchen. "Lady slaving over a hot stove needs a little bit of cheer."

Lacy tried too late to hide the evidence from the supermarket. He set the wine down on the small kitchen table and took the sauce bottle out of her hands, examining it with mock gravity.

"You'd asked me, I could have made a better sauce than this, my dear. But at least we won't get ptomaine."

"I spiced it up," Lacy lied. "Put lots of extra stuff in it. Now let me concentrate on the pasta."

But as she dumped spaghetti in the boiling water, she was thinking less about cooking than about the dicey problem ahead of her. She was not sure how to proceed, but she knew well enough *what* she had to do. As gently as possible, but definitely, she had to put an end to this thing with Speed.

"Did you put some oil in that water?" Speed peered over her shoulder.

She had to end it because the more she thought about it, what the congressman's chiding remark actually had said to her was that maybe she could be more than just an ordinary filing clerk or word processor; maybe she could actually *be* somebody in his office, on his staff, over in the Senate. Make a meaningful place for herself and a name even her bullheaded father would have to hear, all the way up in Vermont.

"What for?"

She did not care about the oil in the water as much as she cared about the possibilities she suddenly had seen. She knew she was observant, diligent, intelligent, and it certainly didn't hurt that men liked her looks since men called all the important shots. She was sure she could do something big if she got the chance—make her father realize somebody else in his family could be all-state, in something besides basketball at that.

"Keeps the pasta from getting so gluey." Speed took a bottle of Wesson oil from a shelf, examined it critically, and shrugged. "Guess it'll have to do." He poured some of the oil in the steaming water, and put the lid back on the pot.

Nothing underhanded or scandalous, of course—Victor T.

Donovan was too honorable to be a party to anything like that, which anyway was not at all what she had in mind. But not like that snotty Josie either. *Imagine* his own wife staying in Washington until yesterday, refusing to help him win the most important contest of his life. Actually, so Rafe Ames had told her, *hurting* the congressman politically.

"You know how long to boil the pasta?" Speed took the wooden spoon out of her hand and stirred, then tasted the sauce.

Lacy glanced at the wall clock. "Six minutes more."

She was so nearly lost in her own thoughts that she did not mind his officiousness. She hardly even noticed as he moved her gently aside from her own stove.

"Scorching on the bottom." Speed turned the heat down under the sauce.

Victor T. Donovan, in Lacy's opinion, was the finest, most conscientious, public-spirited man she'd ever known. Not a cynic like Speed or a sleaze like Ames. If it was her good fortune to work for such a man as the congressman, then surely it was her responsibility to make herself something more than just a flunky around his office. He deserved her best.

"You spiced *this* up?" Speed took the wineglass from the table. "What with? Cornstarch?" He poured the wine into the sauce and stirred.

Somebody a senator could really talk to, Lacy thought, maybe confide in, try out his ideas on. And if to get herself in that position required sending Milo Speed on his way—well, she had no real interest in a man his age anyway, and she was under no illusion that Lacy Farnes was much more to him than one more willing piece. Which was not what she intended to be to any man—certainly not the Honorable Victor T. Donovan.

★

When they had finished dinner and were having the coffee Speed had insisted on brewing himself, he said abruptly: "I can't stay over tonight."

Lacy was startled. She had been mulling the idea of maybe taking him to bed one more time. Soften him up a little before lowering the boom in the morning.

"Who asked you?" Her bantering question was a little lame, she felt, but perhaps sarcastic enough to hide her surprise.

Speed did not reply in kind. "Do you realize," he said seriously, "that I lived practically a whole lifetime before you and I ever met?"

Lacy believed a pretty woman could joke any man out of whatever mood he was in. She tried.

"I know you had a whole lot of girl friends, if you call that a lifetime."

"Maybe not as many as you think."

Speed evidently wanted to stay serious. Lacy quickly dropped her jaunty manner. "I know that, Milo. I know *you*."

"You think you do anyway."

"Well enough to know you only want people to *think* women swoon at the mere sight of you."

Speed shook his head. "As far as I'm concerned, people can think anything they want."

"As long as they don't think you're . . ." She searched for the right word.

"Cheap." He found a word for her, chuckling not quite mirthlessly.

It would do, she thought, and said: "Where we've usually ended up our evenings is a good place to get to know somebody."

"About some things. But not about why I'm going home tonight instead of staying here."

"Nobody *asked* you."

But Lacy felt a vague disquiet. Speed was serious. Maybe too serious for her to deliver the message.

"You see, Lacy, a long time ago, when you probably still were in grammar school, there was a particular woman in my life."

Lacy's disquiet turned into alarm. He sounded as if . . .

The phone rang before she could complete the thought. For once she was glad to be interrupted by the shrill jangle. The phone was on top of a bookcase against the farthest wall.

When she picked up the receiver, she heard the congressman's voice.

"Lacy?"

Instinctively she turned away from Speed, shielding her conversation with her head and body, trying not to give away the caller's identity with her words.

"This is Lacy." She had almost to bite her lip to keep from saying "sir."

"Things are really going well out here, Lacy."

"So I hear. I'm glad."

"So well"—the congressman sounded as cheerful as she had ever heard him—"I want you to get on an airplane and come join us."

I knew it, Lacy thought exultantly. *I* knew *he'd single me out some way*. But she responded carefully.

"What about . . . things in the office?" She kept her voice low, though Speed could hardly help hearing.

"I'll square it with Horn. You get on the plane tomorrow morning, and I'll have you met at the airport on this end. If there's any trouble about the reservation, call Horn and he'll fix it."

"All right, then . . . I'll be there."

If she had tipped Speed to the congressman's identity, there was nothing she could do about it. Excitement swelled in her. Little Lacy Farnes from Winooski. She could hardly wait to hit the campaign trail with the Honorable Victor T. Donovan.

"Listen, Lacy . . . you'll hear about it anyway. I'd better tell you now to make sure you get everything straight."

Behind her, Speed's chair scraped, and she took a quick look around. He was headed for the vodka bottle.

"Shall I take notes?"

"No, no, nothing like that. You see, I just got off the air out here tonight. Made this little speech."

Lacy listened incredulously. By the time he'd finished, she could hardly breathe. The politics of the thing, the possible effect on his campaign, hardly even occurred to her. She was too amazed and impressed by the congressman's determination, the standards he maintained for himself. His sacrifice.

"Lacy, I just couldn't ask people to support me with . . . something ugly hanging over my head."

She'd never dreamed things were so bad for him. Perfectly clear, of course, that Josie was not . . . well . . . exactly the kind of wife the congressman needed. But though he was careful not to say what had caused him to act, from the way he described what he'd said on the air, Lacy could draw only one conclusion. She would never have expected *that* from any woman of Josie's age—certainly not the congressman's wife. But of course, even in crisis, he'd been a gentleman—not saying a word about what his wife obviously had been up to. Or down to.

"I really didn't think I had any choice," Victor T. Donovan said. "But you can imagine how tough a thing it was to do."

Lacy remembered sparring with Rafael Ames, in this very room, about Josie Donovan. Ames had dismissed the idea, but Lacy had seen the way Josie looked at him as if she could eat him up. The hussy—flirting around right in the congressman's own office, with somebody on the congressman's own staff. Shameless.

"I couldn't even bring myself to see her off on the plane today," Victor T. Donovan said. "I just wanted her out of my sight."

"It must have torn you to *pieces*."

Lacy grieved for what the congressman must be feeling, way out there in a crummy hotel room by himself. Then it struck her that maybe it would look funny if she came out to join the campaign practically the minute he'd sent his wife packing. People were so suspicious.

"You don't think," she said, "if I come out, people would maybe . . . talk?"

"About you?"

She did not dare say, nor did she want him to think, "about us." But of course, that was what *she* was thinking.

"There's plenty of work for you to do, Lacy, believe me. Real work. Nobody'll think anything because there won't be anything for anybody to think."

Of course, there wouldn't be. Lacy was abashed even to

have brought it up when he was too straightforward for anything like that even to have occurred to him. It shouldn't have to her. She wanted, suddenly, to make amends. For something. Everything. By then, in her excitement and concern, she had forgotten that Speed was in the room.

"I'm *so* sorry you had to go through a crisis like this, and I just don't see, I really don't, how your wife could have done something like that to you when you're out there fighting for—"

"How do you know what Josie did?" The congressman's voice was not accusing but a little harder, sharper than it had been.

"I don't know *anything* except what you told me." Lacy was certain she could guess what Josie had done; what else did wives do? But in her anxiety not to trouble him further, her words came in a rush. "I just know how . . . difficult it must have been for you. Right in the middle of your campaign and all."

"No, no . . . it was a long time ago. Years ago." Victor T. Donovan paused; then his words came in a rush, as if long dammed up: "The only thing that really hurts, the other guy was Milo Speed."

★

"What the hell's going on?" Speed demanded when Lacy came back to the table. "Was that your hero? What crisis?"

Lacy sat down and took a generous drink of wine. She put the glass down and looked at him levelly, accusingly.

"You're a real shit, Milo."

Speed sat up straighter. "Guilty, I guess . . . but maybe not on whatever grounds *you* mean."

"You're not to come here anymore, damn you," Lacy said. "Don't you dare even to call me."

Speed was in no mood to be denounced by a kid, which he suddenly remembered Lacy was not much more than. In the body of a woman, he told himself apologetically.

"I wasn't going to anyway. But what in *hell* did Vic say to get your back up like this?"

Lacy's green eyes were flashing; her breasts heaved beautifully but were no longer of interest to Speed. He was looking at her face, mottled red with anger.

"He told me all about you and his tramp of a wife. That's what."

Speed was astounded—not that the cat was out of the bag since Josie had flown out there specifically to warn her husband, or even that Victor T. Donovan had been foolish enough to tell one of his office girls—people mostly *were* foolish—but that Lacy apparently was taking it so personally. He realized he had never seen her really angry; now the red hair looked like a warning.

"Lacy, that was a long time ago. What I was about to tell you about when the phone rang. It didn't have anything to do with you." He added, belligerently: "And Josie's not a tramp."

"I don't know what you'd call her then. Cheating on her husband like that."

"Which *you*, I suppose, would never do." It came to Speed that he was infinitely tired of righteousness.

"Cheat on a decent, honorable man like the congressman? You *bet* I wouldn't."

"If he's that kind," Speed said, "he's the kind that *usually* gets cheated on."

He got up and poured another vodka. When he turned back to the table, he saw that the flush had gone out of Lacy's face. She looked as if she were about to cry; she looked about thirteen years old. He wondered what there was about her that once had aroused him. It was an unwelcome thought; having made love to her seemed not far from incest, from molesting his own child, if he'd had one. He wished suddenly, desperately, that he *had* had a child, a daughter; maybe everything would have been different.

"Do you know what he did?" Lacy said. "That poor, tormented man out there trying to run an honorable campaign?"

With a quick flash of insight, Speed saw that she had not really been angry at him for having had an affair with another woman years earlier; why had he thought she would be? No, Lacy had been angry at what she saw as the harm he'd done Victor T. Donovan.

"He didn't tell me how he found out what she did, but—"

"*Josie* told him. That's why she went out there, to tell him."

Lacy looked at him malevolently. "As if that made it right. And I suppose she talked it all over with *you* first."

Speed said nothing. The story—Bender, Kyle, his meeting in Montrose Park with Josie—was too complicated to tell; besides, he owed Lacy no explanations. Certainly not about Josie.

"Anyway, when he found out about you and her," Lacy said, "he sent her straight home on today's plane and—"

Speed stole a look at his wristwatch. Only one plane a day, he thought. If on time, it would be landing at National Airport in just over an hour.

"—went on TV a few minutes ago. He told everybody straight out that he was separating from his wife."

"Good God!" Speed was astounded again, this time at the temerity of the man. "Did he tell them *why*?"

"He said he didn't feel he could set the kind of moral example he wanted to if he had a cloud hanging over his head."

Even in the circumstances, the political reporter lurking just under Speed's human surface could not help a certain abstract admiration, like that of a man for a winning horse he had not had the courage to bet on. Victor T. Donovan had moved quickly, maybe effectively, to preempt a story that could ruin him. Speed *hoped* it would, but he shrank from the idea of his own involvement.

"I'm sure that's exactly what he did say. But what I meant . . . did he say on the air what caused this cloud?"

"Did he name you, you mean? I don't think so." Lacy's eyes shone, whether with admiration or brimming tears he could not tell. "The congressman's too much of a gentleman to tell on her in public. Or to mention *you*." The last word was full of distaste.

Speed refrained from saying what he thought: that it would take an utter damn fool to believe a Senate candidate had ditched his wife a few days before a close election because she had bad breath or was overdrawn at the bank. Everybody would know, or at least would think they knew, the truth, and maybe, just maybe, their hearts—like Lacy's—would go out to poor, grieving, righteous Victor T. Donovan. Maybe, just maybe, he would get away with his peculiar kind of moral example.

Speed put his glass down and stood up. "I'm sorry to have to leave on that note, Lacy."

She looked up at him stonily; though her eyes were calm now and her face pale, her voice was weaker than usual, a trifle querulous. "Did you really mean you weren't going to come back anyway? Even if I hadn't . . ."

"That's what I came over to tell you."

Lacy did not ask him why. "Funny," she said. "*I* was going to break it off with *you*. That's why I wanted you to come here instead of going out."

Speed did not ask why either; he was afraid he knew.

"So your boss did the job for both of us." He moved toward the door. "We can thank him for that, even if he didn't know he was doing it."

Lacy's green eyes flashed at him again. "You never could give him any credit, could you? Not even for being the gentleman he is."

"If Victor T. Donovan's a gentleman"—Speed opened the door—"then I'm your father."

He saw her mouth open to speak, but she closed it again and glared at him so intensely that as he stood in the doorway, he could not take his eyes away from hers. He hesitated, wanting to leave, but feeling something dangling, unfinished.

Finally she said, viciously: "You're *old* enough to be my father . . . I found that out in bed. Thirty minutes to get it up, thirty seconds to get it off."

★

On his way to the airport Speed wondered whether a daughter of his would have turned out like Lacy Farnes, going to bed with overage men, setting them up a little, then saying things to hurt them. Maybe, maybe not. His daughter would have been Nancy's child, and Nancy had not been much interested or interesting in bed, but when it suited her, Nancy had known how to say things that hurt.

"You just don't want to take the trouble," she'd said to Speed in one of their fights about her desire to have children. "Or time off from that work of yours you think is so important."

"So what if I don't?" he'd demanded. "My work *is* important. And I can't do it the way I need to, the way I'm *expected* to, if I'm having to stay home and change diapers."

His work *had* seemed that important at the time, though Nancy had never conceded it. And he *had* expected himself to do it better than anyone else.

"You'll have lots of time one of these days," Nancy had warned him. "When they throw you on the ash heap, the way they do. You'll have plenty of time to wish you had children around to give a damn whether you live or die."

Now he had time, all right, and a lonely life, as Nancy had foreseen. In retrospect, when she had said things like that, he should have known she would leave him. But he had been too busy with his work, for a time too entranced by Josie, and too certain that life would go on rewarding him, as it always had.

Odd, he thought, to be on his way to meet Josie and thinking about Nancy. The Girl Next Door. She had married again, a rich old lawyer in Nashville, inherited the works when he died; she was still childless, still occasionally sharp-tongued, still drinking too much, as Josie had seen before he did. The last time he'd talked to Nancy long distance, she had not been speaking clearly, but he had managed to understand her.

"Always wanted t'be famous, didn' you? Worked so hard t'be famous. And don' want it now you got it."

He shook himself, like a dog emerging from water, as if he actually might shake off thoughts of Nancy. He did not like to think about her because that was inevitably to think of youth, dreams, wastage: time irretrievable.

The lights of Washington burned across the Potomac, casting long, glistening paths on the black river. A plane slid past overhead, its roar so near the rooftop of his car that he instinctively pulled his head down between his shoulders. Other cars hurtled past on the parkway as he eased into the right lane for the turnoff to the airport. A glance at his watch reassured him; even if Josie's plane was on time, he should be able to meet her at the gate.

In the tightly closed world of the airliner she would not have heard what Victor T. Donovan had said on the air, and he would have been too cautious to risk a leak by telling her in advance. And too vindictive. So Speed had sped from Lacy's apartment to the Washington *Post* building and double-parked while he ran upstairs to check the wire service ticker.

The report, datelined from Capital City, was sketchy and studiously hedged:

> In a move that stunned political observers, Rep. Victor T. Donovan tonight announced that he was separating from his wife, perhaps jeopardizing what political observers had considered the strong possibility of an upset in his underdog campaign against Sen. O. Mack Bender.
>
> Rep. Donovan, appearing to some TV viewers on the verge of tears, gave no specific reason for his unprecedented action, saying only that he wanted to be able to set a "moral example" in the Senate.
>
> Speculation began immediately, centering on Mrs. Josephine Donovan's absence in Washington during most of a hotly contested campaign. Neither she nor Rep. Donovan could be reached for comment. Spokesmen for Rep. Donovan would not say why the candidate had acted or why he had done so on the eve of an election in which most observers had expected him to make a strong showing.
>
> One state political figure who supports Rep. Donovan but who spoke on condition of anonymity said the congressman, little known before his denunciation last spring of the financier J. Conrad Cramer, was "heartsick but determined to keep on fighting." This source predicted voters would rally to the support of "a man who proved he will tell the truth even when it hurts."
>
> But Mayor Chester "Chet" Blade of this city, a Bender backer, told reporters that the Donovan announce-

> ment was a "cheap, last-minute effort to get off the low road and take the high ground that won't fool the voters. If a man can't manage his own family, how's he going to manage this state's business in the Senate?"

An obliging copyboy had photocopied the report for him. Speed had raced back to his car and off for the airport. There he parked in a space reserved for members of Congress and Supreme Court justices and hurried into the terminal. Having no ticket, he could not go all the way to Josie's gate; he waited, instead, by the baggage-checking machine. At that hour of the night, its operators in their lurid uniforms seemed more nearly comatose than usual.

Victor T. Donovan on the verge of tears? Crocodile, Speed thought.

That was just the sort of thing, however, that a lot of voters would eat up. Lacy Farnes, the little fool, apparently had swallowed it whole. Mayor Blade undoubtedly had the straight of Victor T. Donovan's motive, but Speed remembered the mayor's display, in Pioneer Park, of loyalty to Bender. He mistrusted Blade's judgment that the speech "wouldn't fool the voters."

Nobody ever lost an election, Speed thought, *overestimating the sentimentality of the American voter.*

★

Josie was the first passenger off the plane; later she told Speed that she'd used Victor T. Donovan's American Express card for a first-class ticket, taking a sort of final jab at him. He'd always insisted that they fly tourist, to show solidarity with the common man.

"And anyway," Josie said, "Vic's cheaper than dime-store perfume."

That night she came swinging easily along the airport corridor, dressed for travel in slacks, a black sweater, and a light coat, a light dress bag slung from her shoulder. He might, Speed thought, have been seeing her in one of his countless dreams.

When Josie saw him waiting, surprise spread across her

face; her eyes seemed to Speed to turn a lighter blue. Without a word he took the bag from her shoulder.

"Is this all your luggage?"

"I travel light," Josie said.

They walked along the narrow, nearly empty cinder-block corridor, her heels echoing, toward an escalator; as they neared it, Josie began to laugh. Speed stood aside to let her on the escalator first; as they went up, she turned to look at him, still laughing.

"I never thought . . . imagine Milo Speed meeting me at the airport after all these years."

I'd have met you in the Sahara, Speed thought. But he only said, carefully: "I'm not trying to force myself on you. I had a reason to come."

"How'd you know which plane I was on?"

"There's only one. When I heard you were coming back, it had to be this flight."

They got off the escalator and went through the echoing terminal to the sidewalk.

"You heard I was coming back?"

He did not answer; the ground, he told himself, needed to be prepared first. Carrying the dress bag in one hand, he touched her elbow lightly with the other, steering her toward his car.

"There's something I thought maybe it'd be better you heard it from me."

"Then that story about us must be out," she said. "Kyle floated it, didn't he?"

"Not yet." They walked along in silence. "But you're close."

"I doubt if whatever it is can top what I've got to tell you," Josie said. "You're not going to believe it, but Vic knew about you and me all along. Right from the start."

Speed stopped and stared at her. "But he never said anything?"

"Not a word. It must have been eating on him all the time. Inside, like acid. The minute I opened the subject, it all came out." She shuddered and took his arm, pulling herself close. "It was pretty terrible, Speed."

He had never thought she would be so close again. The

feel of her warmth, the movements of her body against his, made him light-headed.

"I don't see how he *could* have known. I mean, a cop like Kyle could dig it up, I guess. But we never . . . Josie, we were so *careful*."

"If you think it was careful making love in the back seat of that old car you had," Josie said, "I guess we were. But Vic knew." She walked along quietly for a moment. Then: "He said he could smell sex on me after I'd been with you."

"How would he even know what it was?"

The remark came out of his ancient and accustomed contempt for Josie's husband. But even as he spoke, he felt a wary respect—not unlike that he would accord a menacing dog or the IRS—for the lately formidable Victor T. Donovan.

"Oh, he knew," Josie said. "Don't forget I was married to him quite awhile before I met you at that party."

"Married *then* . . ." Speed realized he wanted badly to know. "How about *recently*?"

They had reached the reserved parking area, and Speed was guiding them toward his car before she answered.

"Not for years. He never seemed to miss it . . . not till he got into this campaign anyway. That seems to have turned him on a little." She looked up at him candidly. "But not me."

Warm satisfaction, even gratification rose in Speed like the flush of wine. Suddenly Josie stopped, looked around, and laughed. "They'll get you for impersonating a member of Congress."

"Considering most of the ones I know"—he spoke happily—"I'd plead not guilty."

But his car's dark interior dimmed Speed's mood. He switched on the dome light and pulled the wire copy from his pocket.

"This'll be sort of a shock, Josie. But I don't know any easy way to break the news."

He held out the folded paper.

"Well, I've got a little shock for *you*." Josie fumbled in her pocketbook, brought out eyeglasses, and set them carefully on her nose. "Ballplayers say the legs go first, but I think it's the eyes."

"Certainly not *your* legs."

"Don't be gallant," Josie said. "It's not your style."

Speed had not spoken for effect; Josie's legs were still splendid, and he did not think her unexpected eyeglasses were unbecoming. They gave her, he thought, a touch of frailty that made him want more than ever to take care of her. But then, he had to admit, nothing about Josie ever was likely to seem unbecoming to him—not after the empty years without her. In the dim glow of the dome light, he watched her strain to read the wire copy.

"That son of a bitch," she said at once, then read on.

"Verge of tears," she said a moment later. "Bullshit."

She finished the story, read it again, and handed it back.

"If there's anything I hate, it's being called Josephine."

"I thought of that when I read it."

"The rest of it's kind of a shock, I admit. Not so much what he did. I knew that would have to happen sooner or later, though I guess I'd rather have done it myself. The worst is *publicly* like that. Before Kyle's story even came out."

Speed explained that Victor T. Donovan undoubtedly was trying to diminish the political impact of that story, when and if it did appear.

"This way, if it does, he's already as good as told the voters out there that he's too almighty righteous to stay married to a . . . uh . . . fallen woman like you. He hopes that'll make people think more about him as an upright Christian than about a . . . ah . . . wayward wife."

"He doesn't care a rap what they think about me."

"Right. He's angling for the sympathy vote for himself. You're his bait."

He told Josie how Lacy Farnes had called Victor T. Donovan "that poor, tormented man." He did not tell her what Lacy had called Josie. His story apparently meant to her mostly that he had been with Lacy earlier that night.

"Speed, are you screwing that child?"

He had felt sure the question would come—he had asked Josie much the same thing about Victor T. Donovan—and was ready with an answer: "Not anymore."

Into the ensuing silence he added: "And she's a child about like Lizzie Borden."

Josie went directly to the main point. "Why not anymore?"

"For one thing," Speed said, "I'm an old fart now. Can't cut the mustard anymore." He took a deep breath and plunged on. "But the main thing is I don't care about any woman but you."

Again Josie seemed to ignore his last words. After a while she said: "She'll go for Vic now. She'll be on the plane tomorrow."

"Do you care?"

"Only for one thing," Josie said. "With that story on the ticker, the damn TV's going to be camped out in my front yard."

"You don't have to say anything to those guys." Speed felt protective; he wanted to clear the way for her. "Just keep right on walking, and don't even look at 'em."

"*That's* not what bothers me." She took off the eyeglasses and tucked them in her handbag. "I mean, if the cameras are in the front yard, I can hardly take you in the house with me."

Speed thought he might choke on his own expanding heart. "Goddammit, Josie, I—"

"Don't take it too hard. I'll think of something else."

"Josie . . . I'm just so *happy*."

He had thought he never could be so happy again or perhaps at all. He looked past Josie, to the lights of cars moving on the airport roadway, a train moving like a long string of glittering beads on the Metro; it seemed to him that he had not *seen* such sights in a long time, that his eyes had been opened to a different, brighter world.

"Let's see," Josie said, as if studying a grocery list, "at your place I'd see tracks from some of those other women everywhere I looked."

"No, no . . . I told you . . . that was mostly talk. I never really—"

"*Some* women anyway. And Speed . . . the way I feel tonight, even some others are too many."

In the still-burning dome light, he could see the serious

look on her face, the way her delicious lips pursed as she thought. He felt the richness of being with her, as if the years never had been.

Josie snapped her fingers, as if coming to a decision. "The George Washington Parkway—do they still keep that parking lot open at night?"

8.

Within twenty-four hours the impact of Victor T. Donovan's speech had spilled far beyond his state and the first careful wire service accounts.

WHAT DID SHE DO? demanded the New York *Post* in eighty-four-point type surrounding a head-and-cleavage shot of Josie Donovan, taken years earlier.

As if in echo, the *Daily News* in equally huge letters suggested JOSIE TOO COZY? The full-length *News* photo, also from the files, was less sexy but more suggestive; the lens had caught Josie coming out of an unspecified doorway, looking nervous and a little disheveled.

The Chicago *Daily News* took the whole thing lightly, heading its story: DID VIC MAKE/SUPREME SACRIFICE? The New York *Times*, on the other hand, declared without irony: MORAL TONE/STRESSED IN/SENATE BID.

The Miami *Herald* indicated mystery: DONOVAN'S VOWS DISSOLVED/DONOVAN'S CASE UNSOLVED. The Boston *Globe* hinted at scandal: SHAPELY WIFE/HEATS UP/SENATE RACE. The San Francisco *Chronicle* resorted to a pun; its main headline proclaimed: HOUSE FRAU DITCHED. A smaller subhead more or less explained: SEEKS SEAT IN SENATE/SEVERS TIES THAT BIND.

A television gossipist, broadcasting from Hollywood, suggested with a superior smirk on her lifted face that "when it becomes known" the story behind Victor T. Donovan's speech would "awaken echoes of fun-and-games on the *Monkey Business*." Sally Jessy Raphael scheduled a show on "Political Wives: Why Must Hubby Come First?"

Prime Time and *20/20* frantically sought interviews with Josie Donovan, but *Geraldo* went on the air with three sex therapists, two men and a woman, who solemnly discussed the question of whether political involvement enhanced, exaggerated, or inhibited the libido. The debate ended in a draw, aided and abetted by stock film about Chappaquiddick, Wayne Hays, Wilbur Mills, Gary Hart, and Nelson Rockefeller's divorce and death.

Reporters from *People* and *Time* burned up telephone wires in Washington and anywhere else they hoped to pick up Josie Donovan's sexual trail, for everyone assumed that she must have done *something* to cause her husband's action, and everybody knew what it was that wives usually had done in such cases. On Josie's block, television remote trucks hindered traffic; in front of the Donovan house, cameras lined the sidewalk like awkward cranes.

In the cramped Rayburn Building offices of the Honorable Victor T. Donovan, Mister Horn deeply resented the absence of Lacy Farnes. It meant that he and the two remaining girls could hardly keep up with phones that rang constantly.

"It's like that darned Cramer business all over again," Mr. Horn lamented to his counterpart in the office of Chairman Hartley G. Flander. "I do think the congressman might have given us some warning."

In the state where it mattered most, Victor T. Donovan's speech was, of course, a sensation, and the conversion of J. Carson Ritch and the Bedrock *Crusher* to the Donovan cause was headline news in other state papers. But Bryce Powers, in his influential *Ledger* column, took the view that no candidate could announce such a shattering personal development a few days before an election and hope to prosper with the voters. Theo Keller had none too subtly suggested this approach.

Powers did slip in the point that to his credit, Victor T. Donovan had *acted,* whereas Senator O. Mack Bender had only denied the Gabriella Lukes story, none too convincingly at that. Art Mingo, reading this, wondered whether Victor T. Donovan benefited more from the compliment than he suffered from the clear implication that he had acted because of some scandal akin to the Lukes affair.

"Damned if I do and damned if I don't," Senator Bender himself complained, by telephone to Bucky Overholt, who had returned to Washington. "I accuse Donovan of hot-dogging this moral example bilge, they claim I didn't exactly set one myself, no matter how I deny I had anything to do with Gabby Lukes. But if I don't say anything, that asshole maybe gets away with what amounts to grand larceny. The hell of it is, I knew the whole story all along."

"You *what*?" Overholt demanded.

"Don't get excited. It's not the kind of thing I could honorably use. It—"

"*Honorably!*" Overholt's scream nearly shattered the senator's eardrum. "What the fuck are you talking about?"

"I've got *some* standards, Overholt, even if—"

"Goddammit, Senator!" Overholt interrupted. "You think you're maybe Abe Lincoln? Let *me* figure out what we do with whatever you've got."

The Washington *Post*'s political correspondent in Capital City worked the phone from his room in the Lewis & Clark. Checking his best sources—Raymond Goodwood, Mayor Blade, Art Mingo, and Bryce Powers—he then filed an "interpretive":

> In the wake of Victor T. Donovan's startling and largely unexplained decision to part from his statuesque wife, this state's overheated Senate race has exploded into confusion.
>
> No polls are yet available, so no one seems certain whether Rep. Donovan self-destructed or scored a ten-

> strike with his claim to be setting a "moral example" for his state and, inferentially, the U.S. Senate. Many voters here have made it clear, however, that they think the latter, at least, could use such an example.
>
> A weak and tentative consensus seemed to be emerging today that Sen. O. Mack Bender's challenger, by his dramatic renunciation of a woman whose absence from this campaign has been widely noted, had made a favorable impression on many of what are often described as "God-fearing" voters across this strongly conservative state.
>
> In these parts, local sources say, marital problems are generally considered moral problems, more nearly the preacher's province than the psychiatrist's.

The *Post* interpretive reflected, in large part, the favorable spin Art Mingo had put on the ball. As Mingo had queried the extensive network of operatives and informants he had erected across the state, he found that these sources—discounted for partisanship—largely confirmed the heavy telephone traffic following Victor T. Donovan's performance.

Not that everyone had believed or approved the candidate's words or action—far from it—but Mingo was honestly able to tell the *Post* correspondent—not, of course, for attribution—that voter interest was widespread and that voter reception seemed rather more than narrowly favorable. He could report more specifically to Darwin John his rough but careful estimate that at least three voters in five, some of them nominal supporters of Senator Bender, had been impressed or moved by Victor T. Donovan's dramatic action.

"Or conned," said Rafael Ames, on hearing the same report over drinks in the lobby of the Lewis & Clark. Ames, Mingo, and Floyd Finch were taking a break while Victor T. Donovan—so his schedule declared—was "studying the issues" in his room. The candidate insisted that this entry appear at least once on every day's listing of his activities

"That, too," Mingo conceded. "And I'm not saying they'll all *vote* for 'im."

Floyd Finch secretly, and in contradiction of a lifetime's loyalty to the party, hoped they wouldn't.

"If they don't," he said, "then that damn speech cost 'im his wife *and* a Senate seat." In his private view Victor T. Donovan deserved both losses.

"What's the Chief think?" With one hand Ames fiddled with the glass of Gatorade that stood unsipped in front of him; with the other he raised and lowered the zipper on a warm-up jacket labeled across the back "Portland Trail Blazers."

"Flabbergasted at first. He came around a little when I told 'im how it looked." Mingo shrugged. "He's like everybody else, trying to guess who she was balling."

"Now you don't know that," Floyd Finch protested, setting down his Carta Blanca. "*He* could of been playing around, and it was her that canned him, for all we really know."

"The Honorable?" Ames, aching to reveal his own limited knowledge, found this doubly ridiculous. "Playing around?"

"Could be," Finch insisted. "That redhead out from Washington's got knockers on 'er like a movie star."

"That's just Lacy from the office." Ames looked knowing. "She swore to me there was nothing doing."

But it occurred to him that maybe Finch was on to something. Lacy was alone up there in the room with the Honorable, wasn't she? Maybe he was capable even of that.

Sometimes, Ames thought, *Victor T. Donovan seemed capable of anything.*

"What else would she tell you?" Finch said. "Anyway, I don't think we ought to jump to conclusions about a nice lady like Miz Donovan."

"You may think so, but everybody's doing it." Mingo downed the last of his scotch and soda and signaled the doeskin waitress to bring another. "The one thing everybody *thinks* is, she was back there in Washington cheating on the candidate while he's running his ass off out here. And the one thing everybody wants to *know* is who with."

"First thing *I* thought," Ames said, "I heard him make that speech, 'My God, he's suiciding out.' But I got to hand it to 'im. Sharp fucking instincts. Here's an election right on top of us, and who's everybody talking about? The Honorable. Who's getting all the ink and TV? The Honorable." He winked at Floyd Finch. "Not because of you and me, Floyd."

"Yeah, but look at the way he got the ink." Finch poured the last of his beer. "And a lot of it he could do without."

"That's the real question." Mingo watched the doeskin set down another scotch and another Carta Blanca. "Do most voters think he's made a noble sacrifice and risked his whole career to uphold moral standards? Or do they think he's a nerd who can't control his wife, just grandstanding when he threw her over?"

"You mean Tricky Vic?" the waitress asked.

"If it's any of your business," Ames said.

"For my two cents"—the waitress braced the edge of her tray against her outthrust doeskin hip—"that was a line of bull you could smell a mile off. On the TV, I mean."

"Two miles off." Floyd Finch put his fingers to his nose.

"But my husband—the deputy sheriff over there at the bar—*he* thinks it was real straight stuff. He thinks Tricky Vic's the greatest thing since Barry Goldwater."

"Your husband ever leave that bar?" Ames asked.

The waitress glared down at him. "To vote," she said. "He's the one in the family that always votes."

★

Soon after Victor T. Donovan's renunciation of his wife, Darwin John entertained a few major contributors in his private dining room. The Chief was famous for these small dinners, at which his chef always outdid himself (a coulibiac of salmon featured the night's menu), the wines were memorable, and an exciting guest—the secretary of defense this time—was on hand to lead the conversation. The take never failed to reach the high six figures. Sometimes more.

Through dessert, the SECDEF had kept the conversation focused on the continuing necessity for aircraft carriers to project American power throughout the world.

"And there's just no doubt," he said in summation, as white-jacketed waiters brought in coffee, "we really need the two more the President asked Congress for. After all, the Russkies may be over the hill, but there's plenty of trouble left in this old world Uncle Sam may have to take a hand in. Like the Horn of Africa."

"Well, the President usually gets what he wants," said Ginger Toon, the blond and diamond-ringed widow of a canned tuna fortune. Ginger was a reliable source of big money ("a cash cow," Darwin John was apt to call her in private) for any cause that she thought her late husband would have regarded as anti-Communist—a standard easily met.

"But what I'm wondering . . ." Ginger Toon shifted her heavily shadowed blue eyes to Darwin John. "What's going to happen to our man Donovan's Senate race?"

"Ah," said the Chief, "a fascinating story. I was wondering when somebody would bring it up."

Just then a waiter whispered in his ear that an urgent call awaited him in the outer office.

"I mean"—Ginger Toon's plump cheeks wobbled under daubs of rouge—"your people kept getting money out of me because they said Vic Donovan had that liberal Bender on the ropes. But this crazy business—"

"If you'll excuse me," said Darwin John, "I have to take a quick call. *Then* we'll talk about Vic Donovan all you want."

He hurried to the door but heard Welles Jason, a wheel in multinational forest products, pick up Ginger's question. "It did seem crazy, I admit, but don't you think the voters out there can draw the conclusion—"

The Chief emerged from the dining room and picked up a white phone. He knew whoever was calling had to be official to have that particular number.

"John here."

"Sorry to disturb you at dinner, Mister John, but I thought you'd want to know right away that—"

"Who's this?" Darwin John had not recognized the voice and was annoyed to be called by some underling.

"Arthur F. Pritchett, Mister John. I work in the press office."

"What is it, Pritchett? I've only got a minute."

"Lee Lestark's column, Mister John. In the early editions. He's got this story."

"*What* story, Pritchett?" The Chief made a mental note to have somebody jack up Pritchett, teach him to get to the point.

"Well, you know Congressman Donovan's speech, Mister John? In the Senate race out there?"

"Go on," said Darwin John, his attention suddenly riveted.

"Lestark's got this story, he says the reason Congressman Donovan announced the separation, he found out his wife had this . . . ah . . . this affair. I mean . . . Lestark says a love affair."

"Well, of course, goddammit," said Darwin John. "Who with?"

"That's Lestark's main story, Mister John."

Darwin John listened avidly, at first hardly believing what Pritchett said. Then, as details from Lestark's story mounted, John's doubts disappeared, and his agile mind began calculating political consequences.

"There's even this quote from some motel clerk, Mister John. He remembered once checking them in. . . ."

By the time Pritchett completed his recital, the Chief saw clearly that Victor T. Donovan somehow must have known what was coming and had taken the only course open to him. A cold-blooded piece of work at that. The man was a gut fighter, the kind Darwin John liked. But how had he found out the danger in time to take preemptive action?

"Pritchett," said the Chief, "you did the right thing calling me." He remembered that the impressive Rafael Ames had once been just such an unknown gofer in the press office. Hard to tell about these kids. "Come up to the office sometime and get acquainted."

"Oh . . . I'd like that . . . ah . . . Chief."

When Darwin John returned to his place at the dining table, the SECDEF was twiddling his spoon in his coffee. The talk was not about aircraft carriers.

"A woman who won't go to bat for her husband," Ginger Toon was saying, "frankly, in my opinion, that's hardly a woman at all."

"Well," said Darwin John, resuming his seat, "according to what I just heard, I don't think you can really say *that* about Josie Donovan."

At approximately the same moment, though it was two

hours earlier on their watches, Senator O. Mack Bender and Ernest Fulton, the senator's issues man, arrived at the Prairie Schooner Motel in the small city of Fort Ida. They were to spend the night at the Prairie Schooner, but Bender was first to do a call-in show on local radio. The next morning he was to attend the Fort Ida Lions Club Prayer Breakfast.

"Ernie," the senator said, as their youthful driver—who was studying political science at the state university—let them out at the motel entrance, "my ass is dragging. I'll be glad when this damn thing is over, win, lose, or draw."

"You don't mean that, Senator. You aren't going to lose."

Ernest Fulton wished he were as sure as he had tried to sound. It was no secret to him, as the race narrowed, that his excellent job—not to mention his putative future as a White House special assistant—depended on the senator's reelection.

"I wish I were as sure as you are," Bender said.

They entered the motel lobby, which featured mounted cattle horns, an elk head on the wall, and a chandelier adapted from a wagon wheel. Theo Keller sat on a sofa upholstered in what might have been a pinto pony's hide. His presence instantly alerted Mack Bender to news—probably bad, he thought, the way things were going.

"Theo . . . you're a long way from home."

"I figured you might not hear about it tonight if I didn't drive over here, tell you myself."

"Donovan's dropped dead?"

"No such luck, Mack." Theo handed him three sheets of paper. "This stuff will be in tomorrow morning's papers all over the country, including the *Ledger*."

Senator Bender studied the syndicate distribution of Lee Lestark's column. Ernest Fulton read over his shoulder.

"All these years I've known that guy," Theo said, "he never said a word to me about her. Not even a hint."

Damn that Overholt, Bender thought. *I* told *him not to*—

"Christ," Ernest Fulton said, "so *that*'s what it was all about."

Bender handed him the papers and strode toward the telephone booth under the elk's head.

"Mack!" Theo Keller called. "Where you going?"

Bender did not answer but went into the phone booth and closed the door. He sat still a moment, composing himself, anger like heartburn in his chest—not so much at Bucky Overholt as at himself.

Overholt's home phone rang three times before a sleepy voice answered.

"Did you give Lestark that goddam story?" Bender demanded.

The sleepy voice became Bucky Overholt's quick bark. "What story? Donovan's wife?"

"What else? Did you leak it?"

"Not yet," Overholt said. "You say Lestark's got it?"

"In tomorrow morning's papers."

"Shit. I had it lined up for Sunday and a lot more circulation than Lestark's got."

"Didn't I tell you I didn't want you to do that?"

Silence fell briefly on the line.

"Not that it matters now," Overholt said, "but I thought that was some kind of self-protection. Otherwise why'd you tell me the story at all?"

Why indeed?

Bender stared at the advertisement on the wall of the booth. "Reach Out and Touch Someone." Of course, Overholt had assumed that he wanted the story out but didn't want to smirch his "honor" with responsibility for leaking it. How could Overholt, with his long political experience, his view of the world he shared with Mack Bender, have assumed anything else?

And how could I assume he'd think anything else?

"I wish you'd told me sooner, Senator. We could of got more mileage out of it."

Or did I assume he would think anything else?

Bender said: "Let it go, Bucky. The story's out, and that's that."

"Gives me a few ideas anyway. Couple of spots for the finishing kick."

Bender closed his eyes and rubbed them with his fingers, wishing for sleep, rest, to have it all over and done. He had seldom been so dispirited, or dreamed of such pressures. He had never conceived of his own susceptibilities. Things for so long had seemed so easy.

"I don't want to see any more of your goddam spots," he said.

Theo and Fulton were waiting for him under an enormous spread of cattle horns that clung to a paneled wall.

"I'm glad of one thing," Bender said. "Overholt tells me we didn't have anything to do with this—" he took the paper from Fulton and looked it over again—"this rot. I was afraid maybe it was some of his work."

That I put him up to.

"Nobody would believe *you'd* let anything like that happen." Theo Keller's face and voice were full of veneration. "Besides, the way it looks to me, this story tends to vindicate Donovan. For giving her the gate, I mean."

That was also the way it looked to Victor T. Donovan, when Lacy Farnes brought the news to his door at the Lewis & Clark. She'd had it from Mr. Horn, who'd called her as soon as the first reporter had called him, seeking comment from the congressman on Lestark's column.

Lacy had been working in her own room, compiling voter lists by street address on a laptop computer. After Mr. Horn's call she ran immediately for the elevator, then along the hall to Victor T. Donovan's door. When he opened it, tightly belted in a maroon robe, she gave him a breathless report, worded as tactfully as the news permitted.

"Call Horn back and tell him I won't have any comment on that." The congressman shook his head sadly. "I suppose it had to come out. Poor Josie. Her secret spread out for the world to see."

In Lacy's face, he was gratified to see no such sympathy as he had felt it judicious to fake.

"Not because of anything *you* did," Lacy said. "You did your best to protect her." Her tone suggested that he had, in fact, done more than Josie Donovan deserved.

Victor T. Donovan carefully kept his face neutral, no hint on his bland countenance of the resentment seething in him—resentment he had kept bottled, like some toxic gas he feared would destroy him if loosed, eat from within at the blameless image he had carefully erected, in all those patient years of waiting for his chance. He had done what he could, but he knew Josie might yet bring him down. The bitch.

"Do you think," Lacy said tentatively, "I mean, I don't want to be crass about anything that's hurt you so much, but what will it mean about the election?"

He let his shoulders slump in weary resignation. "I'm not sure I care anymore, Lacy. But I guess at least it tells people I really was doing what I had to do. I couldn't let them send me to the Senate in good faith and then take *her* along with me with this kind of thing hanging over us."

He looked at Lacy with grave sincerity. "I just hope this Lestark story is all. I hope nobody catches her actually in bed with Speed."

Lacy stared at him, horror on her face. "You mean . . . they're still—"

"Sure they are. I could tell *that* the night she talked to me." He added, taking pleasure in the lie, in paying Josie back in the only way he could: "Probably never stopped."

Lacy burst out: "How could she *do* this to a man like you? *Hurt* you this way?"

For just a moment Victor T. Donovan considered asking this warm and caring girl into his room, maybe feeding her a drink from the supplies he kept for contributors, seeing what might happen. He thought about Josie's whorish tits bulging under the jumping horse; Lacy's were just as big and maybe softer.

"Lacy . . ." But he quickly realized as he spoke that it was too soon, would be too abrupt; besides, it might be risky. Get the election out of the way first.

He tried to look and sound forgiving. "Maybe I wasn't such a great husband either. Only thing is . . . I guess I wouldn't have been so friendly with *him* if I'd known what I know now."

"Neither would I," Lacy said.

Victor T. Donovan was elated to hear it. It would salve the wound a little, he thought, if he could turn the tables. Let Speed have a taste of what it did to a man to have his woman stolen.

★

Lacy walked slowly back to her room, thinking hard. No wonder that stinking newspaper son of a bitch had had so much trouble getting it up; all the time he was fucking *her,* he had been fucking the roundheels wife, too. Maybe on the same nights.

I hope his limp old prick falls off. Gets caught in his zipper. Permanently.

Lacy's anger rose with each step along the corridor. Milo Speed needn't think he could get away with two-timing Lacy Farnes. Not to mention the damage to an honorable gentleman and public servant like the congressman. She'd show Speed, just the way she aimed to show her rinky-dink father and that filthy scum of a brother, now that she was getting to be *somebody* on the Hill. With a congressman who was going to be a senator.

Speed would have to pay, she thought as she unlocked her door. No question about it. He *would* pay.

Once she was alone in the solitude of her own room, her anger welled into hot tears. But not for long. Lacy dried her eyes, balled up a fist, and shook it at the dark, unwinking eye of the TV, imagining Speed's hateful face leering from it.

"You wait," she said out loud. "You just wait, asshole!"

She tried to finish her work on the laptop, but it was no use. She kept thinking of Speed rutting around on top of her even while he was thinking about that slut of a wife.

As Lacy began to take off her clothes for bed, she could not help wondering if maybe Mrs. Roundheels was doing the same exact thing in front of Milo Speed. Showing her sleazy stuff, right that minute. As she thought of them together, the idea came to Lacy: how she would make Speed pay.

Perfect.

But it would have to be timed right. So it couldn't hurt the congressman in the election.

Lacy pondered the problem as she continued slowly to undress. She always slept nude, and by the time her underwear puddled pinkly at her feet, she had hit on the way to do it. She pulled down the covers and switched off the bedside lamp; as she slipped between the sheets, cool and soothing against her flesh, she was no longer angry—only determined.

★

Speed and Josie did not learn that Lestark had exposed their long-ago affair until the next morning, when his column appeared in newspapers all over the country. Ordinarily Speed's syndicate editors would have informed him immediately of anything concerning himself that might be in the early editions, and no doubt they had tried. But after bringing Josie to his apartment, he had turned off the telephone, first calling Evangeline to come in late the next day.

So he and Josie were side by side in bed, reading the papers that had been left at Speed's door, when Josie let out a yelp. Speed turned his head in alarm.

"Lestark," she cried. "The story's in Lestark!"

That explained, Speed realized at once, the several loud knocks at the door they had managed to ignore. He felt a sharp, stabbing pain—not so much that the story was out, as they had expected, as that Lee Lestark had come up with an exclusive to match or top the Gabby Lukes story.

"It *would* be Lestark," he growled.

"Now it can be told . . ." the column began, with what Speed scorned as a typical cliché:

> . . . the seamy, steamy story behind Rep. Victor T. Donovan's amazing decision to separate from his shapely wife only days before his election challenge to the popular and respected Sen. O. Mack Bender.
>
> This reporter can exclusively reveal the reason, hush-hush till now—a sizzling love affair between Mrs. Josie Donovan, a statuesque brunette, and the once widely read Washington columnist Milo Speed . . .

"*Once* widely read!" Speed exclaimed. "I've got twice that little fart's circulation!"

"And you have to read all the way down to here"—Josie complained, pointing with her finger—"to find out it was years ago what he's writing about."

> ... well known to Washington and on the campaign trail as a womanizer of unsavory personal repute.
>
> Rep. Donovan, reported to be the frequent source of supposedly exclusive items in Speed's column, belatedly learned of ...

"That mealymouth bastard!" Speed erupted. "He knows I never needed Vic Donovan or anybody else to beat *his* pants off."

"Speed," Josie said, "please don't comment on every word about you while I'm reading about me."

> ... his buxom wife's illicit liaison with a man he is thought to have befriended.

"Does 'buxom' mean big tits or a big behind?" Josie asked, and read on:

> This reporter is not at liberty to say how Rep. Donovan learned the truth, but insiders say he several times expressed the fear that Lee Lestark's column soon would tell the world about curvaceous Josie Donovan's torrid sexual games.

"Torrid?" Josie shook the paper in irritation. "Before these last two nights with you, I can't even re*mem*ber the last time I was in bed with a man."

> Thus, these sources say, Rep. Donovan went on the air and renounced his aging but well-endowed wife "to beat Lestark to the punch," and in hopes of retaining a chance to defeat Sen. Bender, who is widely considered to be presidential timber and a man of principle.

Speed read to the end, then slammed down the paper in disgust.

"I can see Lestark laughing over every line. And he didn't do a damn thing but swallow a leak from Calvin Kyle."

Josie did not look up from her second reading of the column. "How do you know it wasn't Bender?"

"Because I read Lestark like a book. When he says here he's not at liberty to say how Vic found out, he might as well have told me *he doesn't know*. Kyle can't know either. But Bender knows I told you, and it wouldn't have been hard for him to figure out that *you* must have told Vic. So if Bender had leaked this garbage, it stands to reason he'd have leaked the other."

Josie threw the paper aside, as if it were a dirty stocking.

"I *hate* this part about 'aging but well-endowed.' Makes me sound like Elizabeth Taylor on her sixth marriage. But Lestark doesn't make Vic look exactly like a white knight either."

"Oh, Kyle's got the red ass because Vic canned him. Lestark ordinarily wouldn't give a damn one way or the other, but he's already ripped Vic up in a few pieces Connie Cramer obviously touted him on to. They'd both be pulling for Bender to plow Vic under."

"Well, anyway"—Josie turned on her hip to face him—"the suspense is over, isn't it? We knew we'd have to go through this sooner or later."

Speed put his arm around her bare shoulders, reassuring himself by the warm touch of her skin that Josie really was there in bed with him, where he'd thought she'd never be again. It seemed a miracle, *had* seemed a miracle ever since they'd talked in his car at National Airport.

They had not, in the end, risked the parking lot beside the George Washington Parkway—"You got to be younger than we are to be that crazy," Speed insisted—but had wound up in a dank motel off the interstate near Manassas.

"You got to be as old as we are to be *this* careful," Josie said as she glumly inspected, in the dim motel light, the plastic blanket, the plastic chairs, the plastic bathtub.

But the motel had enabled them to dodge the television cameras, and the next day Speed had persuaded a lawyer, whose failed appointment to the D.C. court of appeals he had vainly supported, to escort Josie into her own house. The lawyer had subjected reporters to a barrage of stolid "no comment," while Josie slipped unquestioned up the front steps.

Speed called later. A woman from the lawyer's office answered, but Josie quickly came on the line. She said at once:

"Why'd you give me that bullshit you couldn't cut the mustard anymore?"

Speed laughed, a little unsettled. Over the years he had forgotten how direct Josie could be.

"Wasn't it . . . ah . . . obvious?"

"What was obvious," Josie said, "was that now you really know how to please a woman. More than you used to. Which is something we *both* can be happy about."

Speed swelled with a mixture of happiness and pride, how much of each he could not tell. He was the eternal male, he thought, never more apt to prance and preen than when he thought he was satisfying his woman.

As if sensing his mood, Josie punctured it. "The little redhead gave you that idea about the mustard, didn't she?"

Speed thought of the night Victor T. Donovan had announced his candidacy for the Senate, while he lay on Lacy's bed listening to the radio, highly conscious of her body beside him.

"It was already in my mind," Speed said. "Maybe she did sort of stimulate the thought. But a man can't help knowing he's not getting any younger."

He might have succumbed to almost any pretty woman, he supposed, that night, in that situation, after his reawakening to Josie had met only with her seeming indifference. But something other than disappointment had been deceptively at work: Lacy's youth, her fresh attitudes, her seeming interest in him.

"I checked with Mr. Horn," Josie said, "just in case you're still interested. She's already gone out to Vic's campaign, like I expected. Mr. Horn's not happy about it."

He had been reaching back, Speed knew, for youth, at a time when supposedly ripe maturity had seemed particularly empty, even though he well knew the obvious truth that there was no going back. Now, miraculously, maturity meant Josie. Maturity was ripe after all.

"You want to know," he said, "I'll tell you exactly what it means to me she's gone out there."

"You don't have to," Josie said. "I was just being bitchy. A little jealous."

He was elated again, to think that Josie was jealous of Lacy, over him. He had a continuing sense of a miracle happening.

"It means," he managed to say, "no more bottled spaghetti sauce."

Josie laughed out loud, the old hearty go-to-hell laugh that he remembered from so many ecstatic times, that he had heard so often in his dreams.

"Did she give you jug wine, too?"

"Oh, no . . . not *that*."

They chuckled together for a moment, long enough for him to remember with embarrassment the near-comic spectacle of his last meeting with Lacy—each trying round about and for different reasons to tell the other that their affair was over.

Josie suddenly turned serious. "Lacy was off her rocker, Speed. A woman doesn't need a pole vaulter in bed. I'm not exactly a bouncy little cheerleader myself, but I've learned a few things about women and men."

"You're . . ." He knew *what* he felt but was not sure *how* to say it. "Josie, you were wonderful last night. Even in that lousy motel. Not just because of the sex. It *was* sex, of course, but . . ."

He groped for the words he needed. He was a man of words, he thought desperately, but they were failing him, as so many things had.

"Sex, but more than sex," Josie said. "I guess we both needed to find out that it could be."

The words he wanted came to him, awkward but true: "You're the only thing I ever dreamed of having . . . that didn't fail me when I got it."

He heard her catch her breath.

"Ah, you lovely man," Josie whispered. "Give me a little time."

★

Before hanging up, they had arranged for Speed to pick her up after dark, on the block behind her house; Josie said she could reach it undetected by reporters, via a back alley. She did, dressed romantically all in black, including a scarf around her head. He had driven her quickly to his apartment, where —he assured her—only a quiet bachelor and professional existence had left any traces. There he prepared a roast chicken— with expertise derived from years of lonely dinners—while Josie looked over the many shelves of books assiduously dusted by Evangeline.

Now, with the morning papers carrying Lestark's column strewn over the bed, his arm around Josie, she turned her face up to him. Her eyes were sky blue. When he kissed her, the coverlet fell away to their waists. After a while when he took his lips away from hers, she looked down at herself.

"Remember you told me I had the most beautiful breasts in the world? Are they still?"

"Of course." Speed kissed one, then the other, nibbling happily.

"Seems to me they droop a little," Josie said. "I've been thinking about a silicon job."

Speed moved his head away, horrified. "Don't you dare!"

Josie covered herself. "I've already had this little tuck around the eyes. You couldn't tell that, so what's the difference?"

"If you have to ask," Speed said, "you'll never know. Probably because you're not a man."

"Probably because you're not a woman, *you'll* never know why I'm thinking about it."

Just then Evangeline—making much unnecessary noise to alert them—entered the apartment. Speed pulled on the Italian silk robe with which he had indulged himself on his last trip to Europe and went out to clear the way for Josie.

"You must of got this Donovan lady that's in the papers with you," Evangeline said. "I couldn't hardly drive by on the street, all those TV trucks blocking the way."

"You've read Lestark's story?"

"I'm kind of put out, too. How come you never even mention that lady's name to me?"

"Because it was all a long time ago. And it hurt too much to think about her. Much less talk."

Evangeline looked knowing. "So she was the one all along?"

"She was the one."

Even when I didn't know it. When I wouldn't let myself know it.

Evangeline hung up her coat decisively. "I knew it was somebody. Not one of *them*."

Her voice was edged with the old contempt she had shown for women who had spent a night in Speed's apartment.

"You say TV's waiting outside?"

"But I got it figured how we can get 'er out without they know it." Evangeline was as calm as if discussing the price of asparagus. "Take the elevator straight down to the garage and drive out in my old car. You ain't too high-and-mighty for an eighty-one Dart."

But Speed had no intention of ducking other reporters. He was one himself—one of the breed. Nor did he aim to run from a story because it had unexpectedly involved him.

"You should be in the CIA, Evangeline. But I've got to go down there and face the music. Maybe you'll let Josie take your car."

Before Evangeline could answer, Josie came out of the bedroom in her black escape outfit, the scarf dangling from her hand. She looked, Speed thought, as she always had looked in his mind's eye. He wanted to touch her again, make sure that she was real, not a miracle, that she really was there with him.

"Uh-huh," Evangeline said. "I can see in your face she's the one."

★

Just after noon Rafael Ames found Lacy Farnes in the Chuck Wagon Grill; without asking, he sat down at her table. Over her tepee-shaped menu, through her granny glasses, Lacy looked at him with cold green eyes.

"I told you," Ames said.

She stared a moment longer, then looked at the menu again.

"Told me what?"

Above jeans faded nearly white, Ames wore a striped rugby shirt; even in the Chuck Wagon Grill he had not removed a blue baseball cap emblazoned: "HONORARY ASTRONAUT, Huntsville, Ala."

"What I could see through those old lady glasses."

He watched her struggle to let nothing show on her face, in the green eyes. She put down the menu calmly and said: "I remember what you said. You were wrong then, and you're wrong now."

Ames pushed the cap on the back of his head and leaned his folded arms on the table.

"One day the old lady goes home. The next day you're on the first plane in. You think I'm thick in the skull?"

Lacy shook her head. "Not thick. Sick."

"Touché," Ames said. "But you want to bet you and the Honorable don't celebrate election night in the sack?"

He expected her to flare at him. But she only said: "He'll have a lot to celebrate."

A waitress came to take their orders. Lacy asked for a spinach salad. Ames had not looked at the menu.

"Roast beef sandwich," he said. "Rare on white."

"No roast beef today."

"Corned beef then."

"No corned beef either."

Ames sighed. "Just a few more days," he told Lacy, "and we can go back East to civilization."

"We got tuna melt," the waitress said. "Or turkey breast."

"Bring me the tuna. No melt."

"It don't come that way."

Ames glared at her. "Just a cup of coffee then. Piece of apple pie. You got apple pie?"

The waitress snarled something that sounded like yes and went away.

"Your manners don't get any better," Lacy said.

Her continued calm irritated him. "Fuck my manners, Red. Let's make a deal."

Lacy shook her head. "I don't even like you."

Who cares? Ames thought. *When there's yardage to gain.*

"But you got the Honorable wrapped around your little

finger, Red. Maybe you don't know it yet, but his tongue's hanging out."

That got to her, and he saw with satisfaction her little face of disgust. *Not just his tongue,* Ames wanted to add. But instinct told him that would push things too far.

"On the other hand, when he moves into the big time over in the Senate, he'll need somebody knows where the bodies're buried. Somebody that maybe even buried some of 'em. Not that old has-been Horn."

"You mean somebody like you?"

"Not just somebody *like* me." Ames grinned at her, believing from her inquiry that he was getting somewhere.

The waitress brought the spinach salad and the apple pie and a coffee cup for Ames.

"Problem is . . ." He waited until the waitress went away. "The Honorable's got maybe a little big for his britches these days. Ever since he fired Cal Kyle."

"Which you advised him *not* to do."

Ames was taken aback, but he quickly realized that only the Honorable himself could have clued her to that. Which proved his theory that she had his Honorable pecker practically in her hand.

"Like this business with his old lady. He didn't ask a soul about that, and it could've blown him out of the water. It maybe did."

"But you just suggested he was going to win."

"Because of my spots. *If* he does."

Lacy munched spinach, looking at him solemnly through the granny glasses before she spoke.

"Let me get this straight, Ames. You want Mister Horn's job, and you think I can help you get it?"

"You could, all right. But I wouldn't have that asshole job on a cross of gold. Too much paper work and not enough . . ." Ames held up thumb and fingers, rubbing them together.

The waitress came back, poured coffee in Ames's cup, and left without a word. His untouched pie looked glutinous on the saucer.

"Easier than that," Ames said. "Except lately I get the feeling the Honorable thinks he can get along without what I do for him."

Lacy put her spinach salad aside and her elbows on the table, looking interested.

"Just a little contract's all I need, Red. For the company I'm going to form after we win. Then I can represent Senator Honorable the way he ought to be represented. Polls, spots, advice, speeches, the works. Whatever he needs."

He grinned again, his confidence rising. "Whatever he needs that *you* aren't giving him." He leaned farther across the table and whispered: "To go beyond the Senate. With you along for the ride."

That, he thought, would get her if anything would.

But Lacy pushed back her chair and stood up. "You can shove your contract, Ames. I'm not interested."

He was flabbergasted. "But . . . all you got to do is put the bug in his ear. Maybe stroke him a little."

"I told you"—Lacy dropped her napkin in the spinach salad—"never to call me Red."

★

The night before the state's voters went to the polls, Theo Keller found it necessary to kill the headline—DOWN TO THE WIRE!—his slot man had penciled in for the *Ledger*'s election day lead. Keller subbed different racing slang that put his favorite's name in seventy-two-point type: BENDER IN STRETCH RUN.

"Theo," the slot man said, "we put Bender's name up there like that, maybe at least we should get Donovan in the subhead."

Theo Keller eyed him belligerently. "I'm not trying to balance the scales of justice, Umstead. I'm an editor, not a poll-taker."

Umstead's proposal might have been a shade more objective, but Theo Keller knew from experience that journalism is a highly subjective craft. Anyway, no reasonable person could say that his substitute was inaccurate. O. Mack Bender *had* come on strongly in the last few days of the Senate campaign, even after Victor T. Donovan had dumped his wife and grabbed the headlines. The trend to the challenger that briefly resulted had been halted, then turned, with the repeated appearance on statewide TV of a few gripping seconds that Rafael Ames enviously considered vintage Bucky Overholt.

A bloodhound bayed across the state's screens, its nose to the ground, pulling by its leash a reluctant handler, seen only in shadowy glimpses or indistinct profile. The bloodhound ran past the Washington Monument, sniffing a fugitive trail, pulling the handler along.

"Where is she?" inquired a voice as resonant as James Earl Jones's.

The bloodhound, baying fiercely, invaded a posh restaurant, the handler hanging on as startled patrons reared away from the lunging dog.

"Where can she be?" the resounding voice asked.

The scene shifted to a tropical beach, with the bloodhound sniffing among startled sunbathers. The handler lurched frantically behind, barely hanging on.

"Where, oh, where can she *be*?"

In a flash the baying hound was charging into a hotel lobby, with a bellboy leaping for the cover of a sofa. The hound made straight for an open elevator door, dragging his handler behind. Viewers then could see a hand-printed sign pinned to the handler's back: TRICKY VIC.

Just as the dog reached the elevator door, it slid shut in his face. While the bloodhound sniffed the door, the handler slowly turned to show a strange resemblance to Victor T. Donovan. Wearily he pleaded with the audience:

"Has *anybody* seen my wife?"

Tipplers at the Lewis & Clark's lobby bar agreed with an irate Deputy Sheriff Blanton F. Hollis that this commercial was in execrable taste, even as they chuckled at its content. Senator Bender, enraged when he first saw it broadcast in his behalf, ordered Bucky Overholt to pull it off the air.

"It's not ours to pull," Overholt insisted. "It's made and paid for by this PAC that's like a hundred ten percent for you. Calls itself Better American Morals."

BAM, Bender soon learned, was a front for a few business leaders, but mostly for J. Conrad Cramer. BAM, or Cramer, or both refused all entreaties to pull the bloodhound spot, which Bender could not actually prove—though like Ames, he believed it—to have been made at Cramer's order by Bucky Overholt.

Overnight polls paid for by Darwin John disclosed the ominous information that Lee Lestark's column and the bloodhound spot had made Josie Donovan's imagined transgression as notorious as Mack Bender's supposed one-night stand with Gabby Lukes.

"That goddam dog's wiping us out," Art Mingo groaned. "Everything we gained since the candidate threw his wife to the wolves."

Rafael Ames stayed cool. "When you get kicked in the balls," he told Mingo, "best thing to do is call in old Doctor Video."

Working around the clock, Ames got out a depth charge to counter the bloodhound. It opened quietly, innocuously, with film of an opulent house amid lush gardens. No music.

"It was in this house," a mild voice related, "at a plush Florida resort, that Senator Mack Bender spent the night with the notorious Washington lobbyist Gabriella Lukes."

Old film of Gabby, blond and low-cut, glass in hand, entertaining at a cocktail party.

"Senator Bender would have us believe he didn't know *she* was in the house."

News film of an angry Mack Bender: ". . . just a low political attack. I don't think I even saw the woman that night."

The opulent house again; cut to black-and-white still of busty Gabby, looking seductive; while it remained on-screen, the mild voice resumed: "Who does he think he's kidding?"

Quick cut to the Honorable Victor T. Donovan declaring: ". . . that shining moral example that means more to me, and I know to you, than anything else."

Film freezes on his sincere face. The mild voice again: "Wouldn't you rather have a senator who sets a Christian moral example for our time . . . for *your* children?"

After this commercial's first airing, Mayor Blade demanded at a hastily called news conference: "When is Tricky Vic Donovan going to stop these underhanded smears, these

. . . these flat-out *lies* about a man who's worked overtime for the people of this state?"

To which bait, the Honorable Victor T. Donovan refused to rise.

"I guess the mayor got up on the wrong side of the bed this morning," he told a rally later in Oxbow. "Or maybe he's been a politician himself long enough to know that the man he used to work for is getting whipped."

Once again, as the Chief's overnight polls showed, the race swung back and forth. Published polls continued to show the senator slightly ahead, but the outcome was well within the margin of error; apparently knowing political sources said this was not just the result of *choice* but also of name recognition and familiarity. Lunch counter analysis considered the election too close to call. At the Exxon station in Yellowtail, Slim Chance inelegantly summed up his pinochle buddies' views:

"Tighter than teenage pussy!"

Art Mingo agreed. He spent the last few days tirelessly organizing to produce a heavy turnout, hoping to bring out not only Victor T. Donovan's supporters but voters who had not voted or who in the past had backed Senator Bender for lack of an alternative. Mingo's strategy assumed that they would welcome the appeal of a new face. A small turnout, on the other hand, was likely to favor the candidate with the longer-known image.

"Turnout shmernout," Ames complained. "They'll be voting in mobs because of Overholt and me. They can't look at the set, they don't see the campaign."

"Rafe . . ." One of Mingo's virtues was patience. "One thing I learned the hard way, in this business there's no such thing as a sure thing."

Telephone banks, door-to-door canvassers, a flock of cars with drivers ready to transport the elderly and infirm to the polls, a flurry of radio appeals (ostensibly nonpartisan but paid for by Darwin John) to vote like good citizens for "the man of your choice," as well as huge ads to the same point in every newspaper in the state, the Jaycees mobilized in Capital City for the worthy purpose of getting out the vote—Mingo resorted to every device gleaned from his long experience at winning elections. He paid particular attention to the efficient distribution of absentee ballots.

"Some guy's too busy to go to the polls," he explained to Bryce Powers, who had become an admirer, "maybe travels a lot, got a secretary doing his chores, bet your ass he won't back a liberal like Bender. Absentees'll go three to one for my man."

Focus groups organized by both campaigns reflected the sentiment that Lee Lestark's column had justified Victor T. Donovan's decision to separate from his wife and his proclaimed desire to set a high moral example. In contrast, and despite the bloodhound, many thought Mack Bender would have done better to confess his sin—as Victor T. Donovan had more or less confessed his wife's—and ask the people's forgiveness.

"Like hell," Bender said to Theo Keller when told of this attitude. "If I admit I shacked up with that bunny-looking babe, they'd sooner forgive Hitler."

Cinema Center, which operated five screens in the former Roller Rink on the outskirts of Capital City, advertised the results of its Popcorn Poll: Over the final weeks of the campaign, 2,222 moviegoers had bought popcorn in Bender Bags, while 2,116 had chosen Donovan Druthers. Nearly 3,000 had purchased popcorn in sacks labeled "NO."

"Which only means," Bart Goings declared after reading the tally in the *Ledger*, "they're selling a shitload of popcorn over there."

National reporters, flocking in for the election, thought it significant that Chief Sam Runninglegs finally came out for Victor T. Donovan. These reporters did not know that Chief Runninglegs's endorsement had been negotiated by Art Mingo, to be announced when Mingo thought it most effective, in return for unspecified future considerations that Runninglegs in past years had failed to extract from O. Mack Bender.

"Either of these assholes wins," Carl Fulk told his wife, as they watched *The Simpsons* after his hard day's work weatherstripping the Bullseye Bar and Grill in Broken Axle, "the rest of us better keep a-holt our wallets."

In a noon speech to the combined civic clubs of Appaloosa,

Victor T. Donovan accused Senator Bender of opposition to the death penalty. Bender, in fact, had voted some years before against capital punishment for the federal crime of sodomy in the toilet of any airliner that flew across state borders.

Victor T. Donovan, on the other hand, stood foursquare for the death penalty as a demonstration of "society's moral outrage" at crime—though his state already decreed the electric chair for offenses ranging from breaking and entering at night to serial murder.

"We've got to get *serious* about crime," the congressman declared. "I say an eye for an eye and a tooth for a tooth!"

The Appaloosa speech was a setup that gave Rafael Ames the launching pad for the rocket he had been saving for the finale of the campaign. He immediately aired a long-prepared spot that opened with the outraged face of Victor T. Donovan demanding: "What does Mack Bender say *now* about the death penalty?"

Quick cut to film of black-tied Senator Bender speaking to a banquet group in impenetrable gobbledygook about the Uruguay Round.

Back to Victor T. Donovan, angrier now: "Why won't Mack Bender tell you where he stands *now* on the death penalty?"

Bender appeared shirt-sleeved at a political rally, promising in ringing tones to promote the welfare, pursue the happiness, etc., of every living American, without regard to race, color, or creed.

Victor T. Donovan again, sounding resigned: "But what this state wants to know, Senator—are you for or against the death penalty *now*?"

Bender on-screen to respond emphatically: "Better the criminal should go free—"

Here the sound track became fuzzy; the closing words were barely comprehensible to close listeners: "—than the innocent be convicted."

Small letters overlay this film clip, which gave no hint that it was six years old: "From Campaign Debate."

Victor T. Donovan finally, vigorously: "Vic Donovan doesn't think the criminal should go free! Vic Donovan's *for* the death penalty!"

The last-minute impact was considerable in a state where men carried rifles in racks behind the seats of their pickup trucks, and John Wayne was revered. Raymond Goodwood advised Art Mingo that the spot had swung a number of his constituents off the fence.

"That thing's a real killer," Goodwood declared.

The timing was shrewd, too, leaving Bucky Overholt no chance to prepare an explicit response, though Senator Bender himself lamely declared that the death penalty was a state, not a federal, issue, and their state already imposed it. Overholt resorted to his backlog—to a spot that was not a direct response or the sort of brass-knuckle blow he usually favored, but that he thought would have substantial cornball effect.

Senator Bender and his motherly wife, she wearing her familiar apron, strolled across the lawn of a nineteenth-century gingerbread house, presumably theirs—though actually they had lived for years in the Methodist Building in Washington, maintaining only an apartment with a kitchenette in Capital City.

A preteenage girl in a western outfit, astride a black animal with one white foot, trotted up to the couple and dismounted. Mrs. Bender put a motherly arm around the child.

"This is our daughter, Belinda."

"And this"—Senator Bender grasped the bridle of the little animal; the camera moved in close on both their heads—"is Hotfoot, Belinda's pride and joy. Some easterners might think he's a horse. Around here we know Hotfoot's just a pony."

He stroked Hotfoot's nose. "So it pays to be careful when people who don't know what they're talking about start throwing a lot of charges around."

Bender turned away from Hotfoot and stood beside his daughter and white-haired Mrs. Bender, beaming in her apron.

"Like my opponents. Why, if even half of what they say about me were true, the wife here wouldn't let me come home for dinner."

Fade out on a smiling three-shot, Bender's arm around his motherly wife, her arm around Belinda. Hotfoot looks around cutely at the camera.

"So if Betty Crocker and her little girl don't seem to care if the Gummer dicked Gabby or protects criminals," Ames told Floyd Finch, with a hint of admiration, "why should anybody else? That's what Overholt's trying to put across, my man."

The fate of Josie Donovan still rankled Finch. "If we could put *our* wife on TV," he said, "she'd run rings around that old bag in the apron."

"Floyd"—Ames's voice was mocking—"that's not the kind of running around Josie Baby's famous for."

Some local reporters thought an editorial in the Oakwood *Messenger*, a pro-Donovan weekly in his old district, virtually conceded defeat when it claimed for him "a moral victory no matter how the actual vote turns out." On the other hand, J. Carson Ritch seemed confident in his final *Crusher* editorial. "Though not a landslide," he wrote, "the Donovan victory now in the making will be decisive."

On election eve Penny Burd expressed to her husband, Steve, the fear that not enough right-thinking women would exercise their voting privilege to defeat that old lech Bender, with all his whores. But Bryce Powers, tirelessly working the phones to sources around the state, knew better than to tell Theo Keller that he sensed the tide running again for Victor T. Donovan.

"I got to make a living," he told Umstead, the slot man. "And the *Ledger* pays a lot better than working nights in a steam laundry."

★

Both candidates campaigned throughout election day, right up to the closing of the polls. Mack Bender toured senior citizens' centers, trying to get right with the old folks, many of whom had been shocked by the Gabby Lukes story; politicians, they thought, had not gone tomcatting around in *their* day.

Victor T. Donovan attended a prayer breakfast in Capital City and a prayer lunch in Bedrock, emphasizing his moral example theme; both affairs had been arranged by Art Mingo and featured Protestant and Catholic clerics. Then the congressman donned a cowboy hat and rode a white horse before a rodeo crowd at Indian Trail.

Mingo's turnout arrangements functioned like well-oiled gears. His fleets of autos hauled voters to the polls in a never-ending flow. Scarcely a household in the state, in which was known to reside a Donovan supporter or leaner, or an undecided, went untelephoned by well-paid volunteers. The pitch was direct and insistent, but if a determined Bender voter was on the line, he or she got only a cursory reminder that it was election day. None of the latter was urged to vote.

Taking care not to encounter each other in person, O. Mack Bender and Victor T. Donovan appeared in sequence on the popular statewide TV program *Under the Dome*, aired from the old redstone state capitol building. Senator Bender, designated by protocol to go first, said he was flattered by the suggestion of host Oliver Swan that he might run for President. But, he assured Swan and his listeners, he had "absolutely no plans to do anything but serve the good people of this state for the next six years."

Victor T. Donovan later told Swan and the audience that anyone who believed Bender's pledge "would buy Yellowstone Park, Ollie, for ten dollars down."

Throughout election day spots for both sides flooded the state's airwaves—most prominently, the BAM bloodhound, Victor T. Donovan's death penalty declaration, and Ames's recap of the Gabby Lukes caper. Deputy Sheriff Blanton F. Hollis, who had voted as soon as the polls opened at 6:30 A.M., was offended by another spot, in which Senator Bender charged that his "slippery" opponent had voted for antipollution laws, then flip-flopped to accept contributions from PACs representing corporations charged with polluting.

"You show me a man always whining about this pollution crap," Deputy Sheriff Hollis assured his wife, the doeskin waitress—both were at home, since the Lewis & Clark's lobby bar was closed on election day—"I'll show you a bleeding heart that's against *jobs*."

Sam Stennis, one of nine candidates for five places on the Pinto County Commission, voted a straight party ticket, which included himself and Mack Bender. Stennis had little hope of winning a seat on the commission, since he had never run for office before, was little known, and had spent only $275, all to print wallet-size campaign cards. But he calculated his campaign had been worth the money in publicity for Sam's Salvage, his auto graveyard.

So as he sipped a Coors Light and watched late-afternoon TV in the old school bus body that served as the graveyard office, Sam Stennis only chuckled at a commercial that featured the four familiar presidential faces on Mount Rushmore, then joined them with a mock-up of O. Mack Bender.

"But in this state we don't need a monument," Victor T. Donovan came on to declare. "We need a *senator*!"

"Not you, we don't," Sam Stennis replied, jovially waving his Coors at the screen. But he could not help wondering if maybe Senator Bender *had* got maybe a little too far above himself to touch base with ordinary folks like salvage customers.

The candidates kept doggedly at it as the sun slipped lower in the brilliant blue sky of election day; so did Mingo's volunteers. Bender had no get-out-the-vote operation since he privately agreed with Mingo that the lower the turnout, the better his chances. The senator himself, however, walked along downtown streets in Capital City and through the stores that lined them, shaking every hand in sight, as cheery as if he had not been at it for hours.

"My best shot," he had said to Ernest Fulton, "is eyeball to eyeball with the folks that got me here."

Victor T. Donovan did a final radio turn with Country Rhodes, who asked him to tell listeners what would be his first priority in the Senate. To the surprise of no one, least of all Country Rhodes, the congressman replied: "To make this state proud of a clean-living senator."

Voter turnout, all reporters noted as the polls finally closed across the state, had been heavy.

★

Late in the afternoon, as she had planned, Lacy Farnes slipped out of Donovan headquarters in one end of the Lewis & Clark ballroom and went up to her own room. Without hesitation, she picked up the telephone, punched eight, got the tone for long distance, and tapped in 1-202-555-1212 for District of Columbia information. In a moment an operator asked: "What city, please?"

"Washington," Lacy said, wondering what other city was in the District. "I want the office number for the newspaper columnist Lee Lestark."

She was too cautious to jot down the number on the bedside pad, committing it at once to memory. A secretary's voice responded after three rings.

"Mister Lestark, please." Remembering how Milo Speed felt about Lestark, Lacy considered it an act of revenge even to phone the man's office. She shivered with pleasure.

"May I say who's calling?"

"Somebody with information about Milo Speed."

A brief silence, then: "He'll be right with you."

More silence. Then a click and a hum and another click.

"Lady, this better not be a gag," Lestark said. "I'm a busy man."

He sounded as nasty as Speed had made him out to be. But Lacy had expected that. If Lee Lestark was a nice guy, he would not be the one she needed.

"You wrote about what Speed *used* to do. Don't you want to know what he's doing *now*?"

"That stud act of his is a bore, lady. No news in it."

"Not even," Lacy said, "if he's still getting it on with Josie Donovan?"

That stopped him, she thought, with satisfaction.

"Who is this anyway?"

Lacy had expected the question and had decided in advance on her answer.

"A friend of Calvin Kyle."

Silence. Then: "Why didn't Cal call himself?"

"Because he doesn't know what I know."

"Which is?"

"That you've got a better story than you thought you had."

But now you can't get it out in time to affect the vote out here, she thought. Not in time to stop the congressman from winning. Just in time to strip down Milo Speed and Mrs. Roundheels for all the world to see.

She had never felt so powerful, so much like *somebody*. It was, Lacy thought, a really good feeling, as if for once she had told her father off and made him listen or kicked her dirty little flasher of a brother in the balls.

"Tell me more," said Lee Lestark, making Lacy feel even better.

★

There were no voting machines and no central system for counting votes. Returns came in to Capital City slowly, indecisively, in no particular order, no clear pattern forming on the blackboards each campaign had set up at either end of the Lewis & Clark's ballroom—divided, for the occasion, down the middle by partisanship and sliding plastic panels.

"They do it better in Panama," Ames remarked to Floyd Finch. "When the spics get to vote down there, you know who wins before the polls open."

Morning would dawn before all returns, or even most of them, were counted. The attention of the throngs at either end of the ballroom, and of interested persons all over the state and the nation, therefore focused on the television networks. Which would "call it" first? And for whom?

Raymond Goodwood telephoned Art Mingo ninety minutes after the polls closed, to inquire when Mingo wanted Goodwood's precincts reported.

"I can hold 'em as long as you want," Goodwood said. "Give you any majority you need."

"Don't bet the farm just yet," Mingo nevertheless reported to Darwin John. "These Bender guys like that goddam mayor"—he spoke with undue modesty—"they maybe got some local tricks I don't know yet."

Theo Keller inserted at the top of the *Ledger*'s page one a two-column photo of a woman voting with a baby in her arms. Cute shot and good citizenship. Besides, if Mack Bender was reelected, a proper two-column mug shot of the future presidential candidate could be subbed. If Victor T. Donovan pulled off an upset, the lady with the baby could run through all editions.

J. Carson Ritch had no such election night considerations to worry him; the weekly *Crusher* would not come out until Thursday evening. He had organized a viewing party at his house and had rented two extra TVs so that his guests could see election reports from all three networks and their local affiliates.

"Be all over by ten o'clock," he predicted as he greeted each arrival. "Grab yourself a drink, Durward. Been a long, dry day."

"Still looks too close to call," Bryce Powers hedged when interviewed on KPEP; he had no doubt Theo Keller was watching. At about the same time, on another channel, a network correspondent who had been several days in Capital City was explaining an exit poll:

"Precincts voting for Bender by more than fifty-five percent six years ago are backing him this year by only fifty-two-point-six percent. We extrapolate that to an overall decline of—"

Mayor Chet Blade had a low opinion of exit polls because he believed people seldom told the polltakers the truth. "They don't want to fess up," he told Ernest Fulton. "They want to act like they made up their minds only on the issues."

As he watched Mack Bender striding impatiently about his headquarters suite at the Lewis & Clark, the mayor was uneasily optimistic Bender would be reelected, though in a squeak. Enough voters would honor his integrity and his years of service, his high standing in the country. In the end they wouldn't turn such a man out of office for a jackleg congressman most of them had barely heard of six months ago. Still . . .

The mayor whispered nervously to Ernest Fulton: "That Gabriella cunt really shafted us."

Two floors above, meanwhile, Rafael Ames secretly admired the calm demeanor of Victor T. Donovan. *Ice water,* Ames kept thinking; *he got cut, he'd bleed ice water.*

After the rigors of the campaign, however, Ames hardly cared anymore whether the Honorable or the Gummer won the election. The hard-eyed redhead was going to bad-mouth him—probably already had. He knew it in his bones. And there went the future he'd been counting on, right down the tubes.

"Think we got it made," Floyd Finch, who was heavily into Carta Blanca, told Ames around nine-thirty. "Too bad that little honeysuckle rose ain't here. Help us cel'brate."

Sometime after that Lacy Farnes called Mr. Horn in Washington, using one of the several phones installed in Victor T. Donovan's suite at the Lewis & Clark. Behind her, Mingo, Ames, Finch, and one or two local men, whose names Lacy was trying hard to memorize, were clustered around the television set. The congressman—the coolest person in the room, she was proud to see—chatted on another phone.

Mr. Horn took several rings to answer. "Sorry, Lacy, I was watching TV."

"The congressman wants me to tell you he thinks we're in."

There was a pause on the line. "What makes him think so?" Mr. Horn sounded faintly skeptical.

"He's talking to one of the networks now." Lacy was so excited her words ran together. "I think they're getting ready to call it." She told him which channel to watch.

"How do those TV people *do* it?" Mr. Horn said. "Pick a winner so early?"

"The congressman says computers. He says they're almost never wrong."

"My word," Mr. Horn said, "I never really believed—" He broke off abruptly.

Lacy's excitement cooled. She spoke more sharply than she had intended.

"You didn't think we'd win?" If the congressman's *own people* didn't believe in him . . .

"Oh, of course I did, it was just that . . . I mean, sometimes it was hard to take in it was really happening. Listen . . ." Mr. Horn stopped again, then resumed in a rush: "Lacy, would you . . . I mean, if you don't mind . . . maybe you could find out if I'm going over there with him?"

"To the Senate?" Lacy was surprised. She was not accustomed to Mr. Horn in the role of supplicant and had not doubted that he would move with the congressman.

"I've worked over there before, you know. For old Senator Capps."

The Sagebrush Solon. *A long time ago,* Lacy thought. *A different ball game.* Maybe Mr. Horn had more to worry about than she'd thought.

"I don't have any way of knowing what the congressman intends, Mister Horn."

"But you've got a real . . . uh, *in* with him, Lacy. You could find out."

Lacy did not know whether to be angered at his assumption or gratified at what she was coming to see as her new status. Her excitement rose again. First Ames, now this.

But Mr. Horn was a different cup of tea. Mr. Horn could never be a threat to her; he would never see anything through her glasses but a pleasant young woman's pleasant green eyes. She listened for a moment to his anxious breathing on the other end of the line.

"I'll see what I can do, Mister Horn."

She accepted in silence and with faint impatience Mr. Horn's fervent thanks.

★

Senator O. Mack Bender swore at the television set, with feeling.

"Those pricks don't know what they're talking about!" he exclaimed to Bucky Overholt.

Overholt looked quizzical. "I wouldn't count on *that.*"

Ernest Fulton protested: "There's not even a quarter of the vote counted yet. How can they know?"

Mayor Blade looked up from a tally sheet on a clipboard: "Some of your best precincts are still out, Mack."

But Bucky Overholt said: "Time to concede, Senator. Don't drag out the misery."

"Concede?" Bender threw himself back in his chair, glaring at Overholt. "I'm not even sure I'm whipped, Bucky. And I'm damned if I'll give that sleazy bastard the satisfaction of hearing me concede."

He could scarcely believe it was all over. It couldn't be. The third term. The White House. His plans to focus on global

warming, the rain forests. How could Tricky Vic's lies and chicanery have won out? How could people he knew have done this to him—people he loved, people he'd served well?

"It's protocol to concede," Overholt said. "But you don't want to, nobody makes you."

Ernest Fulton coughed, holding the side of his fist to his mouth. "I say it's too early, Senator. Way too early. But when the time comes . . . *if* it comes . . . you don't want to look like a bad loser."

"Mack's *not* a bad loser," Mayor Blade said. "He's not *any* kind of a loser. Not yet."

Bucky Overholt downed the last of his gin and tonic, took his jacket from the back of his chair, and said to the group: "Well, gents, we gave it our best shot. But I learned long ago you can't win 'em all."

"You aren't the one running," Mayor Blade said. "You aren't the one that matters."

Overholt had started out of the room. He turned, at these words, but his manner clearly shut out the mayor and Fulton.

"Senator . . . can I speak to you a minute?"

O. Mack Bender hesitated, looked again at the solemn anchorman in the faraway newsroom, all the way across the continent, repeating his incredible call. How *could* he know?

Bender got up and went to the door where Overholt waited for him. He felt unreal.

This can't be happening. Not this way, he thought, just all at once. All over with and done.

Behind him, Ernest Fulton said to Mayor Blade: "The issues didn't matter a damn, Chet. Not a good goddam. I had position papers ready on every issue conceivable. Stacks of position papers still in our press room. Nobody even looked at 'em. Nobody *cared* about the issues."

"Next time," Mayor Blade said, "forget the position papers. Use sound bites."

Nobody had cared either, he thought, about Mack Bender's character and integrity and his years of service. What he could offer in the future. Not enough voters had cared about any of that. What they cared about, instead, was Gabby Lukes. And Tricky Vic's bullshit moral example.

Ernest Fulton shook his head. "Not me, Chet. I wouldn't want anything to do with that kind of a campaign."

"It's what works," Mayor Blade said. *And it looks to me like what works is all that counts.*

At the door Bucky Overholt was saying confidentially: "I know how you feel, Senator. But my last campaign advice to you—much good the rest did, huh?—go down there and concede. Congratulate the bastard, like they'll expect you to."

But it's only a network call, Bender thought. *Just out of thin air.*

"I'll think about it, Bucky. When I have to. Right now I'm just remembering all the things I wanted to say. All the questions I intended to raise and never . . ." His words trailed away.

"You did your best," Overholt said.

"No." Bitter awareness tinged Bender's voice. "I let *him* carry the ball. I let him set the tone, and he cut me to pieces."

Overholt touched his arm. "Tell me just one thing, now it's all over."

Bender winced at the phrase, still hoping desperately for something to happen: the anchorman to renege, some forgotten county to come in big for him, maybe even the computer to admit error. Garbage in, garbage out. But he knew in his anguished heart that none of it would happen, any more than he would ever have it all to do again, the right way, the way he'd really wanted to do it.

"What's left to tell, Bucky?"

Overholt winked suggestively. "How was it that time with Gabby?"

O. Mack Bender looked at him with tired, defeated eyes. That was the worst of it, he thought. He had done it to himself.

"Tell you the truth, Bucky . . . I've had better."

★

"But listen," Floyd Finch was saying, two floors above. "You've *got* to. The Gummer comes down to concede, you got to be there to say something nice about 'im."

"About *him*? No way. I'll demand a recount first."

There was a tap at the door; Lacy Farnes answered it. She

signed for a telegram and handed it to Victor T. Donovan, who tore it open and read quickly. He knew, then, that it was certain: no mere network prediction.

"Darwin John," he said.

"Wha'd he say?" The awestruck local who asked was known to Lacy Farnes only as the president of the Capital City Chamber of Commerce.

"Great candidate," read Victor T. Donovan. "Great victory." He paused dramatically. "Great future. Darwin John."

Everyone was silent, as if a voice had rolled down from above. Finally, reverently, clearly reluctant to intrude on echoes of the Chief, Art Mingo said: "It would be the gracious thing if you'd go down there for his concession, Senator. Maybe some bad press if you don't."

The Honorable Victor T. Donovan ostentatiously folded the telegram and put it in his breast pocket, over his heart. He would remember, he thought, that Art Mingo had put the heat on him.

"What does the press know?" he said. "That monkey with his bloodhound accused me one too many times of taking the low road. Somebody else can go down to receive the surrender."

"But that's not the way it's *done,*" Finch said. "I never been in a campaign the winner didn't—"

Rafael Ames interrupted: "You don't want to do it, Senator, nobody makes you."

★

In Washington Milo Speed looked away from the television toward Josie; she lay on his sofa, her legs cocked up on its back.

"So much for American politics," Speed said. "The people, yes."

He thought of calling Theo Keller, maybe Bender himself. But what did he need to learn from them that he did not already know? He decided against being a journalist and focused, instead, on his own concerns.

"Maybe you wish you were out there with him now."

Josie made a face. "It makes me sick to think about it. To

remember all the years I . . ." She put her arm over her eyes. "The years I threw away."

Speed decided to have it over with.

"Which makes it as good a time as any to ask you why the hell you stayed with Vic? Instead of me."

She moved her arm and looked up at him—a little evasively, he thought. Her voice was slightly edged.

"I never heard you say anything serious about getting a divorce, did I?"

"Maybe not. But that wasn't it."

He sat on the edge of the sofa; Josie lowered her legs until one knee touched his hip. The soft contact reassured him; she really *was* there on his sofa. A smooth television voice droned on in the background.

"It just about killed me, Josie. When you left."

"Me, too."

"You couldn't have proved it by me."

"I wasn't about to let *you* know." Josie flung her arm across her eyes again, as if unwilling to look at the past.

He waited, puzzled, putting his hand on her thigh to reassure himself further. Josie took her arm away and looked into his eyes—directly this time. Her own eyes, in the half-light of the room, were the blue of night against the window.

"I was about to drown, Speed. I was going under for the third time."

"Because of me?"

"Sex," Josie said. "I couldn't think about anything else. I couldn't do anything, I couldn't control what I thought or did. It wasn't *just* you; it was what we had together, what it did to *me*."

Her eyes, he saw, had changed again, to a lighter, more brilliant blue.

"I thought if if I stayed with you, I'd drown. Something like that. The only thing I'd ever do was . . ."

Speed waited. The voice on TV said something about the upset of the year. Finally he asked: "Was what?"

"Make love with you. Like I wanted to do all the time. Even right there in the booth that last day with the rain running down the window."

"So did I."

He took her hand as before and closed her fist around his forefinger. She squeezed his finger spasmodically.

"And you said, 'Maybe that's all there is.' I thought if I didn't get away from . . . what we were . . . that really *was* all there ever would be."

"I'm not so sure anymore, Josie. That that's all there is."

"Funny." Josie looked up at him with eyes darkening again. "Sometimes, after that, I thought maybe it *was* true."

Remembering so much, the hurt of that day in the Georgetown café an actual ache in his bones, recalling the blunt weapons of the words she'd used, he was sure there was more to come. Too easy, so far.

"You said Vic needed you and I didn't."

Josie's finger twisted in his grip.

"I was pregnant," she said.

The words were like drumbeats, pounding in his ears. *But why,* he wondered, bewildered, almost disoriented, *didn't she tell me then? I'd have . . .*

Hastily, as if reading his thoughts or forcing herself to go on, Josie said: "Remember you were away on a trip? For about a month?" Her second's hesitation seemed an age. "That's when it happened."

Vic . . . needs me.

He let go of her finger, grasping at her meaning, as if at a slashing blade. "With Vic," he said. "While I was away."

She seized his hand in both of her own. "Speed, I was his wife . . . I couldn't . . . I didn't think I could just . . ."

Josie looked at him over their clasped hands, her vein blue eyes pleading. He felt the blade slashing, its edge searing, knowing before he heard it what she was going to say next, what in the cruel flux of life it was inevitable she would say: "You were away so long, and I was lonely. That night . . ."

He finished for her. "You wanted it."

"I wanted you."

For a moment he thought he would not be able to bear the hurt. He closed his eyes, bearing it anyway. For a long time only the anchorman's well-informed voice broke the silence.

"Look at me," Josie said, after a while. "Don't close your eyes like that."

He looked at her, saw tears brimming on her lashes. Their hands were still clasped.

"I couldn't go on with you while . . ." Then, in a rush: "I had Vic's baby inside me. And I thought . . . maybe a child, a family would hold Vic and me together."

So, after all the echoing years, after so much of his life, he knew the truth.

What fools we are! he thought. *For wanting the truth. When nothing is harder to bear.*

"Then I lost the baby," Josie said. "Maybe if he had been yours, like he should have been, everything would have been all right."

But of course, everything had not been all right. The stars had moved in their relentless courses, of which he had known nothing, guessed nothing. He had been wrapped in his own loss, cloaked in the vast ignorance that shielded men from truth. Until truth at last, like the anchorman's drone in the background, had shattered silence.

"If it had been mine, I'd have liked a girl." He knew as he said it that he was years too late. The futility of the words was leaden in his mouth. "A girl like you."

Josie let go his hands, put hers to his cheeks, and pulled his head down. He felt the tears wet on her face, his own mingling with them. He held her close and whispered into the fragrance of her hair, feeling its tickle miraculously on his lips: "Maybe we're better for the way things happened."

He did not believe his own words. They left him, nevertheless, a kind of peace, as if he had borne the worst.

"No," Josie said, "we're just older."

He kissed her, stirred by the remembered hunger of her mouth, real again. He was holding Josie, not in a dream or a memory but in his arms. He had his life again. It hardly seemed to matter, anymore, that he had missed so much of it.

★

Well after midnight Lacy Farnes went back to her own room. Tired but happy, she started to undress for bed. The campaign trail had been every bit as exciting as she'd expected. And they'd won!

She was getting into bed when the phone rang. She knew before she picked it up who'd be on the line.

"I thought maybe you'd come back down and we could celebrate with a drink," Victor T. Donovan said.

Since Ames's prediction Lacy had expected just this call, and had rehearsed her lines to be ready when it came.

"Oh . . . I don't . . . who else is with you, Senator?"

"Nobody. Last well-wisher just straggled out. But I'm not quite ready to let this evening fade away."

"Well, if you're alone," Lacy said, "I mean, that talk we had in your office after we went out to dinner that time . . . do you really think it's all right?"

"Lacy, we won! And you know me well enough by now to know that *of course* it's all right."

Lacy did not know him that well. She knew, instead, exactly what he had in mind, though she conceded he might not know it himself. Victor T. Donovan, after all, was a male as well as a gentleman—and now a senator. Because he was all of those things, she had no doubt what he really wanted—what they all wanted—or that she could handle him.

"If you really think so, I'll be right down."

Victor T. Donovan said the most daring thing she had ever heard from him: "Come as you are."

She decided to give him a thrill and whispered reproachfully: "Oh, Senator . . . if you could see me, you'd know I couldn't do *that*."

To let his imagination work, she took plenty of time dressing. Rejecting her office hours bra, she chose one that lifted her breasts; otherwise she carefully dressed in sedate clothes. After checking herself in the mirror, she hurried two flights down the stairwell, made sure the corridor was empty, and trotted along it to tap at the new senator's door.

Victor T. Donovan was fully clothed, too, as she had expected; he was not a precipitate man. He did have a drink ready for her, a weak gin and tonic like the one she'd nursed through the long wait for the returns to come in.

"Quite an evening," he said, sitting stiffly beside her on the sofa. "Quite an evening! I think the vote's just about confirmed the network."

Lacy had been sure it would. It was beyond her imagination that the network could be wrong.

"I didn't get a chance to tell you earlier, Senator. I'm glad you didn't go down to accept his concession. After all the mean things he's said and that bloodhound and all."

"I just couldn't have done it, Lacy. And anyway . . . did you know Bender turned out to be too sorry a loser to concede? Maybe he couldn't face me. Ames found out he sneaked out of the hotel through the kitchen."

To be a spy was a fitting role for that snake Ames. Lacy said: "You're bound to be good in the Senate, sir, the way you make so many hard decisions for yourself. Like not going down there."

He smiled and sipped his gin and tonic—the first, Lacy was sure, he'd had that night.

"I'll have plenty of help over there."

"Of course. Mister Horn and me and the other girls for the office work. But for the big questions, with all your political experience, I don't think you really need anybody else."

"I'm thinking of this Ritch fellow over in Bedrock for press relations," Victor T. Donovan said. "Seems pretty savvy, knows the state like a book. Good insurance for next time, when Chet Blade takes me on. He will, you know."

Lacy could barely remember who Chet Blade was; she only marveled that the senator was already thinking six years ahead.

She also seized her chance. "What about Ames?"

"Well . . . I really don't know about Rafe. Sometimes he's brilliant, I give him that. What do you think?"

"Well, it's not my place to . . ."

"No, no . . . I really want to know." Victor T. Donovan tipped his glass to her. "I've learned to respect your judgment, Lacy." He glanced not too obviously at her uplifted breasts.

"Well, if you really . . ." She set her glass on the coffee table, leaning forward to give him a more rounded view. "I think Rafe Ames is kind of beneath you."

Victor T. Donovan looked puzzled.

"Now that you're going to be in the Senate, I mean. In my judgment, he'd try to drag you down with him."

"Down?"

"To the low road," Lacy said.

Victor T. Donovan shook his head decisively. "I couldn't have that. I guess I'll have to think hard about Ames. But listen . . . let's don't talk politics anymore." He tipped his glass again, and she saw him swallow. "You look extraordinarily beautiful tonight."

Coming on.

She said: "That must be because you won. I'm so excited I could die!"

She really was. She wished her father could see her in the senator's room. And her asshole brother. Of course, with their dirty minds . . .

"We must have dinner again," Victor T. Donovan said. "That was more fun that night than I can remember."

"I'd like that."

Lacy measured the moment and decided it was ripe. He had shown his hand but would be too much of a gentleman to push it. If anything further were to happen, it would be up to her. But that might jeopardize the future.

She stood up. "I really have to go now." She giggled expertly. "Get my beauty rest."

"Oh, you hardly need *that*."

Victor T. Donovan walked with her to the door, trying but failing to hide the disappointment that would have disclosed his thwarted hope.

"I meant it about dinner," he said.

The wistful note in his voice told her she had gauged him correctly. She opened the door, turned, and held out her hand; Victor T. Donovan took it, swallowed again, and leaned forward as if to kiss her.

Lacy inclined her head toward him but at the last second turned it so that his lips only brushed her cheek; then she stepped back and looked at him with wide, direct green eyes.

"I know you meant it, Senator. But there'll be plenty of time for . . . all that."

The Morning After

Josie and Speed had stayed up late, lying together on the sofa, watching election returns from around the nation. Josie slept late the next morning. But with a column to write, Milo Speed began making phone calls by 9:00 A.M.

A polltaker for each party, a White House assistant, a former Cabinet officer now lobbying for communications industries, and the Speaker's right-hand man all confirmed Speed's opinion that the defeat of O. Mack Bender, reverberating into the next presidential election, was more than merely the upset of the decade.

"I'm already trying to get the TV clips," said a senator of Victor T. Donovan's party. "A lot of us around here are going to want to know how this guy managed to pull this off. Something might rub off on the rest of us."

"Just a damn tragedy," a senator of Bender's party lamented. "A man of principle like Mack. Could of won the next nomination, easy. And you better believe it, Speed, that lying son of a bitch that ambushed him out there, he shows his face in the Senate, he's gonna get a reception with icicles on it."

Yes, Speed thought as he hung up. But before he'd been there a year, Victor T. Donovan would be a member of the Club, just like the other ninety-nine.

Of all the calls Speed placed that morning, only Darwin John did not come on the line at once.

"Mister John," a distant female voice informed him, "is with the President." As, she seemed to be saying, you should have expected.

Speed hated to leave his telephone number anywhere. Even though his quarry usually called back right away, he still dreaded the possibility that someone might not. When it occasionally happened, he brooded as if over a slight.

"Maybe I'll call him again," he told the cool voice. "And then again maybe I won't."

Since the Lestark column had appeared and until he had started making his own calls that morning, Speed had kept his telephone turned off, in order to frustrate reporters trying to reach him. He had told them all he intended to—which was not much—when he had faced them the day before, while Josie drove away in Evangeline's car.

"Some things are private," he had insisted. "Even from you servants of the people."

"But she's a congressman's wife," one reporter insisted, and another said righteously:

"The people have a right to know what—"

Speed had cut him off. "All the people have a *right* to know, I've been trying to tell them for years. And it's got nothing to do with anybody's sex life."

Now, after his fruitless call to Darwin John, he had hardly taken his hand off the phone before it rang. Instinctively he picked it up.

"This Speed?"

Speed regretted at once that he had answered when he knew the press still had his building staked out.

"Get lost, will you? I knew all those reporters' tricks before you were born."

"This's Calvin Kyle," said the voice on the other end of the line.

Speed reacted cautiously. "Yeah?"

"Got something you'll want to know about."

Speed was instantly angry. "I'm not Lee Lestark, Kyle. You're wasting your time."

"Suit yourself. But Tricky Vic's about to dump on the lady again."

Speed hesitated. He doubted there was any limit to what Victor T. Donovan would do to get even with Josie. Or with him. But what else might be coming?

"Could be a way for you to stop it."

"I'm listening," Speed said, in spite of his lingering anger.

"Not on the telephone."

"Then where?"

"I'm down in your building garage. Using a cellular phone. I could take the elevator right up."

"The TV guys didn't see you come in?"

Kyle's voice dripped with disdain. "Those assholes couldn't spot an elephant in an outhouse."

"All right." Speed had a sense of impending disaster, but his stronger intuition was that Calvin Kyle already had been spurned once too often. "Knock twice, then wait, and knock three times. I want to be sure it's you and not some amateur Winchell."

Kyle hung up. Speed went immediately to the bedroom door and checked to make sure Josie still slept. She was beautiful, there in bed with her long dark hair spread on the pillow; the sight made him catch his breath. He wanted nothing more, he thought, than to be sure she would always be there when he woke.

He left her breathing quietly in sleep and went back to the living room. When he heard the prescribed sequence of knocks, he went quickly to the door and opened it.

Two men he did not know stood in the corridor; between them, grinning, was Lee Lestark.

★

Far to the west and two hours earlier by the clock, Rafael Ames was just then tapping at Bucky Overholt's door in the

Lewis & Clark. Overholt, in his shorts, opened it, turned his back, and went to a room service table on which were numerous covered food dishes, a thermos of coffee, and a carafe of orange juice. He poured two glasses of juice and held out one to Ames, who had followed him into the room.

" 'Preciate you asking me up, Mister Overholt." Ames took the proffered glass.

"Bucky to you." Overholt drank down his own orange juice in one gulp. "Let's not beat around the bush, kid. You showed me a lot in this campaign. I'd of had a sharper candidate, I'd of whipped your ass. But you showed me plenty."

"Thanks a lot, uh, Bucky."

"I asked you for breakfast"—Overholt indicated the laden table with its covered dishes—" 'cause I been thinking. You want to make a deal?"

He poured coffee from the thermos into a cup and held it out.

"With you?"

Ames put down his juice glass and took the cup, thinking fast. The Honorable had his pecker up for the Lacy snatch; probably been in there all night long. Ames knew she could torpedo him; so of course she would. Scratch *that* contract.

If he went independent, there'd surely be others. But Bucky Overholt was the old master of the trade; Overholt already had the kind of business signed up that Ames knew he'd have to dig to attract. People whose names were household words.

"Junior partner," Overholt said.

Ames sipped his coffee and started at Overholt over the rim of the cup. Payday had arrived; Big Casino was at hand. He was dazzled but not too much to calculate the angles. Overholt could talk all he wanted, but he'd got his butt royally kicked in the Bender campaign, by a newcomer at that. Not only lost a race but blown the career of a Senator mentioned for President. So the bottom line was that Overholt had fallen on his ass, and no pratfall was lost on the trade. No doubt about it: Bucky Overholt was leading from weakness.

"No way, Jose," Ames said. "Make it even-steven."

Overholt eyed him sourly and made a show of hesitation,

enough to cause Ames to hold his breath. Then he put his coffee on the table, slopping a little over into the saucer.

"All right, smartass. Even up."

Ames breathed again. "Great, Bucky! It's a real honor."

"Kid," Bucky Overholt said, "we both know honor's got nothing to do with it. Have some eggs."

★

"Don't look so surprised," said Lee Lestark to Milo Speed. "I always did run rings around you in the tricks department."

Speed did not wish to dispute the claim. He looked at one of the other men, the one wearing a dingy Panama hat.

"You're Kyle, right?"

The brim of the Panama dipped an inch.

"Who tipped you?"

Calvin Kyle considered the question before replying: "Ames. He just thought there might be something."

"There always is," said Lee Lestark. "Isn't there?"

Speed ignored him and the third man. "And now Ames's got something else?"

"Not Ames." Lee Lestark turned to Calvin Kyle and tucked a greenback into the breast pocket of the investigator's tight-fitting suit. "See you later, Cal, and thanks a whole heap."

He elbowed his way past Speed into the living room and the other man followed. Speed had wanted instinctively to stop them; then he thought that the less disturbance, the better. Besides, using force on Lee Lestark might be satisfying, but it would only dodge the issue of whatever he and the other man wanted.

Calvin Kyle's gaze followed Lestark. Then he looked at Speed, and the brim of the Panama dipped again.

"Just doing my job," Kyle said, and turned away.

Speed closed the door and faced around to his visitors.

"Have we got a deal for you!" Lestark was as hearty as if offering Super Bowl tickets.

"Not likely," Speed said.

Lestark was tall and beefy but richly tailored; fat bulged

above the white collar of his striped shirt, but his well-cut suit concealed what Speed knew to be a spreading waistline, in which he longed to bury his fist. The other man was slender, unobtrusive in gray flannel, a subdued tie. He looked uncomfortable.

"Where's the lady?" Lestark's black wing tip shoes shone brilliantly.

Even if Josie awoke, Speed thought, she would be too wary to show herself outside the bedroom. He stonewalled.

"What lady?"

Lestark lowered himself jauntily to the sofa. "Galahad suit looks good on you, lover boy. But I got the real skinny."

"Not if you think there's a woman here."

Lestark sighed. "You mean there's not a dish named Josie—" he jerked his barbered head toward the bedroom door—"in there ready for Freddy?" He grinned salaciously at the third man. "Or maybe I should say needy for Speedy."

Speed pointed at the door. "Let's just say you can get your ass out of here right now. And take your friend with you."

Lestark kept on grinning. The other man still was standing, and still looked uncomfortable.

"But maybe Josie *is* in there . . . like I heard from a certain voice on the phone." Lestark settled himself more comfortably on the sofa. "Which it was easy for a smart guy like me to have traced while that certain voice was still talking. Guess where from, lover boy?"

"I'm not playing guessing games with you, Lestark. Or any other kind."

"Does the Lewis and Clark Hotel ring a bell?"

"Ames again?" Speed immediately regretted even this small response to Lestark's suggestions.

"Oh, no, no." Lestark shook his head vigorously. "So you'll know my bona fides, lover boy . . ."

He put his hands around his mouth and stage-whispered across the room: "A little birdie on the line."

Lacy, Speed thought. *Why would she leak to this creep?*

Lestark waggled a finger. "Singing sweetly. And we know what little redheaded twat just flew out there the other day, don't we?"

Speed was saddened for Lacy, by her; he remembered the day they had touched hands in the office of Victor T. Donovan, what that had meant to him at the time. But he could not doubt, after Lestark's hints, that Lacy Farnes had given the oily bastard some kind of information he thought he could use—apparently that Josie was still, or again, involved with him, Milo Speed.

Victor T. Donovan, Speed thought. *Just like him to tell Lacy that, even when he couldn't have known it was true.*

"Now we both know I'm serious, don't we?"

The third man coughed, a delicate sound muffled against the back of his hand.

"We *are* serious," he said. "So maybe we ought to get down to business."

Lestark gestured carelessly at the man. "Quentin Leech. Best editor in the business."

Leech smiled tentatively. "Not really. Not exactly."

Speed offered no smile in return. "Even if you're Max Perkins come back to life, you handle what *he* writes . . ." He nodded at Lee Lestark. "You got to do it with a shovel."

Lestark held up both hands as if to ward off a blow. "Never mind what *I* write, lover boy. Let's talk about what *you're* going to write."

★

The Honorable Victor T. Donovan's call, unlike Milo Speed's, went right through to Darwin John. For three minutes they exchanged hearty congratulations and cheerful views of the future. Then the Chief turned serious.

"That was a shame . . . a tough break, I mean, about your wife. Looks to me like you handled it just right, but it must have been hard on you."

"Not easy," Victor T. Donovan said. "But once I made up my mind, something just told me it was the right thing to do. The *only* thing."

In Darwin John's private view, Victor T. Donovan was well rid of Josie; no candidate needed a wife that fucked around. But the Chief assumed that anytime a man broke off with a woman he'd been married to for a long time, especially if he'd caught her cheating, it had to be a kick in the ass. And who'd want to lose a looker like Josie Donovan?

"I'm not going to forget it, Vic. All you did for us out there. The sacrifice you made for the party."

"I know you won't, Chief. Oh, there *was* one little thing I wanted to mention to you."

"What's that, Vic?"

"Well . . . at first I didn't want to say anything. Then I thought you really needed to know."

Darwin John waited. He never made it easier for anyone to call a due bill on him.

"I had a lot of trouble with Art Mingo."

The Chief was not easily shocked; this time he was.

"The best operator we've got, Vic. I can't imagine—"

"He's got that reputation, but I think maybe it's gone to his head, Chief."

"I'll talk to him," said Darwin John, intending to do no such thing. "Maybe dress him down a little."

"I want him fired."

Darwin John was shocked again. "What the hell did he *do*, Vic? I can't just—"

"Insolent, insubordinate, uncooperative, maybe disloyal. I don't want to bother you with details, but *I'll* never work with him again."

The Chief understood immediately that for whatever reasons, real or imagined, Victor T. Donovan wanted his pound of flesh from Art Mingo. And he had timed his request precisely, in the very echoes of a promise from the top that his sacrifice for the party would not be forgotten.

Time to punt, thought Darwin John. "I hear you, Vic. I'll look into it."

He thought wearily that it did not take much to make a tiger out of a house cat, a warlord from common clay. He had seen it before, applause at the curtain turning an understudy into a prima donna. Victor T. Donovan apparently was no exception; coming from so far down to so far up, he might even be harder than most to hold in line.

"Give me the word, Chief"—Victor T. Donovan's voice was quietly insistent—"I'll do it myself. Today."

Christ, said Darwin John to himself, though nearly aloud: *Who's this prick think he is*?

"Vic . . ." But even as the Chief started to speak irately, it was he who remembered:

Victor T. Donovan might in the flush of victory be a prick, but he was also the conqueror of O. Mack Bender, hence the man who had made victory in the next presidential election considerably more likely. He was a television star, a new party hero, one of its hopes for the future, maybe someday a national asset.

And who, in contrast, the Chief asked himself, reining in his anger, was Art Mingo? An advance man, a sharp operator, a loyal old hand. One of many. In the final analysis, an interchangeable part.

"You're sure that's what you want?"

"Dead sure, Chief."

Now was not the time, thought Darwin John, to fight it out. On what was, after all, a minor issue, with a man for the moment on top. Now was not the time.

"Then go ahead."

The Chief spoke decisively, conclusively, the way he always announced decisions, and hung up abruptly. In his long memory he marked it down carefully that the party's debt to Victor T. Donovan had been paid.

★

As much as he hated the sight of Lee Lestark perched on his sofa, Milo Speed—listening in spite of himself—had become curious to know what his visitors were up to. Surely nothing good.

"Six figures." Lestark spoke reverently. "Maybe seven."

"I'm sure . . ." Quentin Leech broke in smoothly. "Mister Speed must be wondering what we're here for." He looked with distaste at the empty seat on the sofa beside Lestark, then at a chair across the room.

"Sit down and tell me." Speed's abrupt tone was intended for Lestark, but it seemed to spur on Leech, who began talking even before he was seated:

"The whole story. How it all began. Right up to the minute

the husband finds out. Tough reporter and politico's wife. Congress and the press . . ."

"Plenty of Romeo and Juliet," Lee Lestark broke in breathlessly. "Star-crossed lovers, hands under the table. Secret codes, if you had 'em."

Speed stared in amazement, from one to the other.

"Love inside the Beltway," Lestark said. "Not to mention below the belt. It'll be the hottest thing since my best seller."

Lestark's best seller had recounted the sensational story of a Soviet defector, whose identity and experiences had been entirely invented by the CIA, then confided by the agency's disinformation experts only to Lee Lestark. Other writers, disgruntled at losing such a plum for themselves, had publicly cried foul; but Langley, at the highest levels, had denied all.

Owing to his own inquiries, Speed had no doubt that the charge was true. Nevertheless, Lestark's book had stayed atop the New York *Times* best-seller list for thirty-seven weeks. Including his take from the subsequent movie, *Freedom's Flame*, to Speed's disgust, had fixed Lestark financially for life.

"The minute that chick phoned me, I saw where this thing could go," Lestark said. "She's not hardly hung up, I'm on the horn to New York. I got a hot track record, y'know. So just on my sayso, tongues're hanging out up there for your book."

"*My* book? Goddammit, I'm not writing—"

"New York's already calling it *House Divided*. Because the other guy was an Emcee, you get it? Myself, I like *Potomac Passion*. Ties Washington right into the title, see what I'm saying?"

"Mister Lestark," said Quentin Leech, mildly but with force that surprised Milo Speed. "Let me handle this. *If* you don't mind?"

Lestark looked annoyed but slumped back on the sofa. "Didn't think you'd ever get down to the nut-cutting."

"What we'd like," Quentin Leech said, "ah . . . Arnold and Pound, that is. You know the house?"

Speed knew Arnold and Pound had published *Freedom's Flame*, and no questions asked. He felt he needed to know little more, but Quentin Leech pushed hurriedly on:

"We'd like your personal story, Mister Speed. A *love* story, the way we see it. Seems a natural, now that . . . ah . . . the other man's going to the Senate. It's . . . uh . . . promotable, Mister Speed, *très* promotable. Vast interest to a public that sees Washington . . . as, well . . ."

"Sex and scratch," Lee Lestark said. "They're thinking big in New York, Speed. Donahue, Oprah, spin-offs, ten-city tour, the whole shmear. And . . ."

"Mister Lestark." Quentin Leech spoke less mildly, more forcefully. Lestark lapsed sullenly into silence.

"We *would* put our . . . um . . . considerable resources behind your book, Mister Speed. It could be *the* Washington love story the public's been waiting for."

The man, Speed realized, was *serious*. His eyes, fixed on Speed's, glinted with interest, passion—with something that might even have passed for sincerity. Except that he was, at least to some extent, in league with Lee Lestark.

"What's the catch?" Speed said.

Quentin Leech shook his head sadly. "No catch, Mister Speed. Only one little point maybe I ought to mention."

"I think you should," Speed said, sympathetically.

"No holds barred," said Lee Lestark. "The real nitty-gritty, right down to her bra size."

"Lestark . . ." Quentin Leech's voice was no longer mild at all. "Just shut the fuck up!"

"But what he's saying . . ." Speed did not even look toward the sofa. "You'd want all the intimate details?"

Quentin Leech seemed offended. "*I* was only going to suggest . . ." He searched for words. "The story we at Arnold and Pound think we see . . . I mean, a lady of rather, eh, spectacular appearance, a famous journalist . . ."

Lee Lestark made a retching sound, which Quentin Leech and Milo Speed chose to ignore.

"And a top political figure . . . well, a triangle like that would almost *dictate* a little spice. Wouldn't you say so, Mister Speed?"

Speed was amazed to find that he preferred Lestark's open vulgarity to Quentin Leech's delicate suggestiveness.

He wondered how far these bizarre messengers were prepared to go.

"Suppose," he said, "the lady won't play ball?"

Quentin Leech's left hand lashed out, forestalling whatever Lee Lestark had been about to say.

"In that unfortunate case," he told Speed, his hand figuratively in Lestark's face, "you might want to tell her that Hollywood has been sounded out. And I think I may say that one of the most successful studios is . . . well . . ." He barely suppressed a smirk. "Hot to trot."

"I'll want a veto," Speed said, "on who plays me."

Quentin Leech pondered the idea, his face serious. "We can give it our best shot, Mister Speed. But you know how they are on the Coast."

"And did I hear something about seven figures?"

"Oh, well," Quentin Leech said. "Possibly you could haggle that out with New York." He looked pensive. "Considering taxes, if I were in your shoes, I'd take the eight-fifty I'm authorized to offer."

"Eight hundred fifty *thousand*?"

"Minus the tax bite, of course." Quentin Leech pulled a sheaf of papers from an inside pocket of his gray suit coat and put them on the coffee table. "The minute you sign"—a manicured forefinger indicated the line—"right here, I can put a check for that amount in your hands."

"This cheapo never had a wad like that in his life," Lee Lestark said from the sofa.

"I wouldn't think, really, even half." Quentin Leech's voice was earnest, persuasive. "Not when you figure tie-ins, magazines, paperback, Hollywood, maybe Broadway, foreign rights, possibly a sequel—"

"Grand opera?" Speed asked.

Lestark snorted, but Quentin Leech appeared to take the question seriously.

"Except I'm not sure you could get a big enough name to do the music," he said. "And not that a proven writer like you would need help, Mister Speed, but I'd be there as editor if . . . I mean, I could . . . if it needed a little juicing up. Some . . . ah

. . . excitement you might be a little too close to the story to see that it needed?"

"Red meat," said Lee Lestark. "Between the sheets."

Speed picked up the papers from the table, tore them in two, and let the strips flutter to the floor.

"You can tear up the check, too."

Quentin Leech looked sadly down at the strewn paper.

"For a minute there, Mister Speed, I thought you were going along. When you asked for the veto on the actor." He leaned over to pick up the scraps.

"I told'em it was a long shot." Lestark stood up, glaring at Speed. "I told'em you'd be too fucking snooty to deal."

"But they'll pay your finders' fee anyway. You arranged that, didn't you?"

"Bet your sweet ass." Lestark went to the door and opened it. "So it's nobody's funeral but yours, lover boy." He nodded at the bedroom. "Yours and that six-figure piece you're hiding back there." He went on out into the hall.

Quentin Leech put his hand on Speed's arm, as if to restrain him. Speed looked coldly down at the polished fingernails.

"I only wanted Lestark to get me in to see you, Mister Speed." His voice was mild again, pleading; and Speed saw in his eyes that what might have been sincerity was only adaptability. "I didn't expect . . ."

"Lie down with dogs," Speed said, "you got to expect to get up with fleas."

★

After Quentin Leech had left, too, Josie appeared from the bedroom, without makeup and wrapped in Speed's robe. He thought he had never seen her more beautiful. Her eyes were blue and glistening as a sea in sunlight.

"Lestark's going to write we're still together?"

He had suspected she was listening at the bedroom door.

"Seems to be what he aims to do."

"But you could have stopped him," Josie said. "And put eight hundred fifty thousand dollars in the bank."

"Less the tax bite. But grand opera killed the deal, Josie. If Leech had guaranteed Menotti to do the music, I might have signed up."

Josie put her arms around him and held up her face. Her eyes seemed darker, deep and warm.

"Not even Mozart. You'd still be too snooty to deal."